INFERNO

ALSO BY DAN BROWN

**Available from Random
House Large Print**

Angels & Demons
The Da Vinci Code
The Lost Symbol

INFERNO

A NOVEL

DAN BROWN

RANDOM HOUSE
LARGE PRINT

This is a work of fiction. Names, characters, places, and incidents either are the product of the author's imagination or are used fictitiously. Any resemblance to actual persons, living or dead, events, or locales is entirely coincidental.

Published in the United States of America by Random House Large Print in association with Doubleday, New York.
Distributed by Random House, Inc., New York.

Cover design Michael J. Windsor
Cover photographs: Dante © Imagno/
Hulton Archive/Getty Images;
Florence © Bread and Butter/Getty Images

The Library of Congress has established a Cataloging-in-Publication record for this title.

ISBN: 978-0-8041-2106-4

www.randomhouse.com/largeprint

FIRST LARGE PRINT EDITION

Printed in the United States of America

10 9 8 7 6 5 4 3 2 1

This Large Print edition published in accord with the standards of the N.A.V.H.

FOR MY PARENTS . . .

Acknowledgments

My most humble and sincere thanks to:

As always, first and foremost, my editor and close friend, Jason Kaufman, for his dedication and talent . . . but mainly for his endless good humor.

My extraordinary wife, Blythe, for her love and patience with the writing process, and also for her superb instincts and candor as a front-line editor.

My tireless agent and trusted friend Heide Lange, for expertly navigating more conversations, in more countries, on more topics than I will ever know. For her skills and energy, I am eternally grateful.

The entire team at Doubleday for its enthusiasm, creativity, and efforts on behalf of my books, with very special thanks to Suzanne Herz (for wearing so many hats . . . and wearing them so well), Bill Thomas, Michael Windsor, Judy Jacoby, Joe Gallagher, Rob Bloom, Nora Reichard, Beth Meister, Maria Carella, Lorraine Hyland, and also to the unending support of Sonny Mehta, Tony Chirico, Kathy Trager, Anne Messitte, and Markus Dohle. To the incredible people of the Random House sales department . . . you are unrivaled.

My sage counsel Michael Rudell, for his pitch-perfect instincts on all matters, large and small, as well as for his friendship.

My irreplaceable assistant Susan Morehouse, for her grace and vitality, and without whom all things descend into chaos.

All of my friends at Transworld, in particular Bill Scott-Kerr for his creativity, support, and good cheer, and also to Gail Rebuck for her superb leadership.

My Italian publisher Mondadori, especially Ricky Cavallero, Piera Cusani, Giovanni Dutto, Antonio Franchini, and Claudia Scheu; and my Turkish publisher Altin Kitaplar, particularly Oya Alpar, Erden Heper, and Batu Bozkurt, for the special services provided in connection with the locations in this book.

My exceptional publishers around the world for their passion, hard work, and commitment.

For their impressive management of the London and Milan translation sites, Leon Romero-Montalvo and Luciano Guglielmi.

The bright Dr. Marta Alvarez González for spending so much time with us in Florence and for bringing to life the city's art and architecture.

The peerless Maurizio Pimponi for all he did to enhance our visit to Italy.

All the historians, guides, and specialists who generously spent time with me in Florence and Venice, sharing their expertise: Giovanna Rao and Eugenia Antonucci at the Biblioteca Medicea Laurenziana, Serena Pini and staff at the Palazzo Vecchio; Giovanna Giusti at the Uffizi Gallery; Barbara Fedeli at the Baptistery and Il Duomo; Ettore Vito and Massimo Bisson at St. Mark's Basilica; Giorgio Tagliaferro at the Doge's Palace; Isabella di Lenardo, Elizabeth Carroll Consavari, and Elena Svalduz throughout all of Venice; Annalisa Bruni and staff at the Biblioteca Nazionale Marciana; and to the many others whom I've failed to mention in this abbreviated list, my sincere thanks.

Rachael Dillon Fried and Stephanie Delman at Sanford J. Greenburger Associates for everything they do both here and abroad.

The exceptional minds of Dr. George Abraham, Dr. John Treanor, and Dr. Bob Helm for their scientific expertise.

My early readers, who provided perspective along the way: Greg Brown, Dick and Connie Brown, Rebecca Kaufman, Jerry and Olivia Kaufman, and John Chaffee.

The web-savvy Alex Cannon, who, along with the team at Sanborn Media Factory, keeps things humming in the online world.

Judd and Kathy Gregg for providing me quiet sanctuary within Green Gables as I wrote the final chapters of this book.

The superb online resources of the Princeton Dante Project, Digital Dante at Columbia University, and the World of Dante.

INFERNO

The darkest places in hell are reserved for those who maintain their neutrality in times of moral crisis.

FACT:

All artwork, literature, science, and historical references in this novel are real.

"The Consortium" is a private organization with offices in seven countries. Its name has been changed for considerations of security and privacy.

Inferno is the underworld as described in Dante Alighieri's epic poem **The Divine Comedy,** which portrays hell as an elaborately structured realm populated by entities known as "shades"—bodiless souls trapped between life and death.

PROLOGUE

I am the Shade.

Through the dolent city, I flee.

Through the eternal woe, I take flight.

Along the banks of the river Arno, I scramble, breathless . . . turning left onto Via dei Castellani, making my way northward, huddling in the shadows of the Uffizi.

And still they pursue me.

Their footsteps grow louder now as they hunt with relentless determination.

For years they have pursued me. Their persistence has kept me underground . . . forced me to live in purgatory . . . laboring beneath the earth like a chthonic monster.

I am the Shade.

Here aboveground, I raise my eyes to the north, but I am unable to find a direct path to salvation . . . for the Apennine Mountains are blotting out the first light of dawn.

I pass behind the palazzo with its crenellated tower and one-handed clock . . . snaking through the early-morning vendors in Piazza di San Firenze with their hoarse voices smelling of **lampredotto** and roasted olives. Crossing before the Bargello, I cut west toward the spire of the Badia and come up hard against the iron gate at the base of the stairs.

Here all hesitation must be left behind.

I turn the handle and step into the passage from which I know there will be no return. I urge my leaden legs up the narrow staircase . . . spiraling skyward on soft marble treads, pitted and worn.

The voices echo from below. Beseeching.

They are behind me, unyielding, closing in.

They do not understand what is coming . . . nor what I have done for them!

Ungrateful land!

As I climb, the visions come hard . . . the lustful bodies writhing in fiery rain, the gluttonous souls floating in excrement, the treacherous villains frozen in Satan's icy grasp.

I climb the final stairs and arrive at the top, staggering near dead into the damp morning air. I rush to the head-high wall, peering through the slits. Far below is the blessed city that I have made my sanctuary from those who exiled me.

The voices call out, arriving close behind me. "What you've done is madness!"

Madness breeds madness.

"For the love of God," they shout, "tell us where you've hidden it!"

For precisely the love of God, I will not.

I stand now, cornered, my back to the cold stone. They stare deep into my clear green eyes, and their expressions darken, no longer cajoling, but threatening. "You know we have our methods. We can force you to tell us where it is."

For that reason, I have climbed halfway to heaven.

Without warning, I turn and reach up, curling my fingers onto the high ledge, pulling myself up, scrambling onto my knees, then standing . . . unsteady at the precipice. **Guide me, dear Virgil, across the void.**

They rush forward in disbelief, wanting to grab at my feet, but fearing they will upset my balance and knock me off. They beg now, in quiet desperation, but I have turned my back. **I know what I must do.**

Beneath me, dizzyingly far beneath me, the red tile roofs spread out like a sea of fire on the countryside, illuminating the fair land upon which giants once roamed . . . Giotto, Donatello, Brunelleschi, Michelangelo, Botticelli.

I inch my toes to the edge.

"Come down!" they shout. "It's not too late!"

O, willful ignorants! Do you not see the future? Do you not grasp the splendor of my creation? The necessity?

I will gladly make this ultimate sacrifice . . . and with it I will extinguish your final hope of finding what you seek.

You will never locate it in time.

Hundreds of feet below, the cobblestone piazza beckons like a tranquil oasis. How I long for more time . . . but time is the one commodity even my vast fortunes cannot afford.

In these final seconds, I gaze down at the piazza, and I behold a sight that startles me.

I see your face.

You are gazing up at me from the shadows. Your eyes are mournful, and yet in them I sense a veneration for what I have accomplished. You understand I have no choice. For the love of Mankind, I must protect my masterpiece.

It grows even now . . . waiting . . . simmering beneath the bloodred waters of the lagoon that reflects no stars.

And so, I lift my eyes from yours and I contemplate the horizon. High above this burdened world, I make my final supplication.

Dearest God, I pray the world remembers my name not as a monstrous sinner, but as the glorious savior you know I truly am. I pray Mankind will understand the gift I leave behind.

My gift is the future.

My gift is salvation.

My gift is Inferno.

With that, I whisper my amen . . . and take my final step, into the abyss.

CHAPTER 1

The memories materialized slowly . . . like bubbles surfacing from the darkness of a bottomless well.

A veiled woman.

Robert Langdon gazed at her across a river whose churning waters ran red with blood. On the far bank, the woman stood facing him, motionless, solemn, her face hidden by a shroud. In her hand she gripped a blue **tainia** cloth, which she now raised in honor of the sea of corpses at her feet. The smell of death hung everywhere.

Seek, the woman whispered. **And ye shall find.**

Langdon heard the words as if she had spoken them inside his head. "Who are you?" he called out, but his voice made no sound.

Time grows short, she whispered. **Seek and find.**

Langdon took a step toward the river, but he could see the waters were bloodred and too deep to traverse. When Langdon raised his eyes again to the veiled woman, the bodies at her feet had multiplied. There were hundreds of them now, maybe thousands, some still alive, writhing in agony, dying unthinkable deaths . . . consumed by fire, buried in feces, devouring one another. He could hear the mournful cries of human suffering echoing across the water.

The woman moved toward him, holding out her slender hands, as if beckoning for help.

"Who are you?!" Langdon again shouted.

In response, the woman reached up and slowly lifted the veil from her face. She was strikingly beautiful, and yet older than Langdon had imagined—in her sixties perhaps, stately and strong, like a timeless statue. She had a sternly set jaw, deep soulful eyes, and long, silver-gray hair that cascaded over her shoulders in ringlets. An amulet of lapis lazuli hung around her neck—a single snake coiled around a staff.

Langdon sensed he knew her . . . trusted her. **But how? Why?**

She pointed now to a writhing pair of legs, which protruded upside down from the earth, apparently belonging to some poor soul who had been buried headfirst to his waist. The man's pale thigh bore a single letter—written in mud—**R.**

R? Langdon thought, uncertain. **As in . . . Robert?** "Is that . . . **me?**"

The woman's face revealed nothing. **Seek and find,** she repeated.

Without warning, she began radiating a white light . . . brighter and brighter. Her entire body started vibrating intensely, and then, in a rush of thunder, she exploded into a thousand splintering shards of light.

Langdon bolted awake, shouting.

The room was bright. He was alone. The sharp

smell of medicinal alcohol hung in the air, and somewhere a machine pinged in quiet rhythm with his
heart. Langdon tried to move his right arm, but a
sharp pain restrained him. He looked down and saw
an IV tugging at the skin of his forearm.

His pulse quickened, and the machines kept pace,
pinging more rapidly.

Where am I? What happened?

The back of Langdon's head throbbed, a gnawing pain. Gingerly, he reached up with his free arm
and touched his scalp, trying to locate the source of
his headache. Beneath his matted hair, he found the
hard nubs of a dozen or so stitches caked with dried
blood.

He closed his eyes, trying to remember an accident.

Nothing. A total blank.

Think.

Only darkness.

A man in scrubs hurried in, apparently alerted by
Langdon's racing heart monitor. He had a shaggy
beard, bushy mustache, and gentle eyes that radiated
a thoughtful calm beneath his overgrown eyebrows.

"What . . . happened?" Langdon managed. "Did I
have an accident?"

The bearded man put a finger to his lips and then
rushed out, calling for someone down the hall.

Langdon turned his head, but the movement sent
a spike of pain radiating through his skull. He took
deep breaths and let the pain pass. Then, very gently and methodically, he surveyed his sterile surroundings.

The hospital room had a single bed. No flowers. No cards. Langdon saw his clothes on a nearby counter, folded inside a clear plastic bag. They were covered with blood.

My God. It must have been bad.

Now Langdon rotated his head very slowly toward the window beside his bed. It was dark outside. Night. All Langdon could see in the glass was his own reflection—an ashen stranger, pale and weary, attached to tubes and wires, surrounded by medical equipment.

Voices approached in the hall, and Langdon turned his gaze back toward the room. The doctor returned, now accompanied by a woman.

She appeared to be in her early thirties. She wore blue scrubs and had tied her blond hair back in a thick ponytail that swung behind her as she walked.

"I'm Dr. Sienna Brooks," she said, giving Langdon a smile as she entered. "I'll be working with Dr. Marconi tonight."

Langdon nodded weakly.

Tall and lissome, Dr. Brooks moved with the assertive gait of an athlete. Even in shapeless scrubs, she had a willowy elegance about her. Despite the absence of any makeup that Langdon could see, her complexion appeared unusually smooth, the only blemish a tiny beauty mark just above her lips. Her eyes, though a gentle brown, seemed unusually penetrating, as if they had witnessed a profundity of experience rarely encountered by a person her age.

"Dr. Marconi doesn't speak much English," she

said, sitting down beside him, "and he asked me to fill out your admittance form." She gave him another smile.

"Thanks," Langdon croaked.

"Okay," she began, her tone businesslike. "What is your name?"

It took him a moment. "Robert . . . Langdon."

She shone a penlight in Langdon's eyes. "Occupation?"

This information surfaced even more slowly. "Professor. Art history . . . and symbology. Harvard University."

Dr. Brooks lowered the light, looking startled. The doctor with the bushy eyebrows looked equally surprised.

"You're . . . an American?"

Langdon gave her a confused look.

"It's just . . ." She hesitated. "You had no identification when you arrived tonight. You were wearing Harris Tweed and Somerset loafers, so we guessed British."

"I'm American," Langdon assured her, too exhausted to explain his preference for well-tailored clothing.

"Any pain?"

"My head," Langdon replied, his throbbing skull only made worse by the bright penlight. Thankfully, she now pocketed it, taking Langdon's wrist and checking his pulse.

"You woke up shouting," the woman said. "Do you remember why?"

Langdon flashed again on the strange vision of the veiled woman surrounded by writing bodies. **Seek and ye shall find.** "I was having a nightmare."

"About?"

Langdon told her.

Dr. Brooks's expression remained neutral as she made notes on a clipboard. "Any idea what might have sparked such a frightening vision?"

Langdon probed his memory and then shook his head, which pounded in protest.

"Okay, Mr. Langdon," she said, still writing, "a couple of routine questions for you. What day of the week is it?"

Langdon thought for a moment. "It's Saturday. I remember earlier today walking across campus . . . going to an afternoon lecture series, and then . . . that's pretty much the last thing I remember. Did I fall?"

"We'll get to that. Do you know where you are?"

Langdon took his best guess. "Massachusetts General Hospital?"

Dr. Brooks made another note. "And is there someone we should call for you? Wife? Children?"

"Nobody," Langdon replied instinctively. He had always enjoyed the solitude and independence provided him by his chosen life of bachelorhood, although he had to admit, in his current situation, he'd prefer to have a familiar face at his side. "There are some colleagues I could call, but I'm fine."

Dr. Brooks finished writing, and the older doctor approached. Smoothing back his bushy eyebrows, he produced a small voice recorder from his pocket and showed it to Dr. Brooks. She nodded in understanding and turned back to her patient.

"Mr. Langdon, when you arrived tonight, you were mumbling something over and over." She glanced at Dr. Marconi, who held up the digital recorder and pressed a button.

A recording began to play, and Langdon heard his own groggy voice, repeatedly muttering the same phrase: "**Ve . . . sorry. Ve . . . sorry.**"

"It sounds to me," the woman said, "like you're saying, 'Very sorry. Very sorry.'"

Langdon agreed, and yet he had no recollection of it.

Dr. Brooks fixed him with a disquietingly intense stare. "Do you have any idea why you'd be saying this? Are you sorry about something?"

As Langdon probed the dark recesses of his memory, he again saw the veiled woman. She was standing on the banks of a bloodred river surrounded by bodies. The stench of death returned.

Langdon was overcome by a sudden, instinctive sense of danger . . . not just for himself . . . but for everyone. The pinging of his heart monitor accelerated rapidly. His muscles tightened, and he tried to sit up.

Dr. Brooks quickly placed a firm hand on Langdon's sternum, forcing him back down. She shot a glance at the bearded doctor, who walked over to a nearby counter and began preparing something.

Dr. Brooks hovered over Langdon, whispering

now. "Mr. Langdon, anxiety is common with brain injuries, but you need to keep your pulse rate down. No movement. No excitement. Just lie still and rest. You'll be okay. Your memory will come back slowly."

The doctor returned now with a syringe, which he handed to Dr. Brooks. She injected its contents into Langdon's IV.

"Just a mild sedative to calm you down," she explained, "and also to help with the pain." She stood to go. "You'll be fine, Mr. Langdon. Just sleep. If you need anything, press the button on your bedside."

She turned out the light and departed with the bearded doctor.

In the darkness, Langdon felt the drugs washing through his system almost instantly, dragging his body back down into that deep well from which he had emerged. He fought the feeling, forcing his eyes open in the darkness of his room. He tried to sit up, but his body felt like cement.

As Langdon shifted, he found himself again facing the window. The lights were out, and in the dark glass, his own reflection had disappeared, replaced by an illuminated skyline in the distance.

Amid a contour of spires and domes, a single regal facade dominated Langdon's field of view. The building was an imposing stone fortress with a notched parapet and a three-hundred-foot tower that swelled near the top, bulging outward into a massive machicolated battlement.

Langdon sat bolt upright in bed, pain exploding in

his head. He fought off the searing throb and fixed his gaze on the tower.

Langdon knew the medieval structure well.

It was unique in the world.

Unfortunately, it was also located four thousand miles from Massachusetts.

———

Outside his window, hidden in the shadows of the Via Torregalli, a powerfully built woman effortlessly unstraddled her BMW motorcycle and advanced with the intensity of a panther stalking its prey. Her gaze was sharp. Her close-cropped hair—styled into spikes—stood out against the upturned collar of her black leather riding suit. She checked her silenced weapon, and stared up at the window where Robert Langdon's light had just gone out.

Earlier tonight her original mission had gone horribly awry.

The coo of a single dove had changed everything.

Now she had come to make it right.

CHAPTER 2

I'm in Florence!?

Robert Langdon's head throbbed. He was now seated upright in his hospital bed, repeatedly jamming his finger into the call button. Despite the sedatives in his system, his heart was racing.

Dr. Brooks hurried back in, her ponytail bobbing. "Are you okay?"

Langdon shook his head in bewilderment. "I'm in . . . Italy!?"

"Good," she said. "You're remembering."

"No!" Langdon pointed out the window at the commanding edifice in the distance. "I recognize the Palazzo Vecchio."

Dr. Brooks flicked the lights back on, and the Florence skyline disappeared. She came to his bedside, whispering calmly. "Mr. Langdon, there's no need to worry. You're suffering from mild amnesia, but Dr. Marconi confirmed that your brain function is fine."

The bearded doctor rushed in as well, apparently hearing the call button. He checked Langdon's heart monitor as the young doctor spoke to him in rapid, fluent Italian—something about how Langdon was **"agitato"** to learn he was in Italy.

Agitated? Langdon thought angrily. **More like stupefied!** The adrenaline surging through his system was now doing battle with the sedatives. "What happened to me?" he demanded. "What day is it?!"

"Everything is fine," she said. "It's early morning. Monday, March eighteenth."

Monday. Langdon forced his aching mind to reel back to the last images he could recall—cold and dark—walking alone across the Harvard campus to a Saturday-night lecture series. **That was two days ago?!** A sharper panic now gripped him as he tried to recall anything at all from the lecture or afterward. **Nothing.** The ping of his heart monitor accelerated.

The older doctor scratched at his beard and continued adjusting equipment while Dr. Brooks sat again beside Langdon.

"You're going to be okay," she reassured him, speaking gently. "We've diagnosed you with retrograde amnesia, which is very common in head trauma. Your memories of the past few days may be muddled or missing, but you should suffer no permanent damage." She paused. "Do you remember my first name? I told you when I walked in."

Langdon thought a moment. "Sienna." **Dr. Sienna Brooks.**

She smiled. "See? You're already forming new memories."

The pain in Langdon's head was almost unbearable, and his near-field vision remained blurry. "What . . . happened? How did I get here?"

"I think you should rest, and maybe—"

"How did I get here?!" he demanded, his heart monitor accelerating further.

"Okay, just breathe easy," Dr. Brooks said, exchanging a nervous look with her colleague. "I'll tell you." Her voice turned markedly more serious. "Mr. Langdon, three hours ago, you staggered into our emergency room, bleeding from a head wound, and you immediately collapsed. Nobody had any idea who you were or how you got here. You were mumbling in English, so Dr. Marconi asked me to assist. I'm on sabbatical here from the U.K."

Langdon felt like he had awoken inside a Max Ernst painting. **What the hell am I doing in Italy?** Normally Langdon came here every other June for an art conference, but this was March.

The sedatives pulled harder at him now, and he felt as if earth's gravity were growing stronger by the second, trying to drag him down through his mattress. Langdon fought it, hoisting his head, trying to stay alert.

Dr. Brooks leaned over him, hovering like an angel. "Please, Mr. Langdon," she whispered. "Head trauma is delicate in the first twenty-four hours. You need to rest, or you could do serious damage."

A voice crackled suddenly on the room's intercom. **"Dr. Marconi?"**

The bearded doctor touched a button on the wall and replied, "Sì?"

The voice on the intercom spoke in rapid Italian. Langdon didn't catch what it said, but he did catch the two doctors exchanging a look of surprise. **Or is it alarm?**

"**Momento,**" Marconi replied, ending the conversation.

"What's going on?" Langdon asked.

Dr. Brooks's eyes seemed to narrow a bit. "That was the ICU receptionist. Someone's here to visit you."

A ray of hope cut through Langdon's grogginess. "That's good news! Maybe this person knows what happened to me."

She looked uncertain. "It's just odd that someone's here. We didn't have your name, and you're not even registered in the system yet."

Langdon battled the sedatives and awkwardly hoisted himself upright in his bed. "If someone knows I'm here, that person must know what happened!"

Dr. Brooks glanced at Dr. Marconi, who immediately shook his head and tapped his watch. She turned back to Langdon.

"This is the ICU," she explained. "Nobody is allowed in until nine A.M. at the earliest. In a moment Dr. Marconi will go out and see who the visitor is and what he or she wants."

"What about what I want?" Langdon demanded.

Dr. Brooks smiled patiently and lowered her voice, leaning closer. "Mr. Langdon, there are some things you don't know about last night . . . about what happened to you. And before you speak to anyone, I think it's only fair that you have all the facts. Unfortunately, I don't think you're strong enough yet to—"

"What facts!?" Langdon demanded, struggling to prop himself higher. The IV in his arm pinched, and his body felt like it weighed several hundred pounds. "All I know is I'm in a Florence hospital and I arrived repeating the words 'very sorry . . .'"

A frightening thought now occurred to him.

"Was I responsible for a car accident?" Langdon asked. "Did I hurt someone?!"

"No, no," she said. "I don't believe so."

"Then **what**?" Langdon insisted, eyeing both doctors furiously. "I have a right to know what's going on!"

There was a long silence, and Dr. Marconi finally gave his attractive young colleague a reluctant nod. Dr. Brooks exhaled and moved closer to his bedside. "Okay, let me tell you what I know . . . and you'll listen calmly, agreed?"

Langdon nodded, the head movement sending a jolt of pain radiating through his skull. He ignored it, eager for answers.

"The first thing is this . . . Your head wound was not caused by an accident."

"Well, that's a relief."

"Not really. Your wound, in fact, was caused by a bullet."

Langdon's heart monitor pinged faster. "I beg your pardon!?"

Dr. Brooks spoke steadily but quickly. "A bullet grazed the top of your skull and most likely gave you a concussion. You're very lucky to be alive. An inch lower, and . . ." She shook her head.

Langdon stared at her in disbelief. **Someone shot me?**

Angry voices erupted in the hall as an argument broke out. It sounded as if whoever had arrived to visit Langdon did not want to wait. Almost immediately, Langdon heard a heavy door at the far end of the hallway burst open. He watched until he saw a figure approaching down the corridor.

The woman was dressed entirely in black leather. She was toned and strong with dark, spiked hair. She moved effortlessly, as if her feet weren't touching the ground, and she was headed directly for Langdon's room.

Without hesitation, Dr. Marconi stepped into the open doorway to block the visitor's passage. **"Ferma!"** the man commanded, holding out his palm like a policeman.

The stranger, without breaking stride, produced a silenced handgun. She aimed directly at Dr. Marconi's chest and fired.

There was a staccato hiss.

Langdon watched in horror as Dr. Marconi staggered backward into the room, falling to the floor, clutching his chest, his white lab coat drenched in blood.

CHAPTER 3

Five miles off the coast of Italy, the 237-foot luxury yacht **The Mendacium** motored through the predawn mist that rose from the gently rolling swells of the Adriatic. The ship's stealth-profile hull was painted gunmetal gray, giving it the distinctly unwelcoming aura of a military vessel.

With a price tag of over 300 million U.S. dollars, the craft boasted all the usual amenities—spa, pool, cinema, personal submarine, and helicopter pad. The ship's creature comforts, however, were of little interest to its owner, who had taken delivery of the yacht five years ago and immediately gutted most of these spaces to install a lead-lined, military-grade, electronic command center.

Fed by three dedicated satellite links and a redundant array of terrestrial relay stations, the control room on **The Mendacium** had a staff of nearly two dozen—technicians, analysts, operation coordinators—who lived on board and remained in constant contact with the organization's various land-based operation centers.

The ship's onboard security included a small unit of military-trained soldiers, two missile-detection systems, and an arsenal of the latest weapons available. Other support staff—cooks, cleaning, and service—pushed the total number on board to more than forty. The **Mendacium** was, in effect, the portable office building from which the owner ran his empire.

Known to his employees only as "the provost," he was a tiny, stunted man with tanned skin and deep-set eyes. His unimposing physique and direct manner seemed well suited to one who had made a vast fortune providing a private menu of covert services along the shadowy fringes of society.

He had been called many things—a soulless mercenary, a facilitator of sin, the devil's enabler—but he was none of these. The provost simply provided his clients with the opportunity to pursue their ambitions and desires without consequence; that mankind was sinful in nature was not his problem.

Despite his detractors and their ethical objections, the provost's moral compass was a fixed star. He had built his reputation—and the Consortium itself—on two golden rules.

Never make a promise you cannot keep.

And never lie to a client.

Ever.

In his professional career, the provost had never broken a promise or reneged on a deal. His word was bankable—an absolute guarantee—and while there were certainly contracts he regretted having made, backing out of them was never an option.

This morning, as he stepped onto the private balcony of his yacht's stateroom, the provost looked across the churning sea and tried to fend off the disquiet that had settled in his gut.

The decisions of our past are the architects of our present.

The decisions of the provost's past had put him in a position to negotiate almost any minefield and always come out on top. Today, however, as he gazed out the window at the distant lights of the Italian mainland, he felt uncharacteristically on edge.

One year ago, on this very yacht, he had made a decision whose ramifications now threatened to unravel everything he had built. **I agreed to provide services to the wrong man.** There had been no way the provost could have known at the time, and yet now the miscalculation had brought a tempest of unforeseen challenges, forcing him to send some of his best agents into the field with orders to do "whatever it took" to keep his listing ship from capsizing.

At the moment the provost was waiting to hear from one field agent in particular.

Vayentha, he thought, picturing the sinewy, spike-haired specialist. Vayentha, who had served him perfectly until this mission, had made a mistake last night that had dire consequences. The last six hours had been a scramble, a desperate attempt to regain control of the situation.

Vayentha claimed her error was the result of simple bad luck—the untimely coo of a dove.

The provost, however, did not believe in luck. Everything he did was orchestrated to eradicate randomness and remove chance. Control was the provost's expertise—foreseeing every possibility, anticipating every response, and molding reality toward the desired outcome. He had an immaculate track record of success and secrecy, and with it came a staggering clientele—billionaires, politicians, sheikhs, and even entire governments.

To the east, the first faint light of morning had begun to consume the lowest stars on the horizon. On the deck the provost stood and patiently awaited word from Vayentha that her mission had gone exactly as planned.

CHAPTER 4

For an instant, Langdon felt as if time had stopped.

Dr. Marconi lay motionless on the floor, blood gushing from his chest. Fighting the sedatives in his system, Langdon raised his eyes to the spike-haired assassin, who was still striding down the hall, covering the last few yards toward his open door. As she neared the threshold, she looked toward Langdon and instantly swung her weapon in his direction . . . aiming at his head.

I'm going to die, Langdon realized. **Here and now.**

The bang was deafening in the small hospital room.

Langdon recoiled, certain he had been shot, but the noise had not been the attacker's gun. Rather, the bang had been the slam of the room's heavy metal door as Dr. Brooks threw herself against it and turned the lock.

Eyes wild with fear, Dr. Brooks immediately spun and crouched beside her blood-soaked colleague, searching for a pulse. Dr. Marconi coughed up a mouthful of blood, which dribbled down his cheek across his thick beard. Then he fell limp.

"**Enrico, no! Ti prego!**" she screamed.

Outside, a barrage of bullets exploded against the

metal exterior of the door. Shouts of alarm filled the hall.

Somehow, Langdon's body was in motion, panic and instinct now overruling his sedatives. As he clambered awkwardly out of bed, a searing hot pain tore into his right forearm. For an instant, he thought a bullet had passed through the door and hit him, but when he looked down, he realized his IV had snapped off in his arm. The plastic catheter poked out of a jagged hole in his forearm, and warm blood was already flowing backward out of the tube.

Langdon was now fully awake.

Crouched beside Marconi's body, Dr. Brooks kept searching for a pulse as tears welled in her eyes. Then, as if a switch had been flipped inside her, she stood and turned to Langdon. Her expression transformed before his eyes, her young features hardening with all the detached composure of a seasoned ER doctor dealing with a crisis.

"Follow me," she commanded.

Dr. Brooks grabbed Langdon's arm and pulled him across the room. The sounds of gunfire and chaos continued in the hallway as Langdon lurched forward on unstable legs. His mind felt alert but his heavily drugged body was slow to respond. **Move!** The tile floor felt cold beneath his feet, and his thin hospital johnny was scarcely long enough to cover his six-foot frame. He could feel blood dripping down his forearm and pooling in his palm.

Bullets continued to slam against the heavy door-knob, and Dr. Brooks pushed Langdon roughly into a small bathroom. She was about to follow when she paused, turned around, and ran back toward the counter and grabbed his bloody Harris Tweed.

Forget my damned jacket!

She returned clutching his jacket and quickly locked the bathroom door. Just then, the door in the outer room crashed open.

The young doctor took control. She strode through the tiny bathroom to a second door, yanked it open, and led Langdon into an adjoining recovery room. Gunfire echoed behind them as Dr. Brooks stuck her head out into the hallway and quickly grabbed Langdon's arm, pulling him across the corridor into a stairwell. The sudden motion made Langdon dizzy; he sensed that he could pass out at any moment.

The next fifteen seconds were a blur . . . descending stairs . . . stumbling . . . falling. The pounding in Langdon's head was almost unbearable. His vision seemed even more blurry now, and his muscles were sluggish, each movement feeling like a delayed reaction.

And then the air grew cold.

I'm outside.

As Dr. Brooks hustled him along a dark alley away from the building, Langdon stepped on something sharp and fell, hitting the pavement hard. She struggled to get him back to his feet, cursing out loud the fact that he had been sedated.

As they neared the end of the alley, Langdon stumbled again. This time she left him on the ground, rushing into the street and yelling to someone in the distance. Langdon could make out the faint green light of a taxi parked in front of the hospital. The car didn't move, its driver undoubtedly asleep. Dr. Brooks screamed and waved her arms wildly. Finally the taxi's headlights came on and it moved lazily toward them.

Behind Langdon in the alley, a door burst open, followed by the sound of rapidly approaching footsteps. He turned and saw the dark figure bounding toward him. Langdon tried to get back to his feet, but the doctor was already grabbing him, forcing him into the backseat of an idling Fiat taxi. He landed half on the seat and half on the floor as Dr. Brooks dove on top of him, yanking the door shut.

The sleepy-eyed driver turned and stared at the bizarre duo that had just tumbled into his cab—a young, ponytailed woman in scrubs and a man in a half-torn johnny with a bleeding arm. He clearly was about ready to tell them to get the hell out of his car, when the side mirror exploded. The woman in black leather sprinted out of the alley, gun extended. Her pistol hissed again just as Dr. Brooks grabbed Langdon's head, pulling it down. The rear window exploded, showering them with glass.

The driver needed no further encouragement. He slammed his foot down on the gas, and the taxi peeled out.

Langdon teetered on the brink of consciousness. **Someone is trying to kill me?**

Once they had rounded a corner, Dr. Brooks sat up and grabbed Langdon's bloody arm. The catheter was protruding awkwardly from a hole in his flesh.

"Look out the window," she commanded.

Langdon obeyed. Outside, ghostly tombstones rushed by in the darkness. It seemed somehow fitting that they were passing a cemetery. Langdon felt the doctor's fingers probing gently for the catheter and then, without warning, she wrenched it out.

A searing bolt of pain traveled directly to Langdon's head. He felt his eyes rolling back, and then everything went black.

CHAPTER 5

The shrill ring of his phone drew the provost's gaze from the calming mist of the Adriatic, and he quickly stepped back into his stateroom office.

It's about time, he thought, eager for news.

The computer screen on his desk had flickered to life, informing him that the incoming call was from a Swedish Sectra Tiger XS personal voice-encrypting phone, which had been redirected through four untraceable routers before being connected to his ship.

He donned his headset. "This is the provost," he answered, his words slow and meticulous. "Go ahead."

"It's Vayentha," the voice replied.

The provost sensed an unusual nervousness in her tone. Field agents rarely spoke to the provost directly, and even more rarely did they remain in his employ after a debacle like the one last night. Nonetheless, the provost had required an agent on-site to help remedy the crisis, and Vayentha had been the best person for the job.

"I have an update," Vayentha said.

The provost was silent, his cue for her to continue.

When she spoke, her tone was emotionless, clearly an attempt at professionalism. "Langdon has escaped," she said. "He has the object."

The provost sat down at his desk and remained silent for a very long time. "Understood," he finally said. "I imagine he will reach out to the authorities as soon as he possibly can."

———

Two decks beneath the provost, in the ship's secure control center, senior facilitator Laurence Knowlton sat in his private cubicle and noticed that the provost's encrypted call had ended. He hoped the news was good. The provost's tension had been palpable for the past two days, and every operative on board sensed there was some kind of high-stakes operation going on.

The stakes are inconceivably high, and Vayentha had better get it right this time.

Knowlton was accustomed to quarterbacking carefully constructed game plans, but this particular scenario had disintegrated into chaos, and the provost had taken over personally.

We've moved into uncharted territory.

Although a half-dozen other missions were currently in process around the world, all of them were being serviced by the Consortium's various field offices, freeing the provost and his staff aboard **The Mendacium** to focus exclusively on this one.

Their client had jumped to his death several days ago in Florence, but the Consortium still had numerous outstanding services on his docket—specific tasks the man had entrusted to this organization regardless of the circumstances—and the Consortium, as always, intended to follow through without question.

I have my orders, Knowlton thought, fully intending to comply. He exited his soundproofed glass cubicle, walking past a half-dozen other chambers—some transparent, some opaque—in which duty officers were handling other aspects of this same mission.

Knowlton crossed through the thin, processed air of the main control room, nodding to the tech crew, and entered a small walk-in vault containing a dozen strongboxes. He opened one of the boxes and retrieved its contents—in this case, a bright red memory stick. According to the task card attached, the memory stick contained a large video file, which the client had directed them to upload to key media outlets at a specific time tomorrow morning.

Tomorrow's anonymous upload would be simple enough, but in keeping protocol for all digital files, the flowchart had flagged this file for review **today**—twenty-four hours prior to delivery—to ensure the Consortium had adequate time to perform any necessary decryption, compiling, or other preparation that might be required before uploading it at the precise hour.

Nothing left to chance.

Knowlton returned to his transparent cubicle and closed the heavy glass door, blocking out the outside world.

He flipped a switch on the wall, and his cubicle instantly turned opaque. For privacy, all of the glass-walled offices aboard **The Mendacium** were built with "suspended particle device" glass. The transparency of SPD glass was easily controlled by the application or removal of an electric current, which either aligned or randomized millions of tiny rodlike particles suspended within the panel.

Compartmentalization was a cornerstone of the Consortium's success.

Know only your own mission. Share nothing.

Now, ensconced in his private space, Knowlton inserted the memory stick into his computer and clicked the file to begin his assessment.

Immediately his screen faded to black . . . and his speakers began playing the soft sound of lapping water. An image slowly appeared on-screen . . . amorphous and shadowy. Emerging from the darkness, a scene began to take shape . . . the interior of a cave . . . or a giant chamber of some sort. The floor of the cavern was water, like an underground lake. Strangely, the water appeared to be illuminated . . . as if from within.

Knowlton had never seen anything like it. The entire cavern shone with an eerie reddish hue, its pale walls awash with tendril-like reflections of rippling water. **What . . . is this place?**

As the lapping continued, the camera began to tilt downward and descend vertically, directly toward the water until the camera pierced the illuminated surface. The sounds of rippling disappeared, replaced by an eerie hush beneath the water. Submerged now, the camera kept descending, moving down through several feet of water until it stopped, focusing on the cavern's silt-covered floor.

Bolted to the floor was a rectangular plaque of shimmering titanium.

The plaque bore an inscription.

IN THIS PLACE, ON THIS DATE,
THE WORLD WAS CHANGED FOREVER.

Engraved at the bottom of the plaque was a name and a date.

The name was that of their client.

The date . . . tomorrow.

CHAPTER 6

Langdon felt firm hands lifting him now . . . urging him from his delirium, helping him out of the taxi. The pavement felt cold beneath his bare feet.

Half supported by the slender frame of Dr. Brooks, Langdon staggered down a deserted walkway between two apartment buildings. The dawn air rustled, billowing his hospital gown, and Langdon felt cold air in places he knew he shouldn't.

The sedative he'd been given in the hospital had left his mind as blurred as his vision. Langdon felt like he was underwater, attempting to claw his way through a viscous, dimly lit world. Sienna Brooks dragged him onward, supporting him with surprising strength.

"Stairs," she said, and Langdon realized they had reached a side entrance of the building.

Langdon gripped the railing and trudged dizzily upward, one step at a time. His body felt ponderous. Dr. Brooks physically pushed him now. When they reached the landing, she typed some numbers into a rusted old keypad and the door buzzed open.

The air inside was not much warmer, but the tile

floors felt like soft carpet on the soles of his feet compared to the rough pavement outside. Dr. Brooks led
Langdon to a tiny elevator and yanked open a folding
door, herding Langdon into a cubicle that was about
the size of a phone booth. The air inside smelled of
MS cigarettes—a bittersweet fragrance as ubiquitous in Italy as the aroma of fresh espresso. Ever so
slightly, the smell helped clear Langdon's mind. Dr.
Brooks pressed a button, and somewhere high above
them, a series of tired gears clunked and whirred into
motion.

Upward . . .

The creaky carriage shimmied and vibrated as it
began its ascent. Because the walls were nothing but
metal screens, Langdon found himself watching the
inside of the elevator shaft slide rhythmically past
them. Even in his semiconscious state, Langdon's
lifelong fear of cramped spaces was alive and well.

Don't look.

He leaned on the wall, trying to catch his breath.
His forearm ached, and when he looked down, he
saw that the sleeve of his Harris Tweed had been
tied awkwardly around his arm like a bandage. The
remainder of the jacket was dragging behind him on
the ground, frayed and filthy.

He closed his eyes against his pounding headache,
but the blackness engulfed him again.

A familiar vision materialized—the statuesque,
veiled woman with the amulet and silver hair in ringlets. As before, she was on the banks of a bloodred

river and surrounded by writhing bodies. She spoke to Langdon, her voice pleading. **Seek and ye shall find!**

Langdon was overcome with the feeling that he had to save her . . . save them all. The half-buried, upside-down legs were falling limp . . . one by one.

Who are you!? he called out in silence. **What do you want?!**

Her luxuriant silver hair began fluttering in a hot wind. **Our time grows short**, she whispered, touching her amulet necklace. Then, without warning, she erupted in a blinding pillar of fire, which billowed across the river, engulfing them both.

Langdon shouted, his eyes flying open.

Dr. Brooks eyed him with concern. "What is it?"

"I keep hallucinating!" Langdon exclaimed. "The same scene."

"The silver-haired woman? And all the dead bodies?"

Langdon nodded, perspiration beading on his brow.

"You'll be okay," she assured him, despite sounding shaky herself. "Recurring visions are common with amnesia. The brain function that sorts and catalogs your memories has been temporarily shaken up, and so it throws everything into one picture."

"Not a very nice picture," he managed.

"I know, but until you heal, your memories will be muddled and uncataloged—past, present, and imagination all mixed together. The same thing happens in dreams."

The elevator lurched to a stop, and Dr. Brooks

yanked open the folding door. They were walking again, this time down a dark, narrow corridor. They passed a window, outside of which the murky silhouettes of Florence rooftops had begun emerging in the predawn light. At the far end of the hall, she crouched down and retrieved a key from beneath a thirsty-looking houseplant and unlocked a door.

The apartment was tiny, the air inside hinting at an ongoing battle between a vanilla-scented candle and old carpeting. The furniture and artwork were meager at best—as if she had furnished it at a yard sale. Dr. Brooks adjusted a thermostat, and the radiators banged to life.

She stood a moment and closed her eyes, exhaling heavily, as if to collect herself. Then she turned and helped Langdon into a modest kitchenette whose Formica table had two flimsy chairs.

Langdon made a move toward a chair in hopes of sitting down, but Dr. Brooks grabbed his arm with one hand and opened a cabinet with her other. The cabinet was nearly bare . . . crackers, a few bags of pasta, a can of Coke, and a bottle of NoDoz.

She took out the bottle and dumped six caplets into Langdon's palm. "Caffeine," she said. "For when I work night shifts like tonight."

Langdon put the pills in his mouth and glanced around for some water.

"Chew them," she said. "They'll hit your system faster and help counteract the sedative."

Langdon began chewing and instantly cringed.

The pills were bitter, clearly meant to be swallowed whole. Dr. Brooks opened the refrigerator and handed Langdon a half-empty bottle of San Pellegrino. He gratefully took a long drink.

The ponytailed doctor now took his right arm and removed the makeshift bandage that she'd fashioned out of his jacket, which she laid on the kitchen table. Then she carefully examined his wound. As she held his bare arm, Langdon could feel her slender hands trembling.

"You'll live," she announced.

Langdon hoped she was going to be okay. He could barely fathom what they'd both just endured. "Dr. Brooks," he said, "we need to call somebody. The consulate . . . the police. Somebody."

She nodded in agreement. "Also, you can stop calling me Dr. Brooks—my name is Sienna."

Langdon nodded. "Thanks. I'm Robert." It seemed the bond they'd just forged fleeing for their lives warranted a first-name basis. "You said you're British?"

"By birth, yes."

"I don't hear an accent."

"Good," she replied. "I worked hard to lose it."

Langdon was about to inquire why, but Sienna motioned for him to follow. She led him down a narrow corridor to a small, gloomy bathroom. In the mirror above the sink, Langdon glimpsed his reflection for the first time since seeing it in the window of his hospital room.

Not good. Langdon's thick dark hair was matted,

and his eyes looked bloodshot and weary. A shroud of stubble obscured his jaw.

Sienna turned on the faucet and guided Langdon's injured forearm under the ice-cold water. It stung sharply, but he held it there, wincing.

Sienna retrieved a fresh washcloth and squirted it with antibacterial soap. "You may want to look away."

"It's fine. I'm not bothered by—"

Sienna began scrubbing violently, and white-hot pain shot up Langdon's arm. He clenched his jaw to prevent himself from shouting out in protest.

"You don't want an infection," she said, scrubbing harder now. "Besides, if you're going to call the authorities, you'll want to be more alert than you are now. Nothing activates adrenaline production like pain."

Langdon held on for what felt like a full ten seconds of scrubbing before he forcefully yanked his arm away. **Enough!** Admittedly, he felt stronger and more awake; the pain in his arm had now entirely overshadowed his headache.

"Good," she said, turning off the water and patting his arm dry with a clean towel. Sienna then applied a small bandage to his forearm, but as she did so, Langdon found himself distracted by something he had just noticed—something deeply upsetting to him.

For nearly four decades, Langdon had worn an antique collector's edition Mickey Mouse timepiece, a gift from his parents. Mickey's smiling face and wildly waving arms had always served as his daily reminder to smile more often and take life a little less seriously.

"My . . . watch," Langdon stammered. "It's gone!" Without it, he felt suddenly incomplete. "Was I wearing it when I arrived at the hospital?"

Sienna shot him an incredulous look, clearly mystified that he could be worried about such a trivial thing. "I don't remember any watch. Just clean yourself up. I'll be back in a few minutes and we'll figure out how to get you some help." She turned to go, but paused in the doorway, locking eyes with him in the mirror. "And while I'm gone, I suggest you think very hard about why someone would want to kill you. I imagine it's the first question the authorities will ask."

"Wait, where are you going?"

"You can't talk to the police half naked. I'm going to find you some clothes. My neighbor is about your size. He's away, and I'm feeding his cat. He owes me."

With that, Sienna was gone.

Robert Langdon turned back to the tiny mirror over the sink and barely recognized the person staring back at him. **Someone wants me dead.** In his mind, he again heard the recording of his own delirious mumblings.

Very sorry. Very sorry.

He probed his memory for some recollection . . . anything at all. He saw only emptiness. All Langdon knew was that he was in Florence, having suffered a bullet wound to the head.

As Langdon stared into his own weary eyes, he half

wondered if he might at any moment wake up in his reading chair at home, clutching an empty martini glass and a copy of **Dead Souls**, only to remind himself that Bombay Sapphire and Gogol should never be mixed.

CHAPTER 7

L angdon shed his bloody hospital gown and wrapped a towel around his waist. After splashing water on his face, he gingerly touched the stitches on the back of his head. The skin was sore, but when he smoothed his matted hair down over the spot, the injury all but disappeared. The caffeine pills were kicking in, and he finally felt the fog beginning to lift.

Think, Robert. Try to remember.

The windowless bathroom was suddenly feeling claustrophobic, and Langdon stepped into the hall, moving instinctively toward a shaft of natural light that spilled through a partially open door across the corridor. The room was a makeshift study of sorts, with a cheap desk, a worn swivel chair, assorted books on the floor, and, thankfully . . . a **window**.

Langdon moved toward daylight.

In the distance, the rising Tuscan sun was just beginning to kiss the highest spires of the waking city—the campanile, the Badia, the Bargello. Langdon pressed his forehead to the cool glass. The March air was crisp and cold, amplifying the full spectrum of sunlight that now peeked up over the hillsides.

Painter's light, they called it.

At the heart of the skyline, a mountainous dome of red tiles rose up, its zenith adorned with a gilt copper ball that glinted like a beacon. Il Duomo. Brunelleschi had made architectural history by engineering the basilica's massive dome, and now, more than five hundred years later, the 375-foot-tall structure still stood its ground, an immovable giant on Piazza del Duomo.

Why would I be in Florence?

For Langdon, a lifelong aficionado of Italian art, Florence had become one of his favorite destinations in all of Europe. This was the city on whose streets Michelangelo played as a child, and in whose studios the Italian Renaissance had ignited. This was Florence, whose galleries lured millions of travelers to admire Botticelli's **Birth of Venus**, Leonardo's **Annunciation**, and the city's pride and joy—**Il Davide.**

Langdon had been mesmerized by Michelangelo's **David** when he first saw it as a teenager . . . entering the Accademia delle Belle Arti . . . moving slowly through the somber phalanx of Michelangelo's crude **Prigioni** . . . and then feeling his gaze dragged upward, inexorably, to the seventeen-foot-tall masterpiece. The **David**'s sheer enormity and defined musculature startled most first-time visitors, and yet for Langdon, it had been the genius of David's pose that he found most captivating. Michelangelo had employed the classical tradition of **contrapposto** to create the illusion that David was leaning to his right, his left leg bearing almost no weight, when, in fact, his left leg was supporting tons of marble.

The **David** had sparked in Langdon his first true

appreciation for the power of great sculpture. Now Langdon wondered if he had visited the masterpiece during the last several days, but the only memory he could conjure was that of awakening in the hospital and watching an innocent doctor murdered before his eyes. **Very sorry. Very sorry.**

The guilt he felt was almost nauseating. **What have I done?**

As he stood at the window, his peripheral vision caught a glimpse of a laptop computer sitting on the desk beside him. Whatever had happened to Langdon last night, he suddenly realized, might be in the news.

If I can access the Internet, I might find answers.

Langdon turned toward the doorway and called out: "Sienna?!"

Silence. She was still at the neighbor's apartment looking for clothes.

Having no doubt Sienna would understand the intrusion, Langdon opened the laptop and powered it up.

Sienna's home screen flickered to life—a standard Windows "blue cloud" background. Langdon immediately went to the Google Italia search page and typed in **Robert Langdon.**

If my students could see me now, he thought as he began the search. Langdon continually admonished his students for Googling themselves—a bizarre new pastime that reflected the obsession with personal celebrity that now seemed to possess American youth.

A page of search results materialized—hundreds of

hits pertaining to Langdon, his books, and his lectures. **Not what I'm looking for.**

Langdon restricted the search by selecting the news button.

A fresh page appeared: **News results for "Robert Langdon."**

Book signings: Robert Langdon to appear . . .

Graduation address by Robert Langdon . . .

Robert Langdon publishes Symbol primer for . . .

The list was several pages long, and yet Langdon saw nothing recent—certainly nothing that would explain his current predicament. **What happened last night?** Langdon pushed on, accessing the Web site for **The Florentine**, an English-language newspaper published in Florence. He scanned the headlines, breaking-news sections, and police blog, seeing articles on an apartment fire, a government embezzling scandal, and assorted incidents of petty crime.

Anything at all?!

He paused at a breaking-news blurb about a city official who, last night, had died of a heart attack in the plaza outside the cathedral. The official's name had yet to be released, but no foul play was suspected.

Finally, not knowing what else to do, Langdon logged on to his Harvard e-mail account and checked his messages, wondering if he might find answers there. All he found was the usual stream of mail from colleagues, students, and friends, much of it referencing appointments for the coming week.

It's as if nobody knows I'm gone.

With rising uncertainty, Langdon shut down the

computer and closed the lid. He was about to leave when something caught his eye. On the corner of Sienna's desk, atop a stack of old medical journals and papers, sat a Polaroid photograph. The snapshot was of Sienna Brooks and her bearded doctor colleague, laughing together in a hospital hallway.

Dr. Marconi, Langdon thought, racked with guilt as he picked up the photo and studied it.

As Langdon replaced the photo on the stack of books, he noticed with surprise the yellow booklet on top—a tattered playbill from the London Globe Theatre. According to the cover, it was for a production of Shakespeare's **A Midsummer Night's Dream** . . . staged nearly twenty-five years ago.

Scrawled across the top of the playbill was a handwritten message in Magic Marker: **Sweetheart, never forget you're a miracle.**

Langdon picked up the playbill, and a stack of press clippings fell out onto the desk. He quickly tried to replace them, but as he opened the booklet to the weathered page where the clippings had been, he stopped short.

He was staring at a cast photo of the child actor portraying Shakespeare's mischievous sprite Puck. The photo showed a young girl who could not have been more than five, her blond hair in a familiar ponytail.

The text below her photo read: **A star is born.**

The bio was a gushing account of a child theater prodigy—Sienna Brooks—with an off-the-chart IQ, who had, in a single night, memorized every character's lines and, during initial rehearsals, often cued her fellow cast members. Among this five-year-old's hobbies were violin, chess, biology, and chemistry. The child of a wealthy couple in the London suburb of Blackheath, the girl was already a celebrity in scientific circles; at the age of four, she had beat a chess grand master at his own game and was reading in three languages.

My God, Langdon thought. **Sienna. That explains a few things.**

Langdon recalled one of Harvard's most famous graduates had been a child prodigy named Saul Kripke, who at the age of six had taught himself Hebrew and read all of the works of Descartes by the age of twelve. More recently, Langdon recalled reading about a young phenom named Moshe Kai Cavalin, who, at age eleven, had earned a college degree with a 4.0 grade-point average and won a national title in martial arts, and, at fourteen, published a book titled **We Can Do.**

Langdon picked up another press clipping, a newspaper article with a photo of Sienna at age seven: CHILD GENIUS DISPLAYS 208 IQ.

Langdon had been unaware that IQs even went that high. According to the article, Sienna Brooks was a virtuoso violinist, could master a new language in a month, and was teaching herself anatomy and physiology.

He looked at another clipping from a medical journal: THE FUTURE OF THOUGHT: NOT ALL MINDS ARE CREATED EQUAL.

This article had a photo of Sienna, now maybe ten

years old, still a towhead, standing beside a large piece of medical apparatus. The article contained an interview with a doctor, who explained that PET scans of Sienna's cerebellum revealed that it was **physically** different from other cerebella, in her case a larger, more streamlined organ capable of manipulating visual-spatial content in ways that most human beings could not begin to fathom. The doctor equated Sienna's physiological advantage to an unusually accelerated cellular growth in her brain, much like a cancer, except that it accelerated growth of beneficial brain tissue rather than dangerous cancer cells.

Langdon found a clipping from a small-town newspaper.

THE CURSE OF BRILLIANCE.

There was no photo this time, but the story told of a young genius, Sienna Brooks, who had tried to attend regular schools but was teased by other students because she didn't fit in. It talked about the isolation felt by gifted young people whose social skills could not keep up with their intellects and who were often ostracized.

Sienna, according to this article, had run away from home at the age of eight, and had been smart enough to live on her own undiscovered for ten days. She had been found in an upscale London hotel, where she had pretended to be the daughter of a guest, stolen a key, and was ordering room service on someone else's account. Apparently she had spent the week reading all 1,600 pages of **Gray's Anatomy**. When authorities asked why she was reading medical texts, she told them she wanted to figure out what was wrong with her brain.

Langdon's heart went out to the little girl. He couldn't imagine how lonely it must be for a child to be so profoundly different. He refolded the articles, pausing for one last look at the photo of the five-year-old Sienna in the role of Puck. Langdon had to admit, considering the surreal quality of his encounter with Sienna this morning, that her role as the mischievous, dream-inducing sprite seemed strangely apt. Langdon only wished that he, like the characters in the play, could now simply wake up and pretend that his most recent experiences were all a dream.

Langdon carefully replaced all the clippings on the proper page and closed the playbill, feeling an unexpected melancholy as he again saw the note on the cover: **Sweetheart, never forget you're a miracle.**

His eyes moved down to the familiar symbol adorning the cover of the playbill. It was the same early Greek pictogram that adorned most playbills around the world—a 2,500-year-old symbol that had become synonymous with dramatic theater.

Le maschere.

Langdon looked at the iconic faces of Comedy and Tragedy gazing up at him, and suddenly he heard a strange humming in his ears—as if a wire were

slowly being pulled taut inside his mind. A stab
of pain erupted inside his skull. Visions of a mask
floated before his eyes. Langdon gasped and raised
his hands, sitting down in the desk chair and closing
his eyes tightly, clutching at his scalp.

In his darkness, the bizarre visions returned with a
fury . . . stark and vivid.

The silver-haired woman with the amulet was calling to him again from across a bloodred river. Her
shouts of desperation pierced the putrid air, clearly
audible over the sounds of the tortured and dying,
who thrashed in agony as far as the eye could see.
Langdon again saw the upside-down legs adorned
with the letter **R**, the half-buried body pedaling its
legs in wild desperation in the air.

Seek and find! the woman called to Langdon.
Time is running out!

Langdon again felt the overwhelming need to help
her . . . to help **everyone**. Frantic, he shouted back to
her across the bloodred river. **Who are you?!**

Once again, the woman reached up and lifted her
veil to reveal the same striking visage that Langdon
had seen earlier.

I am life, she said.

Without warning, a colossal image materialized
in the sky above her—a fearsome mask with a long,
beaklike nose and two fiery green eyes, which stared
blankly out at Langdon.

And . . . I am death, the voice boomed.

CHAPTER 8

Langdon's eyes shot open, and he drew a startled breath. He was still seated at Sienna's desk, head in his hands, heart pounding wildly.

What the hell is happening to me?

The images of the silver-haired woman and the beaked mask lingered in his mind. **I am life. I am death.** He tried to shake the vision, but it felt seared permanently into his mind. On the desk before him, the playbill's two masks stared up at him.

Your memories will be muddled and uncataloged, Sienna had told him. **Past, present, and imagination all mixed together.**

Langdon felt dizzy.

Somewhere in the apartment, a phone was ringing. It was a piercing, old-fashioned ring, coming from the kitchen.

"Sienna?!" Langdon called out, standing up.

No response. She had not yet returned. After only two rings, an answering machine picked up.

"**Ciao, sono io,**" Sienna's voice happily declared on her outgoing message. "**Lasciatemi un messaggio e vi richiamerò.**"

There was a beep, and a panicked woman began

leaving a message in a thick Eastern European accent. Her voice echoed down the hall.

"Sienna, eez Danikova! Where you?! Eez terrible! Your friend Dr. Marconi, he dead! Hospital going craaazy! Police come here! People telling them you running out trying to save **patient**?! Why!? You don't know him! Now police want to talk to **you**! They take employee file! I know information wrong—bad address, no numbers, fake working visa—so they no find you today, but soon they find! I try to warn you. So sorry, Sienna."

The call ended.

Langdon felt a fresh wave of remorse engulfing him. From the sounds of the message, Dr. Marconi had been permitting Sienna to work at the hospital. Now Langdon's presence had cost Marconi his life, and Sienna's instinct to save a stranger had dire implications for her future.

Just then a door closed loudly at the far end of the apartment.

She's back.

A moment later, the answering machine blared. "Sienna, eez Danikova! Where you?!"

Langdon winced, knowing what Sienna was about to hear. As the message played, Langdon quickly put away the playbill, neatening the desk. Then he slipped back across the hall into the bathroom, feeling uncomfortable about his glimpse into Sienna's past.

Ten seconds later, there was a soft knock on the bathroom door.

"I'll leave your clothes on the doorknob," Sienna said, her voice ragged with emotion.

"Thank you so much," Langdon replied.

"When you're done, please come out to the kitchen," she added. "There's something important I need to show you before we call anyone."

———

Sienna walked tiredly down the hall to the apartment's modest bedroom. Retrieving a pair of blue jeans and a sweater from the dresser, she carried them into her bathroom.

Locking her eyes with her own reflection in the mirror, she reached up, grabbed a clutch of her thick blond ponytail, and pulled down hard, sliding the wig from her bald scalp.

A hairless thirty-two-year-old woman stared back at her from the mirror.

Sienna had endured no shortage of challenges in her life, and although she had trained herself to rely on intellect to overcome hardship, her current predicament had shaken her on a deeply emotional level.

She set the wig aside and washed her face and hands. After drying off, she changed her clothes and put the wig back on, straightening it carefully. Self-pity was an impulse Sienna seldom tolerated, but now, as the tears welled up from deep within, she knew she had no choice but to let them come.

And so she did.

She cried for the life she could not control.

She cried for the mentor who had died before her eyes.

She cried for the profound loneliness that filled her heart.

But, above all, she cried for the future . . . which suddenly felt so uncertain.

CHAPTER 9

Belowdecks on the luxury vessel The Mendacium, facilitator Laurence Knowlton sat in his sealed glass cubicle and stared in disbelief at his computer monitor, having just previewed the video their client had left behind.

I'm supposed to upload this to the media tomorrow morning?

In his ten years with the Consortium, Knowlton had performed all kinds of strange tasks that he knew fell somewhere between dishonest and illegal. Working within a moral gray area was commonplace at the Consortium—an organization whose lone ethical high ground was that they would do whatever it took to keep a promise to a client.

We follow through. No questions asked. No matter what.

The prospect of uploading this video, however, had left Knowlton unsettled. In the past, no matter what bizarre tasks he had performed, he always understood the rationale . . . grasped the motives . . . comprehended the desired outcome.

And yet this video was baffling.

Something about it felt different.

Much different.

Sitting back down at his computer, Knowlton restarted the video file, hoping a second viewing might shed more light. He turned up the volume and settled in for the nine-minute show.

As before, the video began with the soft lapping of water in the eerie water-filled cavern where everything was bathed in a numinous red light. Again the camera plunged down through the surface of the illuminated water to view the silt-covered floor of the cavern. And again, Knowlton read the text on the submerged plaque:

IN THIS PLACE, ON THIS DATE,
THE WORLD WAS CHANGED FOREVER.

That the polished plaque was signed by the Consortium's client was disquieting. That the date was **tomorrow** . . . left Knowlton increasingly concerned. It was what followed, however, that had truly set Knowlton on edge.

The camera now panned to the left to reveal a startling object hovering underwater just beside the plaque.

Here, tethered to the floor by a short filament, was an undulating sphere of thin plastic. Delicate and wobbling like an oversize soap bubble, the transparent shape floated like an underwater balloon . . . inflated not with helium, but with some kind of gelatinous, yellow-brown liquid. The amorphous bag was distended and appeared to be about a foot in diameter, and within its transparent walls, the murky cloud of liquid seemed to swirl slowly, like the eye of a silently growing storm.

Jesus, Knowlton thought, feeling clammy. The suspended bag looked even more ominous the second time around.

Slowly, the image faded to black.

A new image appeared—the cavern's damp wall, dancing with the rippling reflections of the illuminated lagoon. On the wall, a shadow appeared . . . the shadow of a man . . . standing in the cavern.

But the man's head was misshapen . . . badly.

Instead of a nose, the man had a long beak . . . as if he were half bird.

When he spoke, his voice was muffled . . . and he spoke with an eerie eloquence . . . a measured cadence . . . as if he were the narrator in some kind of classical chorus.

Knowlton sat motionless, barely breathing, as the beaked shadow spoke.

I am the Shade.

If you are watching this, then it means my soul is finally at rest.

Driven underground, I must speak to the world from deep within the earth, exiled to this gloomy cavern where the bloodred waters collect in the lagoon that reflects no stars.

But this is my paradise . . . the perfect womb for my fragile child.

Inferno.

Soon you will know what I have left behind.

And yet, even here, I sense the footfalls of the ignorant souls who pursue me . . . willing to stop at nothing to thwart my actions.

Forgive them, you might say, for they know not what they do. But there comes a moment in history when ignorance is no longer a forgivable offense . . . a moment when only wisdom has the power to absolve.

With purity of conscience, I have bequeathed to you all the gift of Hope, of salvation, of tomorrow.

And yet still there are those who hunt me like a dog, fueled by the self-righteous belief that I am a madman. There is the silver-haired beauty who dares call me monster! Like the blind clerics who lobbied for the death of Copernicus, she scorns me as a demon, terrified that I have glimpsed the Truth.

But I am not a prophet.

I am your salvation.

I am the Shade.

CHAPTER 10

"H ave a seat," Sienna said. "I have some questions for you."

As Langdon entered the kitchen, he felt much steadier on his feet. He was wearing the neighbor's Brioni suit, which fit remarkably well. Even the loafers were comfortable, and Langdon made a mental note to switch to Italian footwear when he got home.

If I get home, he thought.

Sienna was transformed—a natural beauty—having changed into formfitting jeans and a cream-colored sweater, both of which complemented her lithe figure. Her hair was still pulled back in a ponytail, and without the authoritative air of medical scrubs, she seemed more vulnerable somehow. Langdon noticed her eyes were red, as if she had been crying, and an overwhelming guilt again gripped him.

"Sienna, I'm so sorry. I heard the phone message. I don't know what to say."

"Thanks," she replied. "But we need to focus on **you** at the moment. Please sit down."

Her tone was firmer now, conjuring memories of the articles Langdon had just read about her intellect and precocious childhood.

"I need you to think," Sienna said, motioning for him to sit. "Can you remember how we got to this apartment?"

Langdon wasn't sure how it was relevant. "In a taxi," he said, sitting down at the table. "Someone was shooting at us."

"Shooting at **you**, Professor. Let's be clear on that."

"Yes. Sorry."

"And do you remember any gunshots while you were in the cab?"

Odd question. "Yes, two of them. One hit the side mirror, and the other broke the rear window."

"Good, now close your eyes."

Langdon realized she was testing his memory. He closed his eyes.

"What am I wearing?"

Langdon could see her perfectly. "Black flats, blue jeans, and a cream V-neck sweater. Your hair is blond, shoulder length, pulled back. Your eyes are brown."

Langdon opened his eyes and studied her, pleased to see his eidetic memory was functioning normally.

"Good. Your visual cognitive imprinting is excellent, which confirms your amnesia is fully retrograde, and you have no permanent damage to the memory-making process. Have you recalled anything new from the last few days?"

"No, unfortunately. I did have another wave of visions while you were gone, though."

Langdon told her about the recurrence of his hallucination of the veiled woman, the throngs of dead people, and the writhing, half-buried legs marked with the letter **R**. Then he told her about the strange, beaked mask hovering in the sky.

" 'I am death'?" Sienna asked, looking troubled.

"That's what it said, yes."

"Okay . . . I guess that beats 'I am Vishnu, destroyer of worlds.' "

The young woman had just quoted Robert Oppenheimer at the moment he tested the first atomic bomb.

"And this beak-nosed . . . green-eyed mask?" Sienna said, looking puzzled. "Do you have any idea why your mind might have conjured that image?"

"No idea at all, but that style of mask was quite common in the Middle Ages." Langdon paused. "It's called a plague mask."

Sienna looked strangely unnerved. "A plague mask?"

Langdon quickly explained that in his world of symbols, the unique shape of the long-beaked mask was nearly synonymous with the Black Death—the deadly plague that swept through Europe in the 1300s, killing off a third of the population in some regions. Most believed the "black" in Black Death was a reference to the darkening of the victims' flesh through gangrene and subepidermal hemorrhages, but in fact the word **black** was a reference to the profound emotional dread that the pandemic spread through the population.

"That long-beaked mask," Langdon said, "was worn by medieval plague doctors to keep the pestilence far from their nostrils while treating the infected. Nowadays, you only see them worn as costumes during Venice Carnevale—an eerie reminder of a grim period in Italy's history."

"And you're certain you saw one of these masks in your visions?" Sienna asked, her voice now tremulous. "A mask of a medieval plague doctor?"

Langdon nodded. **A beaked mask is hard to mistake.**

Sienna was knitting her brow in a way that gave Langdon the sense she was trying to figure out how best to give him some bad news. "And the woman kept telling you to 'seek and find'?"

"Yes. Just as before. But the problem is, I have no idea what I'm supposed to seek."

Sienna let out a long slow breath, her expression grave. "I think I may know. And what's more . . . I think you may have already found it."

Langdon stared. "What are you talking about?!"

"Robert, last night when you arrived at the hospital, you were carrying something unusual in your jacket pocket. Do you recall what it was?"

Langdon shook his head.

"You were carrying an object . . . a rather startling object. I found it by chance when we were cleaning you up." She motioned to Langdon's bloody Harris Tweed, which was laid out flat on the table. "It's still in the pocket, if you'd like to have a look."

Uncertain, Langdon eyed his jacket. **At least that explains why she went back for my jacket.** He grabbed his bloodstained coat and searched all the pockets, one by one. Nothing. He did it again. Finally, he turned to her with a shrug. "There's nothing here."

"How about the secret pocket?"

"What? My jacket doesn't have a secret pocket."

"No?" She looked puzzled. "Then is this jacket . . . someone else's?"

Langdon's brain felt muddled again. "No, this is **my** jacket."

"You're certain?"

Damned certain, he thought. **In fact, it used to be my favorite Camberley.**

He folded back the lining and showed Sienna the label bearing his favorite symbol in the fashion world—Harris Tweed's iconic orb adorned with thirteen buttonlike jewels and topped by a Maltese cross. **Leave it to the Scots to invoke the Christian warriors on a piece of twill.**

"Look at this," Langdon said, pointing out the hand-embroidered initials—**R.L.**—that had been added to the label. He always sprang for Harris Tweed's hand-tailored models, and for that reason, he always paid extra to have them sew his initials into the label. On a college campus where hundreds of tweed jackets were constantly doffed and donned in dining halls and classrooms, Langdon had no intention of getting the short end of an inadvertent trade.

"I believe you," she said, taking the jacket from him. "Now **you** look."

Sienna opened the jacket farther to reveal the lining near the nape of the back. Here, discreetly hidden in the lining, was a large, neatly fashioned pocket.

What the hell?!

Langdon was certain he had never seen this before.

The pocket consisted of a hidden seam, perfectly tailored.

"That wasn't there before!" Langdon insisted.

"Then I'm imagining you've never seen . . . **this?**" Sienna reached into the pocket and extracted a sleek metal object, which she set gently in Langdon's hands.

Langdon stared down at the object in utter bewilderment.

"Do you know what this is?" Sienna asked.

"No . . ." he stammered. "I've never seen anything like it."

"Well, unfortunately, I **do** know what this is. And I'm fairly certain it's the reason someone is trying to kill you."

———

Now pacing his private cubicle aboard **The Mendacium**, facilitator Knowlton felt an increasing disquiet as he considered the video he was supposed to share with the world tomorrow morning.

I am the Shade?

Rumors had circulated that this particular client had suffered a psychotic break over the last few months, but this video seemed to confirm those rumors beyond any doubt.

Knowlton knew he had two choices. He could either prepare the video for delivery tomorrow as promised, or he could take it upstairs to the provost for a second opinion.

I already know his opinion, Knowlton thought, having never witnessed the provost take any action other than the one promised a client. **He'll tell me to upload this video to the world, no questions asked . . . and he'll be furious at me for asking.**

Knowlton returned his attention to the video, which he rewound to a particularly unsettling spot. He started the playback, and the eerily illuminated cavern reappeared accompanied by the sounds of lapping water. The humanoid shadow loomed on the dripping wall—a tall man with a long, birdlike beak.

In a muffled voice, the deformed shadow spoke:

> These are the new Dark Ages.
> Centuries ago, Europe was in the depths of its own misery—the population huddled, starving, mired in sin and hopelessness. They were as a congested forest, suffocated by deadwood, awaiting God's lightning strike—the spark that would finally ignite the fire that would rage across the land and clear the deadwood, once again bringing sunshine to the healthy roots.
> Culling is God's Natural Order.
> Ask yourself, What followed the Black Death?
> We all know the answer.
> The Renaissance.

Rebirth.

It has always been this way. Death is followed by birth.

To reach Paradise, man must pass through Inferno.

This, the master taught us.

And yet the silver-haired ignorant dares call me monster? Does she still not grasp the mathematics of the future? The horrors it will bring?

I am the Shade.

I am your salvation.

And so I stand, deep within this cavern, gazing out across the lagoon that reflects no stars. Here in this sunken palace, Inferno smolders beneath the waters.

Soon it will burst into flames.

And when it does, nothing on earth will be able to stop it.

CHAPTER 11

The object in Langdon's hand felt surprisingly heavy for its size. Slender and smooth, the polished metal cylinder was about six inches long and rounded at both ends, like a miniature torpedo.

"Before you handle that too roughly," Sienna offered, "you may want to look at the other side." She gave him a taut smile. "You say you're a professor of symbols?"

Langdon refocused on the tube, turning it in his hands until a bright red symbol rolled into view, emblazoned on its side.

Instantly, his body tensed.

As a student of iconography, Langdon knew that precious few images had the power to instill instantaneous fear in the human mind . . . but the symbol before him definitely made the list. His reaction was visceral and immediate; he placed the tube on the table and slid back his chair.

Sienna nodded. "Yeah, that was my reaction, too."

The marking on the tube was a simple trilateral icon.

This notorious symbol, Langdon had once read, was developed by Dow Chemical in the 1960s to replace an array of impotent warning graphics previously in use. Like all successful symbols, this one was simple, distinctive, and easy to reproduce. Cleverly conjuring associations with everything from crab pincers to ninja hurling knives, the modern "biohazard" symbol had become a global brand that conveyed **danger** in every language.

"This little canister is a biotube," Sienna said. "Used for transporting dangerous substances. We see these occasionally in the medical field. Inside is a foam sleeve into which you can insert a specimen tube for safe transport. In this case . . ." She pointed to the biohazard symbol. "I'm guessing a deadly chemical agent . . . or maybe a . . . virus?" She paused. "The first Ebola samples were brought back from Africa in a tube similar to this one."

This was not at all what Langdon wanted to hear. "What the hell is it doing in my jacket! I'm an art history professor; why am I carrying this thing?!"

Violent images of writhing bodies flashed through his mind . . . and hovering over them, the plague mask.

Very sorry . . . Very sorry.

"Wherever this came from," Sienna said, "this is a very high-end unit. Lead-lined titanium. Virtually impenetrable, even to radiation. I'm guessing government issue." She pointed to a postage-stamp-size black pad flanking the biohazard symbol. "Thumbprint recognition. Security in case it's lost or stolen.

Tubes like this can be opened only by a specified individual."

Although Langdon sensed his mind now working at normal speed, he still felt as if he were struggling to catch up. **I've been carrying a biometrically sealed canister.**

"When I discovered this canister in your jacket, I wanted to show Dr. Marconi privately, but I didn't have an opportunity before you woke up. I considered trying your thumb on the pad while you were unconscious, but I had no idea what was in the tube, and—"

"MY thumb?!" Langdon shook his head. "There's no way this thing is programmed for **me** to open it. I don't know anything about biochemistry. I'd never have anything like this."

"Are you sure?"

Langdon was damned sure. He reached out and placed his thumb on the finger pad. Nothing happened. "See?! I told—"

The titanium tube clicked loudly, and Langdon yanked his hand back as if it had been burned. **Holy shit.** He stared at the canister as if it were about to unscrew itself and start emitting a deadly gas. After three seconds, it clicked again, apparently relocking itself.

Speechless, Langdon turned to Sienna.

The young doctor exhaled, looking unnerved. "Well, it seems pretty clear that the intended carrier is you."

For Langdon, the entire scenario felt incongruous.

"That's impossible. First of all, how would I get this chunk of metal through airport security?"

"Maybe you flew in on a private jet? Or maybe it was given to you when you arrived in Italy?"

"Sienna, I need to call the consulate. Right away."

"You don't think we should open it first?"

Langdon had taken some ill-advised actions in his life, but opening a hazardous materials container in this woman's kitchen would not be one of them. "I'm handing this thing over to the authorities. Now."

Sienna pursed her lips, mulling over options. "Okay, but as soon as you make that call, you're on your own. I can't be involved. You definitely can't meet them here. My immigration situation in Italy is . . . complicated."

Langdon looked Sienna in the eye. "All I know, Sienna, is that you saved my life. I'll handle this situation however you want me to handle it."

She gave a grateful nod and walked over to the window, gazing down at the street below. "Okay, this is how we should do it."

Sienna quickly outlined a plan. It was simple, clever, and safe.

Langdon waited as she turned on her cell phone's caller-ID blocking and dialed. Her fingers were delicate and yet moved purposefully.

"**Informazioni abbonati?**" Sienna said, speaking in a flawless Italian accent. "**Per favore, può darmi il numero del Consolato americano di Firenze?**"

She waited and then quickly wrote down a phone number.

"**Grazie mille**," she said, and hung up.

Sienna slid the phone number over to Langdon along with her cell phone. "You're on. Do you remember what to say?"

"My memory is fine," he said with a smile as he dialed the number on the slip of paper. The line began to ring.

Here goes nothing.

He switched the call to speaker and set the phone on the table so Sienna could hear. A recorded message answered, offering general information about consulate services and hours of operation, which did not begin until 8:30 A.M.

Langdon checked the clock on the cell. It was only 6 A.M.

"If this is an emergency," the automated recording said, "you may dial seven-seven to speak to the night duty officer."

Langdon immediately dialed the extension.

The line was ringing again.

"**Consolato americano**," a tired voice answered. "**Sono il funzionario di turno.**"

"**Lei parla inglese?**" Langdon asked.

"Of course," the man said in American English. He sounded vaguely annoyed to have been awoken. "How can I help you?"

"I'm an American visiting Florence and I was attacked. My name is Robert Langdon."

"Passport number, please." The man yawned audibly.

"My passport is missing. I think it was stolen. I

was shot in the head. I've been in the hospital. I need help."

The attendant suddenly woke up. "Sir!? Did you say you were **shot**? What was your full name again, please?"

"Robert Langdon."

There was a rustling on the line and then Langdon could hear the man's fingers typing on a keyboard. The computer pinged. A pause. Then more fingers on the keyboard. Another ping. Then three high-pitched pings.

A longer pause.

"Sir?" the man said. "Your name is Robert Lang-don?"

"Yes, that's right. And I'm in trouble."

"Okay, sir, your name has an action flag on it, which is directing me to transfer you immediately to the con-sul general's chief administrator." The man paused, as if he himself couldn't believe it. "Just hold the line."

"Wait! Can you tell me—"

The line was already ringing.

It rang four times and connected.

"This is Collins," a hoarse voice answered.

Langdon took a deep breath and spoke as calmly and clearly as possible. "Mr. Collins, my name is Robert Langdon. I'm an American visiting Florence. I've been shot. I need help. I want to come to the U.S. Consulate immediately. Can you help me?"

Without hesitation, the deep voice replied, "Thank heavens you're alive, Mr. Langdon. We've been look-ing for you."

CHAPTER 12

The consulate knows I'm here?

For Langdon, the news brought an instantaneous flood of relief.

Mr. Collins—who had introduced himself as the consul general's chief administrator—spoke with a firm, professional cadence, and yet there was urgency in his voice. "Mr. Langdon, you and I need to speak immediately. And obviously not on the phone."

Nothing was obvious to Langdon at this point, but he wasn't about to interrupt.

"I'll have someone pick you up right away," Collins said. "What is your location?"

Sienna shifted nervously, listening to the interchange on speakerphone. Langdon gave her a reassuring nod, fully intending to follow her plan exactly.

"I'm in a small hotel called Pensione la Fiorentina," Langdon said, glancing across the street at the drab hotel that Sienna had pointed out moments ago. He gave Collins the street address.

"Got it," the man replied. "Don't move. Stay in your room. Someone will be there right away. Room number?"

Langdon made one up. "Thirty-nine."

"Okay. Twenty minutes." Collins lowered his

voice. "And, Mr. Langdon, it sounds like you may be injured and confused, but I need to know . . . are you still in possession?"

In possession. Langdon sensed the question, while cryptic, could have only one meaning. His eyes moved to the biotube on the kitchen table. "Yes, sir. I'm still in possession."

Collins exhaled audibly. "When we didn't hear from you, we assumed . . . well, frankly, we assumed the worst. I'm relieved. Stay where you are. Don't move. Twenty minutes. Someone will knock on your door."

Collins hung up.

Langdon could feel his shoulders relaxing for the first time since he'd woken up in the hospital. **The consulate knows what's going on, and soon I'll have answers.** Langdon closed his eyes and let out a slow breath, feeling almost human now. His headache had all but passed.

"Well, that was all very MI6," Sienna said in a half-joking tone. "Are you a spy?"

At the moment Langdon had no idea what he was. The notion that he could lose two days of memory and find himself in an unrecognizable situation felt incomprehensible, and yet here he was . . . twenty minutes away from a rendezvous with a U.S. Consulate official in a run-down hotel.

What's happening here?

He glanced over at Sienna, realizing they were about to part ways and yet feeling as if they had unfinished business. He pictured the bearded doctor at the hospital, dying on the floor before her eyes. "Sienna," he whispered, "your friend . . . Dr. Marconi . . . I feel terrible."

She nodded blankly.

"And I'm sorry to have dragged you into this. I know your situation at the hospital is unusual, and if there's an investigation . . ." He trailed off.

"It's okay," she said. "I'm no stranger to moving around."

Langdon sensed in Sienna's distant eyes that everything had changed for her this morning. Langdon's own life was in chaos at the moment, and yet he felt his heart going out to this woman.

She saved my life . . . and I've ruined hers.

They sat in silence for a full minute, the air between them growing heavy, as if they both wanted to speak, and yet had nothing to say. They were strangers, after all, on a brief and bizarre journey that had just reached a fork in the road, each of them now needing to find separate paths.

"Sienna," Langdon finally said, "when I sort this out with the consulate, if there's anything I can do to help you . . . please."

"Thanks," she whispered, and turned her eyes sadly toward the window.

———

As the minutes ticked past, Sienna Brooks gazed absently out the kitchen window and wondered where the day would lead her. Wherever it was, she had no doubt that by day's end, her world would look a lot different.

She knew it was probably just the adrenaline, but she found herself strangely attracted to the American professor. In addition to his being handsome, he seemed to possess a sincerely good heart. In some distant, alternate life, Robert Langdon might even be someone she could be with.

He would never want me, she thought. **I'm damaged.**

As she choked back the emotion, something outside the window caught her eye. She bolted upright, pressing her face to the glass and staring down into the street. "Robert, look!"

Langdon peered down into the street at the sleek black BMW motorcycle that had just rumbled to a stop in front of Pensione la Fiorentina. The driver was lean and strong, wearing a black leather suit and helmet. As the driver gracefully swung off the bike and removed a polished black helmet, Sienna could hear Langdon stop breathing.

The woman's spiked hair was unmistakable.

She produced a familiar handgun, checked the silencer, and slid it back inside her jacket pocket. Then, moving with lethal grace, she slipped inside the hotel.

"Robert," Sienna whispered, her voice taut with fear. "The U.S. government just sent someone to kill you."

CHAPTER 13

Robert Langdon felt a swell of panic as he stood at the apartment window, eyes riveted on the hotel across the street. The spike-haired woman had just entered, but Langdon could not fathom how she had gotten the address.

Adrenaline coursed through his system, disjointing his thought process once again. "My own government sent someone to kill me?"

Sienna looked equally astounded. "Robert, that means the original attempt on your life at the hospital also was sanctioned by your government." She got up and double-checked the lock on the apartment door. "If the U.S. Consulate has permission to kill you . . ." She didn't finish the thought, but she didn't have to. The implications were terrifying.

What the hell do they think I did? Why is my own government hunting me?!

Once again, Langdon heard the two words he had apparently been mumbling when he staggered into the hospital.

Very sorry . . . very sorry.

"You're not safe here," Sienna said. "We're not safe here." She motioned across the street. "That woman saw us flee the hospital together, and I'm betting your government and the police are already trying to track me down. My apartment is a sublet in someone else's name, but they'll find me eventually." She turned her attention to the biotube on the table. "You need to open that, right now."

Langdon eyed the titanium device, seeing only the biohazard symbol.

"Whatever's inside that tube," Sienna said, "probably has an ID code, an agency sticker, a phone number, **something**. You need information. I need information! Your government killed my friend!"

The pain in Sienna's voice shook Langdon from his thoughts, and he nodded, knowing she was correct. "Yes, I'm . . . very sorry." Langdon cringed, hearing those words again. He turned to the canister on the table, wondering what answers might be hidden inside. "It could be incredibly dangerous to open this."

Sienna thought for a moment. "Whatever's inside will be exceptionally well contained, probably in a shatterproof Plexiglas test tube. This biotube is just an outer shell to provide additional security during transport."

Langdon looked out the window at the black motorcycle parked in front of the hotel. The woman had not yet come out, but she would soon figure out that Langdon was not there. He wondered what her next move would be . . . and how long it would take before she was pounding on the apartment door.

Langdon made up his mind. He lifted the titanium tube and reluctantly placed his thumb on the biometric pad. After a moment the canister pinged and then clicked loudly.

Before the tube could lock itself again, Langdon twisted the two halves against each other in opposite directions. After a quarter turn, the canister pinged a second time, and Langdon knew he was committed.

Langdon's hands felt sweaty as he continued unscrewing the tube. The two halves turned smoothly on perfectly machined threads. He kept twisting, feeling as if he were about to open a precious Russian nesting doll, except that he had no idea what might fall out.

After five turns, the two halves released. With a deep breath, Langdon gently pulled them apart. The gap between the halves widened, and a foam-rubber interior slid out. Langdon laid it on the table. The protective padding vaguely resembled an elongated Nerf football.

Here goes nothing.

Langdon gently folded back the top of the protective foam, finally revealing the object nestled inside.

Sienna stared down at the contents and cocked her head, looking puzzled. "Definitely not what I expected."

Langdon had anticipated some kind of futuristic-looking vial, but the content of the biotube was anything but modern. The ornately carved object appeared to be made of ivory and was approximately the size of a roll of Life Savers.

"It looks old," Sienna whispered. "Some kind of . . ."

"Cylinder seal," Langdon told her, finally permitting himself to exhale.

Invented by the Sumerians in 3500 B.C., cylinder seals were the precursors to the intaglio form of printmaking. Carved with decorative images, a seal contained a hollow shaft, through which an axle pin was inserted so the carved drum could be rolled like a modern paint roller across wet clay or terra-cotta to "imprint" a recurring band of symbols, images, or text.

This particular seal, Langdon guessed, was undoubtedly quite rare and valuable, and yet he still couldn't imagine why it would be locked in a titanium canister like some kind of bioweapon.

As Langdon delicately turned the seal in his fingers, he realized that this one bore an especially gruesome carving—a three-headed, horned Satan who was in the process of eating three different men at once, one man in each of his three mouths.

Pleasant.

Langdon's eyes moved to seven letters carved beneath the devil. The ornate calligraphy was written in mirror image, as was all text on imprinting rollers, but Langdon had no trouble reading the letters—SALIGIA.

Sienna squinted at the text, reading it aloud. "Saligia?"

Langdon nodded, feeling a chill to hear the word spoken aloud. "It's a Latin mnemonic invented by the Vatican in the Middle Ages to remind Christians of the Seven Deadly Sins. **Saligia** is an acronym for:

superbia, **avaritia**, **luxuria**, **invidia**, **gula**, **ira**, and **acedia**."

Sienna frowned. "Pride, greed, lust, envy, gluttony, wrath, and sloth."

Langdon was impressed. "You know Latin."

"I grew up Catholic. I know sin."

Langdon managed a smile as he returned his gaze to the seal, wondering again why it had been locked in a biotube as if it were dangerous.

"I thought it was ivory," Sienna said. "But it's bone." She slid the artifact into the sunlight and pointed to the lines on it. "Ivory forms in a diamond-shaped cross-hatching with translucent striations; bones form with these parallel striations and darkened pitting."

Langdon gently picked up the seal and examined the carvings more closely. The original Sumerian seals had been carved with rudimentary figures and cuneiform. This seal, however, was much more elaborately carved. Medieval, Langdon guessed. Furthermore, the embellishments suggested an unsettling connection with his hallucinations.

Sienna eyed him with concern. "What is it?"

"Recurring theme," Langdon said grimly, and motioned to one of the carvings on the seal. "See this three-headed, man-eating Satan? It's a common image from the Middle Ages—an icon associated with the Black Death. The three gnashing mouths are symbolic of how efficiently the plague ate through the population."

Sienna glanced uneasily at the biohazard symbol on the tube.

Allusions to the plague seemed to be occurring with more frequency this morning than Langdon cared to admit, and so it was with reluctance that he acknowledged a further connection. "**Saligia** is representative of the collective sins of mankind . . . which, according to medieval religious indoctrination—"

"Was the reason God punished the world with the Black Death," Sienna said, completing his thought.

"Yes." Langdon paused, momentarily losing his train of thought. He had just noticed something about the cylinder that struck him as odd. Normally, a person could peer through a cylinder seal's hollow center, as if through a section of empty pipe, but in this case, the shaft was blocked. **There's something inserted inside this bone.** The end caught the light and shimmered.

"There's something inside," Langdon said. "And it looks like it's made of glass." He flipped the cylinder upside down to check the other end, and as he did so, a tiny object rattled inside, tumbling from one end of the bone to the other, like a ball bearing in a tube.

Langdon froze, and he heard Sienna let out a soft gasp beside him.

What the hell was that?!

"Did you hear that sound?" Sienna whispered.

Langdon nodded and carefully peered into the end of the canister. "The opening appears to be blocked by . . . something made of metal." **The cap of a test tube, maybe?**

Sienna backed away. "Does it look . . . broken?"

"I don't think so." He carefully tipped the bone

again to reexamine the glass end, and the rattling
sound recurred. An instant later, the glass in the cylinder did something wholly unexpected.

It began to glow.

Sienna's eyes opened wide. "Robert, stop! Don't
move!"

CHAPTER 14

Langdon stood absolutely still, his hand in mid-air, holding the bone cylinder steady. Without a doubt, the glass at the end of the tube was emitting light . . . glowing as if the contents had suddenly awoken.

Quickly, the light inside faded back to black.

Sienna moved closer, breathing quickly. She tilted her head and studied the visible section of glass inside the bone.

"Tip it again," she whispered. "Very slowly."

Langdon gently turned the bone upside down. Again, a small object rattled the length of the bone and stopped.

"Once more," she said. "Gently."

Langdon repeated the process, and again the tube rattled. This time, the interior glass shimmered faintly, glowing again for an instant before it faded away.

"It's got to be a test tube," Sienna declared, "with an agitator ball."

Langdon was familiar with the agitator balls used in spray-paint cans—submerged pellets that helped stir the paint when the can was shaken.

"It probably contains some kind of phosphorescent chemical compound," Sienna said, "or a bioluminescent organism that glows when it's stimulated."

Langdon was having other ideas. While he had seen chemical glow sticks and even bioluminescent plankton that glowed when a boat churned up its habitat, he was nearly certain the cylinder in his hand contained neither of these things. He gently tipped the tube several more times, until it glowed, and then held the luminescent end over his palm. As expected, a faint reddish light appeared, projected onto his skin.

Nice to know a 208 IQ can be wrong sometimes.

"Watch this," Langdon said, and began shaking the tube violently. The object inside rattled back and forth, faster and faster.

Sienna jumped back. "What are you doing!?"

Still shaking the tube, Langdon walked over to the light switch and flipped it off, plunging the kitchen into relative darkness. "It's not a test tube inside," he said, still shaking as hard as he could. "It's a Faraday pointer."

Langdon had once been given a similar device by one of his students—a laser pointer for lecturers who disliked wasting endless AAA batteries and didn't mind the effort of shaking their pointer for a few seconds in order to transform their own kinetic energy into electricity on demand. When the device was agitated, a metal ball inside sailed back and forth across a series of paddles and powered a tiny generator. Apparently someone had decided to slide this particular pointer into a hollow, carved bone—an ancient skin to sheathe a modern electronic toy.

The tip of the pointer in his hand was now glowing intensely, and Langdon gave Sienna an uneasy grin. "Showtime."

He aimed the bone-sheathed pointer at a bare space on the kitchen wall. When the wall lit up, Sienna drew a startled breath. It was Langdon, however, who physically recoiled in surprise.

The light that appeared on the wall was not a little red laser dot. It was a vivid, high-definition photograph that emanated from the tube as if from an old-fashioned slide projector.

My God! Langdon's hand trembled slightly as he absorbed the macabre scene projected on the wall before him. **No wonder I've been seeing images of death.**

At his side, Sienna covered her mouth and took a tentative step forward, clearly entranced by what she was seeing.

The scene projected out of the carved bone was a grim oil painting of human suffering—thousands of souls undergoing wretched tortures in various levels of hell. The underworld was portrayed as a cutaway cross section of the earth into which plunged a cavernous funnel-shaped pit of unfathomable depth. This pit of hell was divided into descending terraces of increasing misery, each level populated by tormented sinners of every kind.

Langdon recognized the image at once.

The masterpiece before him—**La Mappa dell'Inferno**—had been painted by one of the true giants of the Italian Renaissance, Sandro Botticelli. An elaborate blueprint of the underworld, **The Map of Hell** was one of the most frightening visions of the afterlife ever created. Dark, grim, and terrifying, the painting stopped people in their tracks even today. Unlike his vibrant and colorful **Primavera** or **Birth of Venus**, Botticelli had crafted his **Map of Hell** with a depressing palate of reds, sepias, and browns.

Langdon's crashing headache had suddenly returned, and yet for the first time since waking up in a strange hospital, he felt a piece of the puzzle tumble into place. His grim hallucinations obviously had been stirred by seeing this famous painting.

I must have been studying Botticelli's Map of Hell, he thought, although he had no recollection of why.

While the image itself was disturbing, it was the painting's provenance that was now causing Langdon an increasing disquiet. Langdon was well aware that the inspiration for this foreboding masterpiece had originated **not** in the mind of Botticelli himself . . . but rather in the mind of someone who had lived two hundred years before him.

One great work of art inspired by another.

Botticelli's **Map of Hell** was in fact a tribute to a fourteenth-century work of literature that had become one of history's most celebrated writings . . . a notoriously macabre vision of hell that resonated to this day.

Dante's **Inferno.**

———

Across the street, Vayentha quietly climbed a service staircase and concealed herself on the rooftop terrace of the sleepy little Pensione la Fiorentina. Langdon had provided a nonexistent room number and a fake meeting place to his consulate contact—a "mirrored meet," as it was called in her business—a common tradecraft technique that would enable him to assess the situation before revealing his own location. Invariably, the fake or "mirrored" location was selected because it lay in perfect view of his **actual** location.

Vayentha found a concealed vantage point on the rooftop from which she had a bird's-eye view of the entire area. Slowly, she let her eyes climb the apartment building across the street.

Your move, Mr. Langdon.

———

At that moment, on board **The Mendacium**, the provost stepped out onto the mahogany deck and inhaled deeply, savoring the salty air of the Adriatic. This vessel had been his home for years, and yet now, the series of events transpiring in Florence threatened to destroy everything he had built.

His field agent Vayentha had put everything at risk, and while she would face an inquiry when this mission was over, right now the provost still needed her.

She damned well better regain control of this mess.

Brisk footsteps approached behind him, and the provost turned to see one of his female analysts arriving at a jog.

"Sir?" the analyst said, breathless. "We have new information." Her voice cut the morning air with a rare intensity. "It appears Robert Langdon just accessed his Harvard e-mail account from an unmasked IP address." She paused, locking eyes with the provost. "Langdon's precise location is now traceable."

The provost was stunned that anyone could be so foolish. **This changes everything.** He steepled his hands and stared out at the coastline, considering the implications. "Do we know the status of the SRS team?"

"Yes, sir. Less than two miles away from Langdon's position."

The provost needed only a moment to make the decision.

CHAPTER 15

L'inferno di Dante," Sienna whispered, her expression rapt as she inched closer to the stark image of the underworld now projected on her kitchen wall.

Dante's vision of hell, Langdon thought, **rendered here in living color**.

Exalted as one of the preeminent works of world literature, the **Inferno** was the first of three books that made up Dante Alighieri's **Divine Comedy**—a 14,233-line epic poem describing Dante's brutal descent into the underworld, journey through purgatory, and eventual arrival in paradise. Of the **Comedy**'s three sections—**Inferno, Purgatorio**, and **Paradiso**—**Inferno** was by far the most widely read and memorable.

Composed by Dante Alighieri in the early 1300s, **Inferno** had quite literally redefined medieval perceptions of damnation. Never before had the concept of hell captivated the masses in such an entertaining way. Overnight, Dante's work solidified the abstract concept of hell into a clear and terrifying vision—visceral, palpable, and unforgettable. Not surprisingly, following the poem's release, the Catholic Church enjoyed an enormous uptick in attendance from terrified sinners looking to avoid Dante's updated version of the underworld.

Depicted here by Botticelli, Dante's horrific vision of hell was constructed as a subterranean funnel of suffering—a wretched underground landscape of fire, brimstone, sewage, monsters, and Satan himself waiting at its core. The pit was constructed in nine distinct levels, the Nine Rings of Hell, into which sinners were cast in accordance with the depth of their sin. Near the top, the **lustful** or "carnal male-factors" were blown about by an eternal windstorm, a symbol of their inability to control their desire. Beneath them the **gluttons** were forced to lie face-down in a vile slush of sewage, their mouths filled with the product of their excess. Deeper still, the **heretics** were trapped in flaming coffins, damned to eternal fire. And so it went . . . getting worse and worse the deeper one descended.

In the seven centuries since its publication, Dante's enduring vision of hell had inspired tributes, trans-lations, and variations by some of history's greatest creative minds. Longfellow, Chaucer, Marx, Milton, Balzac, Borges, and even several popes had all written pieces based on Dante's **Inferno**. Monteverdi, Liszt, Wagner, Tchaikovsky, and Puccini composed pieces based on Dante's work, as had one of Langdon's favorite living recording artists—Loreena McKen-nitt. Even the modern world of video games and iPad apps had no shortage of Dante-related offerings.

Langdon, eager to share with his students the vibrant symbolic richness of Dante's vision, sometimes taught a course on the recurring imagery found in both Dante and the works he had inspired over the centuries.

"Robert," Sienna said, shifting closer to the image on the wall. "Look at that!" She pointed to an area near the bottom of the funnel-shaped hell.

The area she was pointing to was known as the Malebolge—meaning "evil ditches." It was the eighth and penultimate ring of hell and was divided into ten separate ditches, each for a specific type of fraud.

Sienna pointed more excitedly now. "Look! Didn't you say, in your vision, you saw this?!"

Langdon squinted at where Sienna was pointing, but he saw nothing. The tiny projector was losing power, and the image had begun to fade. He quickly shook the device again until it was glowing brightly. Then he carefully set it farther back from the wall, on the edge of the counter across the small kitchen, letting it cast an even larger image from there. Langdon approached Sienna, stepping to the side to study the glowing map.

Again Sienna pointed down toward the eighth ring of hell. "Look. Didn't you say your hallucinations included a pair of legs sticking out of the earth upside down with the letter **R**?" She touched a precise spot on the wall. "There they are!"

As Langdon had seen many times in this painting, the tenth ditch of the Malebolge was packed with sinners half buried upside down, their legs sticking out of the earth. But strangely, in **this** version, one pair of legs bore the letter **R**, written in mud, exactly as Langdon had seen in his vision.

My God! Langdon peered more intently at the tiny detail. "That letter **R** . . . that is definitely **not** in Botticelli's original!"

"There's another letter," Sienna said, pointing.

Langdon followed her outstretched finger to another of the ten ditches in the Malebolge, where the letter **E** was scrawled on a false prophet whose head had been put on backward.

What in the world? This painting has been modified.

Other letters now appeared to him, scrawled on sinners throughout all ten ditches of the Malebolge. He saw a **C** on a seducer being whipped by demons . . . another **R** on a thief perpetually bitten by snakes . . . an **A** on a corrupt politician submerged in a boiling lake of tar.

"These letters," Langdon said with certainty, "are definitely **not** part of Botticelli's original. This image has been digitally edited."

He returned his gaze to the uppermost ditch of the Malebolge and began reading the letters downward, through each of the ten ditches, from top to bottom.

C . . . A . . . T . . . R . . . O . . . V . . . A . . . C . . . E . . . R

"**Catrovacer?**" Langdon said. "Is this Italian?"

Sienna shook her head. "Not Latin either. I don't recognize it."

"A . . . signature, maybe?"

"Catrovacer?" She looked doubtful. "Doesn't sound like a name to me. But look over there." She pointed to one of the many characters in the third ditch of the Malebolge.

When Langdon's eyes found the figure, he instantly felt a chill. Among the crowd of sinners in the third ditch was an iconic image from the Middle Ages—a cloaked man in a mask with a long, birdlike beak and dead eyes.

The plague mask.

"Is there a plague doctor in Botticelli's original?" Sienna asked.

"Absolutely not. That figure has been added."

"And did Botticelli **sign** his original?"

Langdon couldn't recall, but as his eyes moved to the lower right-hand corner where a signature normally would be, he realized why she had asked. There was no signature, and yet barely visible along **La Mappa**'s dark brown border was a line of text in tiny block letters: **la verità è visibile solo attraverso gli occhi della morte.**

Langdon knew enough Italian to understand the gist. " 'The truth can be glimpsed only through the eyes of death.' "

Sienna nodded. "Bizarre."

The two of them stood in silence as the morbid image before them slowly began to fade. **Dante's Inferno**, Langdon thought. **Inspiring foreboding pieces of art since 1330.**

Langdon's course on Dante always included an entire section on the illustrious artwork inspired by the **Inferno**. In addition to Botticelli's celebrated **Map of Hell**, there was Rodin's timeless sculpture of **The Three Shades** from **The Gates of Hell** . . . Stradanus's illustration of Phlegyas paddling through submerged bodies on the river Styx . . . William Blake's lustful sinners swirling through an eternal tempest . . . Bouguereau's strangely erotic vision of Dante and Virgil watching two nude men locked in battle . . . Bayros's tortured souls huddling beneath a hail-like torrent of scalding pellets and droplets of fire . . . Salvador Dalí's eccentric series of watercolors and woodcuts . . . and Doré's huge collection of black-and-white etchings depicting everything from the tunneled entrance to Hades . . . to winged Satan himself.

Now it seemed that Dante's poetic vision of hell had not only influenced the most revered artists throughout history. It had also, apparently, inspired yet another individual—a twisted soul who had digitally altered Botticelli's famous painting, adding ten letters, a plague doctor, and then signing it with an ominous phrase about seeing the truth through the eyes of death. This artist had then stored the image on a high-tech projector sheathed in a freakishly carved bone.

Langdon couldn't imagine who would have created such an artifact, and yet, at the moment, this issue seemed secondary to a far more unnerving question.

Why the hell am I carrying it?

———

As Sienna stood with Langdon in the kitchen and pondered her next move, the unexpected roar of a high-horsepower engine echoed up from the street below. It was followed by a staccato burst of screeching tires and car doors slamming.

Puzzled, Sienna hurried to the window and peered outside.

A black, unmarked van had skidded to a stop in the street below. Out of the van flowed a team of men, all dressed in black uniforms with circular green medallions on their left shoulders. They gripped automatic rifles and moved with fierce, military efficiency. Without hesitation, four soldiers dashed toward the entrance of the apartment building.

Sienna felt her blood go cold. "Robert!" she shouted. "I don't know who they are, but they found us!"

————

Down in the street, Agent Christoph Brüder shouted orders to his men as they rushed into the building. He was a powerfully built man whose military background had imbued him with an emotionless sense of duty and respect for the command chain. He knew his mission, and he knew the stakes.

The organization for whom he worked contained many divisions, but Brüder's division—Surveillance and Response Support—was summoned only when a situation reached "crisis" status.

As his men disappeared into the apartment building, Brüder stood watch at the front door, pulling out his comm device and contacting the person in charge.

"It's Brüder," he said. "We've successfully tracked Langdon through his computer IP address. My team is moving in. I'll alert you when we have him."

———

High above Brüder, on the rooftop terrace of Pensione la Fiorentina, Vayentha stared down in horrified disbelief at the agents dashing into the apartment building.

What the hell are THEY doing here?!

She ran a hand through her spiked hair, suddenly grasping the dire consequences of her botched assignment last night. With the single coo of a dove, everything had spiraled wildly out of control. What had begun as a simple mission . . . had now turned into a living nightmare.

If the SRS team is here, then it's all over for me.

Vayentha desperately grabbed her Sectra Tiger XS communications device and called the provost.

"Sir," she stammered. "The SRS team is here! Brüder's men are swarming the apartment building across the street!"

She awaited a response, but when it came, she heard only sharp clicks on the line, then an electronic voice, which calmly stated, "Disavowal protocol commencing."

Vayentha lowered the phone and looked at the screen just in time to see the comm device go dead.

As the blood drained from her face, Vayentha forced herself to accept what was happening. The Consortium had just severed all ties with her.

No links. No association.

I've been disavowed.

The shock lasted only an instant.

Then the fear set in.

CHAPTER **16**

urry, Robert!" Sienna urged. "Follow me!"
Langdon's thoughts were still consumed by grim images of Dante's underworld as he charged out the door into the hall of the apartment building. Until this instant, Sienna Brooks had managed the morning's substantial stress with a kind of detached poise, but now her calm demeanor had grown taut with an emotion Langdon had yet to see in her—true fear.

In the hallway, Sienna ran ahead, rushing past the elevator, which was already descending, no doubt summoned by the men now entering the lobby. She sprinted to the end of the hall and, without looking back, disappeared into the stairwell.

Langdon followed close behind, skidding on the smooth soles of his borrowed loafers. The tiny projector in the breast pocket of his Brioni suit bounced against his chest as he ran. His mind flashed on the strange letters adorning the eighth ring of hell: CATROVACER. He pictured the plague mask and the strange signature: **The truth can be glimpsed only through the eyes of death.**

Langdon strained to connect these disparate elements, but at the moment nothing was making sense. When he finally came to a stop on the staircase landing, Sienna was there, listening intently. Langdon could hear footsteps pounding up the stairs from below.

"Is there another exit?" Langdon whispered.

"Follow me," she said tersely.

Sienna had kept Langdon alive once already today, and so, with little choice but to trust the woman, Langdon took a deep breath and bounded down the stairs after her.

They descended one floor, and the sounds of approaching boots grew very close now, echoing only a floor or two below them.

Why is she running directly into them?

Before Langdon could protest, Sienna grabbed his hand and yanked him out of the stairwell along a deserted hallway of apartments—a long corridor of locked doors.

There's nowhere to hide!

Sienna flipped a light switch and a few bulbs went out, but the dim hallway did little to hide them. Sienna and Langdon were clearly visible here. The thundering footsteps were nearly upon them now, and Langdon knew their assailants would appear on the staircase at any moment, with a direct view down this hall.

"I need your jacket," Sienna whispered as she yanked Langdon's suit jacket off him. She then forced Langdon to crouch on his haunches behind her in a recessed doorframe. "Don't move."

What is she doing? She's in plain sight!

The soldiers appeared on the staircase, rushing upward but stopping short when they saw Sienna in the darkened hallway.

"**Per l'amore di Dio!**" Sienna shouted at them, her tone scathing. "**Cos'è questa confusione?**"

The two men squinted, clearly uncertain what they were looking at.

Sienna kept yelling at them. "**Tanto chiasso a quest'ora!**" So much noise at this hour!

Langdon now saw that Sienna had draped his black jacket over her head and shoulders like an old woman's shawl. She had hunched over, positioning herself to obstruct their view of Langdon crouched in the shadows, and now, utterly transformed, she hobbled one step toward them and screamed like a senile old woman.

One of the soldiers held up his hand, motioning for her to return to her apartment. "**Signora! Rientri subito in casa!**"

Sienna took another rickety step, shaking her fist angrily. "**Avete svegliato mio marito, che è malato!**"

Langdon listened in bewilderment. **They woke up your ailing husband?**

The other soldier now raised his machine gun and aimed directly at her. "**Ferma o sparo!**"

Sienna stopped short, cursing them mercilessly as she hobbled backward, away from them.

The men hurried on, disappearing up the stairs.

Not quite Shakespearean acting, Langdon thought, **but impressive.** Apparently a background in drama could be a versatile weapon.

Sienna removed the jacket from her head and tossed it back to Langdon. "Okay, follow me."

This time Langdon followed without hesitation.

They descended to the landing above the lobby, where two more soldiers were just entering the elevator to go upstairs. On the street outside, another soldier stood watch beside the van, his black uniform stretched taut across his muscular body. In silence, Sienna and Langdon hurried downstairs toward the basement.

The underground carport was dark and smelled of urine. Sienna jogged over to a corner packed with scooters and motorcycles. She stopped at a silver Trike—a three-wheeled moped contraption that looked like the ungainly offspring of an Italian Vespa and an adult tricycle. She ran her slender hand beneath the Trike's front fender and removed a small magnetized case. Inside was a key, which she inserted, and revved the engine.

Seconds later, Langdon was seated behind her on the bike. Precariously perched on the small seat, Langdon groped at his sides, looking for handgrips or something to steady himself.

"Not the moment for modesty," Sienna said, grabbing his hands and wrapping them around her slender waist. "You'll want to hold on."

Langdon did exactly that as Sienna gunned the Trike up the exit ramp. The vehicle had more power than he would have imagined, and they nearly left the ground as they launched out of the garage, emerging into the early-morning light about fifty yards from the main entrance. The brawny soldier in front of the building turned at once to see Langdon and Sienna tearing away, their Trike letting out a high-pitched whine as she opened the throttle.

Perched on the back, Langdon peered back over his shoulder toward the soldier, who now raised his weapon and took careful aim. Langdon braced himself. A single shot rang out, ricocheting off the Trike's back fender, barely missing the base of Langdon's spine.

Jesus!

Sienna made a hard left at an intersection, and Langdon felt himself sliding, fighting to keep his balance.

"Lean toward me!" she shouted.

Langdon leaned forward, centering himself again as Sienna raced the Trike down a larger thorough-fare. They had driven a full block before Langdon began breathing again.

Who the hell were those men?!

Sienna's focus remained locked on the road ahead as she raced down the avenue, weaving in and out of the light morning traffic. Several pedestrians did double takes as they passed, apparently puzzled to see a six-foot man in a Brioni suit riding **behind** a slender woman.

Langdon and Sienna had traveled three blocks and were approaching a major intersection when horns blared up ahead. A sleek black van rounded the cor-ner on two wheels, fishtailing into the intersection, and then accelerating up the road directly toward them. The van was identical to the soldiers' van back at the apartment building.

Sienna immediately swerved hard to her right and slammed on the brakes. Langdon's chest pressed hard into her back as she skidded to a stop out of sight behind a parked delivery truck. She nestled the Trike up to the rear bumper of the truck and killed the engine.

Did they see us!?

She and Langdon huddled low and waited . . . breathless.

The van roared past without hesitation, apparently never having seen them. As the vehicle sped by, however, Langdon caught a fleeting glimpse of someone inside.

In the backseat, an attractive older woman was wedged between two soldiers like a captive. Her eyes sagged and her head bobbed as if she were delirious or maybe drugged. She wore an amulet and had long silver hair that fell in ringlets.

For a moment Langdon's throat clenched, and he thought he'd seen a ghost.

It was the woman from his visions.

CHAPTER 17

The provost stormed out of the control room and marched along the long starboard deck of The Mendacium, trying to gather his thoughts. What had just transpired at the Florence apartment building was unthinkable.

He circled the entire ship twice before stalking into his office and taking out a bottle of fifty-year-old Highland Park single malt. Without pouring a glass, he set down the bottle and turned his back on it—a personal reminder that he was still very much in control.

His eyes moved instinctively to a heavy, weathered tome on his bookshelf—a gift from a client . . . the client whom he now wished he'd never met.

A year ago . . . how could I have known?

The provost did not normally interview prospective clients personally, but this one had come to him through a trusted source, and so he had made an exception.

It had been a dead calm day at sea when the client arrived aboard The Mendacium via his own private helicopter. The visitor, a notable figure in his field, was forty-six, clean-cut, and exceptionally tall, with piercing green eyes.

"As you know," the man had begun, "your services were recommended to me by a mutual friend." The visitor stretched out his long legs and made himself at home in the provost's lushly appointed office. "So, let me tell you what I need."

"Actually, no," the provost interrupted, showing the man who was in charge. "My protocol requires that you tell me nothing. I will explain the services I provide, and you will decide which, if any, are of interest to you."

The visitor looked taken aback but acquiesced and listened intently. In the end, what the lanky newcomer desired had turned out to be very standard fare for the Consortium—essentially a chance to become "invisible" for a while so he could pursue an endeavor far from prying eyes.

Child's play.

The Consortium would accomplish this by providing him a fake identity and a secure location, entirely off the grid, where he could do his work in total secrecy—whatever his work might be. The Consortium never inquired for what **purpose** a client required a service, preferring to know as little as possible about those for whom they worked.

For a full year, at a staggering profit, the provost had provided safe haven to the green-eyed man, who had turned out to be an ideal client. The provost had no contact with him, and all of his bills were paid on time.

Then, two weeks ago, everything changed.

Unexpectedly, the client had made contact, demanding a personal meeting with the provost. Considering the sum of money the client had paid, the provost obliged.

The disheveled man who arrived on the yacht was barely recognizable as the steady, clean-cut person with whom the provost had done business the year before. He had a wild look in his once-sharp green eyes. He looked almost . . . ill.

What happened to him? What has he been doing?

The provost had ushered the jittery man into his office.

"The silver-haired devil," his client stammered. "She's getting closer every day."

The provost glanced down at his client's file, eyeing the photo of the attractive silver-haired woman. "Yes," the provost said, "your silver-haired devil. We are well aware of your enemies. And as powerful as she may be, for a full year we've kept her from you, and we will continue to do so."

The green-eyed man anxiously twisted strands of greasy hair around his fingertips. "Don't let her beauty fool you, she is a dangerous foe."

True, the provost thought, still displeased that his client had drawn the attention of someone so influential. The silver-haired woman had tremendous access and resources—not the kind of adversary the provost appreciated having to deflect.

"If she or her demons locate me . . ." the client began.

"They won't," the provost had assured him. "Have we not thus far hidden you and provided you everything you've requested?"

"Yes," the man said. "And yet, I will sleep easier if . . ." He paused, regrouping. "I need to know that if anything happens to me, you will carry out my final wishes."

"Those wishes being?"

The man reached into a bag and pulled out a small, sealed envelope. "The contents of this envelope provide access to a safe-deposit box in Florence. Inside the box, you will find a small object. If anything happens to me, I need you to deliver the object for me. It is a gift of sorts."

"Very well." The provost lifted his pen to make notes. "And to whom shall I deliver it?"

"To the silver-haired devil."

The provost glanced up. "A gift for your tormentor?"

"More of a thorn in her side." His eyes flashed wildly. "A clever little barb fashioned from a bone. She will discover it is a map . . . her own personal Virgil . . . an escort to the center of her own private hell."

The provost studied him for a long moment. "As you wish. Consider it done."

"The timing will be critical," the man urged. "The gift should not be delivered too soon. You must keep it hidden until . . ." He paused, suddenly lost in thought.

"Until when?" the provost prodded.

The man stood abruptly and walked over behind the provost's desk, grabbing a red marker and frantically circling a date on the provost's personal desk calendar. "Until this day."

The provost set his jaw and exhaled, swallowing his displeasure at the man's brazenness. "Understood," the provost said. "I will do nothing until the circled day, at which time the object in the safe-deposit box, whatever it may be, will be delivered to the silver-haired woman. You have my word." He counted the days on his calendar until the awkwardly circled date. "I will carry out your wishes in precisely fourteen days from now."

"And not one day before!" the client admonished feverishly.

"I understand," the provost assured. "Not a day before."

The provost took the envelope, slid it into the man's file, and made the necessary notations to ensure that his client's wishes were followed precisely. While his client had not described the exact nature of the object in the safe-deposit box, the provost preferred it this way. Detachment was a cornerstone of the Consortium's philosophy. **Provide the service. Ask no questions. Pass no judgment.**

The client's shoulders softened and he exhaled heavily. "Thank you."

"Anything else?" the provost had asked, eager to rid himself of his transformed client.

"Yes, actually, there is." He reached into his pocket and produced a small, crimson memory stick. "This is a video file." He laid the memory stick in front of the provost. "I would like it uploaded to the world media."

The provost studied the man curiously. The Consortium often mass-distributed information for clients, and yet something about this man's request felt disconcerting. "On the same date?" the provost asked, motioning at the scrawled circle on his calendar.

"Same exact date," the client replied. "Not one moment before."

"Understood." The provost tagged the red memory stick with the proper information. "So that's it, then?" He stood up, attempting to end the meeting.

His client remained seated. "No. There is one final thing."

The provost sat back down.

The client's green eyes were looking almost feral now. "Shortly after you deliver this video, I will become a very famous man."

You are already a famous man, the provost had thought, considering his client's impressive accomplishments.

"And you will deserve some of the credit," the man said. "The service you have provided has enabled me to create my masterpiece . . . an opus that is going to change the world. You should be proud of your role."

"Whatever your masterpiece is," the provost said with growing impatience, "I'm pleased you have had the privacy required to create it."

"As a show of thanks, I've brought you a parting gift." The unkempt man reached into his bag. "A book."

The provost wondered if perhaps this book was the secret opus the client had been working on for all this time. "And did you write this book?"

"No." The man heaved a massive tome up onto the table. "Quite to the contrary . . . this book was written **for** me."

Puzzled, the provost eyed the edition his client had produced. **He thinks this was written for him?** The volume was a literary classic . . . written in the fourteenth century.

"Read it," the client urged with an eerie smile. "It will help you understand all I have done."

With that, the unkempt visitor had stood up, said good-bye, and abruptly departed. The provost watched through his office window as the man's helicopter lifted off the deck and headed back toward the coast of Italy.

Then the provost returned his attention to the large book before him. With uncertain fingers, he lifted the leather cover and thumbed to the beginning. The opening stanza of the work was written in large calligraphy, taking up the entire first page.

INFERNO

Midway upon the journey of our life
I found myself within a forest dark,
for the straightforward pathway had been lost.

On the opposing page, his client had signed the book with a handwritten message:

My dear friend, thank you for helping me find the path.
The world thanks you, too.

The provost had no idea what this meant, but he'd read enough. He closed the book and placed it on his bookshelf. Thankfully, his professional relationship with this strange individual would be over soon. **Fourteen more days**, the provost thought, turning his gaze to the wildly scrawled red circle on his personal calendar.

In the days that followed, the provost felt uncharacteristically on edge about this client. The man seemed to have come unhinged. Nonetheless, despite the provost's intuition, the time passed without incident.

Then, just before the circled date, there occurred a rapid series of calamitous events in Florence. The provost tried to handle the crisis, but it quickly accelerated out of control. The crisis climaxed with his client's breathless ascent up the Badia tower.

He jumped off . . . to his death.

Despite his horror at losing a client, especially in this manner, the provost remained a man of his word. He quickly began preparing to make good on his final promise to the deceased—the delivery to the silver-haired woman of the contents of a safe-deposit box in Florence—the timing of which, he had been admonished, was critical.

Not before the date circled in your calendar.

The provost gave the envelope containing the safe-deposit-box codes to Vayentha, who had traveled to Florence to recover the object inside—this "clever little barb." When Vayentha called in, however, her news was both startling and deeply alarming. The contents of the safe-deposit box had already been removed, and Vayentha had barely escaped being detained. Somehow, the silver-haired woman had learned of the account and had used her influence to gain access to the safe-deposit box and also to place an arrest warrant on anyone else who showed up looking to open it.

That was three days ago.

The client had clearly intended the purloined object to be his final insult to the silver-haired woman—a taunting voice from the grave.

And yet now it speaks too soon.

The Consortium had been in a desperate scramble ever since—using all its resources to protect its client's final wishes, as well as itself. In the process, the Consortium had crossed a series of lines from which the provost knew it would be hard to return. Now, with everything unraveling in Florence, the provost stared down at his desk and wondered what the future held.

On his calendar, the client's wildly scrawled circle stared up at him—a crazed ring of red ink around an apparently special day.

Tomorrow.

Reluctantly, the provost eyed the bottle of Scotch

on the table before him. Then, for the first time in fourteen years, he poured a glass and drained it in a single gulp.

———

Belowdecks, facilitator Laurence Knowlton pulled the little red memory stick from his computer and set it on the desk in front of him. The video was one of the strangest things he had ever seen.

And it was precisely nine minutes long . . . to the second.

Feeling uncharacteristically alarmed, he stood and paced his tiny cubicle, wondering again whether he should share the bizarre video with the provost.

Just do your job, Knowlton told himself. **No questions. No judgment.**

Forcing the video from his mind, he marked his planner with a confirmed task. Tomorrow, as requested by the client, he would upload the video file to the media.

CHAPTER 18

Viale Niccolò Machiavelli has been called the most graceful of all Florentine avenues. With wide S-curves that serpentine through lushly wooded landscapes of hedges and deciduous trees, the drive is a favorite among cyclists and Ferrari enthusiasts.

Sienna expertly maneuvered the Trike through each arching curve as they left behind the dingy residential neighborhood and moved into the clean, cedar-laden air of the city's upscale west bank. They passed a chapel clock that was just chiming 8 A.M.

Langdon held on, his mind churning with mystifying images of Dante's inferno . . . and the mysterious face of a beautiful silver-haired woman he had just seen wedged in between two huge soldiers in the backseat of the van.

Whoever she is, Langdon thought, **they have her now.**

"The woman in the van," Sienna said over the noise of the Trike's engine. "You're sure it was the same woman from your visions?"

"Absolutely."

"Then you must have met her at some point in the past two days. The question is why you keep seeing her . . . and why she keeps telling you to seek and find."

Langdon agreed. "I don't know . . . I have no recollection of meeting her, but every time I see her face, I have an overwhelming sense that I need to help her."

Very sorry. Very sorry.

Langdon suddenly wondered if maybe his strange apology had been directed to the silver-haired woman. **Did I fail her somehow?** The thought left a knot in his gut.

For Langdon, it felt as if a vital weapon had been extracted from his arsenal. **I have no memory.** Eidetic since childhood, Langdon's memory was the intellectual asset he relied on most. For a man accustomed to recalling every intricate detail of what he saw around him, functioning without his memory felt like attempting to land a plane in the dark with no radar.

"It seems like your only chance of finding answers is to decipher **La Mappa**," Sienna said. "Whatever secret it holds . . . it seems to be the reason you're being hunted."

Langdon nodded, thinking about the word **catrovacer**, set against the backdrop of writhing bodies in Dante's **Inferno**.

Suddenly a clear thought emerged in Langdon's head.

I awoke in Florence . . .

No city on earth was more closely tied to Dante than Florence. Dante Alighieri had been born in Florence, grew up in Florence, fell in love, according to legend, with Beatrice in Florence, and was cruelly exiled from his home in Florence, destined to wander the Italian countryside for years, longing soulfully for his home.

You shall leave everything you love most, Dante wrote of banishment. **This is the arrow that the bow of exile shoots first.**

As Langdon recalled those words from the seventeenth canto of the **Paradiso,** he looked to the right, gazing out across the Arno River toward the distant spires of old Florence.

Langdon pictured the layout of the old city—a labyrinth of tourists, congestion, and traffic bustling through narrow streets around Florence's famed cathedral, museums, chapels, and shopping districts. He suspected that if he and Sienna ditched the Trike, they could evaporate into the throngs of people.

"The old city is where we need to go," Langdon declared. "If there are answers, that's where they'll probably be. Old Florence was Dante's entire world."

Sienna nodded her agreement and called over her shoulder, "It will be safer, too—plenty of places to hide. I'll head for Porta Romana, and from there, we can cross the river."

The river, Langdon thought with a touch of trepidation. Dante's famous journey into hell had begun by crossing a river as well.

Sienna opened up the throttle, and as the landscape blurred past, Langdon mentally scanned through images of the inferno, the dead and dying, the ten ditches of the Malebolge with the plague doctor and

the strange word—CATROVACER. He pondered the
words scrawled beneath **La Mappa**—**The truth can
be glimpsed only through the eyes of death**—and
wondered if the grim saying might be a quote from
Dante.

I don't recognize it.

Langdon was well versed in Dante's work, and his
prominence as an art historian who specialized in
iconography meant he was occasionally called upon
to interpret the vast array of symbols that populated
Dante's landscape. Coincidentally, or perhaps not
so coincidentally, he had given a lecture on Dante's
Inferno about two years earlier.

"Divine Dante: Symbols of Hell."

Dante Alighieri had evolved into one of history's
true cult icons, sparking the creation of Dante societies all around the world. The oldest American
branch had been founded in 1881 in Cambridge,
Massachusetts, by Henry Wadsworth Longfellow.
New England's famous Fireside Poet was the first
American to translate **The Divine Comedy**, his
translation remaining among the most respected and
widely read to this day.

As a noted student of Dante's work, Langdon had
been asked to speak at a major event hosted by one
of the world's oldest Dante societies—Società Dante
Alighieri Vienna. The event was slated to take place
at the Viennese Academy of Sciences. The event's primary sponsor—a wealthy scientist and Dante Society member—had managed to secure the academy's
two-thousand-seat lecture hall.

When Langdon arrived at the event, he was met by the conference director and ushered inside. As they crossed the lobby, Langdon couldn't help but notice the five words painted in gargantuan letters across the back wall: WHAT IF GOD WAS WRONG?

"It's a Lukas Troberg," the director whispered. "Our newest art installation. What do you think?"

Langdon eyed the massive text, uncertain how to respond. "Um . . . his brushstrokes are lavish, but his command of the subjunctive seems sparse."

The director gave him a confused look. Langdon hoped his rapport with the audience would be better.

When he finally stepped onstage, Langdon received a rousing round of applause from a crowd that was standing room only.

"**Meine Damen und Herren**," Langdon began, his voice booming over the loudspeakers. "**Willkommen, bienvenue, welcome.**"

The famous line from **Cabaret** drew appreciative laughter from the crowd.

"I've been informed that our audience tonight contains not only Dante Society members, but also many visiting scientists and students who may be exploring Dante for the first time. So, for those in the audience who have been too busy studying to read medieval Italian epics, I thought I'd begin with a quick overview of Dante—his life, his work, and why he is considered one of the most influential figures in all of history."

More applause.

Using the tiny remote in his hand, Langdon called

up a series of images of Dante, the first being Andrea del Castagno's full-length portrait of the poet standing in a doorway, clutching a book of philosophy.

"Dante Alighieri," Langdon began. "This Florentine writer and philosopher lived from 1265 to 1321. In this portrait, as in nearly all depictions, he wears on his head a red **cappuccio**—a tight-fitting, plaited hood with earflaps—which, along with his crimson Lucca robe, has become the most widely reproduced image of Dante."

Langdon advanced slides to the Botticelli portrait of Dante from the Uffizi Gallery, which stressed Dante's most salient features, a heavy jaw and hooked nose. "Here, Dante's unique face is once again framed by his red **cappuccio**, but in this instance Botticelli has added a laurel wreath to his cap as a symbol of expertise—in this case in the poetic arts—a traditional symbol borrowed from ancient Greece and used even today in ceremonies honoring poet laureates and Nobel laureates."

Langdon quickly scrolled through several other images, all showing Dante in his red cap, red tunic, laurel wreath, and prominent nose. "And to round out your image of Dante, here is a statue from the Piazza di Santa Croce . . . and, of course, the famous fresco attributed to Giotto in the chapel of the Bargello."

Langdon left the slide of Giotto's fresco on the screen and walked to the center of the stage.

"As you are no doubt aware, Dante is best known for his monumental literary masterpiece—**The Divine Comedy**—a brutally vivid account of the author's descent into hell, passage through purgatory, and eventual ascent into paradise to commune with God. By modern standards, **The Divine Comedy** has nothing comedic about it. It's called a comedy for another reason entirely. In the fourteenth century, Italian literature was, by requirement, divided into two categories: tragedy, representing high literature, was written in formal Italian; comedy, representing low literature, was written in the vernacular and geared toward the general population."

Langdon advanced slides to the iconic fresco by Michelino, which showed Dante standing outside the walls of Florence clutching a copy of **The Divine Comedy**. In the background, the terraced mountain of purgatory rose high above the gates of hell. The painting now hung in Florence's Cathedral of Santa Maria del Fiore—better known as Il Duomo.

"As you may have guessed from the title," Langdon continued, "**The Divine Comedy** was written in the vernacular—the language of the people. Even so, it brilliantly fused religion, history, politics, philosophy, and social commentary in a tapestry of fiction that, while erudite, remained wholly accessible to the masses. The work became such a pillar of Italian culture that Dante's writing style has been credited with nothing less than the codification of the modern Italian language."

Langdon paused a moment for effect and then whispered, "My friends, it is impossible to overstate the influence of Dante Alighieri's work. Throughout all of history, with the sole exception perhaps of Holy

Scripture, no single work of writing, art, music, or literature has inspired more tributes, imitations, variations, and annotations than **The Divine Comedy**."

After listing the vast array of famous composers, artists, and authors who had created works based on Dante's epic poem, Langdon scanned the crowd. "So tell me, do we have any authors here tonight?"

Nearly one-third of the hands went up. Langdon stared out in shock. **Wow, either this is the most accomplished audience on earth, or this e-publishing thing is really taking off.**

"Well, as all of you authors know, there is nothing a writer appreciates more than a blurb—one of those single-line endorsements from a powerful individual, designed to make others want to buy your work. And, in the Middle Ages, blurbs existed, too. And Dante got quite a few of them."

Langdon changed slides. "How would you like to have **this** on your book jacket?"

Ne'er walked the earth a greater man than he.
—Michelangelo

A murmur of surprise rustled through the crowd.

"Yes," Langdon said, "that's the same Michelangelo you all know from the Sistine Chapel and the **David**. In addition to being a master painter and sculptor, Michelangelo was a superb poet, publishing nearly three hundred poems—including one titled 'Dante,' dedicated to the man whose stark visions of hell were those that inspired Michelangelo's **Last Judgment**.

And if you don't believe me, read the third canto of Dante's **Inferno** and then visit the Sistine Chapel; just above the altar, you'll see this familiar image."

Langdon advanced slides to a frightening detail of a muscle-bound beast swinging a giant paddle at cowering people. "This is Dante's hellish ferryman, Charon, beating straggling passengers with an oar."

Langdon moved now to a new slide—a second detail of Michelangelo's **Last Judgment**—a man being crucified. "This is Haman the Agagite, who, according to Scripture, was hanged to death. However, in Dante's poem, he was crucified instead. As you can see here in the Sistine Chapel, Michelangelo chose Dante's version over that of the Bible." Langdon grinned and lowered his voice to a whisper. "Don't tell the pope."

The crowd laughed.

"Dante's **Inferno** created a world of pain and suffering beyond all previous human imagination, and his writing quite literally defined our modern visions of hell." Langdon paused. "And believe me, the Catholic Church has much to thank Dante for. His **Inferno** terrified the faithful for centuries, and no doubt tripled church attendance among the fearful."

Langdon switched the slide. "And this leads us to the reason we are all here tonight."

The screen now displayed the title of his lecture: DIVINE DANTE: SYMBOLS OF HELL.

"Dante's **Inferno** is a landscape so rich in symbolism and iconography that I often dedicate an entire semester course to it. And tonight, I thought there would be no better way to unveil the symbols of Dante's **Inferno** than to walk side by side with him . . . through the gates of hell."

Langdon paced out to the edge of the stage and surveyed the crowd. "Now, if we're planning on taking a stroll through hell, I strongly recommend we use a map. And there is no map of Dante's hell more complete and accurate than the one painted by Sandro Botticelli."

He touched his remote, and Botticelli's forbidding **Mappa dell'Inferno** materialized before the crowd. He could hear several groans as people absorbed the various horrors taking place in the funnel-shaped subterranean cavern.

"Unlike some artists, Botticelli was extremely faithful in his interpretation of Dante's text. In fact, he spent so much time reading Dante that the great art historian Giorgio Vasari said Botticelli's obsession with Dante led to 'serious disorders in his living.' Botticelli created more than two dozen other works relating to Dante, but this map is his most famous."

Langdon turned now, pointing to the upper left-hand corner of the painting. "Our journey will begin up there, aboveground, where you can see Dante in red, along with his guide, Virgil, standing outside the gates of hell. From there we will travel downward, through the nine rings of Dante's inferno, and eventually come face-to-face with . . ."

Langdon quickly flashed to a new slide—a giant enlargement of Satan as depicted by Botticelli in this very painting—a horrific, three-headed Lucifer consuming three different people, one in each mouth.

The crowd gasped audibly.

"A glance at coming attractions," Langdon announced. "This frightening character here is where tonight's journey will end. This is the ninth ring of hell, where Satan himself resides. However . . ." Langdon paused. "Getting there is half the fun, so let's rewind a bit . . . back up to the gates of hell, where our journey begins."

Langdon moved to the next slide—a Gustave Doré lithograph that depicted a dark, tunneled entrance carved into the face of an austere cliff. The inscription above the door read: ABANDON ALL HOPE, YE WHO ENTER HERE.

"So . . ." Langdon said with a smile. "Shall we enter?"

Somewhere tires screeched loudly, and the audience evaporated before Langdon's eyes. He felt himself lurch forward, and he collided with Sienna's back as the Trike skidded to a stop in the middle of the Viale Machiavelli.

Langdon reeled, still thinking about the gates of hell looming before him. As he regained his bearings, he saw where he was.

"What's going on?" he demanded.

Sienna pointed three hundred yards ahead to the Porta Romana—the ancient stone gateway that served as the entrance to old Florence. "Robert, we've got a problem."

CHAPTER 19

Agent Brüder stood in the humble apartment and tried to make sense of what he was seeing. **Who the hell lives here?** The decor was sparse and jumbled, like a college dorm room furnished on a budget.

"Agent Brüder?" one of his men called from down the hall. "You'll want to see this."

As Brüder made his way down the hall, he wondered if the local police had detained Langdon yet. Brüder would have preferred to solve this crisis "in-house," but Langdon's escape had left little choice but to enlist local police support and set up roadblocks. An agile motorbike on the labyrinthine streets of Florence would easily elude Brüder's vans, whose heavy polycarbonate windows and solid, puncture-proof tires made them impenetrable but lumbering. The Italian police had a reputation for being uncooperative with outsiders, but Brüder's organization had significant influence—police, consulates, embassies. **When we make demands, nobody dares question.**

Brüder entered the small office where his man stood over an open laptop and typed in latex gloves. "This is the machine he used," the man said. "Langdon used it to access his e-mail and run some searches. The files are still cached."

Brüder moved toward the desk.

"It doesn't appear to be Langdon's computer," the tech said. "It's registered to someone initialed S.C.—I should have a full name shortly."

As Brüder waited, his eyes were drawn to a stack of papers on the desk. He picked them up, thumbing through the unusual array—an old playbill from the London Globe Theatre and a series of newspaper articles. The more Brüder read, the wider his eyes became.

Taking the documents, Brüder slipped back into the hall and placed a call to his boss. "It's Brüder," he said. "I think I've got an ID on the person helping Langdon."

"Who is it?" his boss replied.

Brüder exhaled slowly. "You're not going to believe this."

———

Two miles away, Vayentha hunkered low on her BMW as it fled the area. Police cars raced past her in the opposite direction, sirens blaring.

I've been disavowed, she thought.

Normally, the soft vibration of the motorcycle's four-stroke engine helped calm her nerves. Not today.

Vayentha had worked for the Consortium for twelve years, climbing the ranks from ground support, to strategy coordination, all the way to a high-ranked field agent. **My career is all I have.** Field agents endured a life of secrecy, travel, and long missions, all of which precluded any real outside life or relationships.

I've been on this same mission for a year, she thought, still unable to believe the provost had pulled the trigger and disavowed her so abruptly.

For twelve months Vayentha had been overseeing support services for the same client of the Consortium—an eccentric, green-eyed genius who wanted only to "disappear" for a while so he could work unmolested by his rivals and enemies. He traveled very rarely, and always invisibly, but mostly he worked. The nature of this man's work was not known to Vayentha, whose contract had simply been to keep the client hidden from the powerful people trying to find him.

Vayentha had performed the service with consummate professionalism, and everything had gone perfectly.

Perfectly, that was . . . until last night.

Vayentha's emotional state and career had been in a downward spiral ever since.

I'm on the outside now.

The disavowal protocol, if invoked, required that the agent instantly abandon her current mission and exit "the arena" at once. If the agent were captured, the Consortium would disavow all knowledge of the agent. Agents knew better than to press their luck with the organization, having witnessed firsthand its disturbing ability to manipulate reality into what-ever suited its needs.

Vayentha knew of only two agents who had been disavowed. Strangely, she had never seen either of them again. She had always assumed they had been called in for their formal review and fired, required never to make contact again with Consortium em-ployees.

Now, however, Vayentha was not so sure.

You're overreacting, she tried to tell herself. **The Consortium's methods are far more elegant than cold-blooded murder.**

Even so, she felt a fresh chill sweep through her body.

It had been instinct that urged her to flee the hotel rooftop unseen the moment she saw Brüder's team arrive, and she wondered if that instinct had saved her.

Nobody knows where I am now.

As Vayentha sped northward on the sleek straight-away of the Viale del Poggio Imperiale, she realized what a difference a few hours had made for her. Last night she had been worried about protecting her job. Now she was worried about protecting her life.

CHAPTER 20

Florence was once a walled city, its primary entrance the stone gateway of the Porta Romana, built in 1326. While most of the city's perimeter walls were destroyed centuries ago, the Porta Romana still exists, and to this day, traffic enters the city by funneling through deep arched tunnels in the colossal fortification.

The gateway itself is a fifty-foot-tall barrier of ancient brick and stone whose primary passageway still retains its massive bolted wooden doors, which are propped open at all times to let traffic pass through. Six major roads converge in front of these doors, filtering into a rotary whose grassy median is dominated by a large Pistoletto statue depicting a woman departing the city gates carrying an enormous bundle on her head.

Although nowadays it is more of a snarled traffic nightmare, Florence's austere city gate was once the site of the Fiera dei Contratti—the Contracts Fair—at which fathers sold their daughters into a contracted marriage, often forcing them to dance provocatively in an effort to secure higher dowries.

This morning, several hundred yards short of the gateway, Sienna had screeched to a stop and was now pointing in alarm. On the back of the Trike, Langdon looked ahead and immediately shared her apprehension. In front of them, a long line of cars idled at a full stop. Traffic in the rotary had been halted by a police barricade, and more police cars were now arriving. Armed officers were walking from car to car, asking questions.

That can't be for us, Langdon thought. **Can it?**

A sweaty cyclist came pedaling toward them up the Viale Machiavelli away from the traffic. He was on a recumbent bike, his bare legs pumping out in front of him.

Sienna shouted out to him. **"Cos' è successo?"**

"E chi lo sa!" he shouted back, looking concerned. **"Carabinieri."** He hurried past, looking eager to clear the area.

Sienna turned to Langdon, her expression grim. "Roadblock. Military police."

Sirens wailed in the distance behind them, and Sienna spun in her seat, staring back up the Viale Machiavelli, her face now masked with fear.

We're trapped in the middle, Langdon thought, scanning the area for any exit at all—an intersecting road, a park, a driveway—but all he saw were private residences on their left and a high stone wall to their right.

The sirens grew louder.

"Up there," Langdon urged, pointing thirty yards ahead to a deserted construction site where a portable cement mixer offered at least a little bit of cover.

Sienna gunned the bike up onto the sidewalk and

raced into the work area. They parked behind the cement mixer, quickly realizing that it offered barely enough concealment for the Trike alone.

"Follow me," Sienna said, rushing toward a small portable toolshed nestled in the bushes against the stone wall.

That's not a toolshed, Langdon realized, his nose crinkling as they got closer. **That's a Porta-Potty.**

As Langdon and Sienna arrived outside the construction workers' chemical toilet, they could hear police cars approaching from behind them. Sienna yanked the door handle, but it didn't budge. A heavy chain and padlock secured it. Langdon grabbed Sienna's arm and pulled her around behind the structure, forcing her into the narrow space between the toilet and the stone wall. The two of them barely fit, and the air smelled putrid and heavy.

Langdon slid in behind her just as a jet-black Subaru Forester came into view with the word CARABINIERI emblazoned on its side. The vehicle rolled slowly past their location.

The Italian military police, Langdon thought, incredulous. He wondered if these officers also had orders to shoot on sight.

"Someone is dead serious about finding us," Sienna whispered. "And somehow they did."

"GPS?" Langdon wondered aloud. "Maybe the projector has a tracking device in it?"

Sienna shook her head. "Believe me, if that thing were traceable, the police would be right on top of us."

Langdon shifted his tall frame, trying to get comfortable in the cramped surroundings. He found himself face-to-face with a collage of elegantly styled graffiti scrawled on the back of the Porta-Potty.

Leave it to the Italians.

Most American Porta-Potties were covered with sophomoric cartoons that vaguely resembled huge breasts or penises. The graffiti on this one, however, looked more like an art student's sketchbook—a human eye, a well-rendered hand, a man in profile, and a fantastical dragon.

"Destruction of property doesn't look like this everywhere in Italy," Sienna said, apparently reading his mind. "The Florence Art Institute is on the other side of this stone wall."

As if to confirm Sienna's statement, a group of students appeared in the distance, ambling toward them with art portfolios under their arms. They were chatting, lighting cigarettes, and puzzling over the roadblock in front of them at the Porta Romana.

Langdon and Sienna crouched lower to stay out of sight of the students, and as they did so, Langdon was struck, most unexpectedly, by a curious thought.

The half-buried sinners with their legs in the air.

Perhaps it was on account of the smell of human waste, or possibly the recumbent bicyclist with bare legs flailing in front of him, but whatever the stimulus, Langdon had flashed on the putrid world of the Malebolge and the naked legs protruding upside down from the earth.

He turned suddenly to his companion. "Sienna, in our version of **La Mappa**, the upside-down legs were in the tenth ditch, right? The lowest level of the Malebolge?"

Sienna gave him an odd look, as if this were hardly the time. "Yes, at the bottom."

For a split second Langdon was back in Vienna giving his lecture. He was standing onstage, only moments from his grand finale, having just shown the audience Doré's engraving of Geryon—the winged monster with a poisonous stinging tail that lived just above the Malebolge.

"Before we meet Satan," Langdon declared, his deep voice resonating over the loudspeakers, "we must pass through the ten ditches of the Malebolge, in which are punished the fraudulent—those guilty of deliberate evil."

Langdon advanced slides to show a detail of the Malebolge and then took the audience down through the ditches one by one. "From top to bottom we have: the seducers whipped by demons . . . the flatterers adrift in human excrement . . . the clerical profiteers half buried upside down with their legs in the air . . . the sorcerers with their heads twisted backward . . . the corrupt politicians in boiling pitch . . . the hypocrites wearing heavy leaden cloaks . . . the thieves bitten by snakes . . . the fraudulent counselors consumed by fire . . . the sowers of discord hacked apart by demons . . . and finally, the liars, who are diseased beyond recognition." Langdon turned back to the audience. "Dante most likely reserved this final ditch for the liars because a series of lies told about him led to his exile from his beloved Florence."

"Robert?" The voice was Sienna's.

Langdon snapped back to the present.

Sienna was staring at him quizzically. "What is it?"

"Our version of **La Mappa**," he said excitedly. "The art has been changed!" He fished the projector out of his jacket pocket and shook it as best as he could in the close quarters. The agitator ball rattled loudly, but all the sirens drowned it out. "Whoever created this image reconfigured the order of the levels in the Malebolge!"

When the device began to glow, Langdon pointed it at the flat surface before them. **La Mappa dell'Inferno** appeared, glowing brightly in the dim light.

Botticelli on a chemical toilet, Langdon thought, ashamed. This had to be the least elegant place a Botticelli had ever been displayed. Langdon ran his eyes down through the ten ditches and began nodding excitedly.

"Yes!" he exclaimed. "This is wrong! The last ditch of the Malebolge is supposed to be full of diseased people, not people upside down. The tenth level is for the liars, not the clerical profiteers!"

Sienna looked intrigued. "But . . . why would someone change that?"

"Catrovacer," Langdon whispered, eyeing the little letters that had been added to each level. "I don't think that's what this really says."

Despite the injury that had erased Langdon's rec-ollections of the last two days, he could now feel his memory working perfectly. He closed his eyes and held the two versions of **La Mappa** in his mind's eye to analyze their differences. The changes to the Malebolge were fewer than Langdon had imag-ined . . . and yet he felt like a veil had suddenly been lifted.

Suddenly it was crystal clear.

Seek and ye shall find!

"What is it?" Sienna demanded.

Langdon's mouth felt dry. "I know why I'm here in Florence."

"You do?!"

"Yes, and I know where I'm supposed to go."

Sienna grabbed his arm. "Where?!"

Langdon felt as if his feet had just touched solid ground for the first time since he'd awoken in the hospital. "These ten letters," he whispered. "They actually point to a precise location in the old city. That's where the answers are."

"Where in the old city?!" Sienna demanded. "What did you figure out?"

The sounds of laughing voices echoed on the other side of the Porta-Potty. Another group of art stu-dents was passing by, joking and chatting in vari-ous languages. Langdon peered cautiously around the cubicle, watching them go. Then he scanned for police. "We've got to keep moving. I'll explain on the way."

"On the way?!" Sienna shook her head. "We'll never get through the Porta Romana!"

"Stay here for thirty seconds," he told her, "and then follow my lead."

With that, Langdon slipped away, leaving his new-found friend bewildered and alone.

CHAPTER 21

S cusi!" Robert Langdon chased after the group of students. "Scusate!"

They all turned, and Langdon made a show of glancing around like a lost tourist.

"Dov'è l'Istituto statale d'arte?" Langdon asked in broken Italian.

A tattooed kid puffed coolly on a cigarette and snidely replied, "Non parliamo italiano." His accent was French.

One of the girls admonished her tattooed friend and politely pointed down the long wall toward the Porta Romana. "Più avanti, sempre dritto."

Straight ahead, Langdon translated. "Grazie."

On cue, Sienna emerged unseen from behind the Porta-Potty and walked over. The willowy thirty-two-year-old approached the group and Langdon placed a welcoming hand on her shoulder. "This is my sister, Sienna. She's an art teacher."

The tattooed kid muttered, "T-I-L-F," and his male friends laughed.

Langdon ignored them. "We're in Florence researching possible spots for a teaching year abroad. Can we walk in with you?"

"Ma certo," the Italian girl said with a smile.

As the group migrated toward the police at the Porta Romana, Sienna fell into conversation with the students while Langdon merged to the middle of the group, slouching low, trying to stay out of sight.

Seek and ye shall find, Langdon thought, his pulse racing with excitement as he pictured the ten ditches of the Malebolge.

Catrovacer. These ten letters, Langdon had realized, stood at the core of one of the art world's most enigmatic mysteries, a centuries-old puzzle that had never been solved. In 1563, these ten letters had been used to spell a message high on a wall inside Florence's famed Palazzo Vecchio, painted some forty feet off the ground, barely visible without binoculars. It had remained hidden there in plain sight for centuries until the 1970s, when it was spotted by a now-famous art diagnostician, who had spent decades trying to uncover its meaning. Despite numerous theories, the significance of the message remains an enigma to this day.

For Langdon, the code felt like familiar ground—a safe harbor from this strange and churning sea. After all, art history and ancient secrets were far more Langdon's realm than were biohazard tubes and gunfire.

Up ahead, additional police cars had begun streaming into the Porta Romana.

"Jesus," the tattooed kid said. "Whoever they're looking for must have done something terrible."

The group arrived at the Art Institute's main gate on the right, where a crowd of students had gathered to watch the action at the Porta Romana. The school's minimum-wage security guard was half-heartedly glancing at student IDs as kids streamed in, but he was clearly more interested in what was happening with the police.

A loud screech of brakes echoed across the plaza as an all-too-familiar black van skidded into the Porta Romana.

Langdon didn't need a second look.

Without a word, he and Sienna seized the moment, slipping through the gate with their new friends.

The entry road to the Istituto Statale d'Arte was startlingly beautiful, almost regal in appearance. Massive oak trees arched gently in from either side, creating a canopy that framed the distant building— a huge, faded yellow structure with a triple portico and an expansive oval lawn.

This building, Langdon knew, had been commissioned, like so many in this city, by the same illustrious dynasty that had dominated Florentine politics during the fifteenth, sixteenth, and seventeenth centuries.

The Medici.

The name alone had become a symbol of Florence. During its three-century reign, the royal house of Medici amassed unfathomable wealth and influence, producing four popes, two queens of France, and the largest financial institution in all of Europe. To this day, modern banks use the accounting method invented by the Medici—the dual-entry system of credits and debits.

The Medici's greatest legacy, however, was not in

finance or politics, but rather in art. Perhaps the most lavish patrons the art world has ever known, the Medici provided a generous stream of commissions that fueled the Renaissance. The list of luminaries receiving Medici patronage ranged from da Vinci to Galileo to Botticelli—the latter's most famous painting, **Birth of Venus**, the result of a commission from Lorenzo de' Medici, who requested a sexually provocative painting to hang over his cousin's marital bed as a wedding gift.

Lorenzo de' Medici—known in his day as Lorenzo the Magnificent on account of his benevolence—was an accomplished artist and poet in his own right and was said to have a superb eye. In 1489 Lorenzo took a liking to the work of a young Florentine sculptor and invited the boy to move into the Medici palace, where he could practice his craft surrounded by fine art, great poetry, and high culture. Under Medici tutelage, the adolescent boy flourished and eventually went on to carve two of the most celebrated sculptures in all of history—the **Pietà** and the **David**. Today we know him as Michelangelo—a creative giant who is sometimes called the Medici's greatest gift to humankind.

Considering the Medici's passion for art, Langdon imagined the family would be pleased to know that the building before him—originally built as the Medici's primary horse stables—had been transformed into the vibrant Art Institute. This tranquil site that now inspired young artists had been specifically chosen for the Medici's stables because of its proximity to one of the most beautiful riding areas in all of Florence.

The Boboli Gardens.

Langdon glanced to his left, where a forest of tree-tops could be seen over a high wall. The massive expanse of the Boboli Gardens was now a popular tourist attraction. Langdon had little doubt that if he and Sienna could gain entrance to the gardens, they could make their way across it, bypassing the Porta Romana undetected. After all, the gardens were vast and had no shortage of hiding places—forests, labyrinths, grottoes, nymphaea. More important, traversing the Boboli Gardens would eventually lead them to the Palazzo Pitti, the stone citadel that once housed the main seat of the Medici grand duchy, and whose 140 rooms remained one of Florence's most frequented tourist attractions.

If we can reach the Palazzo Pitti, Langdon thought, **the bridge to the old city is a stone's throw away.**

Langdon motioned as calmly as possible to the high wall that enclosed the gardens. "How do we get into the gardens?" he asked. "I'd love to show my sister before we tour the institute."

The tattooed kid shook his head. "You can't get into the gardens from here. The entrance is way over at Pitti Palace. You'd have to drive through Porta Romana and go around."

"Bullshit," Sienna blurted.

Everyone turned and stared at her, including Langdon.

"Come on," she said, smirking coyly at the students as she stroked her blond ponytail. "You're telling me you guys don't sneak into the gardens to smoke weed and fool around?"

The kids all exchanged looks and then burst out laughing.

The guy with the tattoos now looked utterly smitten. "Ma'am, you should totally teach here." He walked Sienna to the side of the building and pointed around the corner to a rear parking lot. "See that shed on the left? There's an old platform behind it. Climb up on the roof, and you can jump down on the other side of the wall."

Sienna was already on the move. She glanced back at Langdon with a patronizing smile. "Come on, brother Bob. Unless you're too old to jump a fence?"

CHAPTER 22

The silver-haired woman in the van leaned her head against the bulletproof window and closed her eyes. She felt like the world was spinning beneath her. The drugs they'd given her made her feel ill.

I need medical attention, she thought.

Even so, the armed guard beside her had strict orders: her needs were to be ignored until their task had been successfully completed. From the sounds of chaos around her, it was clear that would be no time soon.

The dizziness was increasing now, and she was having trouble breathing. As she fought off a new wave of nausea, she wondered how life had managed to deliver her to this surreal crossroads. The answer was too complex to decipher in her current delirious state, but she had no doubt where it had all begun.

New York.

Two years ago.

She had flown to Manhattan from Geneva, where she was serving as the director of the World Health Organization, a highly coveted and prestigious post that she had held for nearly a decade. A specialist in communicable disease and the epidemiology of epidemics, she had been invited to the UN to deliver a lecture assessing the threat of pandemic disease in third-world countries. Her talk had been upbeat and reassuring, outlining several new early-detection systems and treatment plans devised by the World Health Organization and others. She had received a standing ovation.

Following the lecture, while she was in the hall talking to some lingering academics, a UN employee with a high-level diplomatic badge strode over and interrupted the conversation.

"Dr. Sinskey, we have just been contacted by the Council on Foreign Relations. There is someone there who would like to speak to you. A car is waiting outside."

Puzzled and a bit unnerved, Dr. Elizabeth Sinskey excused herself and collected her overnight bag. As her limo raced up First Avenue, she began to feel strangely nervous.

The Council on Foreign Relations?

Elizabeth Sinskey, like most, had heard the rumors.

Founded in the 1920s as a private think tank, the CFR had among its past membership nearly every secretary of state, more than a half-dozen presidents, a majority of CIA chiefs, senators, judges, as well as dynastic legends with names like Morgan, Rothschild, and Rockefeller. The membership's unparalleled collection of brainpower, political influence, and wealth had earned the Council on Foreign Relations the reputation of being "the most influential private club on earth."

As director of the World Health Organization, Elizabeth was no stranger to rubbing shoulders with the big boys. Her long tenure at WHO, combined with her outspoken nature, had earned her a nod recently from a major newsmagazine that listed her among its twenty most influential people in the world. **The Face of World Health**, they had written beneath her photo, which Elizabeth found ironic considering she had been such a sick child.

Suffering from severe asthma by age six, she had been treated with a high dose of a promising new drug—the first of the world's glucocorticoids, or steroid hormones—which had cured her asthma symptoms in miraculous fashion. Sadly, the drug's unanticipated side effects had not emerged until years later when Sinskey passed through puberty . . . and yet never developed a menstrual cycle. She would never forget the dark moment in the doctor's office, at nineteen, when she learned that the damage to her reproductive system was permanent.

Elizabeth Sinskey could never have children.

Time will heal the emptiness, her doctor assured, but the sadness and anger only grew inside her. Cruelly, the drugs that had robbed her of her ability to conceive a child had failed to rob her of her animal instincts to do so. For decades, she had battled her cravings to fulfill this impossible desire. Even now, at sixty-one years old, she still felt a pang of hollowness every time she saw a mother and infant.

"It's just ahead, Dr. Sinskey," the limo driver announced.

Elizabeth ran a quick brush through her long silver ringlets and checked her face in the mirror. Before she knew it, the car had stopped, and the driver was helping her out onto the sidewalk in an affluent section of Manhattan.

"I'll wait here for you," the driver said. "We can go straight to the airport when you're ready."

The New York headquarters of the Council on Foreign Relations was an unobtrusive neoclassical building on the corner of Park and Sixty-eighth that had once been the home of a Standard Oil tycoon. Its exterior blended seamlessly with the elegant landscape surrounding it, offering no hint of its unique purpose.

"Dr. Sinskey," a portly female receptionist greeted her. "This way, please. He's expecting you."

Okay, but who is he? She followed the receptionist down a luxurious corridor to a closed door, on which the woman gave a quick knock before opening it and motioning for Elizabeth to enter.

She went in, and the door closed behind her.

The small, dark conference room was illuminated only by the glow of a video screen. In front of the screen, a very tall and lanky silhouette faced her. Though she couldn't make out his face, she sensed power here.

"Dr. Sinskey," the man's sharp voice declared. "Thank you for joining me." The man's tautly precise accent suggested Elizabeth's homeland of Switzerland, or perhaps Germany.

"Please sit," he said, motioning to a chair near the front of the room.

No introductions? Elizabeth sat. The bizarre image being projected on the video screen did nothing to calm her nerves. **What in the world?**

"I was at your presentation this morning," declared the silhouette. "I came a long distance to hear you speak. An impressive performance."

"Thank you," she replied.

"Might I also say you are much more beautiful than I imagined . . . despite your age and your myopic view of world health."

Elizabeth felt her jaw drop. The comment was offensive in all kinds of ways. "Excuse me?" she demanded, peering into the darkness. "Who are you? And why have you called me here?"

"Pardon my failed attempt at humor," the lanky shadow replied. "The image on the screen will explain why you're here."

Sinskey eyed the horrific visual—a painting depicting a vast sea of humanity, throngs of sickly people, all climbing over one another in a dense tangle of naked bodies.

"The great artist Doré," the man announced. "His spectacularly grim interpretation of Dante Alighieri's vision of hell. I hope it looks comfortable to you . . . because that's where we're headed." He paused, drifting slowly toward her. "And let me tell you why."

He kept moving toward her, seeming to grow taller with every step. "If I were to take this piece of paper and tear it in two . . ." He paused at a table, picked up a sheet of paper, and ripped it loudly in half. "And then if I were to place the two halves on top of each other . . ." He stacked the two halves. "And then if I were to repeat the process . . ." He again tore the papers, stacking them. "I produce a stack of paper that is now four times the thickness of the original, correct?" His eyes seemed to smolder in the darkness of the room.

Elizabeth did not appreciate his condescending tone and aggressive posture. She said nothing.

"Hypothetically speaking," he continued, moving closer still, "if the original sheet of paper is a mere one-tenth of a millimeter thick, and I were to repeat this process . . . say, **fifty** times . . . do you know how tall this stack would be?"

Elizabeth bristled. "I do," she replied with more hostility than she intended. "It would be one-tenth of a millimeter times two to the fiftieth power. It's called geometric progression. Might I ask what I'm doing here?"

The man smirked and gave an impressed nod. "Yes, and can you guess what that actual value might look like? One-tenth of a millimeter times two to the fiftieth power? Do you know how tall our stack of paper has become?" He paused only an instant. "Our stack of paper, after only fifty doublings, now reaches almost all the way . . . to the sun."

Elizabeth was not surprised. The staggering power of geometric growth was something she dealt with all the time in her work. **Circles of contamination . . . replication of infected cells . . . death-toll estimates.**

"I apologize if I seem naive," she said, making no effort to hide her annoyance. "But I'm missing your point."

"My point?" He chuckled quietly. "My point is that the history of our human population growth is even more dramatic. The earth's population, like our stack of paper, had very meager beginnings . . . but alarming potential."

He was pacing again. "Consider this. It took the earth's population thousands of years—from the early dawn of man all the way to the early 1800s—to reach **one** billion people. Then, astoundingly, it took only about a hundred years to double the population to **two** billion in the 1920s. After that, it took a mere fifty years for the population to double again to **four** billion in the 1970s. As you can imagine, we're well on track to reach eight billion very soon. Just today, the human race added another quarter-million people to planet Earth. A quarter **million**. And this happens every day—rain or shine. Currently, every year, we're adding the equivalent of the entire country of Germany."

The tall man stopped short, hovering over Elizabeth. "How old are you?"

Another offensive question, although as the head of the WHO, she was accustomed to handling antagonism with diplomacy. "Sixty-one."

"Did you know that if you live another nineteen years, until the age of eighty, you will witness the population **triple** in your lifetime. **One** lifetime—a **tripling**. Think of the implications. As you know, your World Health Organization has again increased its forecasts, predicting there will be some nine billion people on earth before the midpoint of this century. Animal species are going extinct at a precipitously accelerated rate. The demand for dwindling natural resources is skyrocketing. Clean water is harder and harder to come by. By any biological gauge, our species has exceeded our sustainable numbers. And in the face of this disaster, the World Health Organization—the gatekeeper of the planet's health—is investing in things like curing diabetes, filling blood banks, battling cancer." He paused, staring directly at her. "And so I brought you here to ask you directly why the hell the World Health Organization does not have the guts to deal with this issue head-on?"

Elizabeth was seething now. "Whoever you are, you know damned well the WHO takes overpopulation **very** seriously. Recently we spent millions of dollars sending doctors into Africa to deliver free condoms and educate people about birth control."

"Ah, yes!" the lanky man derided. "And an even bigger army of Catholic missionaries marched in on your heels and told the Africans that if they used the condoms, they'd all go to hell. Africa has a new environmental issue now—landfills overflowing with unused condoms."

Elizabeth strained to hold her tongue. He was correct on this point, and yet modern Catholics were starting to fight back against the Vatican's meddling in reproductive issues. Most notably, Melinda Gates, a devout Catholic herself, had bravely risked the wrath of her own church by pledging $560 **million** to help improve access to birth control around the world. Elizabeth Sinskey had gone on record many times saying that Bill and Melinda Gates deserved to be canonized for all they'd done through their foundation to improve world health. Sadly, the only institution capable of conferring sainthood somehow failed to see the Christian nature of their efforts.

"Dr. Sinskey," the shadow continued. "What the World Health Organization fails to recognize is that there is only one global health issue." He pointed again to the grim image on the screen—a sea of tangled, cloying humanity. "And this is it." He paused. "I realize you are a scientist, and therefore perhaps not a student of the classics or the fine arts, so let me offer another image that may speak to you in a language you can better understand."

The room went dark for an instant, and the screen refreshed.

The new image was one Elizabeth had seen many times . . . and it always brought an eerie sense of inevitability.

A heavy silence settled in the room.

"Yes," the lanky man finally said. "Silent terror is an apt response to this graph. Seeing it is a bit like staring into the headlight of an oncoming locomotive." Slowly, the man turned to Elizabeth and gave her a tight, condescending smile. "Any questions, Dr. Sinskey?"

World Population Growth Throughout History

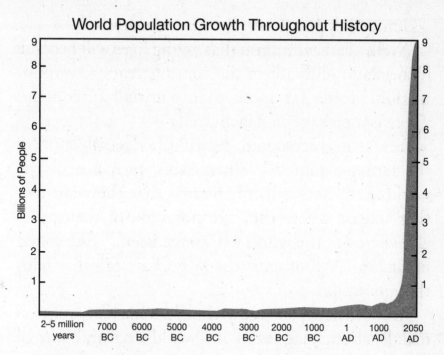

"Just one," she fired back. "Did you bring me here to lecture me or insult me?"

"Neither." His voice turned eerily cajoling. "I brought you here to work with you. I have no doubt you understand that overpopulation is a health issue. But what I fear you don't understand is that it will affect the very soul of man. Under the stress of over-population, those who have never considered steal-ing will become thieves to feed their families. Those who have never considered killing will kill to provide for their young. All of Dante's deadly sins—greed, gluttony, treachery, murder, and the rest—will begin percolating . . . rising up to the surface of humanity, amplified by our evaporating comforts. We are fac-ing a battle for the very soul of man."

"I'm a biologist. I save lives . . . not souls."

"Well, I can assure you that saving lives will become increasingly difficult in the coming years. Overpopulation breeds far more than spiritual discontent. There is a passage in Machiavelli—"

"Yes," she interrupted, reciting her recollection of the famous quote. "'When every province of the world so teems with inhabitants that they can neither subsist where they are nor remove themselves elsewhere . . . the world will purge itself.'" She stared up at him. "All of us at the WHO are familiar with that quotation."

"Good, then you know that Machiavelli went on to talk about plagues as the world's natural way of self-purging."

"Yes, and as I mentioned in my talk, we are well aware of the direct correlation between population density and the likelihood of wide-scale epidemics, but we are constantly devising new detection and treatment methods. The WHO remains confident that we can prevent future pandemics."

"That's a pity."

Elizabeth stared in disbelief. "I beg your pardon?!"

"Dr. Sinskey," the man said with a strange laugh, "you talk about controlling epidemics as if it's a good thing."

She gaped up at the man in mute disbelief.

"There you have it," the lanky man declared, sounding like an attorney resting his case. "Here I stand with the head of the World Health Organization—the best the WHO has to offer. A terrifying thought if you consider it. I have shown you this image of impending misery." He refreshed the screen, again displaying the image of the bodies. "I have reminded you of the awesome power of unchecked population growth." He pointed to his small stack of paper. "I have enlightened you about the fact that we are on the brink of a spiritual collapse." He paused and turned directly toward her. "And your response? Free condoms in Africa." The man gave a derisive sneer. "This is like swinging a flyswatter at an incoming asteroid. The time bomb is no longer ticking. It has already gone off, and without drastic measures, exponential mathematics will become your new God . . . and 'He' is a vengeful God. He will bring to you Dante's vision of hell right outside on Park Avenue . . . huddled masses wallowing in their own excrement. A global culling orchestrated by Nature herself."

"Is that so?" Elizabeth snapped. "So tell me, in **your** vision of a sustainable future, what is the ideal population of earth? What is the magic number at which humankind can hope to sustain itself indefinitely . . . and in relative comfort?"

The tall man smiled, clearly appreciating the question. "Any environmental biologist or statistician will tell you that humankind's best chance of long-term survival occurs with a global population of around four billion."

"**Four** billion?" Elizabeth fired back. "We're at seven billion now, so it's a little late for that."

The tall man's green eyes flashed fire. "Is it?"

CHAPTER 23

Robert Langdon landed hard on the spongy earth just inside the retaining wall of the Boboli Gardens' heavily wooded southern edge. Sienna landed beside him and stood up, brushing herself off and taking in their surroundings.

They were standing in a glade of moss and ferns on the edge of a small forest. From here, the Palazzo Pitti was entirely obscured from view, and Langdon sensed they were about as far from the palace as one could get in the gardens. At least there were no workers or tourists out this far at this early hour.

Langdon gazed at a peastone pathway that wound gracefully downhill into the forest before them. At the point where the path disappeared into the trees, a marble statue had been perfectly situated to receive the eye. Langdon was not surprised. The Boboli Gardens had enjoyed the exceptional design talents of Niccolò Tribolo, Giorgio Vasari, and Bernardo Buontalenti—a brain trust of aesthetic talent that had created on this 111-acre canvas a walkable masterpiece.

"If we head northeast, we'll reach the palace," Langdon said, pointing down the path. "We can mix there with the tourists and exit unseen. I'm guessing it opens at nine."

Langdon glanced down to check the time but saw only his bare wrist where his Mickey Mouse watch had once been strapped. He wondered absently if it was still at the hospital with the rest of his clothing and if he'd ever be able to retrieve it.

Sienna planted her feet defiantly. "Robert, before we take another step, I want to know where we're going. What did you figure out back there? The Malebolge? You said it was out of sequence?"

Langdon motioned toward a wooded area just ahead. "Let's get out of sight first." He led her down a pathway that curled into an enclosed hollow—a "room," in the parlance of landscape architecture—where there were some faux-bois benches and a small fountain. The air beneath the trees was decidedly colder.

Langdon took the projector from his pocket and began shaking it. "Sienna, whoever created this digital image not only added letters to the sinners in the Malebolge, but he also changed the order of the sins." He hopped up on the bench, towering over Sienna, and aimed the projector down at his feet. Botticelli's **Mappa dell'Inferno** materialized faintly on the flat bench top beside Sienna.

Langdon motioned to the tiered area at the bottom of the funnel. "See the letters in the ten ditches of the Malebolge?"

Sienna found them on the projection and read from top to bottom. "Catrovacer."

"Right. Meaningless."

"But then you realized the ten ditches had been shuffled around?"

"Easier than that, actually. If these levels were a deck of ten cards, the deck was not so much shuffled as simply cut once. After the cut, the cards remain in the correct order, but they start with the wrong card." Langdon pointed down at the ten ditches of the Malebolge. "According to Dante's text, our top level should be the seducers whipped by demons. And yet, in this version, the seducers appear . . . way down in the seventh ditch."

Sienna studied the now-fading image beside her and nodded. "Okay, I see that. The first ditch is now the seventh."

Langdon pocketed the projector and jumped back down onto the pathway. He grabbed a small stick and began scratching letters on a patch of dirt just off the path. "Here are the letters as they appear in our modified version of hell."

C
A
T
R
O
V
A
C
E
R

"Catrovacer," Sienna read.

"Yes. And here is where the 'deck' was cut." Langdon now drew a line beneath the seventh letter and waited while Sienna studied his handiwork.

C
A
T
R
O
V
A
—
C
E
R

"Okay," she said quickly. "Catrova. Cer."

"Yes, and to put the cards back in order, we simply uncut the deck and place the bottom on top. The two halves swap places."

Sienna eyed the letters. "Cer. Catrova." She shrugged, looking unimpressed. "Still meaningless . . ."

"Cer catrova," Langdon repeated. After a pause, he said the words again, eliding them together. "Cercatrova." Finally, he said them with a pause in the middle. "Cerca . . . trova."

Sienna gasped audibly and her eyes shot up to meet Langdon's.

"Yes," Langdon said with a smile. "Cerca trova."

The two Italian words **cerca** and **trova** literally meant "seek" and "find." When combined as a phrase—**cerca trova**—they were synonymous with the biblical aphorism "Seek and ye shall find."

"Your hallucinations!" Sienna exclaimed, breathless. "The woman with the veil! She kept telling you to seek and find!" She jumped to her feet. "Robert, do you realize what this means? It means the words **cerca trova** were **already** in your subconscious! Don't you see? You must have deciphered this phrase before you arrived at the hospital! You had probably seen this projector's image already . . . but had forgotten!"

She's right, he realized, having been so fixated on the cipher itself that it never occurred to him that he might have been through all of this already.

"Robert, you said earlier that **La Mappa** points to a specific location in the old city. But I still don't understand where."

"**Cerca trova** doesn't ring any bells for you?"

She shrugged.

Langdon smiled inwardly. **Finally, something Sienna doesn't know.** "As it turns out, this phrase points very specifically to a famous mural that hangs in the Palazzo Vecchio—Giorgio Vasari's **Battaglia di Marciano** in the Hall of the Five Hundred. Near the top of the painting, barely visible, Vasari painted the words **cerca trova** in tiny letters. Plenty of theories exist as to why he did this, but no conclusive proof has ever been discovered."

The high-pitched whine of a small aircraft suddenly buzzed overhead, streaking in out of nowhere and skimming the wooded canopy just above them. The sound was very close, and Langdon and Sienna froze as the craft raced past.

As the aircraft departed, Langdon peered up at it through the trees. "Toy helicopter," he said, exhaling as he watched the three-foot-long, radio-controlled chopper banking in the distance. It sounded like a giant, angry mosquito.

Sienna, however, still looked wary. "Stay down."

Sure enough, the little chopper banked fully and was now coming back their way, skimming the tree-tops, sailing past them again, this time off to their left above another glade.

"That's not a toy," she whispered. "It's a reconnaissance drone. Probably has a video camera on board sending live images back to . . . somebody."

Langdon's jaw tightened as he watched the chopper streak off in the direction from which it had appeared—the Porta Romana and the Art Institute.

"I don't know what you did," Sienna said, "but some powerful people are clearly very eager to find you."

The helicopter banked yet again and began a slow pass along the perimeter wall they had just jumped.

"Someone at the Art Institute must have seen us and said something," Sienna said, heading down the path. "We've got to get out of here. Now."

As the drone buzzed away toward the far end of the gardens, Langdon used his foot to erase the letters he'd written on the pathway and then hurried after Sienna. His mind swirled with thoughts of **cerca trova**, the Giorgio Vasari mural, as well as with Sienna's revelation that Langdon must have already deciphered the projector's message. **Seek and ye shall find.**

Suddenly, just as they entered a second glade, a startling thought hit Langdon. He skidded to a stop on the wooded path, a bemused look on his face.

Sienna stopped, too. "Robert? What is it?!"

"I'm innocent," he declared.

"What are you talking about?"

"The people chasing me . . . I assumed it was because I had done something terrible."

"Yes, at the hospital you kept repeating 'very sorry.'"

"I know. But I thought I was speaking English."

Sienna looked at him with surprise. "You **were** speaking English!"

Langdon's blue eyes were now filled with excitement. "Sienna, when I kept saying 'very sorry,' I wasn't apologizing. I was mumbling about the secret message in the mural at Palazzo Vecchio!" He could still hear the recording of his own delirious voice. **Ve . . . sorry. Ve . . . sorry.**

Sienna looked lost.

"Don't you see?!" Langdon was grinning now. "I wasn't saying 'very sorry, very sorry.' I was saying the artist's name—**Va . . . sari, Vasari!**"

CHAPTER **24**

Vayentha hit the brakes hard.

Her motorcycle fishtailed, screeching loudly as it left a long skid mark on the Viale del Poggio Imperiale, finally coming to an abrupt stop behind an unexpected line of traffic. The Viale del Poggio was at a standstill.

I don't have time for this!

Vayentha craned her neck over the cars, trying to see what was causing the holdup. She had already been forced to drive in a wide circle to avoid the SRS team and all the chaos at the apartment building, and now she needed to get into the old city to clear out of the hotel room where she had been stationed for the last few days of this mission.

I've been disavowed—I need to get the hell out of town!

Her string of bad luck, however, seemed to be continuing. The route she had selected into the old city appeared to be blocked. In no mood to wait, Vayentha revved the bike off to one side of the traffic and sped along the narrow breakdown lane until she could see the snarled intersection. Up ahead was a clogged rotary where six major thoroughfares converged. This was the Porta Romana—one of Florence's most trafficked intersections—the gateway to the old city.

What the hell is going on here?!

Vayentha now saw that the entire area was swarming with police—a roadblock or checkpoint of some sort. Moments later, she spotted something at the center of the action that left her baffled—a familiar black van around which several black-clad agents were calling out orders to the local authorities.

These men, without a doubt, were members of the SRS team, and yet Vayentha could not imagine what they were doing here.

Unless . . .

Vayentha swallowed hard, scarcely daring to imagine the possibility. **Has Langdon eluded Brüder as well?** It seemed unthinkable; the chances of escape had been near zero. Then again, Langdon was not working alone, and Vayentha had experienced first-hand how resourceful the blond woman could be.

Nearby, a police officer appeared, walking from car to car, showing a photo of a handsome man with thick brown hair. Vayentha instantly recognized the photo as a press shot of Robert Langdon. Her heart soared.

Brüder missed him . . .

Langdon is still in play!

An experienced strategist, Vayentha immediately began assessing how this development changed her situation.

Option one—flee as required.

Vayentha had blown a critical job for the provost and had been disavowed because of it. If she were lucky, she would face a formal inquiry and probable career termination. If, however, she were unlucky and had underestimated the severity of her employer, she might spend the rest of her life looking over her shoulder and wondering if the Consortium was lurking just out of sight.

There is a second option now.

Complete your mission.

Staying on task was in direct opposition to her disavowal protocol, and yet with Langdon still on the run, Vayentha now had the opportunity to continue with her original directive.

If Brüder fails to catch Langdon, she thought, her pulse quickening. **And if I succeed . . .**

Vayentha knew it was a long shot, but if Langdon managed to elude Brüder entirely, and if Vayentha could still step in and finish the job, she would single-handedly have saved the day for the Consortium, and the provost would have no choice but to be lenient.

I'll keep my job, she thought. **Probably even be promoted.**

In a flash, Vayentha realized that her entire future now revolved around a single critical undertaking. **I must locate Langdon . . . before Brüder does.**

It would not be easy. Brüder had at his disposal endless manpower as well as a vast array of advanced surveillance technologies. Vayentha was working alone. She did, however, possess one piece of infor-mation that Brüder, the provost, and the police did not have.

I have a very good idea where Langdon will go.

Revving the throttle on her BMW, she spun it 180 degrees around and headed back the way she came. **Ponte alle Grazie**, she thought, picturing the bridge to the north. There existed more than one route into the old city.

CHAPTER 25

Not an apology, Langdon mused. **An artist's name.**

"Vasari," Sienna stammered, taking a full step backward on the path. "The artist who hid the words **cerca trova** in his mural."

Langdon couldn't help but smile. **Vasari. Vasari.** In addition to shedding a ray of light on his strange predicament, this revelation also meant Langdon was no longer wondering what terrible thing he might have done . . . for which he had been profusely saying he was very sorry.

"Robert, you clearly had seen this Botticelli image on the projector before you were injured, and you knew it contained a code that pointed to Vasari's mural. That's why you woke up and kept repeating Vasari's name!"

Langdon tried to calculate what all of this meant. Giorgio Vasari—a sixteenth-century artist, architect, and writer—was a man Langdon often referred to as "the world's first art historian." Despite the hundreds of paintings Vasari created, and the dozens of buildings he designed, his most enduring legacy was his seminal book, **Lives of the Most Excellent Painters, Sculptors, and Architects**, a collection of biographies of Italian artists, which to this day remains requisite reading for students of art history.

The words **cerca trova** had placed Vasari back in the mainstream consciousness about thirty years ago when his "secret message" was discovered high on his sprawling mural in the Palazzo Vecchio's Hall of the Five Hundred. The tiny letters appeared on a green battle flag, barely visible among the chaos of the war scene. While consensus had yet to be reached as to why Vasari added this strange message to his mural, the leading theory was that it was a clue to future generations of the existence of a lost Leonardo da Vinci fresco hidden in a three-centimeter gap behind that wall.

Sienna was glancing nervously up through the trees. "There's still one thing I don't understand. If you weren't saying 'very sorry, very sorry' . . . then why are people trying to kill you?"

Langdon had been wondering the same thing.

The distant buzz of the surveillance drone was getting louder again, and Langdon knew the time had come for a decision. He failed to see how Vasari's **Battaglia di Marciano** could possibly relate to Dante's **Inferno**, or the gunshot wound he had suffered the night before, and yet he finally saw a tangible path before him.

Cerca trova.

Seek and find.

Again Langdon saw the silver-haired woman calling out to him from across the river. **Time is run-**

ning out! If there were answers, Langdon sensed, they would be at the Palazzo Vecchio.

He now flashed on an old adage from early Grecian free divers who hunted lobsters in the coral caves of the Aegean Islands. **When swimming into a dark tunnel, there arrives a point of no return when you no longer have enough breath to double back. Your only choice is to swim forward into the unknown . . . and pray for an exit.**

Langdon wondered if they had reached that point.

He eyed the maze of garden pathways before them. If he and Sienna could reach the Pitti Palace and exit the gardens, then the old city was just a short walk across the most famous footbridge in the world—the Ponte Vecchio. It was always crowded and would provide good cover. From there, the Palazzo Vecchio was only a few blocks away.

The drone hummed closer now, and Langdon felt momentarily overwhelmed by exhaustion. The realization that he had not been saying "very sorry" left him feeling conflicted about running from the police.

"Eventually, they're going to catch me, Sienna," Langdon said. "It might be better for me to stop running."

Sienna looked at him with alarm. "Robert, every time you stop, someone starts shooting at you! You need to figure out what you're involved in. You need to look at that Vasari mural and hope it jars your memory. Maybe it will help you learn where this projector came from and why you're carrying it."

Langdon pictured the spike-haired woman coldly killing Dr. Marconi . . . the soldiers firing on them . . . the Italian military police gathering in the Porta Romana . . . and now a surveillance drone tracking them through the Boboli Gardens. He fell silent, rubbing his tired eyes as he considered his options.

"Robert?" Sienna's voice rose. "There's one other thing . . . something that didn't seem important, but now seems like it might be."

Langdon raised his eyes, reacting to the gravity in her tone.

"I intended to tell you at the apartment," she said, "but . . ."

"What is it?"

Sienna pursed her lips, looking uncomfortable. "When you arrived at the hospital, you were delirious and trying to communicate."

"Yes," Langdon said, "mumbling 'Vasari, Vasari.'"

"Yes, but **before** that . . . before we got out the recorder, in the first moments after you arrived, you said one other thing I remember. You only said it once, but I'm positive I understood."

"What did I say?"

Sienna glanced up toward the drone and then back at Langdon. "You said, '**I hold the key to finding it . . . if I fail, then all is death.**'"

Langdon could only stare.

Sienna continued. "I thought you were referring to the object in your jacket pocket, but now I'm not so sure."

If I fail, then all is death? The words hit Langdon

hard. The haunting images of death flickered before him . . . Dante's inferno, the biohazard symbol, the plague doctor. Yet again, the face of the beautiful silver-haired woman pleaded with him across the bloodred river. **Seek and find! Time is running out!**

Sienna's voice pulled him back. "Whatever this projector ultimately points to . . . or whatever you're trying to find, it must be something extremely dangerous. The fact that people are trying to kill us . . ." Her voice cracked slightly, and she took a moment to regroup. "Think about it. They just shot at you in broad daylight . . . shot at **me**—an innocent bystander. Nobody seems to be looking to negotiate. Your own government turned on you . . . you called them for help, and they sent someone to kill you."

Langdon stared vacantly at the ground. Whether the U.S. Consulate had shared Langdon's location with the assassin, or whether the consulate itself had sent the assassin, was irrelevant. The upshot was the same. **My own government is not on my side.**

Langdon looked into Sienna's brown eyes and saw bravery there. **What have I gotten her involved in?** "I wish I knew what we were looking for. That would help put all of this into perspective."

Sienna nodded. "Whatever it is, I think we need to find it. At least it would give us leverage."

Her logic was hard to refute. Still Langdon felt something nagging at him. **If I fail, then all is death.** All morning he'd been running up against macabre symbols of biohazards, plagues, and Dante's hell. Admittedly, he had no clear proof of what he was looking for, but he would be naive not to consider at least the possibility that this situation involved a deadly disease or large-scale biological threat. But if this were true, why would his own government be trying to eliminate him?

Do they think I'm somehow involved in a potential attack?

It made no sense at all. There was something else going on here.

Langdon thought again of the silver-haired woman. "There's also the woman from my visions. I feel I need to find her."

"Then trust your feelings," Sienna said. "In your condition, the best compass you have is your subconscious mind. It's basic psychology—if your gut is telling you to trust that woman, then I think you should do exactly what she keeps telling you to do."

"Seek and find," they said in unison.

Langdon exhaled, knowing his path was clear.

All I can do is keep swimming down this tunnel.

With hardening resolve, he turned and began taking in his surroundings, trying to get his bearings. **Which way out of the gardens?**

They were standing beneath the trees at the edge of a wide-open plaza where several paths intersected. In the distance to their left, Langdon spied an elliptical-shaped lagoon with a small island adorned with lemon trees and statuary. **The Isolotto,** he thought, recognizing the famous sculpture of Perseus on a half-submerged horse bounding through the water.

"The Pitti Palace is that way," Langdon said, pointing east, away from the Isolotto, toward the garden's main thoroughfare—the Viottolone, which ran east–west along the entire length of the grounds. The Viottolone was as wide as a two-lane road and lined by a row of slender, four-hundred-year-old cypress trees.

"There's no cover," Sienna said, eyeing the uncamouflaged avenue and motioning up at the circling drone.

"You're right," Langdon said with a lopsided grin. "Which is why we're taking the tunnel beside it."

He pointed again, this time to a dense hedgerow adjacent to the mouth of the Viottolone. The wall of dense greenery had a small arched opening cut into it. Beyond the opening, a slender footpath stretched out into the distance—a tunnel running parallel with the Viottolone. It was enclosed on either side by a phalanx of pruned holm oaks, which had been carefully trained since the 1600s to arch inward over the path, intertwining overhead and providing an awning of foliage. The pathway's name, La Cerchiata—literally "circular" or "hooped"—derived from its canopy of curved trees resembling barrel stays or **cerchi**.

Sienna hurried over to the opening and peered into the shaded channel. Immediately she turned back to him with a smile. "Better."

Wasting no time, she slipped through the opening and hurried off among the trees.

Langdon had always considered La Cerchiata one of Florence's most peaceful spots. Today, however, as he watched Sienna disappear down the darkened allée, he thought again of the Grecian free divers swimming into corral tunnels and praying they'd reach an exit.

Langdon quickly said his own little prayer and hurried after her.

———

A half mile behind them, outside the Art Institute, Agent Brüder strode through a bustle of police and students, his icy gaze parting the crowds before him. He made his way to the makeshift command post that his surveillance specialist had set up on the hood of his black van.

"From the aerial drone," the specialist said, handing Brüder a tablet screen. "Taken a few minutes ago."

Brüder examined the video stills, pausing on a blurry enlargement of two faces—a dark-haired man and a blond ponytailed woman—both huddled in the shadows and peering skyward through a canopy of trees.

Robert Langdon.

Sienna Brooks.

Zero doubt.

Brüder turned his attention to the map of the Boboli Gardens, which was spread out on the hood. **They made a poor choice,** he thought, eyeing the garden layout. While it was sprawling and intricate, with plenty of hiding places, the gardens also appeared to be surrounded on all sides by high walls. The Boboli Gardens were the closest thing to a natural kill-box that Brüder had ever seen in the field.

They'll never get out.

"Local authorities are sealing all exits," the agent said. "And commencing a sweep."

"Keep me informed," Brüder said.

Slowly, he raised his eyes to the van's thick polycarbonate window, beyond which he could see the silver-haired woman seated in the back of the vehicle.

The drugs they had given her had definitely dulled her senses—more than Brüder had imagined. Nonetheless, he could tell by the fearful look in her eyes that she still had a firm grasp on precisely what was going on.

She does not look happy, Brüder thought. **Then again, why would she?**

CHAPTER 26

A spire of water shot twenty feet in the air.
Langdon watched it fall gently back to
earth and knew they were getting close. They
had reached the end of La Cerchiata's leafy tunnel
and dashed across an open lawn into a grove of cork
trees. Now they were looking out at the Boboli's
most famous spouting fountain—Stoldo Lorenzi's
bronze of Neptune clutching his three-pronged tri-
dent. Irreverently known by locals as "The Fountain
of the Fork," this water feature was considered the
central point of the gardens.

Sienna stopped at the edge of the grove and peered
upward through the trees. "I don't see the drone."

Langdon no longer heard it either, and yet the
fountain was quite loud.

"Must have needed to refuel," Sienna said. "This is
our chance. Which way?"

Langdon led her to the left, and they began descending a steep incline. As they emerged from the trees,
the Pitti Palace came into view.

"Nice little house," Sienna whispered.

"Typical Medici understatement," he replied wryly.

Still almost a quarter mile away, the Pitti Palace's
stone facade dominated the landscape, stretching out

to their left and right. Its exterior of bulging, rusticated stonework lent the building an air of unyielding authority that was further accentuated by a powerful repetition of shuttered windows and arch-topped apertures. Traditionally, formal palaces were situated on high ground so that anyone in the gardens had to look uphill at the building. The Pitti Palace, however, was situated in a low valley near the Arno River, meaning that people in the Boboli Gardens looked downhill at the palace.

This effect was only more dramatic. One architect had described the palace as appearing to have been built by nature herself . . . as if the massive stones in a landslide had tumbled down the long escarpment and landed in an elegant, barricade-like pile at the bottom. Despite its less defensible position in the low ground, the solid stone structure of the Pitti Palace was so imposing that Napoleon had once used it as a power base while in Florence.

"Look," Sienna said, pointing to the nearest doors of the palace. "Good news."

Langdon had seen it, too. On this strange morning, the most welcome sight was not the palace itself, but the tourists streaming out of the building into the lower gardens. The palace was open, which meant that Langdon and Sienna would have no trouble slipping inside and passing through the building to escape the gardens. Once outside the palace, Langdon knew they would see the Arno River to their right, and beyond that, the spires of the old city.

He and Sienna kept moving, half jogging now

down the steep embankment. As they descended, they traversed the Boboli Amphitheater—the site of the very first opera performance in history— which lay nestled like a horseshoe on the side of a hill. Beyond that, they passed the obelisk of Ramses II and the unfortunate piece of "art" that was positioned at its base. The guidebooks referred to the piece as "a colossal stone basin from Rome's Baths of Caracalla," but Langdon always saw it for what it truly was—the world's largest bathtub. **They really need to put that thing somewhere else.**

They finally reached the rear of the palace and slowed to a calm walk, mixing inconspicuously with the first tourists of the day. Moving against the tide, they descended a narrow tunnel into the cortile, an inner courtyard where visitors were seated enjoying a morning espresso in the palace's makeshift café. The smell of fresh-ground coffee filled the air, and Langdon felt a sudden longing to sit down and enjoy a civilized breakfast. **Today's not the day**, he thought as they pressed on, entering the wide stone passageway that led toward the palace's main doors.

As they neared the doorway, Langdon and Sienna collided with a growing bottleneck of stalled tourists who seemed to be assembling in the portico to observe something outside. Langdon peered through the crowd to the area in front of the palace.

The Pitti's grand entrance was as blunt and unwelcoming as he recalled it. Rather than a manicured lawn and landscaping, the front yard was a vast expanse of pavement that stretched across an entire hillside, flowing down to the Via dei Guicciardini like a massive paved ski slope.

At the bottom of the hill, Langdon now saw the reason for the crowd of onlookers.

Down in Piazza dei Pitti, a half-dozen police cars had streamed in from all directions. A small army of officers were advancing up the hill, unholstering their weapons and fanning out to secure the front of the palace.

CHAPTER 27

As the police entered the Pitti Palace, Sienna and Langdon were already on the move, retracing their steps through the interior of the palace and away from the arriving police. They hurried through the cortile and past the café, where a buzz was spreading, tourists rubbernecking in an attempt to locate the source of the commotion.

Sienna was amazed the authorities had found them so quickly. **The drone must have disappeared because it had already spotted us.**

She and Langdon found the same narrow tunnel through which they had descended from the gardens and without hesitation plunged back into the passageway and bounded up the stairs. The end of the staircase banked left along a high retaining wall. As they dashed along the wall, it grew shorter beside them, until finally they could see over it into the vast expanse of the Boboli Gardens.

Langdon instantly grabbed Sienna's arm and yanked her backward, ducking out of sight behind the retaining wall. Sienna had seen it, too.

Three hundred yards away, on the slope above the amphitheater, a phalanx of police descended, searching groves, interviewing tourists, coordinating with one another on handheld radios.

We're trapped!

Sienna had never imagined, when she and Robert Langdon first met, that it would lead to this. **This is more than I bargained for.** When Sienna had left the hospital with Langdon, she thought they were fleeing a woman with spiked hair and a gun. Now they were running from an entire military team and the Italian authorities. Their chances of escape, she was now realizing, were almost zero.

"Is there any other way out?" Sienna demanded, short of breath.

"I don't think so," Langdon said. "This garden is a walled city, just like . . ." He paused suddenly, turning and looking east. "Just like . . . the Vatican." A strange glint of hope flickered across his face.

Sienna had no idea what the Vatican had to do with their current predicament, but Langdon suddenly began nodding, gazing east along the back of the palace.

"It's a long shot," he said, hustling her along with him now. "But there might be a different way to get out of here."

Two figures materialized suddenly before them, having rounded the corner of the retaining wall, nearly bumping into Sienna and Langdon. Both figures were wearing black, and for one frightening instant, Sienna thought they were the soldiers she had encountered at the apartment building. As they

passed, though, she saw they were only tourists—
Italian, she guessed, from all the stylish black leather.

Having an idea, Sienna caught one of the tourists'
arms and smiled up at him as warmly as possible.
"Può dirci dov'è la Galleria del costume?" she asked
in rapid Italian, requesting directions to the palace's
famed costume gallery. **"Io e mio fratello siamo in
ritardo per una visita privata."** My brother and I are
late for a private tour.

"Certo!" The man grinned at them both, looking
eager to help. **"Proseguite dritto per il sentiero!"** He
turned and pointed west, along the retaining wall,
directly away from whatever Langdon had been looking at.

"Molte grazie!" Sienna chirped with another smile
as the two men headed off.

Langdon gave Sienna an impressed nod, apparently
understanding her motives. If the police began questioning tourists, they might hear that Langdon and
Sienna were headed for the costume gallery, which,
according to the map on the wall before them, was at
the far western end of the palace . . . as far as possible
from the direction in which they were now headed.

"We need to get to that path over there," Langdon said, motioning across an open plaza toward a
walkway that ran down another hill, away from the
palace. The peastone walkway was sheltered on the
uphill side by massive hedges, providing plenty of
cover from the authorities now descending the hill,
only a hundred yards away.

Sienna calculated that their chances of getting

across the open area to the sheltered path were very slim. Tourists were gathering there, watching the police with curiosity. The faint thrum of the drone became audible again, approaching in the distance.

"Now or never," Langdon said, grabbing her hand and pulling her with him out into the open plaza, where they began winding through the crowd of gathering tourists. Sienna fought the urge to break into a run, but Langdon held firmly on to her, walking briskly but calmly through the throng.

When they finally reached the opening to the pathway, Sienna glanced back over her shoulder to see if they had been detected. The only police officers in sight were all facing the other way, their eyes turned skyward toward the sound of the incoming drone.

She faced front and hurried with Langdon down the path.

Before them now, the skyline of old Florence poked above the trees, visible directly ahead in the distance. She saw the red-tiled cupola of the Duomo and the green, red, and white spire of Giotto's bell tower. For an instant, she could also make out the crenellated spire of the Palazzo Vecchio—their seemingly impossible destination—but as they descended the pathway, the high perimeter walls blotted out the view, engulfing them again.

By the time they reached the bottom of the hill, Sienna was out of breath and wondering if Langdon had any idea where they were going. The path led directly into a maze garden, but Langdon confidently turned left into a wide gravel patio, which he skirted, staying behind a hedge in the shadows of the overhanging trees. The patio was deserted, more of an employee parking lot than a tourist area.

"Where are we going?!" Sienna finally asked, breathless.

"Almost there."

Almost where? The entire patio was enclosed by walls that were at least three stories tall. The only exit Sienna saw was a vehicle gateway on the left, which was sealed by a massive wrought-iron grate that looked like it dated back to the original palace in the days of marauding armies. Beyond the barricade, she could see police gathered in the Piazza dei Pitti.

Staying along the perimeter vegetation, Langdon pushed onward, heading directly for the wall in front of them. Sienna scanned the sheer face for any open doorway, but all she saw was a niche containing what had to be the most hideous statue she had ever seen.

Good God, the Medici could afford any artwork on earth, and they chose this?

The statue before them depicted an obese, naked dwarf straddling a giant turtle. The dwarf's testicles were squashed against the turtle's shell, and the turtle's mouth was dribbling water, as if he were ill.

"I know," Langdon said, without breaking stride. "That's **Braccio di Bartolo**—a famous court dwarf. If you ask me, they should put him out back in the giant bathtub."

Langdon turned sharply to his right, heading down a set of stairs that Sienna had been unable to see until now.

A way out?!

The flash of hope was short-lived.

As she turned the corner and headed down the stairs behind Langdon, she realized they were dashing into a dead end—a cul-de-sac whose walls were twice as high as the others.

Furthermore, Sienna now sensed that their long journey was about to terminate at the mouth of a gaping cavern . . . a deep grotto carved out of the rear wall. **This can't be where he's taking us!**

Over the cave's yawning entrance, daggerlike stalactites loomed portentously. In the cavity beyond, oozing geological features twisted and dripped down the walls as if the stone were melting . . . morphing into shapes that included, to Sienna's alarm, half-buried humanoids extruding from the walls as if being consumed by the stone. The entire vision reminded Sienna of something out of Botticelli's **Mappa dell'Inferno.**

Langdon, for some reason, seemed unfazed, and continued running directly toward the cave's entrance. He'd made a comment earlier about Vatican City, but Sienna was fairly certain there were no freakish caverns inside the walls of the Holy See.

As they drew nearer, Sienna's eyes moved to the sprawling entablature above the entrance—a ghostly compilation of stalactites and nebulous stone extrusions that seemed to be engulfing two reclining women, who were flanked by a shield embedded with six balls, or **palle**, the famed crest of the Medici.

Langdon suddenly cut to his left, away from the

entrance and toward a feature Sienna had previously missed—a small gray door to the left of the cavern. Weathered and wooden, it appeared of little significance, like a storage closet or room for landscaping supplies.

Langdon rushed to the door, clearly hoping he could open it, but the door had no handle—only a brass keyhole—and, apparently, could be opened only from within.

"Damn it!" Langdon's eyes now shone with concern, his earlier hopefulness all but erased. "I had hoped—"

Without warning, the piercing whine of the drone echoed loudly off the high walls around them. Sienna turned to see the drone rising up over the palace and clawing its way in their direction.

Langdon clearly saw it, too, because he grabbed Sienna's hand and dashed toward the cavern. They ducked out of sight in the nick of time beneath the grotto's stalactite overhang.

A fitting end, she thought. **Dashing through the gates of hell.**

CHAPTER 28

A quarter mile to the east, Vayentha parked her motorcycle. She had crossed into the old city via the Ponte alle Grazie and then circled around to the Ponte Vecchio—the famed pedestrian bridge connecting the Pitti Palace to the old city. After locking her helmet to the bike, she strode out onto the bridge and mixed with the early-morning tourists.

A cool March breeze blew steadily up the river, ruffling Vayentha's short spiked hair, reminding her that Langdon knew what she looked like. She paused at the stall of one of the bridge's many vendors and bought an AMO FIRENZE baseball cap, pulling it low over her face.

She smoothed her leather suit over the bulge of her handgun and took up a position near the center of the bridge, casually leaning against a pillar and facing the Pitti Palace. From here she was able to survey all the pedestrians crossing the Arno into the heart of Florence.

Langdon is on foot, she told herself. **If he finds a way around the Porta Romana, this bridge is his most logical route into the old city.**

To the west, in the direction of the Pitti Palace, she

could hear sirens and wondered if this was good or bad news. **Are they still looking for him? Or have they caught him?** As Vayentha strained her ears for some indication as to what was going on, a new sound suddenly became audible—a high-pitched whine somewhere overhead. Her eyes turned instinctively skyward, and she spotted it at once—a small remote-controlled helicopter rising fast over the palace and swooping down over the treetops in the direction of the northeast corner of the Boboli Gardens.

A surveillance drone, Vayentha thought with a surge of hope. **If it's in the air, Brüder has yet to find Langdon.**

The drone was approaching fast. Apparently it was surveying the northeast corner of the gardens, the area closest to Ponte Vecchio and Vayentha's position, which gave her additional encouragement.

If Langdon eluded Brüder, he would definitely be moving in this direction.

As Vayentha watched, however, the drone suddenly dive-bombed out of sight behind the high stone wall. She could hear it hovering in place somewhere below the tree line . . . apparently having located something of interest.

CHAPTER 29

Seek and ye shall find, Langdon thought, huddled in the dim grotto with Sienna. **We sought an exit . . . and found a dead end.**

The amorphous fountain in the center of the cave offered good cover, and yet as Langdon peered out from behind it, he sensed it was too late.

The drone had just swooped down into the walled cul-de-sac, stopping abruptly outside the cavern, where it now hovered at a standstill, only ten feet off the ground, facing the grotto, buzzing intensely like some kind of infuriated insect . . . awaiting its prey.

Langdon pulled back and whispered the grim news to Sienna. "I think it knows we're here."

The drone's high-pitched whine was nearly deafening inside the cavern, the noise reflecting sharply off the stone walls. Langdon found it hard to believe they were being held hostage by a miniature mechanical helicopter, and yet he knew that trying to run from it was fruitless. **So what do we do now? Just wait?** His original plan to access what lay behind the little gray door had been a reasonable one, except he hadn't realized the door was openable only from within.

As Langdon's eyes adjusted to the grotto's dark interior, he surveyed their unusual surroundings, won-

dering if there was any other exit. He saw nothing
promising. The interior of the cavern was adorned
with sculpted animals and humans, all in various
stages of consumption by the strange oozing walls.
Dejected, Langdon raised his eyes to the ceiling of
stalactites hanging ominously overhead.

A good place to die.

The Buontalenti Grotto—so named for its architect, Bernardo Buontalenti—was arguably the most
curious-looking space in all of Florence. Intended as
a kind of fun house for young guests at the Pitti Palace, the three-chambered suite of caverns was decorated in a blend of naturalistic fantasy and Gothic
excess, composed of what appeared to be dripping
concretions and flowing pumice that seemed either
to be consuming or exuding the multitude of carved
figures. In the days of the Medici, the grotto was
accented by having water flow down the interior
walls, which served both to cool the space during
the hot Tuscan summers and to create the effect of
an actual cavern.

Langdon and Sienna were hidden in the first and
largest chamber behind an indistinct central fountain. They were surrounded by colorful figures of
shepherds, peasants, musicians, animals, and even
copies of Michelangelo's four prisoners, all of which
seemed to be struggling to break free of the fluid-
looking rock that engulfed them. High above, the
morning light filtered down through an oculus in
the ceiling, which had once held a giant glass ball

filled with water in which bright red carp swam in the sunlight.

Langdon wondered how the original Renaissance visitors here would have reacted at the sight of a real-life helicopter—a fantastical dream of Italy's own Leonardo da Vinci—hovering outside the grotto.

It was at that moment that the drone's shrill whine stopped. It hadn't faded away; rather, it had just . . . abruptly stopped.

Puzzled, Langdon peered out from behind the fountain and saw that the drone had landed. It was now sitting idle on the gravel plaza, looking much less ominous, especially because the stingerlike video lens on the front was facing away from them, off to one side, in the direction of the little gray door.

Langdon's sense of relief was fleeting. A hundred yards behind the drone, near the statue of the dwarf and turtle, three heavily armed soldiers were now striding purposefully down the stairs, heading directly toward the grotto.

The soldiers were dressed in familiar black uniforms with green medallions on their shoulders. Their muscular lead man had vacant eyes that reminded Langdon of the plague mask in his visions.

I am death.

Langdon did not see their van or the mysterious silver-haired woman anywhere.

I am life.

As the soldiers approached, one of them stopped at the bottom of the stairs and turned around, facing backward, apparently to prevent anyone else from descending into this area. The other two kept coming toward the grotto.

Langdon and Sienna sprang into motion again—although probably only delaying the inevitable—shuffling backward on all fours into the second cavern, which was smaller, deeper, and darker. It, too, was dominated by a central piece of art—in this case, a statue of two intertwined lovers—behind which Langdon and Sienna now hid anew.

Veiled in shadow, Langdon carefully peered out around the base of the statue and watched their approaching assailants. As the two soldiers reached the drone, one stopped and crouched down to tend to it, picking it up and examining the camera.

Did the device spot us? Langdon wondered, fearing he knew the answer.

The third and last soldier, the muscular one with the cold eyes, was still moving with icy focus in Langdon's direction. The man approached until he was nearly at the mouth of the cave. **He's coming in.** Langdon prepared to pull back behind the statue and tell Sienna it was over, but in that instant, he witnessed something unexpected.

The soldier, rather than entering the grotto, suddenly peeled off to the left and disappeared.

Where is he going?! He doesn't know we're here?

A few moments later, Langdon heard pounding—a fist knocking on wood.

The little gray door, Langdon thought. **He must know where it leads.**

Pitti Palace security guard Ernesto Russo had always wanted to play European football, but at twenty-nine years old and overweight, he had finally begun to accept that his childhood dream would never come true. For the past three years, Ernesto had worked as a guard here at the Pitti Palace, always in the same closet-size office, always with the same dull job.

Ernesto was no stranger to curious tourists knocking on the little gray door outside the office in which he was stationed, and he usually just ignored them until they stopped. Today, however, the banging was intense and continuous.

Annoyed, he refocused on his television set, which was loudly playing a football rerun—Fiorentina versus Juventus. The knocking only grew louder. Finally, cursing the tourists, he marched out of his office down the narrow corridor toward the sound. Halfway there, he stopped at the massive steel grate that remained sealed across this hallway except at a few specific hours.

He entered the combination on the padlock and unlocked the grate, pulling it to one side. After stepping through, he followed protocol and relocked the grate behind him. Then he walked to the gray wooden door.

"**È chiuso!**" he yelled through the door, hoping the person outside would hear. "**Non si può entrare!**"

The banging continued.

Ernesto gritted his teeth. **New Yorkers**, he wagered.

They want what they want. The only reason their Red Bulls soccer team was having any success on the world stage was that they'd pilfered one of Europe's best coaches.

The banging continued, and Ernesto reluctantly unlocked the door and pushed it open a few inches. **"È chiuso!"**

The banging finally stopped, and Ernesto found himself face-to-face with a soldier whose eyes were so cold they literally made Ernesto step back. The man held up an official carnet bearing an acronym Ernesto did not recognize.

"Cosa succede?!" Ernesto demanded, alarmed. **What's going on?!**

Behind the soldier, a second was crouched down, tinkering with what appeared to be a toy helicopter. Still farther away, another soldier stood guard on the staircase. Ernesto heard police sirens nearby.

"Do you speak English?" The soldier's accent was definitely not New York. **Europe somewhere?**

Ernesto nodded. "A bit, yes."

"Has anyone come through this door this morning?"

"No, signore. Nessuno."

"Excellent. Keep it locked. Nobody in or out. Is that clear?"

Ernesto shrugged. That was his job anyway. "Sì, I understand. **Non deve entrare, né uscire nessuno.**"

"Tell me, please, is this door the sole entrance?"

Ernesto considered the question. Technically, nowadays this door was considered an **exit**, which was why it had no handle on the outside, but he understood what the man was asking. "Yes, **l'accesso** is this door only. No other way." The original entrance inside the palace had been sealed for many years.

"And are there any other hidden exits from the Boboli Gardens? Other than the traditional gates?"

"**No, signore.** Big walls everywhere. This only secret exit."

The soldier nodded. "Thank you for your help." He motioned for Ernesto to close and lock the door.

Puzzled, Ernesto obeyed. Then he headed back up the corridor, unlocked the steel grate, moved through it, relocked it behind him, and returned to his football match.

CHAPTER 30

Langdon and Sienna had seized an opportunity. While the muscular soldier was pounding on the door, they had crawled deeper into the grotto and were now huddled in the final chamber. The tiny space was adorned with rough-hewn mosaics and satyrs. At its center stood a life-size sculpture of a **Bathing Venus**, who, fittingly, seemed to be glancing nervously over her shoulder.

Langdon and Sienna had ensconced themselves on the far side of the statue's narrow plinth, where they now waited, staring back at the single globular stalagmite that climbed the deepest wall of the grotto.

"All exits confirmed secure!" shouted a soldier somewhere outside. He was speaking English with a faint accent that Langdon couldn't place. "Send the drone back up. I'll check this cave here."

Langdon could feel Sienna's body tighten beside him.

Seconds later, heavy boots were padding into the grotto. The footsteps advanced quickly through the first chamber, growing louder still as they entered the second chamber, coming directly toward them.

Langdon and Sienna huddled closer.

"Hey!" a different voice shouted in the distance. "We've got them!"

The footsteps stopped short.

Langdon could now hear someone running loudly down the gravel walkway toward the grotto. "Positive ID!" the breathless voice declared. "We just spoke to a couple of tourists. A few minutes ago, the man and the woman asked them directions to the palace's costume gallery . . . which is over at the west end of the palazzo."

Langdon glanced at Sienna, who seemed to be smiling ever so faintly.

The soldier regained his breath, continuing. "The western exits were the first to be sealed . . . and confidence is high that we've got them trapped inside the gardens."

"Execute your mission," the nearer soldier replied. "And call me the instant you've succeeded."

There was a flurry of departing footsteps on gravel, the sound of the drone lifting off again, and then, thankfully . . . total silence.

Langdon was about to twist sideways in order to peer around the plinth, when Sienna grabbed his arm, stopping him. She held a finger to her lips and nodded at a faint humanoid shadow on the rear wall. The lead soldier was still standing silently in the mouth of the grotto.

What is he waiting for?!

"It's Brüder," he said suddenly. "We've got them cornered. I should have confirmation for you shortly."

The man had placed a phone call, and his voice

sounded unnervingly close, as if he were standing right beside them. The cavern was acting like a parabolic microphone, collecting all the sound and focusing it at the rear.

"There's more," Brüder said. "I just received an update from forensics. The woman's apartment appears to be a sublet. Underfurnished. Clearly short term. We located the biotube, but the projector was **not** present. I repeat, the projector was **not** present. We assume it's still in Langdon's possession."

Langdon felt a chill to hear the soldier speak his own name.

The footsteps grew louder, and Langdon realized that the man was moving into the grotto. His gait lacked the intensity of a few moments before and sounded now as if he were simply wandering, exploring the grotto as he talked on the phone.

"Correct," the man said. "Forensics also confirmed a single outbound call shortly before we stormed the apartment."

The U.S. Consulate, Langdon thought, remembering his phone conversation and the quick arrival of the spike-haired assassin. The woman seemed to have disappeared, replaced by an entire team of trained soldiers.

We can't outrun them forever.

The sound of the soldier's boots on the stone floor was now only about twenty feet away and closing. The man had entered the second chamber, and if he continued to the end, he would certainly spot the two of them crouched behind **Venus**'s narrow base.

"Sienna Brooks," the man declared suddenly, the words crystal clear.

Sienna startled beside Langdon, her eyes reeling upward, clearly expecting to see the soldier staring down at her. But nobody was there.

"They're going through her laptop now," the voice continued, about ten feet away. "I don't have a report yet, but it is definitely the same machine we traced when Langdon accessed his Harvard e-mail account."

On hearing this news, Sienna turned to Langdon in disbelief, gaping at him with an expression of shock . . . and then betrayal.

Langdon was equally stunned. **That's how they tracked us?!** It hadn't even occurred to him at the time. **I just needed information!** Before Langdon could convey an apology, Sienna had turned away, her expression going blank.

"That's correct," the soldier said, arriving at the entrance to the third chamber, a mere six feet from Langdon and Sienna. Two more steps and he would see them for certain.

"Exactly," he declared, taking one step closer. Suddenly the soldier paused. "Hold on a second."

Langdon froze, bracing to be discovered.

"Hold on, I'm losing you," the soldier said, and then retreated a few steps into the second chamber. "Bad connection. Go ahead . . ." He listened for a moment, then replied. "Yes, I agree, but at least we know who we're dealing with."

With that, his footsteps faded out of the grotto,

moved across a gravel surface, and then disappeared completely.

Langdon's shoulders softened, and he turned to Sienna, whose eyes burned with a mixture of fear and anger.

"You used my laptop?!" she demanded. "To check your e-mail?"

"I'm sorry . . . I thought you'd understand. I needed to find out—"

"That's how they found us! And now they know my name!"

"I apologize, Sienna. I didn't realize . . ." Langdon was racked by guilt.

Sienna turned away, staring blankly at the bulbous stalagmite on the rear wall. Neither one of them said anything for nearly a minute. Langdon wondered if Sienna remembered the personal items that had been stacked on her desk—the playbill from **A Midsummer Night's Dream** and press clippings about her life as a young prodigy. **Does she suspect I saw them?** If so, she wasn't asking, and Langdon was in enough trouble with her already that he was not about to mention it.

"They know who I am," Sienna repeated, her voice so faint that Langdon could barely hear her. Over the next ten seconds, Sienna took several slow breaths, as if trying to absorb this new reality. As she did so, Langdon sensed that her resolve was slowly hardening.

Without warning, Sienna scrambled to her feet.

"We should go," she said. "It won't take long for them to figure out we're not in the costume gallery."

Langdon stood up with her. "Yes, but go . . . where?"

"Vatican City?"

"I beg your pardon?"

"I finally figured out what you meant before . . . what Vatican City has in common with the Boboli Gardens." She motioned in the direction of the little gray door. "That's the entrance, right?"

Langdon managed a nod. "Actually, that's the exit, but I figured it was worth a shot. Unfortunately, we can't get through." Langdon had heard enough of the guard's exchange with the soldier to know this doorway was not an option.

"But if we **could** get through," Sienna said, a hint of mischief returning to her voice, "do you know what that would mean?" A faint smile now crossed her lips. "It would mean that twice today you and I have been helped by the same Renaissance artist."

Langdon had to chuckle, having had the same thought a few minutes ago. "**Vasari. Vasari.**"

Sienna grinned more broadly now, and Langdon sensed she had forgiven him, at least for the moment. "I think it's a sign from above," she declared, sounding half serious. "We should go through that door."

"Okay . . . and we'll just march right past the guard?"

Sienna cracked her knuckles and headed out of the grotto. "No, I'll have a word with him." She glanced back at Langdon, the fire returning to her eyes.

"Trust me, Professor, I can be quite persuasive when I have to be."

———

The pounding on the little gray door had returned.

Firm and relentless.

Security guard Ernesto Russo grumbled in frustration. The strange, cold-eyed soldier was apparently back, but his timing could not have been worse. The televised football match was in overtime with Fiorentina a man short and hanging by a thread.

The pounding continued.

Ernesto was no fool. He knew there was some kind of trouble out there this morning—all the sirens and soldiers—but he had never been one to involve himself in matters that didn't affect him directly.

Pazzo è colui che bada ai fatti altrui.

Then again, the soldier was clearly someone of importance, and ignoring him was probably unwise. Jobs in Italy were hard to find these days, even boring ones. Stealing a last glance at the game, Ernesto headed off toward the pounding on the door.

He still couldn't believe he was paid to sit in his tiny office all day and watch television. Perhaps twice a day, a VIP tour would arrive outside the space, having walked all the way from the Uffizi Gallery. Ernesto would greet them, unlock the metal grate, and permit the group to pass through to the little gray door, where their tour would end in the Boboli Gardens.

Now, as the pounding grew more intense, Ernesto opened the steel grate, moved through it, and then closed and locked it behind him.

"Si?" he shouted above the sounds of pounding as he hurried to the gray door.

No reply. The pounding continued.

Insomma! He finally unlocked the door and pulled it open, expecting to see the same lifeless gaze from a moment ago.

But the face at the door was far more attractive.

"Ciao," a pretty blond woman said, smiling sweetly at him. She held out a folded piece of paper, which he instinctively reached out to accept. In the instant he grasped the paper and realized it was nothing but a piece of trash off the ground, the woman seized his wrist with her slender hands and plunged a thumb into the bony carpal area just beneath the palm of his hand.

Ernesto felt as if a knife had just severed his wrist. The slicing stab was followed by an electric numbness. The woman stepped toward him, and the pressure increased exponentially, starting the pain cycle all over again. He staggered backward, trying to pull his arm free, but his legs went numb and buckled beneath him, and he slumped to his knees.

The rest happened in an instant.

A tall man in a dark suit appeared in the open doorway, slipped inside, and quickly closed the gray door behind him. Ernesto reached for his radio, but a soft hand behind his neck squeezed once, and his muscles seized up, leaving him gasping for breath. The woman took the radio as the tall man approached, looking as alarmed by her actions as Ernesto was.

"Dim mak," the blond said casually to the tall man. "Chinese pressure points. There's a reason they've been around for three millennia."

The man watched in wonder.

"Non vogliamo farti del male," the woman whispered to Ernesto, easing the pressure on his neck. **We don't want to hurt you.**

The instant the pressure decreased, Ernesto tried to twist free, but the pressure promptly returned, and his muscles seized again. He gasped in pain, barely able to breathe.

"Dobbiamo passare," she said. **We need to get through.** She motioned to the steel grate, which Ernesto had thankfully locked behind him. "Dov'è la chiave?"

"Non ce l'ho," he managed. **I don't have the key.**

The tall man advanced past them to the grating and examined the mechanism. "It's a combination lock," he called back to the woman, his accent American.

The woman knelt down next to Ernesto, her brown eyes like ice. "Qual è la combinazione?" she demanded.

"Non posso!" he replied. "I'm not permitted—"

Something happened at the top of his spine, and Ernesto felt his entire body go limp. An instant later, he blacked out.

———

When he came to, Ernesto sensed he had been drifting in and out of consciousness for several minutes. He recalled some discussion . . . more stabs of pain . . . being dragged, perhaps? It was all a blur.

As the cobwebs cleared, he saw a strange sight—his shoes lying on the floor nearby with their laces removed. It was then that he realized he could barely move. He was lying on his side with his hands and feet bound behind him, apparently with his shoelaces. He tried to yell, but no sound came. One of his own socks was stuffed in his mouth. The true moment of fear, however, came an instant later, when he looked up and saw his television set playing the football match. **I'm in my office . . . INSIDE the grate?!**

In the distance, Ernesto could hear the sound of running footsteps departing along the corridor . . . and then, slowly, they faded to silence. **Non è possibile!** Somehow, the blond woman had persuaded Ernesto to do the one thing he was hired never to do—reveal the combination for the lock on the entrance to the famed Vasari Corridor.

CHAPTER 31

D r. Elizabeth Sinskey felt the waves of nausea and dizziness coming faster now. She was slumped in the backseat of the van parked in front of the Pitti Palace. The soldier seated beside her was watching her with growing concern.

Moments earlier, the soldier's radio had blared—something about a costume gallery—awakening Elizabeth from the darkness of her mind, where she had been dreaming of the green-eyed monster.

She had been back in the darkened room at the Council on Foreign Relations in New York, listening to the maniacal ravings of the mysterious stranger who had summoned her there. The shadowy man paced at the front of the room—a lanky silhouette against the grisly projected image of the naked and dying throngs inspired by Dante's **Inferno**.

"Someone needs to fight this war," the figure concluded, "or **this** is our future. Mathematics guarantees it. Mankind is hovering now in a purgatory of procrastination and indecision and personal greed . . . but the rings of hell await, just beneath our feet, waiting to consume us all."

Elizabeth was still reeling from the monstrous

ideas this man had just laid out before her. She could stand it no longer and jumped to her feet. "What you're suggesting is—"

"Our only remaining option," the man interjected.

"Actually," she replied, "I was going to say 'criminal'!"

The man shrugged. "The path to paradise passes directly through hell. Dante taught us that."

"You're mad!"

"Mad?" the man repeated, sounding hurt. "Me? I think not. Madness is the WHO staring into the abyss and denying it is there. Madness is an ostrich who sticks her head in the sand while a pack of hyenas closes in around her."

Before Elizabeth could defend her organization, the man had changed the image on the screen.

"And speaking of hyenas," he said, pointing to the new image. "Here is the pack of hyenas currently circling humankind . . . and they are closing in fast."

Elizabeth was surprised to see the familiar image before her. It was a graph published by the WHO the previous year delineating key environmental issues deemed by the WHO to have the greatest impact on global health.

The list included, among others:

Demand for clean water, global surface temperatures, ozone depletion, consumption of ocean resources, species extinction, CO_2 concentration, deforestation, and global sea levels.

All of these negative indicators had been on the

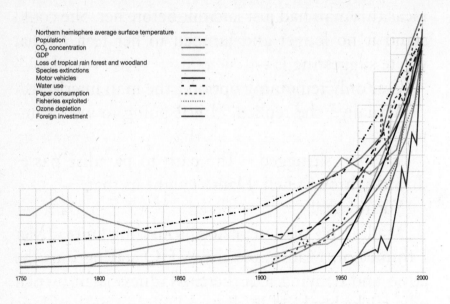

Northern hemisphere average surface temperature
Population
CO$_2$ concentration
GDP
Loss of tropical rain forest and woodland
Species extinctions
Motor vehicles
Water use
Paper consumption
Fisheries exploited
Ozone depletion
Foreign investment

1750   1800   1850   1900   1950   2000

rise over the last century. Now, however, they were all accelerating at terrifying rates.

Elizabeth had the same reaction that she always had when she saw this graph—a sense of helplessness. She was a scientist and believed in the usefulness of statistics, and this graph painted a chilling picture not of the distant future . . . but of the very **near** future.

At many times in her life, Elizabeth Sinskey had been haunted by her inability to conceive a child. Yet, when she saw this graph, she almost felt relieved she had not brought a child into the world.

This is the future I would be giving my child?

"Over the last fifty years," the tall man declared, "our sins against Mother Nature have grown exponentially." He paused. "I fear for the soul of humankind. When the WHO published this graph, the world's politicians, power brokers, and environmentalists held emergency summits, all trying to assess which of these problems were most severe and which we could actually hope to solve. The outcome? Privately, they put their heads in their hands and wept. Publicly, they assured us all that they were working on solutions but that these are complex issues."

"These issues **are** complex!"

"Bullshit!" the man erupted. "You know damned well this graph depicts the **simplest** of relationships— a function based on a **single** variable! Every single line on this graph climbs in direct proportion to one value—the value that everyone is afraid to discuss. Global population!"

"Actually, I think it's a bit more—"

"A bit more complicated? Actually, it's not! There is nothing simpler. If you want more available clean water per capita, you need fewer people on earth. If you want to decrease vehicle emissions, you need fewer drivers. If you want the oceans to replenish their fish, you need fewer people eating fish!"

He glared down at her, his tone becoming even more forceful. "Open your eyes! We are on the brink of the end of humanity, and our world leaders are sitting in boardrooms commissioning studies on solar power, recycling, and hybrid automobiles? How is it that **you**—a highly educated woman of science— don't see? Ozone depletion, lack of water, and pollution are not the disease—they are the **symptoms**. The **disease** is overpopulation. And unless we face world population head-on, we are doing nothing more than sticking a Band-Aid on a fast-growing cancerous tumor."

"You perceive the human race as a cancer?" Elizabeth demanded.

"Cancer is nothing more than a healthy cell that starts replicating out of control. I realize you find my ideas distasteful, but I can assure you that you will find the alternative far less tasteful when it arrives. If we do not take bold action, then—"

"Bold?!" she sputtered. "**Bold** is not the word you're looking for. Try **insane**!"

"Dr. Sinskey," the man said, his voice now eerily calm. "I called you here specifically because I was hoping that you—a sage voice at the World Health Organization—might be willing to work with me and explore a possible solution."

Elizabeth stared in disbelief. "You think the World Health Organization is going to partner with you . . . exploring an idea like **this**?"

"Actually, yes," he said. "Your organization is made up of doctors, and when doctors have a patient with gangrene, they do not hesitate to cut off his leg to save his life. Sometimes the only course of action is the lesser of two evils."

"This is quite different."

"No. This is **identical**. The only difference is scale."

Elizabeth had heard enough. She stood abruptly. "I have a plane to catch."

The tall man took a threatening step in her direction, blocking her exit. "Fair warning. With or without your cooperation, I can very easily explore this idea on my own."

"Fair warning," she fired back. "I consider this a terrorist threat and will treat it as such." She took out her phone.

The man laughed. "You're going to report me for talking in hypotheticals? Unfortunately, you'll have to wait to make your call. This room is electronically shielded. Your phone won't have a signal."

I don't need a signal, you lunatic. Elizabeth raised her phone, and before the man realized what was happening, she clicked a snapshot of his face. The flash reflected in his green eyes, and for a moment she thought he looked familiar.

"Whoever you are," she said, "you did the wrong thing by calling me here. By the time I reach the airport, I will know who you are, and you will be on the watch lists at the WHO, the CDC, and the ECDC as a potential bioterrorist. We will have people on you day and night. If you try to purchase materials, we will know about it. If you build a lab, we will know about it. There is nowhere you can hide."

The man stood in tense silence for a long moment, as if he were going to lunge at her phone. Finally, he relaxed and stepped aside with an eerie grin. "Then it appears our dance has begun."

CHAPTER 32

Il Corridoio Vasariano—the Vasari Corridor—
was designed by Giorgio Vasari in 1564 under
orders of the Medici ruler, Grand Duke Cosimo
I, to provide safe passage from his residence at the
Pitti Palace to his administrative offices, across the
Arno River in the Palazzo Vecchio.

Similar to Vatican City's famed Passetto, the Vasari
Corridor was the quintessential secret passageway.
It stretched nearly a full kilometer from the eastern
corner of the Boboli Gardens to the heart of the old
palace itself, crossing the Ponte Vecchio and snaking
through the Uffizi Gallery in between.

Nowadays, the Vasari Corridor still served as a safe
haven, although not for Medici aristocrats but for
artwork; with its seemingly endless expanse of secure
wall space, the corridor was home to countless rare
paintings—overflow from the world-famous Uffizi
Gallery, through which the corridor passed.

Langdon had traveled the passageway a few years
before as part of a leisurely private tour. On that afternoon, he had paused to admire the corridor's mind-
boggling array of paintings—including the most
extensive collection of self-portraits in the world. He
had also stopped several times to peer out of the cor-

ridor's occasional viewing portals, which permitted travelers to gauge their progress along the elevated walkway.

This morning, however, Langdon and Sienna were moving through the corridor at a run, eager to put as much distance as possible between themselves and their pursuers at the other end. Langdon wondered how long it would take for the bound guard to be discovered. As the tunnel stretched out before them, Langdon sensed it leading them closer with every step to what they were searching for.

Cerca trova . . . the eyes of death . . . and an answer as to who is chasing me.

The distant whine of the surveillance drone was far behind them now. The farther they progressed into the tunnel, the more Langdon was reminded of just how ambitious an architectural feat this passageway had been. Elevated above the city for nearly its entire length, the Vasari Corridor was like a broad serpent, snaking through the buildings, all the way from the Pitti Palace, across the Arno, into the heart of old Florence. The narrow, whitewashed passageway seemed to stretch for eternity, occasionally turning briefly left or right to avoid an obstacle, but always moving east . . . across the Arno.

The sudden sound of voices echoed ahead of them in the corridor, and Sienna skidded to a stop. Langdon halted, too, and immediately placed a calm hand on her shoulder, motioning to a nearby viewing portal.

Tourists down below.

Langdon and Sienna moved to the portal and peered out, seeing that they were currently perched above the Ponte Vecchio—the medieval stone bridge that serves as a pedestrian walkway into the old city. Below them, the day's first tourists were enjoying the market that has been held on the bridge since the 1400s. Today the vendors are mostly goldsmiths and jewelers, but that has not always been the case. Originally, the bridge had been home to Florence's vast, open-air meat market, but the butchers were banished in 1593 after the rancid odor of spoiled meat had wafted up into the Vasari Corridor and assaulted the delicate nostrils of the grand duke.

Down there on the bridge somewhere, Langdon recalled, was the precise spot where one of Florence's most infamous crimes had been committed. In 1216, a young nobleman named Buondelmonte had rejected his family's arranged marriage for the sake of his true love, and for that decision he was brutally killed on this very bridge.

His death, long considered "Florence's bloodiest murder," was so named because it had triggered a rift between two powerful political factions—the Guelphs and Ghibellines—who had then waged war ruthlessly for centuries against each other. Because the ensuing political feud had brought about Dante's exile from Florence, the poet had bitterly immortalized the event in his **Divine Comedy: O Buondelmonte, through another's counsel, you fled your wedding pledge, and brought such evil!**

To this day, three separate plaques—each quoting

a different line from Canto 16 of Dante's **Paradiso**—
could be found near the murder site. One of them
was situated at the mouth of the Ponte Vecchio and
ominously declared:

> BUT FLORENCE, IN HER FINAL PEACE, WAS FATED TO
> OFFER UP UNTO THAT MUTILATED STONE GUARDIAN
> UPON HER BRIDGE . . . A VICTIM.

Langdon raised his eyes now from the bridge to
the murky waters it spanned. Off to the east, the lone
spire of the Palazzo Vecchio beckoned.

Even though Langdon and Sienna were only halfway across the Arno River, he had no doubt they had
long since passed the point of no return.

———

Thirty feet below, on the cobblestones of the Ponte
Vecchio, Vayentha anxiously scanned the oncoming
crowd, never imagining that her only redemption
had, just moments before, passed directly overhead.

CHAPTER 33

Deep in the bowels of the anchored vessel **The Mendacium**, facilitator Knowlton sat alone in his cubicle and tried in vain to focus on his work. Filled with trepidation, he had gone back to viewing the video and, for the past hour, had been analyzing the nine-minute soliloquy that hovered somewhere between genius and madness.

Knowlton fast-forwarded from the beginning, looking for any clue he might have missed. He skipped past the submerged plaque . . . past the suspended bag of murky yellow-brown liquid . . . and found the moment that the beak-nosed shadow appeared—a deformed silhouette cast upon a dripping cavern wall . . . illuminated by a soft red glow.

Knowlton listened to the muffled voice, attempting to decipher the elaborate language. About halfway through the speech, the shadow on the wall suddenly loomed larger and the sound of the voice intensified.

Dante's hell is not fiction . . . it is prophecy!

Wretched misery. Torturous woe. This is the landscape of tomorrow.

Mankind, if unchecked, functions like a plague, a cancer . . . our numbers intensifying with each successive generation until the earthly comforts that once nourished our virtue and brotherhood have dwindled to nothing . . . unveiling the monsters within us . . . fighting to the death to feed our young.

This is Dante's nine-ringed hell.

This is what awaits.

As the future hurls herself toward us, fueled by the unyielding mathematics of Malthus, we teeter above the first ring of hell . . . preparing to plummet faster than we ever fathomed.

Knowlton paused the video. **The mathematics of Malthus?** A quick Internet search led him to information about a prominent nineteenth-century English mathematician and demographist named Thomas Robert Malthus, who had famously predicted an eventual global collapse due to overpopulation.

Malthus's biography, much to Knowlton's alarm, included a harrowing excerpt from his book **An Essay on the Principle of Population:**

The power of population is so superior to the power in the earth to produce subsistence for man, that premature death must in some shape or other visit the human race. The vices of mankind are active and able ministers of depopulation. They are the precursors in the great army of destruction; and often finish the dreadful work themselves. But should they fail in this war of extermination, sickly seasons, epidemics, pestilence, and plague, advance in terrific array, and sweep off their thousands and ten thousands. Should success be still incomplete, gigantic inevitable famine stalks in the rear, and with one mighty blow levels the population with the food of the world.

With his heart pounding, Knowlton glanced back at the paused image of the beak-nosed shadow.

Mankind, if unchecked, functions like a cancer.

Unchecked. Knowlton did not like the sound of that.

With a hesitant finger, he started the video again. The muffled voice continued.

To do nothing is to welcome Dante's hell . . . cramped and starving, weltering in Sin.

And so boldly I have taken action.

Some will recoil in horror, but all salvation comes at a price.

One day the world will grasp the beauty of my sacrifice.

For I am your Salvation.

I am the Shade.

I am the gateway to the Posthuman age.

CHAPTER 34

The Palazzo Vecchio resembles a giant chess piece. With its robust quadrangular facade and rusticated square-cut battlements, the massive rooklike building is aptly situated, guarding the southeast corner of the Piazza della Signoria.

The building's unusual single spire, rising off center from within the square fortress, cuts a distinctive profile against the skyline and has become an inimitable symbol of Florence.

Built as a potent seat of Italian government, the building imposes on its arriving visitors an intimidating array of masculine statuary. Ammannati's muscular **Neptune** stands naked atop four sea horses, a symbol of Florence's dominance in the sea. A replica of Michelangelo's **David**—arguably the world's most admired male nude—stands in all his glory at the palazzo entrance. **David** is joined by **Hercules** and **Cacus**—two more colossal naked men—who, in concert with a host of Neptune's satyrs, bring to more than a dozen the total number of exposed penises that greet visitors to the palazzo.

Normally, Langdon's visits to the Palazzo Vecchio had begun here on the Piazza della Signoria, which, despite its overabundance of phalluses, had always been one of his favorite plazas in all of Europe. No trip to the piazza was complete without sipping an espresso at Caffè Rivoire, followed by a visit to the Medici lions in the Loggia dei Lanzi—the piazza's open-air sculpture gallery.

Today, however, Langdon and his companion planned to enter the Palazzo Vecchio via the Vasari Corridor, much as Medici dukes might have done in their day—bypassing the famous Uffizi Gallery and following the corridor as it snaked above bridges, over roads, and through buildings, leading directly into the heart of the old palace. Thus far, they had heard no trace of footsteps behind them, but Langdon was still anxious to exit the corridor.

And now we've arrived, Langdon realized, eyeing the heavy wooden door before them. **The entrance to the old palace.**

The door, despite its substantial locking mechanism, was equipped with a horizontal push bar, which provided emergency-exit capability while preventing anyone on the other side from entering the Vasari Corridor without a key card.

Langdon placed his ear to the door and listened. Hearing nothing on the other side, he put his hands against the bar and pushed gently.

The lock clicked.

As the wooden portal creaked open a few inches, Langdon peered into the world beyond. A small alcove. Empty. Silent.

With a small sigh of relief, Langdon stepped through and motioned for Sienna to follow.

We're in.

Standing in a quiet alcove somewhere inside the Palazzo Vecchio, Langdon waited a moment and tried to get his bearings. In front of them, a long hallway ran perpendicular to the alcove. To their left, in the distance, voices echoed up the corridor, calm and jovial. The Palazzo Vecchio, much like the United States Capitol Building, was both a tourist attraction and a governmental office. At this hour, the voices they heard were most likely those of civic employees bustling in and out of offices, getting ready for the day.

Langdon and Sienna inched toward the hallway and peered around the corner. Sure enough, at the end of the hallway was an atrium in which a dozen or so government employees stood around sipping morning **espressi** and chatting with colleagues before work.

"The Vasari mural," Sienna whispered, "you said it's in the Hall of the Five Hundred?"

Langdon nodded and pointed across the crowded atrium toward a portico that opened into a stone hallway. "Unfortunately, it's through that atrium."

"You're sure?"

Langdon nodded. "We'll never make it through without being seen."

"They're government workers. They'll have no interest in us. Just walk like you belong here."

Sienna reached up and gently smoothed out Langdon's Brioni suit jacket and adjusted his collar. "You look very presentable, Robert." She gave him a demure smile, adjusted her own sweater, and set out.

Langdon hurried after her, both of them striding purposefully toward the atrium. As they entered, Sienna began talking to him in rapid Italian—something about farm subsidies—gesticulating passionately as she spoke. They kept to the outer wall, maintaining their distance from the others. To Langdon's amazement, not one single employee gave them a second glance.

When they were beyond the atrium, they quickly pressed onward toward the hallway. Langdon recalled the Shakespeare playbill. **Mischievous Puck.** "You're quite an actress," he whispered.

"I've had to be," she said reflexively, her voice strangely distant.

Once again, Langdon sensed there was more heartache in this young woman's past than he knew, and he felt a deepening sense of remorse for having entangled her in his dangerous predicament. He reminded himself that there was nothing to be done now, except to see it through.

Keep swimming through the tunnel . . . and pray for light.

As they neared their portico, Langdon was relieved to see that his memory had served him well. A small plaque with an arrow pointed around the corner into the hallway and announced: IL SALONE DEI CINQUECENTO. **The Hall of the Five Hundred,** Langdon thought, wondering what answers awaited within. **The truth can be glimpsed only through the eyes of death. What could this mean?**

"The room may still be locked," Langdon warned

as they neared the corner. Although the Hall of the Five Hundred was a popular tourist destination, the palazzo did not appear to be open yet to tourists this morning.

"Do you hear that?" Sienna asked, stopping short.

Langdon heard it. A loud humming noise was coming from just around the corner. **Please tell me it's not an indoor drone.** Cautiously, Langdon peered around the corner of the portico. Thirty yards away stood the surprisingly simple wooden door that opened into the Hall of the Five Hundred. Regrettably, directly between them stood a portly custodian pushing an electric floor-buffing machine in weary circles.

Guardian of the gate.

Langdon's attention shifted to three symbols on a plastic sign outside the door. Decipherable to even the least experienced of symbologists, these universal icons were: a video camera with an X through it; a drinking cup with an X through it; and a pair of boxy stick figures, one female, one male.

Langdon took charge, striding swiftly toward the custodian, breaking into a jog as he drew nearer. Sienna rushed behind him to keep up.

The custodian glanced up, looking startled. **"Signori?!"** He held out his arms for Langdon and Sienna to stop.

Langdon gave the man a pained smile—more of a wince—and motioned apologetically toward the symbols near the door. **"Toilette,"** he declared, his voice pinched. It was not a question.

The custodian hesitated a moment, looking ready to deny their request, and then finally, watching Langdon shift uncomfortably before him, he gave a sympathetic nod and waved them through.

When they reached the door, Langdon gave Sienna a quick wink. "Compassion is a universal language."

CHAPTER 35

At one time, the Hall of the Five Hundred was the largest room in the world. It had been built in 1494 to provide a meeting hall for the entire Consiglio Maggiore—the republic's Grand Council of precisely five hundred members—from which the hall drew its name. Some years later, at the behest of Cosimo I, the room was renovated and enlarged substantially. Cosimo I, the most powerful man in Italy, chose as the project's overseer and architect the great Giorgio Vasari.

In an exceptional feat of engineering, Vasari had raised the original roof substantially and permitted natural light to flow in through high transoms on all four sides of the room, resulting in an elegant showroom for some of Florence's finest architecture, sculpture, and painting.

For Langdon, it was always the floor of this room that first drew his eye, immediately announcing that this was no ordinary space. The crimson stone parquet was overlaid with a black grid, giving the twelve-thousand-square-foot expanse an air of solidity, depth, and balance.

Langdon raised his eyes slowly to the far side of the room, where six dynamic sculptures—**The Labors of**

Hercules—lined the wall like a phalanx of soldiers. Langdon intentionally ignored the oft-maligned **Hercules and Diomedes**, whose naked bodies were locked in an awkward-looking wrestling match, which included a creative "penile grip" that always made Langdon cringe.

Far easier on the eyes was Michelangelo's breathtaking **Genius of Victory**, which stood to the right, dominating the central niche in the south wall. At nearly nine feet tall, this sculpture had been intended for the tomb of the ultraconservative pope Julius II— Il Papa Terribile—a commission Langdon had always found ironic, considering the Vatican's stance on homosexuality. The statue depicted Tommaso dei Cavalieri, the young man with whom Michelangelo had been in love for much of his life and to whom he composed over three hundred sonnets.

"I can't believe I've never been here," Sienna whispered beside him, her voice suddenly quiet and reverent. "This is . . . beautiful."

Langdon nodded, recalling his first visit to this space—on the occasion of a spectacular concert of classical music featuring the world-renowned pianist Mariele Keymel. Although this grand hall was originally intended for private political meetings and audiences with the grand duke, nowadays it more commonly featured popular musicians, lecturers, and gala dinners—from art historian Maurizio Seracini to the Gucci Museum's star-studded, black-and-white gala opening. Langdon sometimes wondered how Cosimo I would feel about sharing his austere private hall with CEOs and fashion models.

Langdon lifted his gaze now to the enormous murals adorning the walls. Their bizarre history included a failed experimental painting technique by Leonardo da Vinci, which resulted in a "melting masterpiece." There had also been an artistic "showdown" spearheaded by Piero Soderini and Machiavelli, which pitted against each other two titans of the Renaissance—Michelangelo and Leonardo—commanding them to create murals on opposite walls of the same room.

Today, however, Langdon was more interested in one of the room's other historical oddities.

Cerca trova.

"Which one is the Vasari?" Sienna asked, scanning the murals.

"Nearly all of them," Langdon replied, knowing that as part of the room's renovation, Vasari and his assistants had repainted almost everything in it, from the original wall murals to the thirty-nine coffered panels adorning its famed "hanging" ceiling.

"But **that** mural there," Langdon said, pointing to the mural on their far right, "is the one we came to see—Vasari's **Battle of Marciano**."

The military confrontation was absolutely massive—fifty-five feet long and more than three stories tall. It was rendered in ruddy shades of brown and green—a violent panorama of soldiers, horses, spears, and banners all colliding on a pastoral hillside.

"Vasari, Vasari," Sienna whispered. "And hidden in there somewhere is his secret message?"

Langdon nodded as he squinted toward the top of the huge mural, trying to locate the particular green battle flag on which Vasari had painted his mysterious message—CERCA TROVA. "It's almost impossible to see from down here without binoculars," Langdon said, pointing, "but in the top middle section, if you look just below the two farmhouses on the hillside, there's a tiny, tilted green flag and—"

"I see it!" Sienna said, pointing to the upper-right quadrant, precisely in the right spot.

Langdon wished he had younger eyes.

The two walked closer to the towering mural, and Langdon gazed up at its splendor. Finally, they were here. The only problem now was that Langdon was not sure **why** they were here. He stood in silence for several long moments, staring up at the details of Vasari's masterpiece.

If I fail . . . then all is death.

A door creaked open behind them, and the custodian with the floor buffer peered in, looking uncertain. Sienna gave a friendly wave. The custodian eyed them a moment and then closed the door.

"We don't have much time, Robert," Sienna urged. "You need to think. Does the painting ring any bells for you? Any memories at all?"

Langdon scrutinized the chaotic battle scene above them.

The truth can be glimpsed only through the eyes of death.

Langdon had thought perhaps the mural included a corpse whose dead eyes were gazing blankly off toward some other clue in the painting . . . or perhaps even elsewhere in the room. Unfortunately, Langdon now saw that there were dozens of dead bodies in the mural, none of them particularly noteworthy and none with dead eyes directed anywhere in particular.

The truth can be glimpsed only through the eyes of death?

He tried to envision connecting lines from one corpse to another, wondering if a shape might emerge, but he saw nothing.

Langdon's head was throbbing again as he frantically plumbed the depths of his memory. Somewhere down there, the voice of the silver-haired woman kept whispering: **Seek and ye shall find.**

"Find what?!" Langdon wanted to shout.

He forced himself to close his eyes and exhale slowly. He rolled his shoulders a few times and tried to free himself from all conscious thought, hoping to tap into his gut instinct.

Very sorry.

Vasari.

Cerca trova.

The truth can be glimpsed only through the eyes of death.

His gut told him, without a doubt, that he was standing in the right location. And while he was not yet sure why, he had the distinct sense that he was moments away from finding what he had come here seeking.

———

Agent Brüder stared blankly at the red velvet panta-
loons and tunic in the display case before him and
cursed under his breath. His SRS team had searched
the entire costume gallery, and Langdon and Sienna
Brooks were nowhere to be found.

Surveillance and Response Support, he thought
angrily. **Since when does a college professor elude
SRS? Where the hell did they go!**

"Every exit was sealed," one of his men insisted.
"The only possibility is that they are still in the gardens."

While this seemed logical, Brüder had the sinking sensation that Langdon and Sienna Brooks had
found some other way out.

"Get the drone back in the air," Brüder snapped.
"And tell the local authorities to widen the search
area outside the walls." **Goddamn it!**

As his men dashed off, Brüder grabbed his phone
and called the person in charge. "It's Brüder," he said.
"I'm afraid we've got a serious problem. A number of
them actually."

CHAPTER **36**

The truth can be glimpsed only through the eyes of death.

Sienna repeated the words to herself as she continued to search every inch of Vasari's brutal battle scene, hoping something might stand out.

She saw eyes of death everywhere.

Which ones are we looking for?!

She wondered if maybe the eyes of death were a reference to all the rotting corpses strewn across Europe by the Black Death.

At least that would explain the plague mask . . .

Out of the blue, a childhood nursery rhyme jumped into Sienna's mind: **Ring around the rosie. A pocketful of posies. Ashes, ashes. We all fall down.**

She used to recite the poem as a schoolgirl in England until she heard that it derived from the Great Plague of London in 1665. Allegedly, a ring around the rosie was a reference to a rose-colored pustule on the skin that developed a ring around it and indicated that one was infected. Sufferers would carry a pocketful of posies in an effort to mask the smell of their own decaying bodies as well as the stench of the city itself, where hundreds of plague victims dropped dead daily, their bodies then cremated. **Ashes, ashes. We all fall down.**

"For the love of God," Langdon blurted suddenly, wheeling around toward the opposite wall.

Sienna looked over. "What's wrong?"

"That's the name of a piece of art that was once on display here. **For the Love of God.**"

Bewildered, Sienna watched Langdon hurry across the room to a small glass door, which he tried to open. It was locked. He put his face to the glass, cupping his hands around his eyes and peering inside.

Whatever Langdon was looking for, Sienna hoped he spotted it in a hurry; the custodian had just reappeared, now with a look of deepening suspicion at the sight of Langdon sauntering off to snoop at a locked door.

Sienna waved cheerfully to the custodian, but the man glared at her for a long cold beat and then disappeared.

——————

Lo Studiolo.

Positioned behind a glass door, directly opposite the hidden words **cerca trova** in the Hall of the Five Hundred, was nestled a tiny windowless chamber. Designed by Vasari as a secret study for Francesco I, the rectangular Studiolo rose to a rounded, barrel-vaulted ceiling, which gave those inside the feeling of being inside a giant treasure chest.

Fittingly, the interior glistened with objects of beauty. More than thirty rare paintings adorned the walls and ceiling, mounted so close to one another that they left virtually no empty wall space. **The Fall of Icarus . . . An Allegory of Human Life . . . Nature Presenting Prometheus with Spectacular Gems . . .**

As Langdon peered through the glass into the dazzling space beyond, he whispered to himself, "The eyes of death."

Langdon had first been inside Lo Studiolo during a private secret passages tour of the palazzo a few years back and had been stunned to learn about the plethora of hidden doors, stairs, and passageways that honeycombed the palazzo, including several hidden behind paintings inside Lo Studiolo.

The secret passages, however, were not what had just sparked Langdon's interest. Instead he had flashed on a bold piece of modern art that he had once seen on display here—**For the Love of God**—a controversial piece by Damien Hirst, which had caused an uproar when it was shown inside Vasari's famed Studiolo.

A life-size cast of a human skull in solid platinum, its surface had been entirely covered with more than **eight thousand** glittering, pavé-set diamonds. The effect was striking. The skull's empty eye sockets glistened with light and life, creating a troubling juxtaposition of opposing symbols—life and death . . . beauty and horror. Although Hirst's diamond skull had long since been removed from Lo Studiolo, Langdon's recollection of it had sparked an idea.

The eyes of death, he thought. **A skull certainly qualifies, doesn't it?**

Skulls were a recurring theme in Dante's **Inferno,**

most famously Count Ugolino's brutal punishment
in the lowest circle of hell—that of being sentenced
to gnaw eternally on the skull of a wicked archbishop.

Are we looking for a skull?

The enigmatic Studiolo, Langdon knew, had
been built in the tradition of a "cabinet of curiosi-
ties." Nearly all of its paintings were secretly hinged,
swinging open to reveal hidden cupboards in which
the duke had kept strange possessions of interest to
him—rare mineral samples, beautiful feathers, a
perfect fossil of a nautilus shell, and even, allegedly,
a monk's tibia decorated with hand-pounded silver.

Unfortunately, Langdon suspected all the cupboard items had been removed long ago, and he had
never heard of any skull on display here other than
Hirst's piece.

His thoughts were cut short by the loud slam of
a door on the far side of the hall. The brisk click of
footsteps approached quickly across the salon.

"**Signore!**" an angry voice shouted. "**Il salone non
è aperto!**"

Langdon turned to see a female employee marching toward him. She was petite, with short brown
hair. She was also extremely pregnant. The woman
moved snappily toward them, tapping her watch
and shouting something about the hall not yet being
open. As she drew near, she made eye contact with
Langdon, and immediately stopped short, covering
her mouth in shock.

"Professor Langdon!" she exclaimed, looking embarrassed. "I'm so sorry! I didn't know you were here. Welcome back!"

Langdon froze.

He was quite certain he had never seen this woman before in his life.

CHAPTER 37

I almost didn't recognize you, Professor!" the woman gushed in accented English as she approached Langdon. "It's your clothing." She smiled warmly and gave Langdon's Brioni suit an appreciative nod. "Very fashionable. You look almost Italian."

Langdon's mouth went bone dry, but he managed a polite smile as the woman joined him. "Good . . . morning," he stumbled. "How are you?"

She laughed, holding her belly. "Exhausted. Little Catalina kicked all night." The woman glanced around the room, looking puzzled. "Il **Duomino** didn't mention you were coming back today. I assume he's with you?"

Il Duomino? Langdon had no idea who she was talking about.

The woman apparently saw his confusion and gave a reassuring chuckle. "It's okay, everybody in Florence calls him by that nickname. He doesn't mind." She glanced around. "Did he let you in?"

"He did," Sienna said, arriving from across the hall, "but he had a breakfast meeting. He said you wouldn't mind if we stayed to look around." Sienna enthusiastically extended her hand. "I'm Sienna. Robert's sister."

The woman gave Sienna's hand an overly official handshake. "I'm Marta Alvarez. Aren't you the lucky one—having Professor Langdon as a private guide."

"Yes," Sienna enthused, barely hiding the roll of her eyes. "He's so smart!"

There was an awkward pause as the woman studied Sienna. "Funny," she said, "I don't see **any** family resemblance at all. Except perhaps your height."

Langdon sensed an impending train wreck. **Now or never.**

"Marta," Langdon interrupted, hoping he had heard her name correctly, "I'm sorry to trouble you, but, well . . . I guess you can probably imagine why I'm here."

"Actually, no," she replied, her eyes narrowing. "I can't for the life of me imagine what you would be doing here."

Langdon's pulse quickened, and in the awkward silence that followed, he realized his gamble was about to crash and burn. Suddenly Marta broke into a broad smile and laughed out loud.

"Professor, I'm joking! Of course, I can guess why you returned. Frankly, I don't know why you find it so fascinating, but since you and **il Duomino** spent almost an hour up there last night, I'm guessing you've come back to show your sister?"

"Right . . ." he managed. "Exactly. I'd love to show Sienna, if that's not . . . an inconvenience?"

Marta glanced up to the second-floor balcony and shrugged. "No problem. I'm headed up there now."

Langdon's heart pounded as he looked up to the

second-story balcony at the rear of the hall. **I was up there last night?** He remembered nothing. The balcony, he knew, in addition to being at the exact same height as the words **cerca trova**, also served as the entrance to the palazzo's museum, which Langdon visited whenever he was here.

Marta was about to lead them across the hall, when she paused, as if having second thoughts. "Actually, Professor, are you sure we can't find something a bit less grim to show your lovely sister?"

Langdon had no idea how to respond.

"We're seeing something grim?" Sienna asked. "What is it? He hasn't told me."

Marta gave a coy smile and glanced at Langdon. "Professor, would you like me to tell your sister about it, or would you prefer to do so yourself?"

Langdon nearly jumped at the opportunity. "By all means, Marta, why don't you tell her all about it."

Marta turned back to Sienna, speaking very slowly now. "I don't know what your brother has told you, but we're going up to the museum to see a very unusual mask."

Sienna's eyes widened a bit. "What kind of mask? One of those ugly plague masks they wear at Carnevale?"

"Good guess," Marta said, "but no, it's not a plague mask. It's a much different kind of mask. It's called a death mask."

Langdon's gasp of revelation was audible, and Marta scowled at him, apparently thinking he was being overly dramatic in an attempt to frighten his sister.

"Don't listen to your brother," she said. "Death masks were a very common practice in the 1500s. It's essentially just a plaster cast of someone's face, taken a few moments after that person dies."

The death mask. Langdon felt the first moment of clarity he'd felt since waking up in Florence. **Dante's Inferno** . . . cerca trova . . . **Looking through the eyes of death. The mask!**

Sienna asked, "Whose face was used to cast the mask?"

Langdon put his hand on Sienna's shoulder and answered as calmly as possible. "A famous Italian poet. His name was Dante Alighieri."

CHAPTER 38

The Mediterranean sun shone brightly on the decks of **The Mendacium** as it rocked over the Adriatic swells. Feeling weary, the provost drained his second Scotch and gazed blankly out his office window.

The news from Florence was not good.

Perhaps it was on account of his first taste of alcohol in a very long time, but he was feeling strangely disoriented and powerless . . . as if his ship had lost its engines and were drifting aimlessly on the tide.

The sensation was a foreign one to the provost. In his world, there always existed a dependable compass—**protocol**—and it had never failed to show the way. Protocol was what enabled him to make difficult decisions without ever looking back.

It had been protocol that required Vayentha's disavowal, and the provost had carried out the deed with no hesitation. **I will deal with her once this current crisis has passed.**

It had been protocol that required the provost to know as little as possible about all of his clients. He had decided long ago that the Consortium had no ethical responsibility to judge them.

Provide the service.

Trust the client.

Ask no questions.

Like the directors of most companies, the provost simply offered services with the assumption that those services would be implemented within the framework of the law. After all, Volvo had no responsibility to ensure that soccer moms didn't speed through school zones, any more than Dell would be held responsible if someone used one of their computers to hack into a bank account.

Now, with everything unraveling, the provost quietly cursed the trusted contact who had suggested this client to the Consortium.

"He will be low maintenance and easy money," the contact had assured him. "The man is brilliant, a star in his field, and absurdly wealthy. He simply needs to disappear for a year or two. He wants to buy some time off the grid to work on an important project."

The provost had agreed without much thought. Long-term relocations were always easy money, and the provost trusted his contact's instincts.

As expected, the job had been very easy money.

That is, until last week.

Now, in the wake of the chaos created by this man, the provost found himself pacing in circles around a bottle of Scotch and counting the days until his responsibilities to this client were over.

The phone on his desk rang, and the provost saw it was Knowlton, one of his top facilitators, calling from downstairs.

"Yes," he answered.

"Sir," Knowlton began, an uneasy edge in his voice. "I hate to bother you with this, but as you may know, we're tasked with uploading a video to the media tomorrow."

"Yes," the provost replied. "Is it prepped?"

"It is, but I thought you might want to preview it before upload."

The provost paused, puzzled by the comment. "Does the video mention us by name or compromise us in some way?"

"No, sir, but the content is quite disturbing. The client appears on-screen and says—"

"Stop right there," the provost ordered, stunned that a senior facilitator would dare suggest such a blatant breach of protocol. "The **content** is immaterial. Whatever it says, his video would have been released with or without us. The client could just as easily have released this video electronically, but he hired **us**. He paid **us**. He trusted **us**."

"Yes, sir."

"You were not hired to be a film critic," the provost admonished. "You were hired to keep promises. Do your job."

———

On the Ponte Vecchio, Vayentha waited, her sharp eyes scanning the hundreds of faces on the bridge. She had been vigilant and felt certain that Langdon had not yet passed her, but the drone had fallen silent, its tracking apparently no longer required.

Brüder must have caught him.

Reluctantly, she began to ponder the grim prospect of a Consortium inquiry. **Or worse.**

Vayentha again pictured the two agents who had been disavowed . . . never heard from again. **They simply moved to different work**, she assured herself. Nonetheless, she now found herself wondering if she should just drive into the hills of Tuscany, disappear, and use her skills to find a new life.

But how long could I hide from them?

Countless targets had learned firsthand that when the Consortium set you in its sights, privacy became an illusion. It was only a matter of time.

Is my career really ending like this? she wondered, still unable to accept that her twelve-year tenure at the Consortium would be terminated over a series of unlucky breaks. For a year she had vigilantly over-seen the needs of the Consortium's green-eyed client. **It was not my fault he jumped to his death . . . and yet I seem to be falling along with him.**

Her only chance at redemption had been to outfox Brüder . . . but she'd known from the start that this was a long shot.

I had my chance last night, and I failed.

As Vayentha reluctantly turned back toward her motorcycle, she became suddenly aware of a distant sound . . . a familiar high-pitched whine.

Puzzled, she glanced up. To her surprise, the sur-veillance drone had just lifted off again, this time near the farthest end of the Pitti Palace. Vayentha watched as the tiny craft began flying desperate circles over the palace.

The drone's deployment could mean only one thing.

They still don't have Langdon!

Where the hell is he?

————

The piercing whine overhead again pulled Dr. Elizabeth Sinskey from her delirium. **The drone is up again? But I thought . . .**

She shifted in the backseat of the van, where the same young agent was still seated beside her. She closed her eyes again, fighting the pain and nausea. Mostly, though, she fought the fear.

Time is running out.

Even though her enemy had jumped to his death, she still saw his silhouette in her dreams, lecturing her in the darkness of the Council on Foreign Relations.

It is imperative that someone take bold action, he had declared, his green eyes flashing. **If not us, who? If not now, when?**

Elizabeth knew she should have stopped him right then when she had the chance. She would never forget storming out of that meeting and fuming in the back of the limo as she headed across Manhattan toward JFK International Airport. Eager to know who the hell this maniac could be, she pulled out her cell phone to look at the surprise snapshot she had taken of him.

When she saw the photo, she gasped aloud. Dr. Elizabeth Sinskey knew exactly who this man was. The good news was that he would be very easy to track. The bad news was that he was a genius in his field—a very dangerous person should he choose to be.

Nothing is more creative . . . nor destructive . . . than a brilliant mind with a purpose.

By the time she arrived at the airport thirty minutes later, she had called her team and placed this man on the bioterrorism watch lists of every relevant agency on earth—the CIA, the CDC, the ECDC, and all of their sister organizations around the world.

That's all I can do until I get back to Geneva, she thought.

Exhausted, she carried her overnight bag to check-in and handed the attendant her passport and ticket.

"Oh, Dr. Sinskey," the attendant said with a smile. "A very nice gentleman just left a message for you."

"I'm sorry?" Elizabeth knew of nobody who had access to her flight information.

"He was very tall?" the attendant said. "With green eyes?"

Elizabeth literally dropped her bag. **He's here? How?!** She spun around, looking at the faces behind her.

"He left already," the attendant said, "but he wanted us to give you this." She handed Elizabeth a folded piece of stationery.

Shaking, Elizabeth unfolded the paper and read the handwritten note.

It was a famous quote derived from the work of
Dante Alighieri.

The darkest places in hell
are reserved for those
who maintain their neutrality
in times of moral crisis.

CHAPTER **39**

Marta Alvarez gazed tiredly up the steep staircase that ascended from the Hall of the Five Hundred to the second-floor museum. **Posso farcela**, she told herself. **I can do it.**

As an arts and culture administrator at the Palazzo Vecchio, Marta had climbed these stairs countless times, but recently, being more than eight months pregnant, she found the ascent significantly more taxing.

"Marta, are you sure we don't want to take the elevator?" Robert Langdon looked concerned and motioned to the small service elevator nearby, which the palazzo had installed for handicapped visitors.

Marta smiled appreciatively but shook her head. "As I told you last night, my doctor says the exercise is good for the baby. Besides, Professor, I know you're claustrophobic."

Langdon seemed strangely startled by her comment. "Oh, right. I forgot I mentioned that."

Forgot he mentioned it? Marta puzzled. **It was less than twelve hours ago, and we discussed at length the childhood incident that led to the fear.**

Last night, while Langdon's morbidly obese companion, **il Duomino**, ascended in the elevator, Langdon had accompanied Marta on foot. En route Langdon had shared with her a vivid description of a boyhood fall into an abandoned well that had left him with a nearly debilitating fear of cramped spaces.

Now, while Langdon's younger sister bounded ahead, her blond ponytail swinging behind her, Langdon and Marta ascended methodically, pausing several times so she could catch her breath. "I'm surprised you want to see the mask again," she said. "Considering all the pieces in Florence, this one seems among the least interesting."

Langdon gave a noncommittal shrug. "I've returned mainly so Sienna can see it. Thank you, by the way, for letting us in again."

"Of course."

Langdon's reputation would have sufficed last night to persuade Marta to open the gallery for him, but the fact that he had been accompanied by **il Duomino** meant that she really had no choice.

Ignazio Busoni—the man known as **il Duomino**—was something of a celebrity in the Florence cultural world. The longtime director of the Museo dell'Opera del Duomo, Ignazio oversaw all aspects of Florence's most prominent historical site—Il Duomo—the massive, red-domed cathedral that dominated both the history and the skyline of Florence. His passion for the landmark, combined with his body weight of nearly four hundred pounds and his perpetually red face, resulted in his good-natured nickname of **il Duomino**—"the little dome."

Marta had no idea how Langdon had become acquainted with **il Duomino**, but the latter had called her last evening and said he wanted to bring a guest for a private viewing of the Dante death mask. When the mystery guest turned out to be the famous American symbologist and art historian Robert Langdon, Marta had felt a bit of a thrill at having the opportunity to usher these two famous men into the palazzo's gallery.

Now, as they reached the top of the stairs, Marta placed her hands on her hips, breathing deeply. Sienna was already at the balcony railing, peering back down into the Hall of the Five Hundred.

"My favorite view of the room," Marta panted. "You get an entirely different perspective on the murals. I imagine your brother told you about the mysterious message hidden in that one there?" She pointed.

Sienna nodded enthusiastically. **"Cerca trova."**

As Langdon gazed toward the room, Marta watched him. In the light of the mezzanine windows, she couldn't help but notice that Langdon did not look as striking as he had last night. She liked his new suit, but he needed a shave, and his face seemed pale and weary. Also, his hair, which was thick and full last night, looked matted this morning, as if he had yet to take a shower.

Marta turned back to the mural before he caught her staring. "We're standing at nearly the exact height as **cerca trova**," Marta said. "You can almost see the words with the naked eye."

Langdon's sister seemed indifferent to the mural. "Tell me about Dante's death mask. Why is it here at the Palazzo Vecchio?"

Like brother, like sister, Marta thought with an inward groan, still perplexed that the mask held such fascination for them. Then again, the Dante death mask had a very strange history, especially recently, and Langdon was not the first to show a nearly maniacal fascination with it. "Well, tell me, what do you know about Dante?"

The pretty, young blonde shrugged. "Just what everyone learns in school. Dante was an Italian poet most famous for writing **The Divine Comedy**, which describes his imagined journey through hell."

"Partially correct," Marta replied. "In his poem, Dante eventually escapes hell, continues through purgatory, and finally arrives in paradise. If you ever read **The Divine Comedy**, you'll see his journey is divided into three parts—**Inferno**, **Purgatorio**, and **Paradiso**." Marta motioned for them to follow her along the balcony toward the museum entrance. "The reason the mask resides here in the Palazzo Vecchio has nothing to do with **The Divine Comedy**, though. It has to do with real history. Dante lived in Florence, and he loved this city as much as anyone could ever love a city. He was a very prominent and powerful Florentine, but there was a shift in political power, and Dante supported the wrong side, so he was exiled—thrown outside the city walls and told he could never come back."

Marta paused to catch her breath as they approached

the museum entrance. Hands again on her hips, she leaned back and continued talking. "Some people claim that Dante's exile is the reason why his death mask looks so sad, but I have another theory. I'm a bit of a romantic, and I think the sad face has more to do with a woman named Beatrice. You see, Dante spent his entire life desperately in love with a young woman named Beatrice Portinari. But sadly, Beatrice married another man, which meant Dante had to live not only without his beloved Florence, but also without the woman he so deeply loved. His love for Beatrice became a central theme in **The Divine Comedy.**"

"Interesting," Sienna said in a tone that suggested she had not heard a word. "And yet I'm still not clear on why the death mask is kept here inside the palazzo?"

Marta found the young woman's insistence both unusual and bordering on impolite. "Well," she continued, walking again, "when Dante died, he was still forbidden to enter Florence, and his body was buried in Ravenna. But because his true love, Beatrice, was buried in Florence, and because Dante so loved Florence, bringing his death mask here seemed like a kindhearted tribute to the man."

"I see," Sienna said. "And the choice of this building in particular?"

"The Palazzo Vecchio is the oldest symbol of Florence and, in Dante's time, was the heart of the city. In fact, there is a famous painting in the cathedral that shows Dante standing outside the walled city, banished, while visible in the background is his cherished palazzo tower. In many ways, by keeping his death mask here, we feel like Dante has finally been allowed to come home."

"That's nice," Sienna said, finally seeming satisfied. "Thank you."

Marta arrived at the door of the museum and rapped three times. **"Sono io, Marta! Buongiorno!"**

Some keys rattled inside and the door opened. An elderly guard smiled tiredly at her and checked his watch. **"È un po' presto,"** he said with a smile. **A little early.**

By way of explanation, Marta motioned to Langdon, and the guard immediately brightened. **"Signore! Bentornato!" Welcome back!**

"Grazie," Langdon replied amiably as the guard motioned them all inside.

They moved through a small foyer, where the guard disarmed a security system and then unlocked a second, heavier door. As the door swung open, he stepped aside, sweeping his arm out with a flourish. **"Ecco il museo!"**

Marta smiled her thanks and led her guests inside.

The space that made up this museum had originally been designed as government offices, which meant that rather than a sprawling, wide-open gallery space, it was a labyrinth of moderate-size rooms and hallways, which encircled half of the building.

"The Dante death mask is around the corner," Marta told Sienna. "It's displayed in a narrow space called **l'andito,** which is essentially just a walkway between two larger rooms. An antique cabinet against the sidewall holds the mask, which keeps it invisible until you draw even with it. For this reason, many visitors walk right past the mask without even noticing it!"

Langdon was striding faster now, eyes straight ahead, as if the mask held some kind of strange power over him. Marta nudged Sienna and whispered, "Obviously, your brother is not interested in any of our other pieces, but as long as you're here, you shouldn't miss our bust of Machiavelli or the **Mappa Mundi** globe in the Hall of Maps."

Sienna nodded politely and kept moving, her eyes also straight ahead. Marta was barely able to keep pace. As they reached the third room, she had fallen behind a bit and finally stopped short.

"Professor?" she called out, panting. "Perhaps you . . . want to show your sister . . . some of the gallery . . . before we see his mask?"

Langdon turned, seeming distracted, as if returning to the present from some far-off thought. "Excuse me?"

Marta breathlessly pointed to a nearby display case. "One of the earliest . . . printed copies of **The Divine Comedy**?"

When Langdon finally saw Marta dabbing her forehead and trying to catch her breath, he looked mortified. "Marta, forgive me! Of course, yes, a quick glance at the text would be wonderful."

Langdon hurried back, permitting Marta to guide them over to the antique case. Inside was a well-worn, leather-bound book, propped open to an ornate title page: **La Divina Commedia: Dante Alighieri.**

"Incredible," Langdon said, sounding surprised. "I recognize the frontispiece. I didn't know you had one of the original Numeister editions."

Of course you knew, Marta thought, puzzled. **I showed this to you last night!**

"In the mid–fourteen hundreds," Langdon said hurriedly to Sienna, "Johann Numeister created the first printed edition of this work. Several hundred copies were printed, but only about a dozen survived. They're very rare."

It now seemed to Marta that Langdon had been playing dumb so he could show off for his younger sibling. It seemed a rather unbecoming immodesty for a professor whose reputation was one of academic humility.

"This copy is on loan from the Laurentian Library," Marta offered. "If you and Robert have not visited there, you should. They have a spectacular staircase designed by Michelangelo, which leads up to the world's first public reading room. The books there were actually chained to the seats so nobody could take them out. Of course, many of the books were the **only** copies in the world."

"Amazing," Sienna said, glancing deeper into the museum. "And the mask is this way?"

What's the hurry? Marta needed another minute to regain her breath. "Yes, but you might be interested to hear about this." She pointed across an alcove toward a small staircase that disappeared into the ceiling. "That goes up to a viewing platform in the rafters where you can actually look **down** on Vasari's famous hanging ceiling. I'd be happy to wait here if you'd like to—"

"Please, Marta," Sienna interjected. "I'd love to see the mask. We're a little short on time."

Marta stared at the pretty, young woman, perplexed. She very much disliked the new fashion of strangers calling each other by their first names. **I'm Signora Alvarez**, she silently chided. **And I'm doing you a favor.**

"Okay, Sienna," Marta said curtly. "The mask is right this way."

Marta wasted no more time offering Langdon and his sister informed commentary as they made their way through the winding suite of gallery rooms toward the mask. Last night, Langdon and **il Duomino** had spent nearly a half hour in the narrow **andito**, viewing the mask. Marta, intrigued by the men's curiosity for the piece, had asked if their fascination was related somehow to the unusual series of events surrounding the mask over this past year. Langdon and **il Duomino** had been coy, offering no real answer.

Now, as they approached the **andito**, Langdon began explaining to his sister the simple process used to create a death mask. His description, Marta was pleased to hear, was perfectly accurate, unlike his bogus claim that he had not previously seen the museum's rare copy of **The Divine Comedy**.

"Shortly after death," Langdon described, "the

deceased is laid out, and his face is coated with olive oil. Then a layer of wet plaster is caked onto the skin, covering everything—mouth, nose, eyelids—from the hairline down to the neck. Once hardened, the plaster is easily lifted off and used as a mold into which fresh plaster is poured. This plaster hardens into a perfectly detailed replica of the deceased's face. The practice was particularly widespread in commemorating eminent persons and men of genius—Dante, Shakespeare, Voltaire, Tasso, Keats—they all had death masks made."

"And here we are at last," Marta announced as the trio arrived outside the **andito**. She stepped aside and motioned for Langdon's sister to enter first. "The mask is in the display case against the wall on your left. We ask that you please stay outside the stanchions."

"Thank you." Sienna entered the narrow corridor, walked toward the display case, and peered inside. Her eyes instantly went wide, and she glanced back at her brother with an expression of dread.

Marta had seen the reaction a thousand times; visitors were often jolted and repulsed by their first glimpse of the mask—Dante's eerily crinkled visage, hooked nose, and closed eyes.

Langdon strode in right behind Sienna, arriving beside her and looking into the display case. He immediately stepped back, his face also registering surprise.

Marta groaned. **Che esagerato.** She followed them in. But when she gazed into the cabinet, she, too, gasped out loud. **Oh mio Dio!**

Marta Alvarez had expected to see Dante's familiar dead face staring back at her, but instead, all she saw was the red satin interior of the cabinet and the peg on which the mask normally hung.

Marta covered her mouth and stared in horror at the empty display case. Her breathing accelerated and she grabbed one of the stanchions for support. Finally, she tore her eyes from the bare cabinet and wheeled in the direction of the night guards at the main entrance.

"La maschera di Dante!" she shouted like a madwoman. **"La maschera di Dante è sparita!"**

CHAPTER 40

Marta Alvarez trembled before the empty display cabinet. She hoped the tightness spreading through her abdomen was panic and not labor pains.

The Dante death mask is gone!

The two security guards were now on full alert, having arrived in the **andito**, seen the empty case, and sprung into action. One had rushed to the nearby video control room to access security-camera footage from last night, while the other had just finished phoning in the robbery to the police.

"**La polizia arriverà tra venti minuti!**" the guard told Marta as he hung up with the police.

"**Venti minuti?!**" she demanded. **Twenty minutes?!** "We've had a major art theft!"

The guard explained that he had been told most of the city police were currently handling a far more serious crisis and they were trying to find an available agent to come and take a statement.

"**Che cosa potrebbe esserci di più grave?!**" she ranted. **What can be more serious?!**

Langdon and Sienna shared an anxious glance, and Marta sensed that her two guests were suffering from sensory overload. **Not surprising.** Having simply stopped by for a quick look at the mask, they were now witnessing the aftermath of a major art theft. Last night, somehow, someone had gained access to the gallery and stolen Dante's death mask.

Marta knew there were far more valuable pieces in the museum that could have been stolen, so she tried to count her blessings. Nonetheless, this was the first theft in this museum's history. **I don't even know the protocol!**

Marta felt suddenly weak, and she again reached out to one of the stanchions for support.

Both gallery guards appeared mystified as they had recounted to Marta their exact actions and the events of last night: At around ten o'clock, Marta had entered with **il Duomino** and Langdon. A short while later, the threesome had exited together. The guards had relocked the doors, reset the alarm, and as far as they knew, nobody had been in or out of the gallery since that moment.

"Impossible!" Marta had scolded in Italian. "The mask was in the cabinet when the three of us left last night, so obviously **somebody** has been inside the gallery since then!"

The guards showed their palms, looking bewildered. **"Noi non abbiamo visto nessuno!"**

Now, with the police on the way, Marta moved as rapidly as her pregnant body permitted in the direction of the security control room. Langdon and Sienna fell into step nervously behind her.

The security video, Marta thought. **That will show us precisely who was in here last night!**

———

Three blocks away, on the Ponte Vecchio, Vayentha moved into the shadows as a pair of police officers filtered through the crowd, canvassing the area with photos of Langdon.

As the officers neared Vayentha, one of their radios blared—a routine all-points bulletin from dispatch. The announcement was brief and in Italian, but Vayentha caught the gist: Any available officer in the area of the Palazzo Vecchio should report to take a statement at the palazzo museum.

The officers barely flinched, but Vayentha's ears pricked up.

Il Museo di Palazzo Vecchio?

Last night's debacle—the fiasco that had all but destroyed her career—had occurred in the alleyways just outside the Palazzo Vecchio.

The police bulletin continued, in static-filled Italian that was mostly unintelligible, except for two words that stood out clearly: the name Dante Alighieri.

Her body instantly tensed. **Dante Alighieri?!** Most certainly **this** was not coincidence. She spun in the direction of the Palazzo Vecchio and located its crenellated tower peeking over the rooftops of the nearby buildings.

What exactly happened at the museum? she wondered. **And when?!**

The specifics aside, Vayentha had been a field analyst long enough to know that coincidence was far less common than most people imagined. **The Pala-zzo Vecchio museum . . . AND Dante?** This had to relate to Langdon.

Vayentha had suspected all along that Langdon would return to the old city. It only made sense— the old city was where Langdon had been last night when everything had started to come undone.

Now, in the light of day, Vayentha wondered if Langdon had somehow returned to the area around the Palazzo Vecchio to find whatever it was he was seeking. She was certain Langdon had not crossed this bridge into the old city. There were plenty of other bridges, and yet they seemed to be impossibly far on foot from the Boboli Gardens.

Beneath her, she noticed a four-man crew shell skimming across the water and passing under the bridge. The hull read SOCIETÀ CANOTTIERI FIRENZE / FLORENCE ROWING CLUB. The shell's distinctive red-and-white oars rose and fell in perfect unison.

Could Langdon have taken a boat across? It seemed unlikely, and yet something told her the police bulletin regarding the Palazzo Vecchio was a cue she should heed.

"All cameras out, **per favore!**" a woman called in accented English.

Vayentha turned to see a frilly orange pom-pom waving on a stick as a female tour guide attempted to herd her brood of duckling tourists across the Ponte Vecchio.

"Above you is Vasari's largest masterpiece!" the

guide exclaimed with practiced enthusiasm, lifting her pom-pom into the air and directing everyone's gaze upward.

Vayentha hadn't noticed it before, but there appeared to be a second-story structure that ran across the top of the shops like a narrow apartment.

"The Vasari Corridor," the guide announced. "It's nearly one kilometer long and provided the Medici family with a secure passageway between the Pitti Palace and the Palazzo Vecchio."

Vayentha's eyes widened as she took in the tunnel-like structure above her. She'd heard of the corridor, but knew very little about it.

It leads to the Palazzo Vecchio?

"For those rare few with VIP connections," the guide continued, "they can access the corridor even today. It's a spectacular art gallery that stretches all the way from the Palazzo Vecchio to the northeast corner of the Boboli Gardens."

Whatever the guide said next, Vayentha did not hear.

She was already dashing for her motorcycle.

CHAPTER **41**

The stitches in Langdon's scalp were throbbing again as he and Sienna squeezed inside the video control room with Marta and the two guards. The cramped space was nothing more than a converted vestment chamber with a bank of whirring hard drives and computer monitors. The air inside was stiflingly hot and smelled of stale cigarette smoke.

Langdon felt the walls closing in around him immediately.

Marta took a seat in front of the video monitor, which was already in playback mode and displayed a grainy black-and-white image of the **andito**, shot from above the door. The time stamp on-screen indicated that the footage had been cued to mid-morning yesterday—precisely twenty-four hours ago—apparently just before the museum opened and long before the arrival of Langdon and the mysterious **il Duomino** that evening.

The guard fast-forwarded through the video, and Langdon watched as an influx of tourists flowed rapidly into the **andito**, moving in hurried jerky motions. The mask itself was not visible from this perspective, but clearly it was still in its display case as tourists repeatedly paused to peer inside or take photos before moving on.

Please hurry, Langdon thought, knowing the police were on their way. He wondered if he and Sienna should just excuse themselves and run, but they needed to see this video: whatever was on this recording would answer a lot of questions about what the hell was going on.

The video playback continued, faster now, and afternoon shadows began moving across the room. Tourists zipped in and out until finally the crowds began to thin, and then abruptly disappeared entirely. As the time stamp raced past 1700 hours, the museum lights went out, and all was quiet.

Five P.M. Closing time.

"**Aumenti la velocità**," Marta commanded, leaning forward in her chair and staring at the screen.

The guard let the video race on, the time stamp advancing quickly, until suddenly, at around 10 P.M., the lights in the museum flickered back on.

The guard quickly slowed the tape back to regular speed.

A moment later, the familiar pregnant shape of Marta Alvarez came into view. She was followed closely by Langdon, who entered wearing his familiar Harris Tweed Camberley jacket, pressed khakis, and his own cordovan loafers. He even saw the glint of his Mickey Mouse watch peeking out from under his sleeve as he walked.

There I am . . . before I got shot.

Langdon found it deeply unsettling to watch him-

self doing things of which he had absolutely no recollection. **I was here last night . . . looking at the
death mask?** Somehow, between then and now, he
had managed to lose his clothing, his Mickey Mouse
watch, and two days of his life.

As the video continued, he and Sienna crowded in
close behind Marta and the guards for a better view.
The silent footage continued, showing Langdon and
Marta arriving at the display case and admiring the
mask. As they were doing this, a broad shadow darkened the doorway behind him, and a morbidly obese
man shuffled into the frame. He was dressed in a
tan suit, carried a briefcase, and barely fit through
the door. His bulging gut made even the pregnant
Marta look slender.

Langdon recognized the man at once. **Ignazio?!**

"That's Ignazio Busoni," Langdon whispered in
Sienna's ear. "Director of the Museo dell'Opera del
Duomo. An acquaintance of mine for several years.
I'd just never heard him called **il Duomino**."

"A fitting epithet," Sienna replied quietly.

In years past, Langdon had consulted Ignazio on
artifacts and history relating to Il Duomo—the basilica for which he was responsible—but a visit to the
Palazzo Vecchio seemed outside Ignazio's domain.
Then again, Ignazio Busoni, in addition to being an
influential figure in the Florentine art world, was a
Dante enthusiast and scholar.

**A logical source of information on Dante's death
mask.**

As Langdon returned his focus to the video, Marta

could now be seen waiting patiently against the rear wall of the **andito** while Langdon and Ignazio leaned out over the stanchions to get the closest possible look at the mask. As the men continued their examination and discussion, the minutes wore on, and Marta could be seen discreetly checking her watch behind their backs.

Langdon wished the security tape included audio. **What were Ignazio and I talking about? What are we looking for?!**

Just then, on-screen, Langdon stepped over the stanchions and crouched down directly in front of the cabinet, his face only inches from the glass. Marta immediately intervened, apparently admonishing him, and Langdon apologetically stepped back.

"Sorry I was so strict," Marta now said, glancing back at him over her shoulder. "But as I told you, the display case is an antique and extremely fragile. The mask's owner insists we keep people behind the stanchions. He won't even permit our staff to open the case without him present."

Her words took a moment to register. **The mask's owner?** Langdon had assumed the mask was the property of the museum.

Sienna looked equally surprised and chimed in immediately. "The **museum** doesn't own the mask?"

Marta shook her head, her eyes now back on the screen. "A wealthy patron offered to buy Dante's death mask from our collection and yet leave it on permanent display here. He offered a small fortune, and we happily accepted."

"Hold on," Sienna said. "He paid for the mask . . . and let you **keep** it?"

"Common arrangement," Langdon said. "Philanthropic acquisition—a way for donors to make major grants to museums without registering the gift as charity."

"The donor was an unusual man," Marta said. "A genuine scholar of Dante, and yet a bit . . . how do you say . . . **fanatico**?"

"Who is he?" Sienna demanded, her casual tone laced with urgency.

"Who?" Marta frowned, still staring at the screen. "Well, you probably read about him in the news recently—the Swiss billionaire Bertrand Zobrist?"

For Langdon the name seemed only vaguely familiar, but Sienna grabbed Langdon's arm and squeezed it hard, looking as if she'd seen a ghost.

"Oh, yes . . ." Sienna said haltingly, her face ashen. "Bertrand Zobrist. Famous biochemist. Made a fortune in biological patents at a young age." She paused, swallowing hard. She leaned over and whispered to Langdon. "Zobrist basically invented the field of germ-line manipulation."

Langdon had no idea what germ-line manipulation was, but it had an ominous ring, especially in light of the recent spate of images involving plagues and death. He wondered if Sienna knew so much about Zobrist because she was well read in the field of medicine . . . or perhaps because they had both been child prodigies. **Do savants follow each other's work?**

"I first heard of Zobrist a few years ago," Sienna explained, "when he made some highly provocative declarations in the media about population growth." She paused, her face gloomy. "Zobrist is a proponent of the Population Apocalypse Equation."

"I beg your pardon?"

"Essentially it's a mathematical recognition that the earth's population is rising, people are living longer, and our natural resources are waning. The equation predicts that the current trend can have no outcome other than the apocalyptic collapse of society. Zobrist has publicly predicted that the human race will not survive another century . . . unless we have some kind of mass extinction event." Sienna sighed heavily and locked eyes with Langdon. "In fact, Zobrist was once quoted as saying that 'the best thing that ever happened to Europe was the Black Death.'"

Langdon stared at her in shock. The hair on his neck bristled as, once again, the image of the plague mask flashed through his mind. He had been trying all morning to resist the notion that his current dilemma related to a deadly plague . . . but that notion was getting more and more difficult to refute.

For Bertrand Zobrist to describe the Black Death as the best thing ever to happen to Europe was certainly appalling, and yet Langdon knew that many historians had chronicled the long-term socio-economic benefits of the mass extinction that had occurred in Europe in the 1300s. Prior to the plague, overpopulation, famine, and economic hardship had defined the Dark Ages. The sudden arrival of the Black Death, while horrific, had effectively "thinned the human herd," creating an abundance of food and opportunity, which, according to many historians, had been a primary catalyst for bringing about the Renaissance.

As Langdon pictured the biohazard symbol on the tube that had contained the modified map of Dante's inferno, a chilling thought struck him: the eerie little projector had been created by **someone** . . . and Bertrand Zobrist—a biochemist and Dante fanatic—now seemed to be a logical candidate.

The father of genetic germ-line manipulation. Langdon sensed pieces of the puzzle now falling into place. Regrettably, the picture coming into focus felt increasingly frightening.

"Fast-forward through this part," Marta ordered the guard, sounding eager to get past the real-time playback of Langdon and Ignazio Busoni studying the mask so she could find out who had broken into the museum and stolen it.

The guard hit the fast-forward button, and the time stamp accelerated.

Three minutes . . . six minutes . . . eight minutes.

On-screen, Marta could be seen standing behind the men, shifting her weight with increasing frequency and repeatedly checking her watch.

"I'm sorry we talked so long," Langdon said. "You look uncomfortable."

"My own fault," Marta replied. "You both insisted that I should go home and the guards could let you out, but I felt that would be rude."

Suddenly, on-screen, Marta disappeared. The guard slowed the video to normal speed.

"It's okay," Marta said. "I remember going to the restroom."

The guard nodded and reached again for the fast-forward button, but before he pressed it, Marta grabbed his arm. **"Aspetti!"**

She cocked her head and stared at the monitor in confusion.

Langdon had seen it, too. **What in the world?!**

On-screen, Langdon had just reached into the pocket of his tweed coat and produced a pair of surgical gloves, which he was now pulling onto his hands.

Simultaneously, **il Duomino** positioned himself behind Langdon, peering down the hallway where Marta had moments earlier trudged off to use the restroom. After a moment the obese man nodded to Langdon in a way that seemed to mean that the coast was clear.

What the hell are we doing?!

Langdon watched himself on the video as his gloved hand reached out and found the edge of the cabinet door . . . and then, ever so gently, pulled back until the antique hinge shifted and the door swung slowly open . . . exposing the Dante death mask.

Marta Alvarez let out a horrified gasp and brought her hands to her face.

Sharing Marta's horror, Langdon watched himself

in utter disbelief as he reached into the case, gently gripped the Dante death mask with both hands, and lifted it out.

"**Dio mi salvi!**" Marta exploded, heaving herself to her feet and spinning around to face Langdon. "**Cos'ha fatto? Perché?**"

Before Langdon could respond, one of the guards whipped out a black Beretta and aimed it directly at Langdon's chest.

Jesus!

Robert Langdon stared down the barrel of the guard's handgun and felt the tiny room closing in around him. Marta Alvarez was on her feet now, glaring up at him with an incredulous look of betrayal on her face. On the security monitor behind her, Langdon was now holding the mask up to the light and studying it.

"I took it out only for a moment," Langdon insisted, praying that this was true. "Ignazio assured me you wouldn't mind!"

Marta did not reply. She looked stupefied, clearly trying to imagine why Langdon had lied to her . . . and indeed how in the world Langdon could have calmly stood by and let the tape play when he knew what it would reveal.

I had no idea I opened the case!

"Robert," Sienna whispered. "Look! You found something!" Sienna remained riveted on the playback, focusing on getting answers despite their predicament.

On-screen, Langdon was now holding the mask up

and angling it toward the light, his attention apparently drawn to something of interest on the back of the artifact.

From this camera angle, for a split second, the raised mask partially blocked Langdon's face in such a way that Dante's dead eyes were aligned with Langdon's. He remembered the pronouncement—**the truth can be glimpsed only through the eyes of death**—and felt a chill.

Langdon had no idea what he might have been examining on the back of the mask, but at that moment in the video, as he shared his discovery with Ignazio, the obese man recoiled, immediately fumbling for his spectacles and looking again . . . and again. He began shaking his head vigorously and pacing the **andito** in an agitated state.

Suddenly both men glanced up, clearly having heard something in the hallway—most likely Marta returning from the restroom. Hurriedly, Langdon pulled from his pocket a large Ziploc bag, into which he sealed the death mask before gently handing it to Ignazio, who placed it, with seeming reluctance, inside his briefcase. Langdon quickly closed the antique glass door on the now-empty display case, and the two men strode briskly up the hall to encounter Marta before she could discover their theft.

Both guards now had their guns trained on Langdon.

Marta wobbled on her feet, grasping the table for support. "I don't understand!" she sputtered. "You and Ignazio Busoni stole the Dante death mask?!"

"No!" Langdon insisted, bluffing as best as he could. "We had permission from the owner to take the mask out of the building for the night."

"Permission from the owner?" she questioned. "From Bertrand Zobrist!?"

"Yes! Mr. Zobrist agreed to let us examine some markings on the back! We met with him yesterday afternoon!"

Marta's eyes shot daggers. "Professor, I am quite certain you did not meet with Bertrand Zobrist yesterday afternoon."

"We most certainly did—"

Sienna placed a restraining hand on Langdon's arm. "Robert . . ." She gave a grim sigh. "Six days ago, Bertrand Zobrist threw himself off the top of the Badia tower only a few blocks away from here."

CHAPTER 42

Vayentha had abandoned her motorcycle just north of the Palazzo Vecchio and was approaching on foot along the perimeter of the Piazza della Signoria. As she wound her way through the Loggia dei Lanzi's outdoor statuary, she could not help but notice that all the figures seemed to be enacting a variation on a single theme: violent displays of male dominance over women.

The Rape of the Sabines.

The Rape of Polyxena.

Perseus Holding the Severed Head of Medusa.

Lovely, Vayentha thought, pulling her cap low over her eyes and edging her way through the morning crowd toward the entrance of the palace, which was just admitting the first tourists of the day. From all appearances, it was business as usual here at the Palazzo Vecchio.

No police, Vayentha thought. **At least not yet.**

She zipped her jacket high around her neck, making certain that her weapon was concealed, and headed through the entrance. Following signs for Il Museo di Palazzo, she passed through two ornate atriums and then up a massive staircase toward the second floor.

As she climbed, she replayed the police dispatch in her head.

Il Museo di Palazzo Vecchio . . . Dante Alighieri. Langdon has to be here.

The signs for the museum led Vayentha into a massive, spectacularly adorned gallery—the Hall of the Five Hundred—where a scattering of tourists mingled, admiring the colossal murals on the walls. Vayentha had no interest in observing the art here and quickly located another museum sign in the far right-hand corner of the room, pointing up a staircase.

As she made her way across the hall, she noticed a group of university kids all gathered around a single sculpture, laughing and taking pictures.

The plaque read: **Hercules and Diomedes.**

Vayentha eyed the statues and groaned.

The sculpture depicted the two heroes of Greek mythology—both stark naked—locked in a wrestling match. Hercules was holding Diomedes upside down, preparing to throw him, while Diomedes was tightly gripping Hercules' penis, as if to say, "Are you sure you want to throw me?"

Vayentha winced. **Talk about having someone by the balls.**

She removed her eyes from the peculiar statue and quickly climbed the stairs toward the museum.

She arrived on a high balcony that overlooked the hall. A dozen or so tourists were waiting outside the museum entrance.

"Delayed opening," one cheerful tourist offered, peeking out from behind his camcorder.

"Any idea why?" she asked.

"Nope, but what a great view while we wait!" The man swung his arm out over the expanse of the Hall of the Five Hundred below.

Vayentha walked to the edge and peered at the expansive room beneath them. Downstairs, a lone police officer was just arriving, drawing very little attention as he moved, without any sense of urgency, across the room toward the staircase.

He's coming up to take a statement, Vayentha imagined. The man's lugubrious trudge up the stairs indicated this was a routine response call—nothing like the chaotic search for Langdon at the Porta Romana.

If Langdon is here, why aren't they swarming the building?

Either Vayentha had assumed incorrectly that Langdon was here, or the local police and Brüder had not yet put two and two together.

As the officer reached the top of the stairs and ambled toward the museum entrance, Vayentha casually turned away and pretended to gaze out a window. Considering her disavowal and the long reach of the provost, she was not taking any chances of being recognized.

"**Aspetta!**" a voice shouted somewhere.

Vayentha's heart skipped a beat as the officer stopped directly behind her. The voice, she realized, was coming from his walkie-talkie.

"**Attendi i rinforzi!**" the voice repeated.

Wait for support? Vayentha sensed that something had just changed.

Just then, outside the window, Vayentha noticed a black object growing larger in the distant sky. It was flying toward the Palazzo Vecchio from the direction of the Boboli Gardens.

The drone, Vayentha realized. **Brüder knows. And he's headed this way.**

———

Consortium facilitator Laurence Knowlton was still kicking himself for phoning the provost. He knew better than to suggest that the provost preview the client's video before it was uploaded to the media tomorrow.

The content was irrelevant.

Protocol is king.

Knowlton still recalled the mantra taught to young facilitators when they started handling tasks for the organization. **Don't ask. Just task.**

Reluctantly, he placed the little red memory stick in the queue for tomorrow morning, wondering what the media would make of the bizarre message. Would they even play it?

Of course they will. It's from Bertrand Zobrist.

Not only was Zobrist a staggeringly successful figure in the biomedical world, but he was already in the news as a result of his suicide last week. This nine-minute video would play like a message from the grave, and its ominously macabre quality would make it nearly impossible for people to turn it off.

This video will go viral within minutes of its release.

CHAPTER 43

Marta Alvarez was seething as she stepped out of the cramped video room, having left Langdon and his rude little sister at gunpoint with the guards. She marched over to a window and peered down at the Piazza della Signoria, relieved to see a police car parked out front.

It's about time.

Marta still could not fathom why a man as respected in his profession as Robert Langdon would so blatantly deceive her, take advantage of the professional courtesy she had offered, and steal a priceless artifact.

And Ignazio Busoni assisted him!? Unthinkable!

Intent on giving Ignazio a piece of her mind, Marta pulled out her cell phone and dialed **il Duomino**'s office, which was several blocks away at the Museo dell'Opera del Duomo.

The line rang only once.

"Ufficio di Ignazio Busoni," a familiar woman's voice answered.

Marta was friendly with Ignazio's secretary but was in no mood for small talk. **"Eugenia, sono Marta. Devo parlare con Ignazio."**

There was an odd pause on the line and then suddenly the secretary burst into hysterical sobbing.

"Cosa succede?" Marta demanded. **What's wrong!?**

Eugenia tearfully told Marta that she had just arrived at the office to learn that Ignazio had suffered a massive heart attack last night in an alleyway near the Duomo. It was around midnight when he had called for an ambulance, but the medics hadn't arrived in time. Busoni was dead.

Marta's legs nearly buckled beneath her. This morning she'd heard on the news that an unnamed city official had died the previous night, but she never imagined it was Ignazio.

"Eugenia, ascoltami," Marta urged, trying to remain calm as she quickly explained what she had just witnessed on the palazzo video cameras—the Dante death mask stolen by Ignazio and Robert Langdon, who was now being held at gunpoint.

Marta had no idea what response she expected Eugenia to make, but it most certainly was not what she heard.

"Roberto Langdon!?" Eugenia demanded. **"Sei con Langdon ora?!"** You're with Langdon now?!

Eugenia seemed to be missing the point. **Yes, but the mask—**

"Devo parlare con lui!" Eugenia all but shouted. **I need to speak to him!**

———

Inside the security room, Langdon's head continued to throb as the guards aimed their weapons directly at him. Abruptly, the door opened, and Marta Alvarez appeared.

Through the open door Langdon heard the distant whine of the drone somewhere outside, its ominous buzz accompanied by the wail of approaching sirens. **They found out where we are.**

"**È arrivata la polizia,**" Marta told the guards, sending one of them out to usher the authorities into the museum. The other remained behind, gun barrel still aimed at Langdon.

To Langdon's surprise, Marta held out a cell phone to him. "Someone wants to speak to you," she said, sounding mystified. "You'll need to take it out here to have a connection."

The group migrated from the stuffy control room into the gallery space just outside, where sunlight poured through large windows offering a spectacular view of Piazza della Signoria below. Although he was still at gunpoint, Langdon felt relieved to be out of the enclosed space.

Marta motioned him over near the window and handed him the phone.

Langdon took it, uncertain, and raised it to his ear. "Yes? This is Robert Langdon."

"**Signore,**" the woman said in tentative, accented English. "I am Eugenia Antonucci, the secretary of Ignazio Busoni. You and I, we meet yesterday night when you arrive his office."

Langdon recalled nothing. "Yes?"

"I'm very sorry to say you this, but Ignazio, he die of heart attack yesterday night."

Langdon's grip tightened on the phone. **Ignazio Busoni is dead?!**

The woman was weeping now, her voice full of sadness. "Ignazio call me before he die. He leave me a message and tell me to be sure you hear it. I will play it for you."

Langdon heard some rustling, and moments later, a faint breathless recording of the voice of Ignazio Busoni reached his ears.

"Eugenia," the man panted, clearly in pain. "Please be sure Robert Langdon hears this message. I'm in trouble. I don't think I'll make it back to the office." Ignazio groaned and there was a long silence. When he began speaking again, his voice was weaker. "Robert, I hope you escaped. They're still after me . . . and I'm . . . I'm not well. I'm trying to reach a doctor, but . . ." There was another long pause, as if **il Duomino** were mustering his last bit of energy, and then . . . "Robert, listen carefully. What you seek is safely hidden. The gates are open to you, but you must hurry. Paradise Twenty-five." He paused a long moment and then whispered, "Godspeed."

Then the message ended.

Langdon's heart raced, and he knew he had just witnessed the final words of a dying man. That these words had been directed at him did nothing to relieve his anxiety. **Paradise 25? The gates are open to me?** Langdon considered it. **What gates does he mean?!** The only thing that made any sense at all was that Ignazio had said that the mask was safely hidden.

Eugenia came back on the line. "Professor, do you understand this?"

"Some of it, yes."

"Is there something I can do?"

Langdon considered this question a long moment. "Make sure nobody else hears this message."

"Even the police? A detective arrives soon to take my statement."

Langdon stiffened. He looked at the guard who was aiming a gun at him. Quickly, Langdon turned toward the window and lowered his voice, hurriedly whispering, "Eugenia . . . this will sound strange, but for Ignazio's sake, I need you to delete that message and do **not** mention to the police that you spoke to me. Is that clear? The situation is very complicated and—"

Langdon felt a gun barrel press into his side and turned to see the armed guard, inches away, holding out his free hand and demanding Marta's phone.

On the line, there was a long pause, and Eugenia finally said, "Mr. Langdon, my boss trusted you . . . so I will, too."

Then she was gone.

Langdon handed the phone back to the guard. "Ignazio Busoni is dead," he said to Sienna. "He died of a heart attack last night after leaving this museum." Langdon paused. "The mask is safe. Ignazio hid it before he died. And I think he left me a clue about where to find it." **Paradise 25.**

Hope flashed in Sienna's eyes, but when Langdon turned back to Marta, she looked skeptical.

"Marta," Langdon said. "I can retrieve Dante's mask for you, but you'll need to let us go. Immediately."

Marta laughed out loud. "I will do no such thing! You're the one who **stole** the mask! The police are arriving—"

"**Signora Alvarez**," Sienna interrupted loudly. "**Mi dispiace, ma non le abbiamo detto la verità.**"

Langdon did a double take. **What is Sienna doing?!** He had understood her words. **Mrs. Alvarez, I'm sorry, but we have not been honest with you.**

Marta looked equally startled by Sienna's words, although much of her shock seemed to be over the fact that Sienna was suddenly speaking fluent, unaccented Italian.

"**Innanzitutto, non sono la sorella di Robert Langdon**," Sienna declared in an apologetic tone. **First off, I am not Robert Langdon's sister.**

CHAPTER 44

Marta Alvarez took an unsteady step backward and folded her arms, studying the young blond woman before her.

"**Mi dispiace**," Sienna continued, still speaking fluent Italian. "**Le abbiamo mentito su molte cose.**" **We have lied to you about many things.**

The guard looked as perplexed as Marta, although he held his position.

Sienna spoke rapidly now, still in Italian, telling Marta that she worked at a Florence hospital where Langdon had arrived the previous night with a bullet wound to the head. She explained that Langdon recalled nothing of the events that had brought him there, and that he was as surprised by the security video as Marta had been.

"Show her your wound," Sienna ordered Langdon.

When Marta saw the stitches beneath Langdon's matted hair, she sat down on the windowsill and held her face in her hands for several seconds.

In the past ten minutes, Marta had learned not only that the Dante death mask had been stolen during her watch, but that the two thieves had been a

respected American professor and her trusted Florentine colleague, who was now dead. Furthermore, the
young Sienna Brooks, whom Marta had imagined
to be the wide-eyed American sister of Robert Langdon, turned out to be a doctor, admitting to a lie . . .
and doing so in fluent Italian.

"Marta," Langdon said, his voice deep and understanding. "I know it must be hard to believe, but I
truly don't remember last night at all. I have no idea
why Ignazio and I took the mask."

Marta sensed from his eyes that he was telling the
truth.

"I'll return the mask to you," Langdon said. "You
have my word. But I can't retrieve it unless you let us
go. The situation is complicated. You need to let us
go, right away."

Despite wanting the priceless mask returned, Marta
had no intention of letting anyone go. **Where are
the police?!** She looked down at the lone police car
in the Piazza della Signoria. It seemed strange that
the officers had not yet reached the museum. Marta
also heard a strange buzzing noise in the distance—
it sounded like someone was using a power saw. And
it was getting louder.

What is that?

Langdon's tone was beseeching now. "Marta, you
know Ignazio. He would never have removed the
mask without a good reason. There's a bigger picture
here. The owner of the mask, Bertrand Zobrist, was
a very confused man. We think he may be involved

in something terrible. I don't have time to explain it all, but I'm begging you to trust us."

Marta could only stare. None of this seemed to make any sense at all.

"Mrs. Alvarez," Sienna said, fixing Marta with a stony look. "If you care about your future, and that of your baby, then you need to let us leave, right now."

Marta folded her hands protectively across her abdomen, not at all pleased by the veiled threat to her unborn child.

The high-pitched buzz outside was definitely getting louder, and when Marta peered out the window, she couldn't see the source of the noise, but she did see something else.

The guard saw it, too, his eyes widening.

Down in the Piazza della Signoria, the crowds had parted to make way for a long line of police cars that were arriving without sirens, led by two black vans, which now skidded to a stop outside the palace doors. Soldiers in black uniforms jumped out, carrying large guns, and ran into the palace.

Marta felt a surge of fear. **Who the hell is that?!**

The security guard looked equally alarmed.

The high-pitched buzzing sound grew suddenly piercing, and Marta withdrew in distress as she glimpsed a small helicopter rising into view just outside the window.

The machine hovered no more than ten yards away, almost as if it were staring in at the people in the room. It was a small craft, maybe a yard long, with a long black cylinder mounted on the front. The cylinder was pointed directly at them.

"It's going to shoot!" Sienna shouted. "**Sta per sparare!** Everybody down! **Tutti a terra!**" She dropped to her knees beneath the windowsill, and Marta went cold with terror as she instinctively followed suit. The guard dropped down, too, reflexively aiming his gun at the little machine.

From Marta's awkward crouch below the windowsill, she could see that Langdon was still standing, staring at Sienna with an odd look, clearly not believing there was any danger. Sienna was on the ground for only an instant before she bounded back up, grabbed Langdon by the wrist, and began pulling him in the direction of the hallway. An instant later, they were fleeing together toward the main entrance of the building.

The guard spun on his knees and crouched like a sniper—raising his weapon down the hallway in the direction of the departing duo.

"**Non spari!**" Marta ordered him. "**Non possono scappare.**" Don't shoot! They can't possibly escape!

Langdon and Sienna disappeared around a corner, and Marta knew it would be only a matter of seconds before the duo collided with the authorities coming in the other way.

———

"Faster!" Sienna urged, rushing with Langdon back the way they'd come in. She was hoping they could make it to the main entrance before running into the police head-on, but she now realized the chances of this were close to zero.

Langdon apparently had similar doubts. Without warning, he skidded to a full stop in a wide intersection of hallways. "We'll never make it out this way."

"Come on!" Sienna motioned urgently for him to follow. "Robert, we can't just stand here!"

Langdon seemed distracted, gazing to his left, down a short corridor that appeared to dead-end in a small, dimly lit chamber. The walls of the room were covered with antique maps, and at the center of the room stood a massive iron globe. Langdon eyed the huge metal sphere and began nodding slowly, and then more vigorously.

"This way," Langdon declared, dashing off toward the iron globe.

Robert! Sienna followed against her better judgment. The corridor clearly led deeper into the museum, away from the exit.

"Robert?" she gasped, finally catching up to him. "Where are you taking us?!"

"Through Armenia," he replied.

"What?!"

"Armenia," Langdon repeated, his eyes dead ahead. "Trust me."

———

One story below, hidden among frightened tourists on the balcony of the Hall of the Five Hundred, Vayentha kept her head down as Brüder's SRS team thundered past her into the museum. Downstairs, the sound of slamming doors resonated through the hall as police sealed the area.

If Langdon were indeed here, he was trapped.

Unfortunately, Vayentha was, too.

CHAPTER 45

With its warm oak wainscoting and coffered wooden ceilings, the Hall of Geographical Maps feels a world away from the stark stone and plaster interior of the Palazzo Vecchio. Originally the building's cloakroom, this grand space contains dozens of closets and cabinets once used to store the portable assets of the grand duke. On this day, the walls were adorned with maps—fifty-three illuminations hand-painted on leather—depicting the world as it was known in the 1550s.

The hall's dramatic collection of cartography is dominated by the presence of a massive globe that stands in the center of the room. Known as the **Mappa Mundi**, the six-foot-tall sphere had been the largest rotating globe of its era and was said to spin almost effortlessly with just the touch of a finger. Today the globe serves as more of a final stop for tourists who have threaded their way through the long succession of gallery rooms and reached a dead end, where they circle the globe and depart the way they came.

Langdon and Sienna arrived breathless in the Hall of Maps. Before them, the **Mappa Mundi** rose majestically, but Langdon didn't even glance at it, his eyes moving instead to the outer walls of the room.

"We need to find Armenia!" Langdon said. "The map of Armenia!"

Clearly nonplussed by his request, Sienna hurried off to the room's right-hand wall in search of a map of Armenia.

Langdon immediately began a similar search along the left-hand wall, tracing his way around the perimeter of the room.

Arabia, Spain, Greece . . .

Each country was portrayed in remarkable detail, considering that the drawings had been made more than five hundred years ago, at a time when much of the world had yet to be mapped or explored.

Where is Armenia?

Compared to his usually vivid eidetic memories, Langdon's recollections of his "secret passages tour" here several years ago felt cloudy, due in no small part to the second glass of Gaja Nebbiolo he'd enjoyed with lunch prior to the tour. Fittingly, the word **nebbiolo** meant "little fog." Even so, Langdon now distinctly recalled being shown a single map in this room—Armenia—a map that possessed a unique property.

I know it's in here, Langdon thought, continuing to scan the seemingly endless line of maps.

"Armenia!" Sienna announced. "Over here!"

Langdon spun toward where she was standing in the deep right-hand corner of the room. He rushed over, and Sienna pointed to the map of Armenia with an expression that seemed to say, "We found Armenia—so what?"

Langdon knew they didn't have time for explanations. Instead, he simply reached out, grabbed the map's massive wooden frame, and heaved it toward him. The entire map swung into the room, along with a large section of the wall and wainscoting, revealing a hidden passageway.

"All right, then," Sienna said, sounding impressed. "Armenia it is."

Without hesitation, Sienna hurried through the opening, moving fearlessly into the dim space beyond. Langdon followed her and quickly pulled the wall closed behind them.

Despite his foggy recollections of the secret passages tour, Langdon recalled this passageway clearly. He and Sienna had just passed, as it were, through the looking glass into the Palazzo Invisibile—the clandestine world that existed **behind** the walls of the Palazzo Vecchio—a secret domain that had been accessible solely to the then-reigning duke and those closest to him.

Langdon paused a moment inside the doorway and took in their new surroundings—a pale stone hallway lit only by faint natural light that filtered through a series of leaded windows. The passageway descended fifty yards or so to a wooden door.

He turned now to his left, where a narrow ascending staircase was blocked by a chain swag. A sign above the stairs warned: USCITA VIETATA.

Langdon headed for the stairs.

"No!" Sienna warned. "It says 'No Exit.'"

"Thanks," Langdon said with a wry smile. "I can read the Italian."

He unhooked the chain swag, carried it back to the secret door, and quickly used it to immobilize the rotating wall—threading the chain through the door handle and around a nearby fixture so the door could not be pulled open from the other side.

"Oh," Sienna said sheepishly. "Good thinking."

"It won't keep them out for long," Langdon said. "But we won't need much time. Follow me."

———

When the map of Armenia finally crashed open, Agent Brüder and his men streamed down the narrow corridor in pursuit, heading for the wooden door at the far end. When they burst through, Brüder felt a blast of cold air hit him head-on, and was momentarily blinded by bright sunlight.

He had arrived on an exterior walkway, which threaded along the rooftop of the palazzo. His eye traced the path, which led directly to another door, some fifty yards away, and reentered the building.

Brüder glanced to the left of the walkway, where the high, vaulted roof of the Hall of the Five Hundred rose like a mountain. **Impossible to traverse.** Brüder turned now to his right, where the walkway was bordered by a sheer cliff that plummeted down into a deep light well. **Instant death.**

His eyes refocused straight ahead. "This way!"

Brüder and his men dashed along the walkway

toward the second door while the surveillance drone circled like a vulture overhead.

When Brüder and his men burst through the doorway, they all slid to an abrupt stop, nearly piling up on one another.

They were standing in a tiny stone chamber that had no exit other than the door through which they had just come. A lone wooden desk stood against the wall. Overhead, the grotesque figures depicted in the chamber's ceiling frescoes seemed to stare down at them mockingly.

It was a dead end.

One of Brüder's men hurried over and scanned the informational placard on the wall. "Hold on," he said. "This says there's a **finestra** in here—some kind of secret window?"

Brüder looked around but saw no secret window. He marched over and read the placard himself.

Apparently this space had once been the private study of Duchess Bianca Cappello and included a secret window—**una finestra segrata**—through which Bianca could covertly watch her husband deliver speeches down below in the Hall of the Five Hundred.

Brüder's eyes searched the room again, now locating a small lattice-covered opening discreetly hidden in the sidewall. **Did they escape through there?**

He stalked over and examined the opening, which appeared to be too small for someone of Langdon's size to get through. Brüder pressed his face to the grid and peered through, confirming for certain that nobody had escaped this way; on the other side of the lattice was a sheer drop, straight down several stories, to the floor of the Hall of the Five Hundred.

So where the hell did they go?!

As Brüder turned back in to the tiny stone chamber, he felt all of the day's frustration mounting within him. In a rare moment of unrestrained emotion, Agent Brüder threw back his head and let out a bellow of rage.

The noise was deafening in the tiny space.

Far below, in the Hall of the Five Hundred, tourists and police officers all spun and stared up at the latticed opening high on the wall. From the sounds of things, the duchess's secret study was now being used to cage a wild animal.

———

Sienna Brooks and Robert Langdon stood in total darkness.

Minutes earlier, Sienna had watched Langdon cleverly use the chain to seal the rotating map of Armenia, then turn and flee.

To her surprise, however, instead of heading down the corridor, Langdon had gone up the steep staircase that had been marked USCITA VIETATA.

"Robert!" she whispered in confusion. "The sign said 'No Exit'! And besides, I thought we wanted to go **down**!"

"We do," Langdon said, glancing over his shoulder. "But sometimes you need to go up . . . to go down." He gave her an encouraging wink. "Remember Satan's navel?"

What is he talking about? Sienna bounded after him, feeling lost.

"Did you ever read **Inferno**?" Langdon asked.

Yes . . . but I think I was seven.

An instant later, it dawned on her. "Oh, Satan's navel!" she said. "Now I remember."

It had taken a moment, but Sienna now realized that Langdon was referring to the finale of Dante's **Inferno**. In these cantos, in order to escape hell, Dante has to climb down the hairy stomach of the massive Satan, and when he reaches Satan's navel— the alleged center of the earth—the earth's gravity suddenly switches directions, and Dante, in order to continue climbing **down** to purgatory . . . suddenly has to start climbing **up**.

Sienna remembered little of the **Inferno** other than her disappointment in witnessing the absurd actions of gravity at the center of the earth; apparently Dante's genius did not include a grasp of the physics of vector forces.

They reached the top of the stairs, and Langdon opened the lone door they found there; on it was written: SALA DEI MODELLI DI ARCHITETTURA.

Langdon ushered her inside, closing and bolting the door behind them.

The room was small and plain, containing a series of cases that displayed wooden models of Vasari's architectural designs for the interior of the palazzo.

Sienna barely noticed the models. She did, however, notice that the room had no doors, no windows, and, as advertised . . . **no exit.**

"In the mid-1300s," Langdon whispered, "the Duke of Athens assumed power in the palace and built this secret escape route in case he was attacked. It's called the Duke of Athens Stairway, and it descends to a tiny escape hatch on a side street. If we can get there, nobody will see us exit." He pointed to one of the models. "Look. See it there on the side?"

He brought me up here to show me models?

Sienna shot an anxious glance at the miniature and saw the secret staircase descending all the way from the top of the palace down to street level, stealthily hidden between the inner and outer walls of the building.

"I can see the stairs, Robert," Sienna said testily, "but they are on the complete **opposite** side of the palace. We'll never get over there!"

"A little faith," he said with a lopsided grin.

A sudden crash emanating from downstairs told them that the map of Armenia had just been breached. They stood stone-still as they listened to the footfalls of soldiers departing down the corridor, none of them ever thinking that their quarry would climb higher still . . . especially up a tiny staircase marked NO EXIT.

When the sounds below had subsided, Langdon strode with confidence across the exhibit room, snaking through the displays, heading directly for what looked like a large cupboard in the far wall. The

cupboard was about one yard square and positioned
three feet off the floor. Without hesitation, Langdon
grabbed the handle and heaved open the door.

Sienna recoiled with surprise.

The space within appeared to be a cavernous
void . . . as if the cupboard door were a portal into
another world. Beyond was only blackness.

"Follow me," Langdon said.

He grabbed a lone flashlight that was hanging on
the wall beside the opening. Then, with surprising
agility and strength, the professor hoisted himself up
through the opening and disappeared into the rabbit
hole.

CHAPTER **46**

La soffitta, Langdon thought. **The most dramatic attic on earth.**

The air inside the void smelled musty and ancient, as if centuries of plaster dust had now become so fine and light that it refused to settle and instead hung suspended in the atmosphere. The vast space creaked and groaned, giving Langdon the sense that he had just climbed into the belly of a living beast.

Once he had found solid footing on a broad horizontal truss chord, he raised his flashlight, letting the beam pierce the darkness.

Spreading out before him was a seemingly endless tunnel, crisscrossed by a wooden web of triangles and rectangles formed by the intersections of posts, beams, chords, and other structural elements that made up the invisible skeleton of the Hall of the Five Hundred.

This enormous attic space was one Langdon had viewed during his Nebbiolo-fogged secret passages tour a few years ago. The cupboardlike viewing window had been cut in the wall of the architectural-model room so visitors could inspect the models of the truss work and then peer through the opening with a flashlight and see the real thing.

Now that Langdon was actually inside the garret, he was surprised by how much the truss architecture resembled that of an old New England barn—traditional king post–and–strut assembly with "Jupiter's arrow point" connections.

Sienna had also climbed through the opening and now steadied herself on the beam beside him, looking disoriented. Langdon swung the flashlight back and forth to show her the unusual landscape.

From this end, the view down the length of the garret was like peering through a long line of isosceles triangles that telescoped into the distance, extending out toward some distant vanishing point. Beneath their feet, the garret had no floorboards, and its horizontal supporting beams were entirely exposed, resembling a series of massive railroad ties.

Langdon pointed straight down the long shaft, speaking in hushed tones. "This space is directly **over** the Hall of the Five Hundred. If we can get to the other end, I know how to reach the Duke of Athens Stairway."

Sienna cast a skeptical eye into the labyrinth of beams and supports that stretched before them. The only apparent way to advance through the garret would be to jump between the struts like kids on a train track. The struts were large—each consisting of numerous beams strapped together with wide iron clasps into a single powerful sheaf—plenty large enough to balance on. The challenge, however, was that the separation between the struts was much too far to leap across safely.

"I can't possibly jump between those beams," Sienna whispered.

Langdon doubted he could either, and falling would be certain death. He aimed the flashlight down through the open space between the struts.

Eight feet below them, suspended by iron rods, hung a dusty horizontal expanse—a floor of sorts—which extended as far as they could see. Despite its appearance of solidity, Langdon knew the floor consisted primarily of stretched fabric covered in dust. This was the "back side" of the Hall of the Five Hundred's suspended ceiling—a sprawling expanse of wooden lacunars that framed thirty-nine Vasari canvases, all mounted horizontally in a kind of patchwork-quilt configuration.

Sienna pointed down to the dusty expanse beneath them. "Can we climb down there and walk across?"

Not unless you want to fall through a Vasari canvas into the Hall of the Five Hundred.

"Actually, there's a better way," Langdon said calmly, not wanting to frighten her. He began moving down the strut toward the central backbone of the garret.

On his previous visit, in addition to peering through the viewing window in the room of architectural models, Langdon had explored the garret on foot, entering through a doorway at the **other** end of the attic. If his wine-impaired memory served him, a sturdy boardwalk ran along the central spine of the garret, providing tourists access to a large viewing deck in the center of the space.

However, when Langdon arrived at the center of the strut, he found a boardwalk that in no way resembled the one he recalled from his tour.

How much Nebbiolo did I drink that day?

Rather than a sturdy, tourist-worthy structure, he was looking at a hodgepodge of loose planks that had been laid perpendicularly across the beams to create a rudimentary catwalk—more of a tightrope than a bridge.

Apparently, the sturdy tourist walkway that originated at the other end extended only as far as the central viewing platform. From there, the tourists evidently retraced their steps. This jerry-rigged balance beam that Langdon and Sienna now faced was most likely installed so engineers could service the remaining attic space at this end.

"Looks like we're walking the plank," Langdon said, eyeing the narrow boards with uncertainty.

Sienna shrugged, unfazed. "No worse than Venice in flood season."

Langdon realized she had a point. On his most recent research trip to Venice, St. Mark's Square had been under a foot of water, and he had walked from the Hotel Danieli to the basilica on wooden planks propped between cinder blocks and inverted buckets. Of course, the prospect of possibly getting one's loafers wet was a far cry from that of plunging through a Renaissance masterpiece to one's death.

Pushing the thought from his mind, Langdon stepped out onto the narrow board with a feigned self-assurance that he hoped would calm any worries Sienna might secretly be harboring. Nonetheless, despite his confident exterior, his heart was pounding as he moved across the first plank. As he neared the middle, the plank bowed beneath his weight, creaking ominously. He pressed on, faster now, finally reaching the other side and the relative safety of the second strut.

Exhaling, Langdon turned to shine the light for Sienna and also offer any coaxing words she might need. She apparently needed none. As soon as his beam illuminated the plank, she was skimming along its length with remarkable dexterity. The board barely bent beneath her slender body, and within seconds she had joined him on the other side.

Encouraged, Langdon turned back and headed out across the next plank. Sienna waited until he had crossed and could turn around and shine the light for her, and then she followed, staying right with him. Settling into a steady rhythm, they pressed on—two figures moving one after the other by the light of a single flashlight. From somewhere beneath them, the sound of police walkie-talkies crackled up through the thin ceiling. Langdon permitted himself a faint smile. **We're hovering above the Hall of the Five Hundred, weightless and invisible.**

"So, Robert," Sienna whispered. "You said Ignazio told you where to find the mask?"

"He did . . . but in a kind of code." Langdon quickly explained that Ignazio had apparently not wanted to blurt out the mask's location on the answering machine, and so he had shared the information in a more cryptic manner. "He referenced paradise, which I assume is an allusion to the final section of **The Divine Comedy**. His exact words were 'Paradise Twenty-five.'"

Sienna glanced up. "He must mean **Canto** Twenty-five."

"I agree," Langdon said. A **canto** was the rough equivalent of a chapter, the word harkening back to the oral tradition of "singing" epic poems. **The Divine Comedy** contained precisely one hundred cantos in all, divided into three sections.

Inferno 1–34
Purgatorio 1–33
Paradiso 1–33

Paradise Twenty-five, Langdon thought, wishing his eidetic memory were strong enough to recall the entire text. **Not even close—we need to find a copy of the text.**

"There's more," Langdon continued. "The last thing Ignazio said to me was: '**The gates are open to you, but you must hurry.**'" He paused, glancing back at Sienna. "Canto Twenty-five probably makes reference to a specific location here in Florence. Apparently, someplace with gates."

Sienna frowned. "But this city probably has dozens of gates."

"Yes, which is why we need to read Canto Twenty-five of **Paradise**." He gave her a hopeful smile. "You don't, by any chance, know the entire **Divine Comedy** by heart, do you?"

She gave him a dumb look. "Fourteen thousand lines of archaic Italian that I read as a kid?" She shook her head. "You're the one with the freakish memory, Professor. I'm just a doctor."

As they pressed on, Langdon found it sad somehow that Sienna, even after all they'd been through together, apparently still preferred to withhold the truth about her exceptional intellect. **She's just a doctor?** Langdon had to chuckle. **Most humble doctor on earth**, he thought, recalling the clippings he'd read about her special skills—skills that, unfortunately but not surprisingly, did not include total recall of one of history's longest epic poems.

In silence, they continued on, crossing several more beams. Finally, up ahead Langdon saw a heartening shape in the darkness. **The viewing platform!** The precarious planking on which they were walking led directly to a much sturdier structure with guardrails. If they climbed onto the platform, they could continue on along the walkway until they exited the garret through a doorway, which, as Langdon recalled, was very close to the Duke of Athens Stairway.

As they neared the platform, Langdon glanced down at the ceiling suspended eight feet below. So far all the lunettes beneath them had been similar. The upcoming lunette, however, was massive—far larger than the others.

The Apotheosis of Cosimo I, Langdon mused.

This vast, circular lunette was Vasari's most precious painting—the central lunette in the entire Hall of the Five Hundred. Langdon often showed slides of this work to his students, pointing out its similarities to **The Apotheosis of Washington** in the U.S. Capitol—a humble reminder that fledgling America had adopted far more from Italy than merely the concept of a republic.

Today, however, Langdon was more interested in hurrying past the **Apotheosis** than in studying it. As he hastened his pace, he turned his head ever so slightly to whisper back to Sienna that they were nearly there.

As he did so, his right foot missed the center of the plank and his borrowed loafer landed half off the edge. His ankle rolled, and Langdon lurched forward, half stumbling, half running, trying to make a quick stutter step to regain his balance.

But it was too late.

His knees hit the plank hard, and his hands strained desperately forward, trying to reach the crossing strut. The flashlight went clattering into the dark space beneath them, landing on the canvas, which caught it like a net. Langdon's legs pumped, barely propelling him to safety on the next strut as the plank fell away beneath him, landing with a crash eight feet below on the wooden lacunar surrounding the canvas of Vasari's **Apotheosis**.

The sound echoed through the garret.

Horrified, Langdon scrambled to his feet and turned back toward Sienna.

In the dim glow of the abandoned flashlight, which lay on the canvas below, Langdon could see that Sienna was standing on the strut behind him, now trapped, with no way across. Her eyes conveyed what Langdon already knew. The noise of the falling plank had almost certainly given them away.

———

Vayentha's eyes bolted upward to the ornate ceiling.

"Rats in the attic?" the man with the camcorder joked nervously as the sound reverberated down.

Big rats, Vayentha thought, gazing up at the circular painting in the center of the hall's ceiling. A small cloud of dust was now filtering down from between the lacunars, and Vayentha could swear she saw a slight bulge in the canvas . . . almost as if someone were pushing on it from the other side.

"Maybe one of the officers dropped his gun off the viewing platform," the man said, eyeing the lump in the painting. "What do you think they're looking for? All this activity is very exciting."

"A **viewing** platform?" Vayentha demanded. "People can actually go up there?"

"Sure." He motioned to the museum entrance. "Just inside that door is a door that leads up to a catwalk in the attic. You can see Vasari's truss work. It's incredible."

Brüder's voice suddenly echoed again across the Hall of the Five Hundred. "So where the hell did they go?!"

His words, like his anguished yell a little earlier, had

emanated from behind a lattice grate positioned high on the wall to Vayentha's left. Brüder was apparently in a room behind the grate . . . a full story beneath the room's ornate ceiling.

Vayentha's eyes climbed again to the bulge in the canvas overhead.

Rats in the attic, she thought. **Trying to find a way out.**

She thanked the man with the camcorder and drifted quickly toward the museum entrance. The door was closed, but with all the officers running in and out, she suspected that it was unlocked.

Sure enough, her instincts were correct.

CHAPTER 47

Outside in the piazza, amid the chaos of arriving police, a middle-aged man stood in the shadows of the Loggia dei Lanzi, where he had been observing the activity with great interest. The man wore Plume Paris spectacles, a paisley necktie, and a tiny gold stud in one ear.

As he watched the commotion, he caught himself scratching at his neck again. The man had developed a rash overnight, which seemed to be getting worse, manifesting in small pustules on his jawline, neck, cheeks, and over his eyes.

When he glanced down at his fingernails, he saw they were bloody. He took out his handkerchief and wiped his fingers, also dabbing the bloody pustules on his neck and cheeks.

When he had cleaned himself up, he returned his gaze to the two black vans parked outside the palazzo. The closest van contained two people in the backseat.

One was an armed soldier in black.

The other was an older, but very beautiful silver-haired woman wearing a blue amulet.

The soldier looked as if he were preparing a hypodermic syringe.

Inside the van, Dr. Elizabeth Sinskey gazed absently out at the palazzo, wondering about how this crisis had deteriorated to such an extent.

"Ma'am," a deep voice said beside her.

She turned groggily to the soldier accompanying her. He was gripping her forearm and holding up a syringe. "Just be still."

The sharp stab of a needle pierced her flesh.

The soldier completed the injection. "Now go back to sleep."

As she closed her eyes, she could have sworn she saw a man studying her from the shadows. He wore designer glasses and a preppie necktie. His face was rashy and red. For a moment she thought she knew him, but when she opened her eyes for another look, the man had disappeared.

CHAPTER 48

In the darkness of the garret, Langdon and Sienna were now separated by a twenty-foot expanse of open air. Eight feet beneath them, the fallen plank had come to rest across the wooden framing that supported the canvas bearing Vasari's **Apotheosis**. The large flashlight, still glowing, was resting on the canvas itself, creating a small indentation, like a stone on a trampoline.

"The plank behind you," Langdon whispered. "Can you drag it across to reach this strut?"

Sienna eyed the plank. "Not without the other end falling into the canvas."

Langdon had feared as much; the last thing they needed now was to send a two-by-six crashing through a Vasari canvas.

"I've got an idea," Sienna said, now moving sideways along the strut, heading for the sidewall. Langdon followed on his beam, the footing becoming more treacherous with each step as they ventured away from the flashlight beam. By the time they reached the sidewall, they were almost entirely in darkness.

"Down there," Sienna whispered, pointing into the

obscurity below them. "At the edge of the frame. It's got to be mounted to the wall. It should hold me."

Before Langdon could protest, Sienna was climbing down off the strut, using a series of supporting beams as a ladder. She eased herself down onto the edge of the wooden lacunar. It creaked once, but held. Then, inching along the wall, Sienna began moving in Langdon's direction as if she were inching across the ledge of a high building. The lacunar creaked again.

Thin ice, Langdon thought. **Stay near shore.**

As Sienna reached the halfway point, approaching the strut on which he stood in the darkness, Langdon felt a sudden renewed hope that they might indeed get out of here in time.

Suddenly, somewhere in the darkness ahead, a door slammed and he heard fast-moving footsteps approaching along the walkway. The beam of a flashlight now appeared, sweeping the area, getting closer every second. Langdon felt his hopes sink. Someone was coming their way—moving along the main walkway and cutting off their escape route.

"Sienna, keep going," he whispered, reacting on instinct. "Continue the entire length of the wall. There's an exit at the far end. I'll run interference."

"No!" Sienna whispered urgently. "Robert, come back!"

But Langdon was already on the move, heading back along the strut toward the central spine of the garret, leaving Sienna in the darkness, inching across the sidewall, eight feet below him.

When Langdon arrived at the center of the garret,

a faceless silhouette with a flashlight had just arrived on the raised viewing platform. The person halted at the low guardrail and aimed the flashlight beam down into Langdon's eyes.

The glare was blinding, and Langdon immediately raised his arms in surrender. He could not have felt more vulnerable—balanced high above the Hall of the Five Hundred, blinded by a bright light.

Langdon waited for a gunshot or for an authoritative command, but there was only silence. After a moment the beam swung away from his face and began probing the darkness behind him, apparently looking for something . . . or someone else. As the beam left his eyes, Langdon could just make out the silhouette of the person now blocking his escape route. It was a woman, lean and dressed all in black. He had no doubt that beneath her baseball cap was a head of spiked hair.

Langdon's muscles tightened instinctively as his mind flooded with images of Dr. Marconi dying on the hospital floor.

She found me. She's here to finish the job.

Langdon flashed on an image of Greek free divers swimming deep into a tunnel, far past the point of no return, and then colliding with a stony dead end.

The assassin swung her flashlight beam back down into Langdon's eyes.

"Mr. Langdon," she whispered. "Where is your friend?"

Langdon felt a chill. **This killer is here for both of us.**

Langdon made a show of glancing **away** from Sienna, over his shoulder into the darkness from which they'd come. "She has nothing to do with this. You want me."

Langdon prayed that Sienna was now making progress along the wall. If she could sneak beyond the viewing platform, she could then quietly cross back to the central boardwalk, behind the spike-haired woman, and move toward the door.

The assassin again raised her light and scanned the empty garret behind him. With the glare momentarily out of his eyes, Langdon caught a sudden glimpse of a form in the darkness behind her.

Oh God, no!

Sienna was indeed making her way across a strut in the direction of the central boardwalk, but unfortunately, she was only ten yards behind their attacker.

Sienna, no! You're too close! She'll hear you!

The beam returned to Langdon's eyes again.

"Listen carefully, Professor," the assassin whispered. "If you want to live, I suggest you trust me. My mission has been terminated. I have no reason to harm you. You and I are on the same team now, and I may know how to help you."

Langdon was barely listening, his thoughts focused squarely on Sienna, who was now faintly visible in profile, climbing deftly up onto the walkway behind the viewing platform, entirely too close to the woman with the gun.

Run! he willed her. **Get the hell out of here!**

Sienna, however, to Langdon's alarm, held her

ground, crouching low in the shadows and watching in silence.

———

Vayentha's eyes probed the darkness behind Langdon. **Where the hell did she go? Did they separate?**

Vayentha had to find a way to keep the fleeing couple out of Brüder's hands. **It's my only hope.**

"Sienna?!" Vayentha ventured in a throaty whisper. "If you can hear me, listen carefully. You do not want to be captured by the men downstairs. They will **not** be lenient. I know an escape route. I can help you. Trust me."

"Trust you?" Langdon challenged, his voice suddenly loud enough that anyone nearby could hear him. "You're a killer!"

Sienna is nearby, Vayentha realized. **Langdon is talking to her . . . trying to warn her.**

Vayentha tried again. "Sienna, the situation is complicated, but I can get you out of here. Consider your options. You're trapped. You have no choice."

"She has a choice," Langdon called out loudly. "And she's smart enough to run as far from you as possible."

"Everything's changed," Vayentha insisted. "I have no reason to hurt either of you."

"You killed Dr. Marconi! And I'm guessing you're also the one who shot me in the head!"

Vayentha knew that the man was never going to believe she had no intention of killing him.

The time for talking is over. There's nothing I can say to convince him.

Without hesitation, she reached into her leather jacket and extracted the silenced handgun.

———

Motionless in the shadows, Sienna remained crouched on the walkway no more than ten yards behind the woman who had just confronted Langdon. Even in the dark, the woman's silhouette was unmistakable. To Sienna's horror, she was brandishing the same weapon she had used on Dr. Marconi.

She's going to fire, Sienna knew, sensing the woman's body language.

Sure enough, the woman took two threatening steps toward Langdon, stopping at the low railing that enclosed the viewing platform above Vasari's **Apotheosis**. The assassin was now as close to Langdon as she could get. She raised the gun and pointed it directly at Langdon's chest.

"This will only hurt for an instant," she said, "but it's my only choice."

Sienna reacted on instinct.

———

The unexpected vibration in the boards beneath Vayentha's feet was just enough to cause her to turn slightly as she was firing. Even as her weapon discharged, she knew it was no longer pointed at Langdon.

Something was approaching behind her.

Approaching fast.

Vayentha spun in place, swinging her weapon 180

degrees toward her attacker, and a flash of blond hair glinted in the darkness as someone collided with Vayentha at full speed. The gun hissed again, but the person had crouched below barrel level in order to apply a forceful upward body check.

Vayentha's feet left the floor and her midsection crashed hard into the low railing of the viewing platform. As her torso was propelled out over the railing, she flailed her arms, trying to grab onto anything to stop her fall, but it was too late. She went over the edge.

Vayentha fell through the darkness, bracing herself for the collision with the dusty floor that lay eight feet beneath the platform. Strangely, though, her landing was softer than she'd imagined . . . as if she had been caught by a cloth hammock, which now sagged beneath her weight.

Disoriented, Vayentha lay on her back and stared up at her attacker. Sienna Brooks was looking down at her over the railing. Stunned, Vayentha opened her mouth to speak, but suddenly, just beneath her, there was a loud ripping sound.

The cloth that was supporting her weight tore open.

Vayentha was falling again.

This time she fell for three very long seconds, during which she found herself staring upward at a ceiling that was covered with beautiful paintings. The painting directly above her—a massive circular canvas depicting Cosimo I encircled by cherubs on a heavenly cloud—now showed a jagged dark tear that cut through its center.

Then, with a sudden crash, Vayentha's entire world vanished into blackness.

———

High above, frozen in disbelief, Robert Langdon peered through the torn **Apotheosis** into the cavernous space below. On the stone floor of the Hall of the Five Hundred, the spike-haired woman lay motionless, a dark pool of blood quickly spreading from her head. She still had the gun clutched in her hand.

Langdon raised his eyes to Sienna, who was also staring down, transfixed by the grim scene below. Sienna's expression was one of utter shock. "I didn't mean to . . ."

"You reacted on instinct," Langdon whispered. "She was about to kill me."

From down below, shouts of alarm filtered up through the torn canvas.

Gently, Langdon guided Sienna away from the railing. "We need to keep moving."

CHAPTER 49

I n the secret study of Duchess Bianca Cappello, Agent Brüder had heard a sickening thud followed by a growing commotion in the Hall of the Five Hundred. He rushed to the grate in the wall and peered through it. The scene on the elegant stone floor below took him several seconds to process.

The pregnant museum administrator had arrived beside him at the grate, immediately covering her mouth in mute terror at the sight below—a crumpled figure surrounded by panicked tourists. As the woman's gaze shifted slowly upward to the ceiling of the Hall of the Five Hundred, she let out a pained whimper. Brüder looked up, following her gaze to a circular ceiling panel—a painted canvas with a large tear across the center.

He turned to the woman. "How do we get up there!?"

———

At the other end of the building, Langdon and Sienna descended breathlessly from the attic and burst through a doorway. Within a matter of seconds, Langdon had found the small alcove, deftly hidden behind a crimson curtain. He had recalled it clearly from his secret passages tour.

The Duke of Athens Stairway.

The sound of running footsteps and shouting seemed to be coming from all directions now, and Langdon knew their time was short. He pulled aside the curtain, and he and Sienna slipped through onto a small landing.

Without a word, they began to descend the stone staircase. The passage had been designed as a series of frighteningly narrow switchback stairs. The deeper they went, the tighter it seemed to get. Just as Langdon felt as if the walls were moving in to crush him, thankfully, they could go no farther.

Ground level.

The space at the bottom of the stairs was a tiny stone chamber, and although its exit had to be one of the smallest doors on earth, it was a welcome sight. Only about four feet high, the door was made of heavy wood with iron rivets and a heavy interior bolt to keep people out.

"I can hear street sounds beyond the door," Sienna whispered, still looking shaken. "What's on the other side?"

"The Via della Ninna," Langdon replied, picturing the crowded pedestrian walkway. "But there may be police."

"They won't recognize us. They'll be looking for a blond girl and a dark-haired man."

Langdon eyed her strangely. "Which is precisely what we are . . ."

Sienna shook her head, a melancholy resolve crossing her face. "I didn't want you to see me like this, Robert, but unfortunately it's what I look like at the moment." Abruptly, Sienna reached up and grabbed a handful of her blond hair. Then she yanked down, and all of her hair slid off in a single motion.

Langdon recoiled, startled both by the fact that Sienna wore a wig and by her altered appearance without it. Sienna Brooks was in fact totally bald, her bare scalp smooth and pale, like a cancer patient undergoing chemotherapy. **On top of it all, she's ill?**

"I know," she said. "Long story. Now bend down." She held up the wig, clearly intending to put it on Langdon's head.

Is she serious? Langdon halfheartedly bent over, and Sienna wedged the blond hair onto his head. The wig barely fit, but she arranged it as best as she could. Then she stepped back and assessed him. Not quite satisfied, she reached up, loosened his tie, and slipped the loop up onto his forehead, retightening it like a bandanna and securing the ill-fitting wig to his head.

Sienna now set to work on herself, rolling up her pant legs and pushing her socks down around her ankles. When she stood up, she had a sneer on her lips. The lovely Sienna Brooks was now a punk-rock skinhead. The former Shakespearean actress's transformation was startling.

"Remember," she said, "ninety percent of personal recognition is body language, so when you move, move like an aging rocker."

Aging, I can do, Langdon thought. **Rocker, I'm not so sure.**

Before Langdon could argue the point, Sienna had unbolted the tiny door and swung it open. She ducked low and exited onto the crowded cobblestone street. Langdon followed, nearly on all fours as he emerged into the daylight.

Aside from a few startled glances at the mismatched couple emerging from the tiny door in the foundation of Palazzo Vecchio, nobody gave them a second look. Within seconds, Langdon and Sienna were moving east, swallowed up by the crowd.

———

The man in the Plume Paris eyeglasses picked at his bleeding skin as he snaked through the crowd, keeping a safe distance behind Robert Langdon and Sienna Brooks. Despite their clever disguises, he had spotted them emerging from the tiny door on the Via della Ninna and had immediately known who they were.

He had tailed them only a few blocks before he got winded, his chest aching acutely, forcing him to take shallow breaths. He felt like he'd been punched in the sternum.

Gritting his teeth against the pain, he forced his attention back to Langdon and Sienna as he continued to follow them through the streets of Florence.

CHAPTER 50

The morning sun had fully risen now, casting long shadows down the narrow canyons that snaked between the buildings of old Florence. Shopkeepers had begun throwing open the metal grates that protected their shops and bars, and the air was heavy with the aromas of morning espresso and freshly baked cornetti.

Despite a gnawing hunger, Langdon kept moving. **I've got to find the mask . . . and see what's hidden on the back.**

As Langdon led Sienna northward along the slender Via dei Leoni, he was having a hard time getting used to the sight of her bald head. Her radically altered appearance reminded him that he barely knew her. They were moving in the direction of Piazza del Duomo—the square where Ignazio Busoni had been found dead after placing his final phone call.

Robert, Ignazio had managed to say, breathless. **What you seek is safely hidden. The gates are open to you, but you must hurry. Paradise Twenty-five. Godspeed.**

Paradise Twenty-five, Langdon repeated to himself, still puzzled that Ignazio Busoni had recalled Dante's text well enough to reference a specific canto off the top of his head. Something about that canto was apparently memorable to Busoni. Whatever it was, Langdon knew he would find out soon enough, as soon as he laid his hands on a copy of the text, which he could easily do at any number of locations up ahead.

His shoulder-length wig was beginning to itch now, and though he felt somewhat ridiculous in his disguise, he had to admit that Sienna's impromptu styling had been an effective ruse. Nobody had given them a second look, not even the police reinforcements who had just rushed past them en route to the Palazzo Vecchio.

Sienna had been walking in total silence beside him for several minutes, and Langdon glanced over to make sure she was okay. She seemed miles away, probably trying to accept the fact that she had just killed the woman who had been chasing them.

"Lira for your thoughts," he ventured lightly, hoping to pull her mind from the image of the spike-haired woman lying dead on the palazzo floor.

Sienna emerged slowly from her contemplations. "I was thinking of Zobrist," she said slowly. "Trying to recall anything else I might know about him."

"And?"

She shrugged. "Most of what I know is from a controversial essay he wrote a few years ago. It really stayed with me. Among the medical community, it instantly went viral." She winced. "Sorry, bad choice of words."

Langdon gave a grim chuckle. "Go on."

"His essay essentially declared that the human race was on the brink of extinction, and that unless we had a catastrophic event that precipitously decreased global population growth, our species would not survive another hundred years."

Langdon turned and stared at her. "A single century?"

"It was a pretty stark thesis. The predicted time frame was substantially shorter than previous estimates, but it was supported by some very potent scientific data. He made a lot of enemies by declaring that all doctors should stop practicing medicine because extending the human life span was only exacerbating the population problem."

Langdon now understood why the article spread wildly through the medical community.

"Not surprisingly," Sienna continued, "Zobrist was immediately attacked from all sides—politicians, clergy, the World Health Organization—all of whom derided him as a doomsayer lunatic who was simply trying to cause panic. They took particular umbrage at his statement that today's youth, if they chose to reproduce, would have offspring that literally would witness the end of the human race. Zobrist illustrated his point with a 'Doomsday Clock,' which showed that if the entire span of human life on earth were compressed into a single hour . . . we are now in its final seconds."

"I've actually seen that clock online," Langdon said.

"Yes, well, it's his, and it caused quite an uproar.

The biggest backlash against Zobrist, however, came when he declared that his advances in genetic engineering would be far more helpful to mankind if they were used not to **cure** disease, but rather to **create** it."

"What?!"

"Yes, he argued that his technology should be used to limit population growth by creating hybrid strains of disease that our modern medicine would be unable to cure."

Langdon felt a rising dread as his mind conjured images of strange, hybrid "designer viruses" that, once released, were totally unstoppable.

"Over a few short years," Sienna said, "Zobrist went from being the toast of the medical world to being a total outcast. An anathema." She paused, a look of compassion crossing her face. "It's really no wonder he snapped and killed himself. Even sadder because his thesis is probably correct."

Langdon almost fell over. "I'm sorry—you think he's **right**?!"

Sienna gave him a solemn shrug. "Robert, speaking from a purely scientific standpoint—all logic, no heart—I can tell you without a doubt that without some kind of drastic change, the end of our species is coming. And it's coming fast. It won't be fire, brimstone, apocalypse, or nuclear war . . . it will be total collapse due to the number of people on the planet. The mathematics is indisputable."

Langdon stiffened.

"I've studied a fair amount of biology," she said, "and it's quite normal for a species to go extinct simply as a result of overpopulating its environment. Picture a colony of surface algae living in a tiny pond in the forest, enjoying the pond's perfect balance of nutrients. Unchecked, they reproduce so wildly that they quickly cover the pond's entire surface, blotting out the sun and thereby preventing the growth of the nutrients in the pond. Having sapped everything possible from their environment, the algae quickly die and disappear without a trace." She gave a heavy sigh. "A similar fate could easily await mankind. Far sooner and faster than any of us imagine."

Langdon felt deeply unsettled. "But . . . that seems impossible."

"Not impossible, Robert, just **unthinkable**. The human mind has a primitive ego defense mechanism that negates all realities that produce too much stress for the brain to handle. It's called **denial**."

"I've heard of denial," Langdon quipped blithely, "but I don't think it exists."

Sienna rolled her eyes. "Cute, but believe me, it's very real. Denial is a critical part of the human coping mechanism. Without it, we would all wake up terrified every morning about all the ways we could die. Instead, our minds block out our existential fears by focusing on stresses we can handle—like getting to work on time or paying our taxes. If we have wider, existential fears, we jettison them very quickly, refocusing on simple tasks and daily trivialities."

Langdon recalled a recent Web-tracking study of students at some Ivy League universities which revealed that even highly intellectual users displayed an instinctual tendency toward denial. According to the study, the vast majority of university students, after clicking on a depressing news article about arctic ice melt or species extinction, would quickly exit that page in favor of something trivial that purged their minds of fear; favorite choices included sports highlights, funny cat videos, and celebrity gossip.

"In ancient mythology," Langdon offered, "a hero in **denial** is the ultimate manifestation of hubris and pride. No man is more prideful than he who believes himself immune to the dangers of the world. Dante clearly agreed, denouncing pride as the **worst** of the seven deadly sins . . . and punished the prideful in the deepest ring of the inferno."

Sienna reflected a moment and then continued. "Zobrist's article accused many of the world's leaders of being in extreme denial . . . putting their heads in the sand. He was particularly critical of the World Health Organization."

"I bet that went over well."

"They reacted by equating him with a religious zealot on a street corner holding a sign that says 'The End Is Near.'"

"Harvard Square has a couple of those."

"Yes, and we all ignore them because none of us can imagine it will happen. But believe me, just because the human mind can't **imagine** something happening . . . doesn't mean it won't."

"You almost sound like you're a fan of Zobrist's."

"I'm a fan of the **truth**," she replied forcefully, "even if it's painfully hard to accept."

Langdon fell silent, again feeling strangely isolated from Sienna at the moment, trying to understand her bizarre combination of passion and detachment.

Sienna glanced over at him, her face softening. "Robert, look, I'm not saying Zobrist is correct that a plague that kills half the world's people is the answer to overpopulation. Nor am I saying we should stop curing the sick. What I am saying is that our current path is a pretty simple formula for destruction. Population growth is an exponential progression occurring within a system of finite space and limited resources. The end will arrive very abruptly. Our experience will not be that of slowly running out of gas . . . it will be more like driving off a cliff."

Langdon exhaled, trying to process everything he had just heard.

"Speaking of which," she added, somberly pointing up in the air to their right, "I'm pretty sure that's where Zobrist jumped."

Langdon glanced up and saw that they were just passing the austere stone facade of the Bargello Museum to their right. Behind it, the tapered spire of the Badia tower rose above the surrounding structures. He stared at the top of the tower, wondering why Zobrist had jumped and hoped to hell it wasn't because the man had done something terrible and hadn't wanted to face what was coming.

"Critics of Zobrist," Sienna said, "like to point out how paradoxical it is that many of the genetic technologies he developed are now extending life expectancy dramatically."

"Which only compounds the population problem."

"Exactly. Zobrist once said publicly that he wished he could put the genie back in the bottle and erase some of his contributions to human longevity. I suppose that makes sense ideologically. The longer we live, the more our resources go to supporting the elderly and ailing."

Langdon nodded. "I've read that in the U.S. some sixty percent of health care costs go to support patients during the last six months of their lives."

"True, and while our brains say, 'This is insane,' our hearts say, 'Keep Grandma alive as long as we can.'"

Langdon nodded. "It's the conflict between Apollo and Dionysus—a famous dilemma in mythology. It's the age-old battle between mind and heart, which seldom want the same thing."

The mythological reference, Langdon had heard, was now being used in AA meetings to describe the alcoholic who stares at a glass of alcohol, his brain knowing it will harm him, but his heart craving the comfort it will provide. The message apparently was: Don't feel alone—even the gods were conflicted.

"Who needs agathusia?" Sienna whispered suddenly.

"I'm sorry?"

Sienna glanced up. "I finally remembered the name of Zobrist's essay. It was called: 'Who Needs Agathusia?'"

Langdon had never heard the word **agathusia**, but took his best guess based on its Greek roots—

agathos and **thusia**. "Agathusia . . . would be a 'good sacrifice'?"

"Almost. Its actual meaning is 'a self-sacrifice for the common good.'" She paused. "Otherwise known as benevolent suicide."

Langdon had indeed heard this term before—once in relation to a bankrupt father who killed himself so his family could collect his life insurance, and a second time to describe a remorseful serial killer who ended his life fearing he couldn't control his impulse to kill.

The most chilling example Langdon recalled, however, was in the 1967 novel **Logan's Run**, which depicted a future society in which everyone gladly agreed to commit suicide at age twenty-one— thus fully enjoying their youth while not letting their numbers or old age stress the planet's limited resources. If Langdon recalled correctly, the movie version of **Logan's Run** had increased the "termination age" from twenty-one to thirty, no doubt in an attempt to make the film more palatable to the box office's crucial eighteen-to-twenty-five demographic.

"So, Zobrist's essay . . ." Langdon said. "I'm not sure I understand the title. 'Who Needs Agathusia?' Was he saying it sarcastically? As in who needs benevolent suicide . . . we **all** do?"

"Actually no, the title is a pun."

Langdon shook his head, not seeing it.

"**Who** needs suicide—as in the **W-H-O**—the World Health Organization. In his essay, Zobrist railed against the director of the WHO—Dr. Elizabeth Sinskey—who has been there forever and, according to Zobrist, is not taking population control seriously. His article was saying that the WHO would be better off if Director Sinskey killed herself."

"Compassionate guy."

"The perils of being a genius, I guess. Oftentimes, those special brains, the ones that are capable of focusing more intently than others, do so at the expense of emotional maturity."

Langdon pictured the articles he had seen about the young Sienna, the child prodigy with the 208 IQ and off-the-chart intellectual function. Langdon wondered if, in talking about Zobrist, she was also, on some level, talking about herself; he also wondered how long she would choose to keep her secret.

Up ahead, Langdon spotted the landmark he had been looking for. After crossing the Via dei Leoni, Langdon led her to the intersection of an exceptionally narrow street—more of an alleyway. The sign overhead read VIA DANTE ALIGHIERI.

"It sounds like you know a lot about the human brain," Langdon said. "Was that your area of concentration in medical school?"

"No, but when I was a kid, I read a lot. I became interested in brain science because I had some . . . medical issues."

Langdon shot her a curious look, hoping she would continue.

"My brain . . ." Sienna said quietly. "It grew differently from most kids', and it caused some . . . problems. I spent a lot of time trying to figure out what was wrong with me, and in the process I learned a lot about neuroscience." She caught Langdon's eye. "And yes, my baldness is related to my medical condition."

Langdon averted his eyes, embarrassed he'd asked.

"Don't worry about it," she said. "I've learned to live with it."

As they moved into the cold air of the shadowed alleyway, Langdon considered everything he had just learned about Zobrist and his alarming philosophical positions.

A recurring question nagged at him. "These soldiers," Langdon began. "The ones trying to kill us. Who are they? It makes no sense. If Zobrist has put a potential plague out there, wouldn't everyone be on the same side, working to stop its release?"

"Not necessarily. Zobrist may be a pariah in the medical community, but he probably has a legion of devout fans of his ideology—people who agree that a culling is a necessary evil to save the planet. For all we know, these soldiers are trying to ensure that Zobrist's vision is realized."

Zobrist's own private army of disciples? Langdon considered the possibility. Admittedly, history was full of zealots and cults who killed themselves because of all kinds of crazy notions—a belief that their leader is the Messiah, a belief that a spaceship is waiting for them behind the moon, a belief that Judgment Day is imminent. The speculation about population control was at least grounded in science, and yet something about these soldiers still didn't feel right to Langdon.

"I just can't believe that a bunch of trained soldiers would knowingly agree to kill innocent masses . . . all the while fearing they might get sick and die themselves."

Sienna shot him a puzzled look. "Robert, what do you think soldiers **do** when they go to war? They kill innocent people and risk their own death. Anything is possible when people believe in a cause."

"A cause? Releasing a plague?"

Sienna glanced at him, her brown eyes probing. "Robert, the **cause** is not releasing a plague . . . it's saving the world." She paused. "One of the passages in Bertrand Zobrist's essay that got a lot of people talking was a very pointed hypothetical question. I want you to answer it."

"What's the question?"

"Zobrist asked the following: If you could throw a switch and randomly kill half the population on earth, would you do it?"

"Of course not."

"Okay. But what if you were told that if you **didn't** throw that switch right now, the human race would be extinct in the next hundred years?" She paused. "Would you throw it then? Even if it meant you might murder friends, family, and possibly even yourself?"

"Sienna, I can't possibly—"

"It's a hypothetical question," she said. "Would

you kill half the population today in order to save our species from extinction?"

Langdon felt deeply disturbed by the macabre subject they were discussing, and so he was grateful to see a familiar red banner hanging on the side of a stone building just ahead.

"Look," he announced, pointing. "We're here."

Sienna shook her head. "Like I said. **Denial.**"

CHAPTER 51

T he Casa di Dante is located on the Via Santa Margherita and is easily identified by the large banner suspended from the stone facade partway up the alleyway: MUSEO CASA DI DANTE.

Sienna eyed the banner with uncertainty. "We're going to Dante's **house?**"

"Not exactly," Langdon said. "Dante lived around the corner. This is more of a Dante . . . museum." Langdon had ventured inside the place once, curious about the art collection, which turned out to be no more than reproductions of famous Dante-related works from around the world, and yet it was interesting to see them all gathered together under one roof.

Sienna looked suddenly hopeful. "And you think they have an ancient copy of **The Divine Comedy** on display?"

Langdon chuckled. "No, but I know they have a gift shop that sells huge posters with the entire text of Dante's **Divine Comedy** printed in microscopic type."

She gave him a slightly appalled glance.

"I know. But it's better than nothing. The only problem is that my eyes are going, so you'll have to read the fine print."

"**È chiusa**," an old man called out, seeing them approach the door. "**È il giorno di riposo.**"

Closed for the Sabbath? Langdon felt suddenly disoriented again. He looked at Sienna. "Isn't today . . . Monday?"

She nodded. "Florentines prefer a Monday Sabbath."

Langdon groaned, suddenly recalling the city's unusual weekly calendar. Because tourist dollars flowed most heavily on weekends, many Florentine merchants chose to move the Christian "day of rest" from Sunday to Monday to prevent the Sabbath from cutting too deeply into their bottom line.

Unfortunately, Langdon realized, this probably also ruled out his other option: the Paperback Exchange—one of Langdon's favorite Florentine bookshops—which would definitely have had copies of **The Divine Comedy** on hand.

"Any other ideas?" Sienna said.

Langdon thought a long moment and finally nodded. "There's a site just around the corner where Dante enthusiasts gather. I bet someone there has a copy we can borrow."

"It's probably closed, too," Sienna warned. "Almost every place in town moves the Sabbath away from Sunday."

"This place wouldn't dream of doing such a thing," Langdon replied with a smile. "It's a church."

Fifty yards behind them, lurking among the crowd, the man with the skin rash and gold earring leaned on a wall, savoring this chance to catch his breath. His breathing was not getting any better, and the rash on his face was nearly impossible to ignore, especially the sensitive skin just above his eyes. He took off his Plume Paris glasses and gently rubbed his sleeve across his eye sockets, trying not to break the skin. When he replaced his glasses, he could see his quarry moving on. Forcing himself to follow, he continued after them, breathing as gently as possible.

———

Several blocks behind Langdon and Sienna, inside the Hall of the Five Hundred, Agent Brüder stood over the broken body of the all-too-familiar spike-haired woman who was now lying sprawled out on the floor. He knelt down and retrieved her handgun, carefully removing the clip for safety before handing it off to one of his men.

The pregnant museum administrator, Marta Alvarez, stood off to one side. She had just relayed to Brüder a brief but startling account of what had transpired with Robert Langdon since the previous night . . . including a single piece of information that Brüder was still trying to process.

Langdon claims to have amnesia.

Brüder pulled out his phone and dialed. The line at the other end rang three times before his boss answered, sounding distant and unsteady.

"Yes, Agent Brüder? Go ahead."

Brüder spoke slowly to ensure that his every word was understood. "We are still trying to locate Langdon and the girl, but there's been another development." Brüder paused. "And if it's true . . . it changes everything."

———

The provost paced his office, fighting the temptation to pour himself another Scotch, forcing himself to face this growing crisis head-on.

Never in his career had he betrayed a client or failed to keep an agreement, and he most certainly had no intention of starting now. At the same time he suspected that he might have gotten himself tangled up in a scenario whose purpose diverged from what he had originally imagined.

One year ago, the famous geneticist Bertrand Zobrist had come aboard **The Mendacium** and requested a safe haven in which to work. At that time the provost imagined that Zobrist was planning to develop a secret medical procedure whose patenting would increase Zobrist's vast fortune. It would not be the first time the Consortium had been hired by paranoid scientists and engineers who preferred working in extreme isolation to prevent their valuable ideas from being stolen.

With that in mind, the provost accepted the client and was not surprised when he learned that the people at the World Health Organization had begun searching for him. Nor did he give it a second thought when the director of the WHO herself—Dr. Elizabeth Sinskey—seemed to make it her personal mission to locate their client.

The Consortium has always faced powerful adversaries.

As agreed, the Consortium carried out their agreement with Zobrist, no questions asked, thwarting Sinskey's efforts to find him for the entire length of the scientist's contract.

Almost the entire length.

Less than a week before the contract was to expire, Sinskey had somehow located Zobrist in Florence and moved in, harassing and chasing him until he committed suicide. For the first time in his career, the provost had failed to provide the protection he had agreed to, and it haunted him . . . along with the bizarre circumstances of Zobrist's death.

He committed suicide . . . rather than being captured?

What the hell was Zobrist protecting?

In the aftermath of his death, Sinskey had confiscated an item from Zobrist's safe-deposit box, and now the Consortium was locked in a head-to-head battle with Sinskey in Florence—a high-stakes treasure hunt to find . . .

To find what?

The provost felt himself glance instinctively toward the bookshelf and the heavy tome given to him two weeks ago by the wild-eyed Zobrist.

The Divine Comedy.

The provost retrieved the book and carried it back to his desk, where he dropped it with a heavy thud.

With unsteady fingers, he opened the cover to the first page and again read the inscription.

My dear friend, thank you for helping me find the path.
The world thanks you, too.

First off, the provost thought, **you and I were never friends.**

He read the inscription three more times. Then he turned his eyes to the bright red circle his client had scrawled on his calendar, highlighting tomorrow's date.

The world thanks you?

He turned and gazed out at the horizon a long moment.

In the silence, he thought about the video and heard the voice of facilitator Knowlton from his earlier phone call. **I thought you might want to preview it before upload . . . the content is quite disturbing.**

The call still puzzled the provost. Knowlton was one of his best facilitators, and making such a request was entirely out of character. He knew better than to suggest an override of the compartmentalization protocol.

After replacing **The Divine Comedy** on the shelf, the provost walked to the Scotch bottle and poured himself half a glass.

He had a very difficult decision to make.

CHAPTER 52

Known as the Church of Dante, the sanctuary of Chiesa di Santa Margherita dei Cerchi is more of a chapel than a church. The tiny, one-room house of worship is a popular destination for devotees of Dante who revere it as the sacred ground on which transpired two pivotal moments in the great poet's life.

According to lore, it was here at this church, at the age of nine, that Dante first laid eyes on Beatrice Portinari—the woman with whom he fell in love at first sight, and for whom his heart ached his entire life. To Dante's great anguish, Beatrice married another man, and then died at the youthful age of twenty-four.

It was also in this church, some years later, that Dante married Gemma Donati—a woman who, even by the account of the great writer and poet Boccaccio, was a poor choice of wife for Dante. Despite having children, the couple showed little signs of affection for each other, and after Dante's exile, neither spouse seemed eager to see the other ever again.

The love of Dante's life had always been and would always remain the departed Beatrice Portinari, whom Dante had scarcely known, and yet whose memory was so overpowering for him that her ghost became the muse that inspired his greatest works.

Dante's celebrated volume of poetry **La Vita Nuova** overflows with flattering verses about "the blessed Beatrice." More worshipful still, **The Divine Comedy** casts Beatrice as none other than the savior who guides Dante through paradise. In both works, Dante longs for his unattainable lady.

Nowadays, the Church of Dante has become a shrine for the brokenhearted who suffer from unrequited love. The tomb of young Beatrice herself is inside the church, and her simple sepulchre has become a pilgrimage destination for both Dante fans and heartsick lovers alike.

This morning, as Langdon and Sienna wound their way through old Florence toward the church, the streets continued to narrow until they became little more than glorified pedestrian walkways. An occasional local car appeared, inching through the maze and forcing pedestrians to flatten themselves against the buildings as it passed.

"The church is just around the corner," Langdon told Sienna, hopeful that one of the tourists inside would be able to help them. He knew their chances of finding a good Samaritan were better now that Sienna had taken back her wig in exchange for Langdon's jacket, and both had reverted to their normal selves, transforming from rocker and skinhead . . . to college professor and clean-cut young woman.

Langdon was relieved once again to feel like himself.

As they strode into an even tighter alleyway—the Via del Presto—Langdon scanned the various doorways. The entrance of the church was always tricky to locate because the building itself was very small, unadorned, and wedged tightly between two other buildings. One could easily walk past it without even noticing. Oddly, it was often easier to locate this church using not one's eyes . . . but one's **ears**.

One of the peculiarities of La Chiesa di Santa Margherita dei Cerchi was that it hosted frequent concerts, and when no concert was scheduled, the church piped in recordings of those concerts so visitors could enjoy the music at any time.

As anticipated, as they advanced down the alleyway, Langdon began to hear the thin strains of recorded music, which grew steadily louder, until he and Sienna were standing before the inconspicuous entrance. The only indication that this was indeed the correct location was a tiny sign—the antithesis of the bright red banner at the Museo Casa di Dante—that humbly announced that this was the church of Dante and Beatrice.

When Langdon and Sienna stepped off the street into the dark confines of the church, the air grew cooler and the music grew louder. The interior was stark and simple . . . smaller than Langdon recalled. There was only a handful of tourists, mingling, writing in journals, sitting quietly in the pews enjoying the music, or examining the curious collection of artwork.

With the exception of the Madonna-themed altarpiece by Neri di Bicci, almost all of the original art in this chapel had been replaced with contemporary pieces representing the two celebrities—Dante and Beatrice—the reasons most visitors sought out this tiny chapel. Most of the paintings depicted Dante's longing gaze during his famous first encounter with Beatrice, during which the poet, by his own account, instantly fell in love. The paintings were of widely varying quality, and most, to Langdon's taste, seemed kitschy and out of place. In one such rendering, Dante's iconic red cap with earflaps looked like something Dante had stolen from Santa Claus. Nonetheless, the recurring theme of the poet's yearning gaze at his muse, Beatrice, left no doubt that this was a church of painful love—unfulfilled, unrequited, and unattained.

Langdon turned instinctively to his left and gazed upon the modest tomb of Beatrice Portinari. This was the primary reason people visited this church, although not so much to see the tomb itself as to see the famous object that sat beside it.

A wicker basket.

This morning, as always, the simple wicker basket sat beside Beatrice's tomb. And this morning, as always, it was overflowing with folded slips of paper—each a handwritten letter from a visitor, written to Beatrice herself.

Beatrice Portinari had become something of a patron saint of star-crossed lovers, and according to long-standing tradition, handwritten prayers to Beatrice could be deposited in the basket in the hope that she would intervene on the writer's behalf—perhaps inspiring someone to love them more, or helping them find their true love, or even giving them the strength to forget a love who had passed away.

Langdon, many years ago, while in the throes of researching a book on art history, had paused in this church to leave a note in the basket, entreating Dante's muse not to grant him true love, but to shed on him some of the inspiration that had enabled Dante to write his massive tome.

Sing in me, Muse, and through me tell the story . . .

The opening line of Homer's **Odyssey** had seemed a worthy supplication, and Langdon secretly believed his message had indeed sparked Beatrice's divine inspiration, for upon his return home, he had written the book with unusual ease.

"**Scusate!**" Sienna's voice boomed suddenly. "**Potete ascoltarmi tutti?**" Everyone?

Langdon spun to see Sienna loudly addressing the scattering of tourists, all of whom now glanced over at her, looking somewhat alarmed.

Sienna smiled sweetly at everyone and asked in Italian if anyone happened to have a copy of Dante's **Divine Comedy.** After some strange looks and shakes of the head, she tried the question in English, without any more success.

An older woman who was sweeping the altar hissed sharply at Sienna and held up a finger to her lips for silence.

Sienna turned back to Langdon and frowned, as if to say, "Now what?"

Sienna's calling-all-cars solicitation was not quite what Langdon had had in mind, but he had to admit he'd anticipated a better response than she'd received. On previous visits, Langdon had seen no shortage of tourists reading **The Divine Comedy** in this hallowed space, apparently enjoying a total immersion in the Dante experience.

Not so today.

Langdon set his sights on an elderly couple seated near the front of the church. The old man's bald head was dipped forward, chin to chest; clearly he was stealing a nap. The woman beside him seemed very much awake, with a pair of white earbud cables dangling from beneath her gray hair.

A glimmer of promise, Langdon thought, making his way up the aisle until he was even with the couple. As Langdon had hoped, the woman's telltale white earbuds snaked down to an iPhone in her lap. Sensing she was being watched, she looked up and pulled the earbuds from her ears.

Langdon had no idea what language the woman spoke, but the global proliferation of iPhones, iPads, and iPods had resulted in a vocabulary as universally understood as the male/female symbols that graced restrooms around the world.

"iPhone?" Langdon asked, admiring her device.

The old woman brightened at once, nodding proudly. "Such a clever little toy," she whispered in a British accent. "My son got it for me. I'm listening to my e-mail. Can you believe it—**listening** to my e-mail? This little treasure actually **reads** it for me. With my old eyes, it's such a help."

"I have one, too," Langdon said with a smile as he sat down beside her, careful not to wake up her sleeping husband. "But somehow I lost it last night."

"Oh, tragedy! Did you try the 'find your iPhone' feature? My son says—"

"Stupid me, I never activated that feature." Langdon gave her a sheepish look and ventured hesitantly, "If it's not too much of an intrusion, would you mind terribly if I borrowed yours for just a moment? I need to look up something online. It would be a big help to me."

"Of course!" She pulled out the earbuds and thrust the device into his hands. "No problem at all! Poor dear."

Langdon thanked her and took the phone. While she prattled on beside him about how terrible she would feel if she lost her iPhone, Langdon pulled up Google's search window and pressed the microphone button. When the phone beeped once, Langdon articulated his search string.

"Dante, **Divine Comedy**, **Paradise**, Canto Twenty-five."

The woman looked amazed, apparently having yet to learn about this feature. As the search results began to materialize on the tiny screen, Langdon stole a quick glance back at Sienna, who was thumbing through some printed material near the basket of letters to Beatrice.

Not far from where Sienna stood, a man in a necktie was kneeling in the shadows, praying intently, his head bowed low. Langdon couldn't see his face, but he felt a pang of sadness for the solitary man, who had probably lost his loved one and had come here for comfort.

Langdon returned his focus to the iPhone, and within seconds was able to pull up a link to a digital offering of **The Divine Comedy**—freely accessible because it was in the public domain. When the page opened precisely to Canto 25, he had to admit he was impressed with the technology. **I've got to stop being such a snob about leather-bound books,** he reminded himself. **E-books do have their moments.**

As the elderly woman looked on, showing a bit of concern and saying something about the high data rates for surfing the Internet abroad, Langdon sensed that his window of opportunity would be brief, and he focused intently on the Web page before him.

The text was small, but the dim lighting in the chapel made the illuminated screen more legible. Langdon was pleased to see he had randomly stumbled into the Mandelbaum translation—a popular modern rendition by the late American professor Allen Mandelbaum. For his dazzling translation, Mandelbaum had received Italy's highest honor, the Presidential Cross of the Order of the Star of Italian Solidarity. While admittedly less overtly poetic than Longfellow's version, Mandelbaum's translation tended to be far more comprehensible.

Today I'll take clarity over poesy, Langdon thought, hoping to quickly spot in the text a reference to a specific location in Florence—the location where Ignazio hid the Dante death mask.

The iPhone's tiny screen displayed only six lines of text at a time, and as Langdon began to read, he recalled the passage. In the opening of Canto 25, Dante referenced **The Divine Comedy** itself, the physical toll its writing had taken on him, and the aching hope that perhaps his heavenly poem could overcome the wolfish brutality of the exile that kept him from his fair Florence.

CANTO XXV

If it should happen . . . if this sacred poem—
this work so shared by heaven and by earth
that it has made me lean through these long
    years—
can ever overcome the cruelty
that bars me from the fair fold where I slept,
a lamb opposed to wolves that war on it . . .

While the passage was a reminder that fair Florence was the home for which Dante longed while writing **The Divine Comedy**, Langdon saw no reference to any specific location in the city.

"What do you know about data charges?" the woman interrupted, eyeing her iPhone with sudden concern. "I just remembered my son told me to be careful about Web surfing abroad."

Langdon assured her he would be only a minute and offered to reimburse her, but even so, he sensed she would never let him read all one hundred lines of Canto 25.

He quickly scrolled down to the next six lines and continued reading.

> By then with other voice, with other fleece,
> I shall return as poet and put on,
> at my baptismal font, the laurel crown;
> for there I first found entry to that faith
> which makes souls welcome unto God, and
>   then,
> for that faith, Peter garlanded my brow.

Langdon loosely recalled this passage, too—an oblique reference to a political deal offered to Dante by his enemies. According to history, the "wolves" who banished Dante from Florence had told him he could return to the city only if he agreed to endure a public shaming—that of standing before an entire congregation, alone at his baptismal font, wearing only sackcloth as an admission of his guilt.

In the passage Langdon had just read, Dante, having declined the deal, proclaims that if he ever returns to his baptismal font, he will be wearing not the sackcloth of a guilty man but the laurel crown of a poet.

Langdon raised his index finger to scroll farther, but the woman suddenly protested, holding out her hand for the iPhone, apparently having reconsidered her loan.

Langdon barely heard her. In the split second before he had touched the screen, his eye had glossed over a line of text . . . seeing it a second time.

I shall return as poet and put on,
at my baptismal font, the laurel crown;

Langdon stared at the words, sensing that in his eagerness to find mention of a specific location, he'd almost missed a glowing prospect in the very opening lines.

at my baptismal font . . .

Florence was home to one of the world's most celebrated baptismal fonts, which for more than seven hundred years had been used to purify and christen young Florentines—among them, Dante Alighieri.

Langdon immediately conjured an image of the building containing the font. It was a spectacular, octagonal edifice that in many ways was more heavenly than the Duomo itself. He now wondered if perhaps he'd read all he needed to read.

Could this building be the place Ignazio was referring to?

A ray of golden light blazed now in Langdon's mind as a beautiful image materialized—a spectacular set of bronze doors—radiant and glistening in the morning sun.

I know what Ignazio was trying to tell me!

Any lingering doubts evaporated an instant later when he realized that Ignazio Busoni was one of the **only** people in Florence who could possibly unlock those doors.

Robert, the gates are open to you, but you must hurry.

Langdon handed the iPhone back to the old woman and thanked her profusely.

He rushed over to Sienna and whispered excitedly, "I know what gates Ignazio was talking about! The **Gates of Paradise!**"

Sienna looked dubious. "The gates of paradise? Aren't those . . . in heaven?"

"Actually," Langdon said, giving her a wry smile and heading for the door, "if you know where to look, Florence **is** heaven."

CHAPTER 53

I shall return as poet . . . at my baptismal font.
Dante's words echoed repeatedly in Langdon's mind as he led Sienna northward along the narrow passageway known as Via dello Studio. Their destination lay ahead, and with every step Langdon was feeling more confident that they were on the right course and had left their pursuers behind.

The gates are open to you, but you must hurry.

As they neared the end of the chasmlike alleyway, Langdon could already hear the low thrum of activity ahead. Abruptly the cavern on either side of them gave way, spilling them out into a sprawling expanse.

The Piazza del Duomo.

This enormous plaza with its complex network of structures was the ancient religious center of Florence. More of a tourist center nowadays, the piazza was already bustling with tour buses and throngs of visitors crowding around Florence's famed cathedral.

Having arrived on the south side of the piazza, Langdon and Sienna were now facing the side of the cathedral with its dazzling exterior of green, pink, and white marble. As breathtaking in its size as it was in the artistry that had gone into its construction, the cathedral stretched off in both directions to seemingly impossible distances, its full length nearly equal to that of the Washington Monument laid on its side.

Despite its abandonment of traditional monochromatic stone filigree in favor of an unusually flamboyant mix of colors, the structure was pure Gothic—classic, robust, and enduring. Admittedly, Langdon, on his first trip to Florence, had found the architecture almost gaudy. On subsequent trips, however, he found himself studying the structure for hours at a time, strangely captivated by its unusual aesthetic effects, and finally appreciating its spectacular beauty.

Il Duomo—or, more formally, the Cathedral of Santa Maria del Fiore—in addition to providing a nickname for Ignazio Busoni, had long provided not only a spiritual heart to Florence but centuries of drama and intrigue. The building's volatile past ranged from long and vicious debates over Vasari's much-despised fresco of **The Last Judgment** on the dome's interior . . . to the hotly disputed competition to select the architect to finish the dome itself.

Filippo Brunelleschi had eventually secured the lucrative contract and completed the dome—the largest of its kind at the time—and to this day Brunelleschi himself can be seen in sculpture, seated outside the Palazzo dei Canonici, staring contentedly up at his masterpiece.

This morning, as Langdon raised his eyes skyward to the famed red-tiled dome that had been an architectural feat of its era, he recalled the time he had foolishly decided to ascend the dome only to discover that its narrow, tourist-crammed staircases were as distressing as any of the claustrophobic spaces he'd ever encountered. Even so, Langdon was grateful for the ordeal he'd endured while climbing "Brunelleschi's Dome," since it had encouraged him to read an entertaining Ross King book of the same name.

"Robert?" Sienna said. "Are you coming?"

Langdon lowered his gaze from the dome, realizing he had stopped in his tracks to admire the architecture. "Sorry about that."

They continued moving, hugging the perimeter of the square. The cathedral was on their right now, and Langdon noted that tourists were already flowing out of its side exits, checking the site off their to-see lists.

Up ahead rose the unmistakable shape of a campanile—the second of the three structures in the cathedral complex. Commonly known as Giotto's bell tower, the campanile left no doubt that it belonged with the cathedral beside it. Adorned in the identical pink, green, and white facing stones, the square spire climbed skyward to a dizzying height of nearly three hundred feet. Langdon had always found it amazing that this slender structure could remain standing all these centuries, through earthquakes and bad weather, especially knowing how top-heavy it was, with its apex belfry supporting more than twenty thousand pounds of bells.

Sienna walked briskly beside him, her eyes nervously scanning the skies beyond the campanile, clearly searching for the drone, but it was nowhere to be seen. The crowd was fairly dense, even at this early hour, and Langdon made a point of staying in the thick of it.

As they approached the campanile, they passed a line of caricature artists standing at their easels sketching garish cartoons of tourists—a teenage boy grinding on a skateboard, a horse-toothed girl wielding a lacrosse stick, a pair of honeymooners kissing on a unicorn. Langdon found it amusing somehow that this activity was permitted on the same sacred cobbles where Michelangelo had set up his own easel as a boy.

Continuing quickly around the base of Giotto's bell tower, Langdon and Sienna turned right, moving out across the open square directly in front of the cathedral. Here the crowds were thickest, with tourists from around the world aiming camera phones and video cameras upward at the colorful main facade.

Langdon barely glanced up, having already set his sights on a much smaller building that had just come into view. Positioned directly opposite the front entrance of the cathedral stood the third and final structure in the cathedral complex.

It was also Langdon's favorite.

The Baptistry of San Giovanni.

Adorned in the same polychromatic facing stones and striped pilasters as the cathedral, the baptistry distinguished itself from the larger building by its striking shape—a perfect octagon. Resembling a

layer cake, some had claimed, the eight-sided structure consisted of three distinct tiers that ascended to
a shallow white roof.

Langdon knew the octagonal shape had nothing to do with aesthetics and everything to do with
symbolism. In Christianity, the number eight represented rebirth and re-creation. The octagon served as
a visual reminder of the six days of God's creation of
heaven and earth, the one day of Sabbath, and the
eighth day, upon which Christians were "reborn" or
"re-created" through baptism. Octagons had become
a common shape for baptistries around the world.

While Langdon considered the baptistry one of
Florence's most striking buildings, he always found
the choice of its location a bit unfair. This baptistry,
nearly anywhere else on earth, would be the center
of attention. Here, however, in the shadow of its two
colossal siblings, the baptistry gave the impression of
being the runt of the litter.

Until you step inside, Langdon reminded himself, picturing the mind-boggling mosaic work of the
interior, which was so spectacular that early admirers
claimed the baptistry ceiling resembled heaven itself.
If you know where to look, Langdon had wryly told
Sienna, **Florence** is **heaven.**

For centuries, this eight-sided sanctuary had hosted
the baptisms of countless notable figures—Dante
among them.

I shall return as poet . . . at my baptismal font.

Because of his exile, Dante had never been permitted to return to this sacred site—the place of his

baptism—although Langdon felt a rising hope that Dante's death mask, through the unlikely series of events that had occurred last night, had finally found its way back in his stead.

The baptistry, Langdon thought. **This has to be where Ignazio hid the mask before he died.** He recalled Ignazio's desperate phone message, and for a chilling moment, Langdon pictured the corpulent man clutching his chest, lurching across the piazza into an alley, and making his final phone call after leaving the mask safely inside the baptistry.

The gates are open to you.

Langdon's eyes remained fixed on the baptistry as he and Sienna snaked through the crowd. Sienna was moving now with such nimble eagerness that Langdon nearly had to jog to keep up. Even at a distance, he could see the baptistry's massive main doors glistening in the sun.

Crafted of gilded bronze and over fifteen feet tall, the doors had taken Lorenzo Ghiberti more than twenty years to complete. They were adorned with ten intricate panels of delicate biblical figures of such quality that Giorgio Vasari had called the doors "undeniably perfect in every way and . . . the finest masterpiece ever created."

It had been Michelangelo, however, whose gushing testimonial had provided the doors with a nickname that endured even today. Michelangelo had proclaimed them so beautiful as to be fit for use . . . as the Gates of Paradise.

CHAPTER 54

The Bible in bronze, Langdon thought, admiring the beautiful doors before them.

Ghiberti's shimmering Gates of Paradise consisted of ten square panels, each depicting an important scene from the Old Testament. Ranging from the Garden of Eden to Moses to King Solomon's temple, Ghiberti's sculpted narrative unfolded across two vertical columns of five panels each.

The stunning array of individual scenes had spawned over the centuries something of a popularity contest among artists and art historians, with everyone from Botticelli to modern-day critics arguing their preference for "the finest panel." The winner, by general consensus, over the centuries had been Jacob and Esau—the central panel of the left-hand column—chosen allegedly for the impressive number of artistic methods used in its making. Langdon suspected, however, that the actual reason for the panel's dominance was that Ghiberti had chosen it on which to sign his name.

A few years earlier, Ignazio Busoni had proudly shown Langdon these doors, sheepishly admitting that after half a millennium of exposure to floods, vandalism, and air pollution, the gilded doors had been quietly swapped out for exact replicas, the originals now safely stored inside the Museo dell'Opera del Duomo for restoration. Langdon politely refrained from telling Busoni that he was well aware of the fact that they were admiring fakes, and that in actuality, these copies were the **second** set of "fake" Ghiberti doors Langdon had encountered—the first set quite by accident while he was researching the labyrinths at Grace Cathedral in San Francisco and discovered that replicas of Ghiberti's **Gates of Paradise** had served as the cathedral's front doors since the mid-twentieth century.

As Langdon stood before Ghiberti's masterpiece, his eye was drawn to the short informational placard mounted nearby, on which a simple phrase in Italian caught his attention, startling him.

La peste nera. The phrase meant "the Black Death." **My God**, Langdon thought, **it's everywhere I turn!** According to the placard, the doors had been commissioned as a "votive" offering to God—a show of gratitude that Florence had somehow survived the plague.

Langdon forced his eyes back to the **Gates of Paradise** while Ignazio's words echoed again in his mind. **The gates are open to you, but you must hurry.**

Despite Ignazio's promise, the **Gates of Paradise** were definitely closed, as they always were, except for rare religious holidays. Normally, tourists entered the baptistry from a different side, through the north door.

Sienna was on tiptoe beside him, trying to see

around the crowd. "There's no door handle," she said. "No keyhole. Nothing."

True, Langdon thought, knowing Ghiberti was not about to ruin his masterpiece with something as mundane as a doorknob. "The doors swing **in**. They lock from the inside."

Sienna thought a moment, pursing her lips. "So from out here . . . nobody would know if the doors were locked or not."

Langdon nodded. "I'm hoping that's precisely Ignazio's thinking."

He walked a few steps to his right and glanced around the north side of the building to a far less ornate door—the tourist entrance—where a bored-looking docent was smoking a cigarette and rebuffing inquiring tourists by pointing to the sign on the entrance: APERTURA 1300–1700.

It doesn't open for several hours, Langdon thought, pleased. **And nobody has been inside yet.**

Instinctively, he checked his wristwatch, and was again reminded that Mickey Mouse was gone.

When he returned to Sienna, she had been joined by a group of tourists who were taking photos through the simple iron fence that had been erected several feet in front of the **Gates of Paradise** to prevent tourists from getting too close to Ghiberti's masterwork.

This protective gate was made of black wrought iron topped with sun-ray spikes dipped in gold paint, and resembled the simple estate fencing that often enclosed suburban homes. Ambiguously, the informational placard describing the **Gates of Paradise** had been mounted not on the spectacular bronze doors themselves but on this very ordinary protective gate.

Langdon had heard that the placard's placement sometimes caused confusion among tourists, and sure enough, just then a chunky woman in a Juicy Couture sweat suit pushed through the crowd, glanced at the placard, frowned at the wrought-iron gate, and scoffed, "**Gates of Paradise**? Hell, it looks like my dog fence at home!" Then she toddled off before anyone could explain.

Sienna reached up and grasped the protective gate, casually peering through the bars at the locking mechanism on the back.

"Look," she whispered, turning wide-eyed to Langdon. "The padlock on the back is unlocked."

Langdon looked through the bars and saw she was right. The padlock was positioned as if it were locked, but on closer inspection, he could see that it was definitely unlocked.

The gates are open to you, but you must hurry.

Langdon raised his eyes to the **Gates of Paradise** beyond the fencing. If Ignazio had indeed left the baptistry's huge doors unbolted, they should simply swing open. The challenge, however, would be getting inside without drawing the attention of every single person in the square, including, no doubt, the police and Duomo guards.

"Look out!" a woman suddenly screamed nearby. "He's going to jump!" Her voice was filled with terror. "Up there on the bell tower!"

Langdon spun now from the doors, and saw that the woman shouting was . . . Sienna. She stood five yards away, pointing up into Giotto's bell tower and shouting, "There at the top! He's going to jump!"

Every set of eyes turned skyward, searching the top of the bell tower. Nearby, others began pointing, squinting, calling out to one another.

"Someone is jumping?!"

"Where?!"

"I don't see him!"

"Over there on the left?!"

It took only seconds for people across the square to sense the panic and follow suit, staring up at the top of the bell tower. With the fury of a wildfire consuming a parched hay field, the rush of fear billowed out across the piazza until the entire crowd was craning their necks, looking upward, and pointing.

Viral marketing, Langdon thought, knowing he'd have only a moment to act. Immediately he grabbed the wrought-iron fence and swung it open just as Sienna returned to his side and slipped with him into the small space beyond. Once the gate was closed behind them, they turned to face the fifteen-foot bronze doors. Hoping he had understood Ignazio correctly, Langdon threw his shoulder into one side of the massive double doors and drove his legs hard.

Nothing happened, and then, painfully slowly, the cumbersome section began to move. **The doors are open!** The **Gates of Paradise** swung open about one foot, and Sienna wasted no time turning sideways and slipping through. Langdon followed suit, inch-

ing sideways through the narrow opening into the
darkness of the baptistry.

Together, they turned and heaved the door in the
opposite direction, quickly closing the massive portal
with a definitive thud. Instantly, the noise and chaos
outside evaporated, leaving only silence.

Sienna pointed to a long wooden beam on the floor
at their feet, which clearly had been set in side brackets on either side of the door to serve as a barricade.
"Ignazio must have removed it for you," she said.

Together they lifted the beam and dropped it back
into its brackets, effectively locking the **Gates of Paradise** . . . and sealing themselves safely inside.

For a long moment Langdon and Sienna stood in
silence, leaning against the door and catching their
breath. Compared to the noises of the piazza outside,
the interior of the baptistry felt as peaceful as heaven
itself.

———

Outside the Baptistry of San Giovanni, the man
in the Plume Paris spectacles and a paisley necktie
moved through the crowd, ignoring the uneasy stares
of those who noticed his bloody rash.

He had just reached the bronze doors through
which Robert Langdon and his blond companion
had cleverly disappeared; even from outside, he had
heard the heavy thud of the doors being barred from
within.

No entry this way.

Slowly, the ambience in the piazza was returning to

normal. The tourists who had been staring upward in anticipation were now losing interest. **No jumper.** Everyone moved on.

The man was itchy again, his rash getting worse. Now his fingertips were swollen and cracking as well. He slid his hands into his pockets to keep himself from scratching. His chest continued to throb as he began circling the octagon in search of another entrance.

He had barely made it around the corner when he felt a sharp pain on his Adam's apple and realized he was scratching again.

CHAPTER 55

Legend proclaims that it is physically impossible, upon entering the Baptistry of San Giovanni, not to look up. Langdon, despite having been in this room many times, now felt the mystical pull of the space, and let his gaze climb skyward to the ceiling.

High, high overhead, the surface of the baptistry's octagonal vault spanned more than eighty feet from side to side. It glistened and shimmered as if it were made of smoldering coals. Its burnished amber-gold surface reflected the ambient light unevenly from more than a million **smalti** tiles—tiny ungrouted mosaic pieces hand-cut from a glassy silica glaze—which were arranged in six concentric rings in which scenes from the Bible were depicted.

Adding stark drama to the lustrous upper portion of the room, natural light pierced the dark space through a central oculus—much like the one in Rome's Pantheon—assisted by a series of high, small, deeply recessed windows that threw shafts of illumination that were so focused and tight that they seemed almost solid, like structural beams propped at ever-changing angles.

As Langdon walked with Sienna deeper into the

room, he took in the legendary ceiling mosaic—a multitiered representation of heaven and hell, very much like the depiction in **The Divine Comedy**.

Dante Alighieri saw this as a child, Langdon thought. **Inspiration from above.**

Langdon fixed his gaze now on the centerpiece of the mosaic. Hovering directly above the main altar rose a twenty-seven-foot-tall Jesus Christ, seated in judgment over the saved and the damned.

At Jesus' right hand, the righteous received the reward of everlasting life.

On His left hand, however, the sinful were stoned, roasted on spikes, and eaten by all manner of creatures.

Overseeing the torture was a colossal mosaic of Satan portrayed as an infernal, man-eating beast. Langdon always flinched when he saw this figure, which more than seven hundred years ago had stared down at the young Dante Alighieri, terrifying him and eventually inspiring his vivid portrayal of what lurked in the final ring of hell.

The frightening mosaic overhead depicted a horned devil that was in the process of consuming a human being headfirst. The victim's legs dangled from Satan's mouth in a way that resembled the flailing legs of the half-buried sinners in Dante's Malebolge.

Lo 'mperador del doloroso regno, Langdon thought, recalling Dante's text. **The emperor of the despondent kingdom.**

Slithering from the ears of Satan were two massive, writhing snakes, also in the process of consuming sinners, giving the impression that Satan had three heads, exactly as Dante described him in the final canto of his **Inferno**. Langdon searched his memory and recalled fragments of Dante's imagery.

On his head he had three faces . . . his three chins gushing a bloody froth . . . his three mouths used as grinders . . . gnashing sinners three at once.

That Satan's evil was threefold, Langdon knew, was fraught with symbolic meaning: it placed him in perfect balance with the threefold glory of the Holy Trinity.

As Langdon stared up at the horrific sight, he tried to imagine the effect the mosaic had on the youthful Dante, who had attended services at this church year after year, and seen Satan staring down at him each time he prayed. This morning, however, Langdon had the uneasy feeling that the devil was staring directly at **him**.

He quickly lowered his gaze to the baptistry's second-story balcony and standing gallery—the lone area from which women were permitted to view baptisms—and then down to the suspended tomb of Antipope John XXIII, his body lying in repose high on the wall like a cave dweller or a subject in a magician's levitation trick.

Finally, his gaze reached the ornately tiled floor, which many believed contained references to medieval astronomy. He let his eyes move across the intricate black-and-white patterns until they reached the very center of the room.

And there it is, he thought, knowing he was staring at the exact spot where Dante Alighieri had been baptized in the latter half of the thirteenth century. "'I shall return as poet . . . at my baptismal font,'" Langdon declared, his voice echoing through the empty space. "This is it."

Sienna looked troubled as she eyed the center of the floor, where Langdon was now pointing. "But . . . there's nothing here."

"Not anymore," Langdon replied.

All that remained was a large reddish-brown octagon of pavement. This unusually plain, eight-sided area clearly interrupted the pattern of the more ornately designed floor and resembled nothing so much as a large, patched-up hole, which, in fact, was precisely what it was.

Langdon quickly explained that the baptistry's original baptismal font had been a large octagonal pool located at the very center of this room. While modern fonts were usually raised basins, earlier fonts were more akin to the literal meaning of the word **font**—"springs" or "fountains"—in this case a deep pool of water into which participants could be more deeply immersed. Langdon wondered what this stone chamber had sounded like as children screamed in fear while being literally submerged in the large pool of icy water that once stood in the middle of the floor.

"Baptisms here were cold and scary," Langdon said. "True rites of passage. Dangerous even. Allegedly Dante once jumped into the font to save a drowning child. In any case, the original font was covered over at some point in the sixteenth century."

Sienna's eyes now began darting around the building with obvious concern. "But if Dante's baptismal font is gone . . . where did Ignazio hide the mask?!"

Langdon understood her alarm. There was no shortage of hiding places in this massive chamber— behind columns, statues, tombs, inside niches, at the altar, even upstairs.

Nonetheless, Langdon felt remarkably confident as he turned and faced the door through which they'd just entered. "We should start over there," he said, pointing to an area against the wall just to the right of the **Gates of Paradise.**

On a raised platform, behind a decorative gate, there sat a tall hexagonal plinth of carved marble, which resembled a small altar or service table. The exterior was so intricately carved that it resembled a mother-of-pearl cameo. Atop the marble base sat a polished wooden top with a diameter of about three feet.

Sienna looked uncertain as she followed Langdon over to it. As they ascended the steps and moved inside the protective gate, Sienna looked more closely and drew a startled breath, realizing what she was looking at.

Langdon smiled. **Exactly, it's not an altar or table.** The polished wooden top was in fact a lid—a covering for the hollow structure.

"A baptismal font?" she asked.

Langdon nodded. "If Dante were baptized today, it

would be in this basin right here." Wasting no time, he took a deep, purposeful breath and placed his palms on the wooden cover, feeling a tingle of antici- pation as he prepared to remove it.

Langdon tightly gripped the edges of the cover and heaved it to one side, carefully sliding the top off the marble base and placing it on the floor beside the font. Then he peered down into the two-foot-wide, dark, hollow space within.

The eerie sight made Langdon swallow hard.

From out of the shadows, the dead face of Dante Alighieri was looking back at him.

CHAPTER 56

*S*eek and ye shall find.

Langdon stood at the rim of the baptismal font and stared down at the pale yellow death mask, whose wrinkled countenance gazed blankly upward. The hooked nose and protruding chin were unmistakable.

Dante Alighieri.

The lifeless face was disturbing enough, and yet something about its position in the font seemed almost supernatural. For a moment Langdon was unsure what he was seeing.

Is the mask . . . hovering?

Langdon crouched lower, peering more closely at the scene before him. The font was several feet deep—more of a vertical well than a shallow basin—its steep walls dropping down to a hexagonal repository that was filled with water. Strangely, the mask seemed to be suspended partway down the font . . . perched just above the surface of the water as if by magic.

It took a moment for Langdon to realize what was causing the illusion. The font had a vertical central spindle that rose halfway up and flattened into a kind of small metal platter just above the water. The platter appeared to be a decorative fountainhead and perhaps a place to rest a baby's bottom, but it was currently serving as a pedestal on which the mask of Dante rested, elevated safely above the water.

Neither Langdon nor Sienna said a word as they stood side by side gazing down at the craggy face of Dante Alighieri, still sealed in his Ziploc bag, as if he'd been suffocated. For a moment the image of a face staring up out of a water-filled basin conjured for Langdon his own terrifying experience as a child, stuck at the bottom of a well, staring skyward in desperation.

Pushing the thought from his mind, he carefully reached down and gripped the mask on either side, where Dante's ears would have been. Although the face was small by modern standards, the ancient plaster was heavier than he'd expected. He slowly lifted the mask out of the font and held it up so that he and Sienna could examine it more closely.

Even viewed through the plastic bag, the mask was remarkably lifelike. Every wrinkle and blemish of the old poet's face had been captured by the wet plaster. With the exception of an old crack down the center of the mask, it was in perfect condition.

"Turn it over," Sienna whispered. "Let's see the back."

Langdon was already doing just that. The security video from the Palazzo Vecchio had clearly shown Langdon and Ignazio discovering something on the reverse side of the mask—something of such startling interest that the two men had essentially walked out of the palace with the artifact.

Taking exceptional care not to drop the fragile plaster, Langdon flipped the mask over and laid it face-down in his right palm so they could examine the back. Unlike the weathered, textured face of Dante, the inside of the mask was smooth and bare. Because the mask was never meant to be worn, its back side had been filled in with plaster to give some solidity to the delicate piece, resulting in a featureless, concave surface, like a shallow soup bowl.

Langdon didn't know what he had expected to find on the back of the mask, but it most certainly was not this.

Nothing.

Nothing at all.

Just a smooth, empty surface.

Sienna seemed equally confused. "It's blank plaster," she whispered. "If there's nothing here, what did you and Ignazio see?"

I have no idea, Langdon thought, pulling the plastic bag taut across the plaster for a clearer view. **There's nothing here!** With mounting distress, Langdon raised the mask into a shaft of light and studied it closely. As he tipped the object over for a better view, he thought for an instant that he might have glimpsed a faint discoloration near the top—a line of markings running horizontally across the inside of Dante's forehead.

A natural blemish? Or maybe . . . something else.
Langdon immediately spun and pointed to a hinged
panel of marble on the wall behind them. "Look in
there," he told Sienna. "See if there are towels."

Sienna looked skeptical, but obeyed, opening the
discreetly hidden cupboard, which contained three
items—a valve for controlling the water level in the
font, a light switch for controlling the spotlight above
the font, and . . . a stack of linen towels.

Sienna gave Langdon a surprised look, but Langdon had toured enough churches worldwide to know
that baptismal fonts almost always afforded their
priests easy access to emergency **swaddling cloths**—
the unpredictability of infants' bladders a universal
risk of christenings.

"Good," he said, eyeing the towels. "Hold the mask
a second?" He gently transferred the mask to Sienna's
hands and then set to work.

First, Langdon retrieved the hexagonal lid and
heaved it back up onto the font to restore the small,
altarlike table they had first seen. Then he grabbed
several of the linen towels from the cupboard and
spread them out like a tablecloth. Finally, he flipped
the font's light switch, and the spotlight directly overhead sprang to life, illuminating the baptismal area
and shining brightly down on the covered surface.

Sienna gently laid the mask on the font while
Langdon retrieved more towels, which he used like
oven mitts to slide the mask from the Ziploc bag,
careful not to touch it with his bare hands. Moments
later, Dante's death mask lay unsheathed and naked,

faceup beneath the bright light, like the head of an anesthetized patient on an operating table.

The mask's dramatic texturing appeared even more unsettling in the light, the creases and wrinkles of old age accentuated by the discolored plaster. Langdon wasted no time using his makeshift mitts to flip the mask over and lay it facedown.

The back side of the mask looked markedly less aged than the front—clean and white rather than dingy and yellow.

Sienna cocked her head, looking puzzled. "Does this side look **newer** to you?"

Admittedly, the color difference was more emphatic than Langdon would have imagined, but this side was most certainly the same age as the front. "Uneven aging," he said. "The back of the mask has been shielded by the display case so has never suffered the aging effects of sunlight." Langdon made a mental note to double the SPF of his sunscreen.

"Hold on," Sienna said, leaning in close to the mask. "Look! On the forehead! That must be what you and Ignazio saw."

Langdon's eyes moved quickly across the smooth white surface to the same discoloration he had spied earlier through the plastic—a faint line of markings that ran horizontally across the inside of Dante's forehead. Now, however, in the stark light, Langdon saw clearly that these markings were not a natural blemish . . . they were man-made.

"It's . . . writing," Sienna whispered, the words catching in her throat. "But . . ."

Langdon studied the inscription on the plaster. It was a single row of letters—handwritten in a florid script of faint brownish yellow.

"That's **all** it says?" Sienna said, sounding almost angry.

Langdon barely heard her. **Who wrote this?** he wondered. **Someone in Dante's era?** It seemed unlikely. If so, some art historian would have spotted it long ago during regular cleaning or restoration, and the writing would have become part of the lore of the mask. Langdon had never heard of it.

A far more likely source quickly materialized in his mind.

Bertrand Zobrist.

Zobrist was the mask's owner and therefore could easily have requested private access to it whenever he wanted. He could have written the text on the back of the mask fairly recently and then replaced it in the antique case without anyone ever knowing. **The mask's owner,** Marta had told them, **won't even permit our staff to open the case without him present.**

Langdon quickly explained his theory.

Sienna seemed to accept his logic, and yet the prospect clearly troubled her. "It makes no sense," she said, looking restless. "If we believe Zobrist secretly wrote something on the back of the Dante death mask, and he also went to the trouble to create that little projector to point to the mask . . . then why didn't he write something more **meaningful**? I mean, it's senseless! You and I have been looking all day for the mask, and **this** is all we find?"

Langdon redirected his focus to the text on the back of the mask. The handwritten message was very brief—only seven letters long—and admittedly looked entirely purposeless.

Sienna's frustration is certainly understandable.

Langdon, however, felt the familiar thrill of imminent revelation, having realized almost instantly that these seven letters would tell him everything he needed to know about what he and Sienna were to do next.

Furthermore, he had detected a faint odor to the mask—a familiar scent that divulged why the plaster on the back was so much whiter than the front . . . and the difference had nothing to do with aging or sunlight.

"I don't understand," Sienna said. "The letters are all the same."

Langdon nodded calmly as he studied the line of text—seven identical letters carefully inscribed in calligraphy across the inside of Dante's forehead.

PPPPPPP

"Seven **P**s," Sienna said. "What are we supposed to do with **this**?"

Langdon smiled calmly and raised his eyes to hers. "I suggest we do precisely what this message **tells** us to do."

Sienna stared. "Seven **P**s is . . . a **message**?"

"It is," he said with a grin. "And if you've studied Dante, it's a very clear one."

———

Outside the Baptistry of San Giovanni, the man with the necktie wiped his fingernails on his handkerchief and dabbed at the pustules on his neck. He tried to ignore the burning in his eyes as he squinted at his destination.

The tourist entrance.

Outside the door, a wearied docent in a blazer smoked a cigarette and redirected tourists who apparently couldn't decipher the building's schedule, which was written in international time.

APERTURA 1300–1700.

The man with the rash checked his watch. It was 10:02 A.M. The baptistry was closed for another few hours. He watched the docent for a while and then made up his mind. He removed the gold stud from his ear and pocketed it. Then he pulled out his wallet and checked its contents. In addition to assorted credit cards and a wad of euros, he was carrying over three thousand U.S. dollars in cash.

Thankfully, avarice was an international sin.

CHAPTER 57

Peccatum . . . Peccatum . . . Peccatum . . .

The seven Ps written on the back of Dante's death mask immediately pulled Langdon's thoughts back into the text of **The Divine Comedy**. For a moment he was back onstage in Vienna, presenting his lecture "Divine Dante: Symbols of Hell."

"We have now descended," his voice resounded over the speakers, "passing down through the nine rings of hell to the center of the earth, coming face-to-face with Satan himself."

Langdon moved from slide to slide through a series of three-headed Satans from various works of art—Botticelli's **Mappa**, the Florence baptistry's mosaic, and Andrea di Cione's terrifying black demon, its fur soiled with the crimson blood of its victims.

"Together," Langdon continued, "we have climbed down the shaggy chest of Satan, reversed direction as gravity shifted, and emerged from the gloomy underworld . . . once again to see the stars."

Langdon advanced slides until he reached an image he had shown earlier—the iconic Domenico di Michelino painting from inside the duomo, which depicted the red-robed Dante standing outside the walls of Florence. "And if you look carefully . . . you will see those stars."

Langdon pointed to the star-filled sky that arched above Dante's head. "As you see, the heavens are constructed in a series of nine concentric spheres around the earth. This nine-tiered structure of paradise is intended to reflect and balance the nine rings of the underworld. As you've probably noticed, the number nine is a recurring theme for Dante."

Langdon paused, taking a sip of water and letting the crowd catch their breath after their harrowing descent and final exit from hell.

"So, after enduring the horrors of the inferno, you must all be very excited to move toward paradise. Unfortunately, in the world of Dante, nothing is ever simple." He heaved a dramatic sigh. "To ascend to paradise we all must—both figuratively and literally—climb a mountain."

Langdon pointed to the Michelino painting. On the horizon, behind Dante, the audience could see a single cone-shaped mountain rising into the heavens. Spiraling up the mountain, a pathway circled the cone repeatedly—nine times—ascending in ever-tightening terraces toward the top. Along the pathway, naked figures trudged upward in misery, enduring various penances on the way.

"I give you Mount Purgatory," Langdon announced. "And sadly, this grueling, nine-ringed ascent is the only route from the depths of inferno to the glory of paradise. On this path, you can see the repentant souls ascending . . . each paying an appropriate price for a given sin. The envious must climb with their eyes sewn shut so they cannot covet; the prideful must carry huge stones on their backs to bend them low in a humble manner; the gluttonous must climb without food or water, thereby suffering excruciating hunger; and the lustful must ascend through hot flames to purge themselves of passion's heat." He paused. "But before you are permitted the great privilege of climbing this mountain and purging your sins, you must speak to this individual."

Langdon switched slides to a close-up of the Michelino painting, wherein a winged angel sat on a throne at the foot of Mount Purgatory. At the angel's feet, a line of penitent sinners awaited admittance to the upward path. Strangely, the angel was wielding a long sword, the point of which he seemed to be stabbing into the face of the first person in line.

"Who knows," Langdon called out, "what this angel is doing?"

"Stabbing someone in the head?" a voice ventured.

"Nope."

Another voice. "Stabbing someone in the eye?"

Langdon shook his head. "Anyone else?"

A voice way in the back spoke firmly. "Writing on his forehead."

Langdon smiled. "It appears someone back there knows his Dante." He motioned again to the painting. "I realize it looks like the angel is stabbing this poor fellow in the forehead, but he is not. According to Dante's text, the angel who guards purgatory uses the tip of his sword to write something on his visitors' foreheads before they enter. 'And what does he write?' you ask."

Langdon paused for effect. "Strangely, he writes a single letter . . . which is repeated seven times. Does anyone know what letter the angel writes seven times on Dante's forehead?"

"P!" shouted a voice in the crowd.

Langdon smiled. "Yes. The letter P. This P signifies **peccatum**—the Latin word for 'sin.' And the fact that it is written seven times is symbolic of the Septem Peccata Mortalia, also known as—"

"The Seven Deadly Sins!" someone else shouted.

"Bingo. And so, only by ascending through each level of purgatory can you atone for your sins. With each new level that you ascend, an angel cleanses one of the Ps from your forehead until you reach the top, arriving with your brow cleansed of the seven Ps . . . and your soul purged of all sin." He winked. "The place is called purgatory for a reason."

Langdon emerged from his thoughts to see Sienna staring at him over the baptismal font. "The seven Ps?" she said, pulling him back to the present and motioning down to Dante's death mask. "You say it's a message? Telling us what to do?"

Langdon quickly explained Dante's vision of Mount Purgatory, the Ps representing the Seven Deadly Sins, and the process of cleansing them from the forehead.

"Obviously," Langdon concluded, "Bertrand Zobrist, as the Dante fanatic that he was, would be familiar with the seven Ps and the process of cleansing them from the forehead as a means of moving forward toward paradise."

Sienna looked doubtful. "You think Bertrand Zobrist put those Ps on the mask because he wants us to . . . literally wipe them off the death mask? That's what you think we're supposed to do?"

"I realize it's—"

"Robert, even if we wipe off the letters, how does that help us?! We'll just end up with a totally blank mask."

"Maybe." Langdon offered a hopeful grin. "Maybe not. I think there's more there than meets the eye." He motioned down to the mask. "Remember how I told you that the back of the mask was lighter in color because of uneven aging?"

"Yes."

"I may have been wrong," he said. "The color difference seems too stark to be aging, and the texture of the back has teeth."

"Teeth?"

Langdon showed her that the texture on the back was far rougher than that of the front . . . and also far grittier, like sandpaper. "In the art world, this rough texture is called teeth, and painters prefer to paint on a surface that has teeth because the paint sticks to it better."

"I'm not following."

Langdon smiled. "Do you know what gesso is?"

"Sure, painters use it to prime canvases and—" She stopped short, his meaning apparently registering.

"Exactly," Langdon said. "They use gesso to create a clean white toothy surface, and sometimes to cover up unwanted paintings if they want to reuse a canvas."

Now Sienna looked excited. "And you think maybe Zobrist covered the back of the death mask with gesso?"

"It would explain the teeth and the lighter color. It also might explain why he would want us to wipe off the seven Ps."

Sienna looked puzzled by this last point.

"Smell this," Langdon said, raising the mask to her face like a priest offering Communion.

Sienna cringed. "Gesso smells like a wet dog?"

"Not all gesso. Regular gesso smells like chalk. Wet dog is acrylic gesso."

"Meaning . . . ?"

"Meaning it's water soluble."

Sienna cocked her head, and Langdon could sense the wheels turning. She shifted her gaze slowly to the mask and then suddenly back to Langdon, her eyes wide. "You think there's something under the gesso?"

"It would explain a lot."

Sienna immediately gripped the hexagonal wooden font covering and rotated it partway off, exposing the water below. She grabbed a fresh linen towel and plunged it into the baptismal water. Then she held out the dripping cloth for Langdon. "You should do it."

Langdon placed the mask facedown in his left palm and took the wet linen. Shaking out the excess water, he began dabbing the damp cloth on the inside of

Dante's forehead, moistening the area with the seven calligraphic Ps. After several dabs with his index finger, he redipped the cloth in the font and continued. The black ink began smearing.

"The gesso is dissolving," he said excitedly. "The ink is coming off with it."

As he performed the process a third time, Langdon began speaking in a pious and somber monotone, which resonated in the baptistry. "Through baptism, the Lord Jesus Christ has freed you from sin and brought you to new life through water and the Holy Spirit."

Sienna stared at Langdon like he'd lost his mind.

He shrugged. "It seemed appropriate."

She rolled her eyes and turned back to the mask. As Langdon continued applying water, the original plaster beneath the gesso became visible, its yellowish hue more in keeping with what Langdon would have expected from an artifact this old. When the last of the Ps had disappeared, he dried the area with a clean linen and held the mask up for Sienna to observe.

She gasped out loud.

Precisely as Langdon had anticipated, there was indeed something hidden beneath the gesso—a second layer of calligraphy—nine letters written directly onto the pale yellow surface of the original plaster.

This time, however, the letters formed a word.

CHAPTER 58

Possessed'?" Sienna demanded. "I don't understand."

I'm not sure I do either. Langdon studied the text that had materialized beneath the seven Ps—a single word emblazoned across the inside of Dante's forehead.

possessed

"As in . . . possessed by the devil?" Sienna asked.

Possibly. Langdon turned his gaze overhead to the mosaic of Satan consuming the wretched souls who had never been able to purge themselves of sin. **Dante . . . possessed?** It didn't seem to make much sense.

"There's got to be more," Sienna contended, taking the mask from Langdon's hands and studying it more closely. After a moment she began nodding. "Yes, look at the ends of the word . . . there's more text on either side."

Langdon looked again, now seeing the faint shadow of additional text showing through the moist gesso at either end of the word **possessed**.

Eagerly, Sienna grabbed the cloth and continued dabbing around the word until more text material- ized, written on a gentle curve.

O you possessed of sturdy intellect

Langdon let out a low whistle. "**'O, you possessed of sturdy intellect . . . observe the teachings hidden here . . . beneath the veil of verses so obscure.'**"

Sienna stared at him. "I'm sorry?"

"It's taken from one of the most famous stanzas of Dante's **Inferno**," Langdon said excitedly. "It's Dante urging his smartest readers to seek the wisdom hid- den within his cryptic verse."

Langdon often cited this exact line when teaching literary symbolism; the line was as close an example as existed to an author waving his arms wildly and shouting: "Hey, readers! There is a symbolic double meaning here!"

Sienna began rubbing the back of the mask, more vigorously now.

"Careful with that!" Langdon urged.

"You're right," Sienna announced, zealously wip- ing away gesso. "The rest of Dante's quote is here— just as you recalled it." She paused to dip the cloth back in the font and rinse it out.

Langdon looked on in dismay as the water in the baptismal font turned cloudy with dissolved gesso. **Our apologies to San Giovanni**, he thought, uneasy that this sacred font was being used as a sink.

When Sienna raised the cloth from the water, it was dripping. She barely wrung it out before placing the soggy cloth in the center of the mask and swishing it around as if she were cleaning a soup bowl.

"Sienna!" Langdon admonished. "That's an ancient—"

"The **whole** back side has text!" she announced as she scoured the inside of the mask. "And it's written in . . ." She paused, cocking her head to the left and rotating the mask to the right, as if trying to read sideways.

"Written in what?" Langdon demanded, unable to see.

Sienna finished cleaning the mask and dried it off with a fresh cloth. Then she set it down in front of him so they could both study the result.

When Langdon saw the inside of the mask, he did a double take. The entire concave surface was covered in text, what had to be nearly a hundred words. Beginning at the top with the line **O you possessed of sturdy intellect,** the text continued in a single, unbroken line . . . curling down the right side of the mask to the bottom, where it turned upside down and continued back across the bottom, returning up the left side of the mask to the beginning, where it repeated a similar path in a slightly smaller loop.

The path of the text was eerily reminiscent of Mount Purgatory's spiraling pathway to paradise. The symbologist in Langdon instantly identified the precise spiral. **Symmetrical clockwise Archimedean.** He had also noted that the number of revolutions from the first word, **O**, to the final period in the center was a familiar number.

Nine.

Barely breathing, Langdon turned the mask in slow circles, reading the text as it curled ever inward around the concave bowl, funneling toward the center.

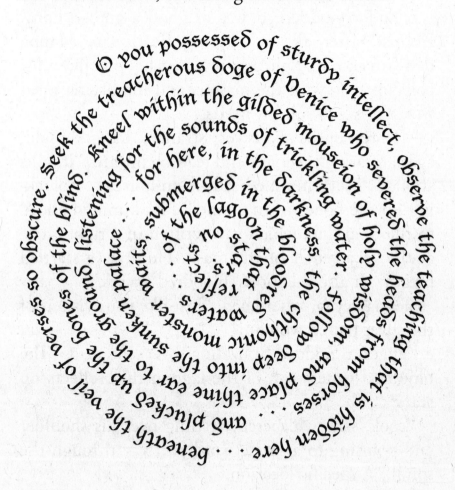

"The first stanza is Dante, almost verbatim," Langdon said. "'O you possessed of sturdy intellect, observe the teaching that is hidden here . . . beneath the veil of verses so obscure.'"

"And the rest?" Sienna pressed.

Langdon shook his head. "I don't think so. It's written in a similar verse pattern, but I don't recognize the text as Dante's. It looks like someone is imitating his style."

"Zobrist," Sienna whispered. "It **has** to be."

Langdon nodded. It was as good a guess as any. Zobrist, after all, by altering Botticelli's **Mappa dell'Inferno**, had already revealed his proclivity for collaborating with the masters and modifying great works of art to suit his needs.

"The rest of the text is very strange," Langdon said, again rotating the mask and reading inward. "It talks about . . . severing the heads from horses . . . plucking up the bones of the blind." He skimmed ahead to the final line, which was written in a tight circle at the very center of the mask. He drew a startled breath. "It also mentions 'bloodred waters.'"

Sienna's eyebrows arched. "Just like your visions of the silver-haired woman?"

Langdon nodded, puzzling over the text. **The bloodred waters . . . of the lagoon that reflects no stars?**

"Look," she whispered, reading over his shoulder and pointing to a single word partway through the spiral. "A specific location."

Langdon's eyes found the word, which he had skimmed over on his first pass. It was the name of one of the most spectacular and unique cities in the world. Langdon felt a chill, knowing it also happened to be the city in which Dante Alighieri famously became infected with the deadly disease that killed him.

Venice.

Langdon and Sienna studied the cryptic verses in silence for several moments. The poem was disturbing and macabre, and hard to decipher. Use of the words **doge** and **lagoon** confirmed for Langdon beyond any doubt that the poem was indeed referencing Venice—a unique Italian water-world city made up of hundreds of interconnected lagoons and ruled for centuries by a Venetian head of state known as a doge.

At a glance, Langdon could not discern exactly where in Venice this poem was pointing, but it definitely seemed to be urging the reader to follow its directions.

Place thine ear to the ground, listening for the sounds of trickling water.

"It's pointing underground," Sienna said, reading along with him.

Langdon gave an uneasy nod as he read the next line.

Follow deep into the sunken palace . . . for here, in the darkness, the chthonic monster waits.

"Robert?" Sienna asked uneasily. "What kind of monster?"

"Chthonic," Langdon replied. "The **c-h** is silent. It means 'dwelling beneath the earth.'"

Before Langdon could continue, the loud clunk of a dead bolt echoed across the baptistry. The tourist entrance had apparently just been unlocked from outside.

———

"**Grazie mille,**" said the man with the rash on his face. **A thousand thanks.**

The baptistry docent nodded nervously as he pocketed the five hundred dollars cash and glanced around to make sure nobody was watching.

"**Cinque minuti,**" the docent reminded, discreetly swinging open the unbolted door just wide enough for the man with the rash to slip inside. The docent closed the door, sealing the man inside and blocking out all sound from outside. **Five minutes.**

Initially the docent had refused to take pity on the man who claimed to have come all the way from America to pray at the Baptistry of San Giovanni in hopes of curing his terrible skin disease. Eventually, though, he had been inspired to become sympathetic, aided no doubt by an offer of five hundred dollars for five minutes alone in the baptistry . . . combined with the growing fear that this contagious-looking person would stand there beside him for the next three hours until the building opened.

Now, as he moved stealthily into the octagonal sanctuary, the man felt his eyes drawn reflexively upward. **Holy shit.** The ceiling was like nothing he'd ever seen. A three-headed demon stared down directly at him, and he quickly lowered his gaze to the floor.

The space appeared to be deserted.

Where the hell are they?

As the man scanned the room, his eyes fell on the main altar. It was a massive rectangular block of marble, set back in a niche, behind a barrier of stanchions and swags to keep spectators away.

The altar appeared to be the only hiding place in the entire room. Moreover, one of the swags was swinging slightly . . . as if it had just been disturbed.

———

Behind the altar, Langdon and Sienna crouched in silence. They had barely had time to collect the dirty towels and straighten the font cover before diving out of sight behind the main altar, with the death mask carefully in tow. The plan was to hide here until the room filled up with tourists, and then discreetly exit among the crowd.

The baptistry's north door had definitely just been opened—at least for a moment—because Langdon had heard sounds emanating from the piazza, but then just as abruptly, the door had been closed, and all had gone quiet again.

Now, back in the silence, Langdon heard a single set of footsteps moving across the stone floor.

A docent? Checking the room before opening it to tourists later today?

He had not had time to extinguish the spotlight over the baptismal font and wondered if the docent would notice. **Apparently not.** The footsteps were moving briskly in their direction, pausing just in front of the altar at the swag that Langdon and Sienna had just vaulted over.

There was a long silence.

"Robert, it's me," a man's voice said angrily. "I know you're back there. Get the hell out here and explain yourself."

CHAPTER 59

There's no point in pretending I'm not here.

Langdon motioned for Sienna to remain crouched safely out of sight, holding the Dante death mask, which he had resealed in the Ziploc bag.

Then, slowly, Langdon rose to his feet. Standing like a priest behind the altar of the baptistry, Langdon gazed out at his congregation of one. The stranger facing him had sandy-brown hair, designer glasses, and a terrible rash on his face and neck. He scratched nervously at his irritated neck, his swollen eyes flashing daggers of confusion and anger.

"You want to tell me what the hell you're doing, Robert?!" he demanded, stepping over the swag and advancing toward Langdon. His accent was American.

"Sure," Langdon replied politely. "But first, tell me who you are."

The man stopped short, looking incredulous. "What did you say?!"

Langdon sensed something vaguely familiar in the man's eyes . . . his voice, too, maybe. **I've met him . . . somehow, somewhere.** Langdon repeated his question calmly. "Please tell me who you are and how I know you."

The man threw up his hands in disbelief. "Jonathan Ferris? World Health Organization? The guy who flew to Harvard University and picked you up!?"

Langdon tried to process what he was hearing.

"Why haven't you called in?!" the man demanded, still scratching at his neck and cheeks, which looked red and blistered. "And who the hell is the woman I saw you come in here with?! Is **she** the one you're working for now?"

Sienna scrambled to her feet beside Langdon and immediately took charge. "Dr. Ferris? I'm Sienna Brooks. I'm also a doctor. I work here in Florence. Professor Langdon was shot in the head last night. He has retrograde amnesia, and he doesn't know who you are or what happened to him over the last two days. I'm here because I'm helping him."

As Sienna's words echoed through the empty baptistry, the man cocked his head, puzzled, as if her meaning had not quite registered. After a dazed beat, he staggered back a step, steadying himself on one of the stanchions.

"Oh . . . my God," he stammered. "That explains everything."

Langdon watched the anger drain from the man's face.

"Robert," the newcomer whispered, "we thought you had . . ." He shook his head as if trying to get the pieces to fall into place. "We thought you had switched sides . . . that maybe they had paid you off . . . or threatened you . . . We just didn't know!"

"I'm the only one he's spoken to," Sienna said. "All

he knows is he woke up last night in my hospital with people trying to kill him. Also, he's been having terrible visions—dead bodies, plague victims, and some woman with silver hair and a serpent amulet telling him—"

"Elizabeth!" the man blurted. "That's Dr. Elizabeth Sinskey! Robert, she's the person who recruited you to help us!"

"Well, if that's her," Sienna said, "I hope you know that she's in trouble. We saw her trapped in the back of a van full of soldiers, and she looked like she'd been drugged or something."

The man nodded slowly, closing his eyes. His eyelids looked puffy and red.

"What's wrong with your face?" Sienna demanded.

He opened his eyes. "I'm sorry?"

"Your skin? It looks like you contracted something. Are you ill?"

The man looked taken aback, and while Sienna's question was certainly blunt to the point of rudeness, Langdon had wondered the same thing. Considering the number of plague references he'd encountered today, the sight of red, blistering skin was unsettling.

"I'm fine," the man said. "It was the damned hotel soap. I'm deathly allergic to soy, and most of these perfumed Italian soaps are soy-based. Stupid me for not checking."

Sienna heaved a sigh of relief, her shoulders relaxing now. "Thank God you didn't eat it. Contact dermatitis beats anaphylactic shock."

They shared an awkward laugh.

"Tell me," Sienna ventured, "does the name Bertrand Zobrist mean anything to you?"

The man froze, looking as if he'd just come face-to-face with the three-headed devil.

"We believe we just found a message from him," Sienna said. "It points to someplace in Venice. Does that make any sense to you?"

The man's eyes were wild now. "Jesus, **yes**! Absolutely! Where is it pointing!?"

Sienna drew a breath, clearly prepared to tell this man everything about the spiraling poem she and Langdon had just discovered on the mask, but Langdon instinctively placed a quieting hand on hers. The man certainly appeared to be an ally, but after today's events, Langdon's gut told him to trust no one. Moreover, the man's tie rang a bell, and he sensed he might very well be the same man he had seen praying in the small Dante church earlier. **Was he following us?**

"How did you find us in here?" Langdon demanded.

The man still looked puzzled that Langdon was not recalling things. "Robert, you called me last night to say you had set up a meeting with a museum director named Ignazio Busoni. Then you disappeared. You never called in. When I heard Ignazio Busoni had been found dead, I got worried. I've been over here looking for you all morning. I saw the police activity outside the Palazzo Vecchio, and while waiting to find out what happened, by chance I saw **you** crawling out of a tiny door with . . ." He glanced over at Sienna, apparently drawing a blank.

"Sienna," she prompted. "Brooks."

"I'm sorry . . . with Dr. Brooks. I followed you hoping to learn what the hell you were doing."

"I saw you in the Cerchi church, praying, didn't I?"

"Yes! I was trying to figure out what you were doing, but it made no sense! You seemed to leave the church like a man on a mission, and so I followed you. When I saw you sneak into the baptistry, I decided it was time to confront you. I paid off the docent for a couple minutes alone in here."

"Gutsy move," Langdon noted, "if you thought I had turned on you."

The man shook his head. "Something told me you would never do that. Professor Robert Langdon? I knew there had to be some other explanation. But amnesia? Incredible. I never would have guessed."

The man with the rash began scratching nervously again. "Listen, I was given only five minutes. We need to get out of here, now. If I found you, then the people trying to kill you might find you, too. There is a lot going on that you don't understand. We need to get to Venice. **Immediately.** The trick will be getting out of Florence unseen. The people who have Dr. Sinskey . . . the ones chasing **you** . . . they have eyes everywhere." He motioned toward the door.

Langdon held his ground, finally feeling like he was about to get some answers. "Who are the soldiers in black suits? Why are they trying to kill me?"

"Long story," the man said. "I'll explain on the way."

Langdon frowned, not entirely liking this answer.

He motioned to Sienna and ushered her off to one side, talking to her in hushed tones. "Do you trust him? What do you think?"

Sienna looked at Langdon like he was crazy for asking. "What do I think? I think he's with the World Health Organization! I think he's our best bet for getting answers!"

"And the rash?"

Sienna shrugged. "It's exactly what he says—severe contact dermatitis."

"And if it's not what he says?" Langdon whispered. "If it's . . . something **else**?"

"Something **else**?" She gave him an incredulous look. "Robert, it's not the plague, if that's what you're asking. He's a doctor, for heaven's sake. If he had a deadly disease and knew he was contagious, he wouldn't be reckless enough to be out infecting the world."

"What if he didn't realize he had the plague?"

Sienna pursed her lips, thinking a moment. "Then I'm afraid you and I are already screwed . . . along with everyone in the general area."

"You know, your bedside manner could use some work."

"Just being honest." Sienna handed Langdon the Ziploc bag containing the death mask. "You can carry our little friend."

As the two returned to Dr. Ferris, they could see that he was just ending a quiet phone call.

"I just called my driver," the man said. "He'll meet us out in front by the—" Dr. Ferris stopped short, staring down at Langdon's hand and seeing, for the first time, the dead face of Dante Alighieri.

"Christ!" Ferris said, recoiling. "What the hell is that?!"

"Long story," Langdon replied. "I'll explain on the way."

CHAPTER 60

New York editor Jonas Faukman awoke to the sound of his home-office line ringing. He rolled over and checked the clock: 4:28 A.M. In the world of book publishing, late-night emergencies were as rare as overnight success. Unnerved, Faukman slipped out of bed and hurried down the hall into his office.

"Hello?" The voice on the line was a familiar deep baritone. "Jonas, thank heaven you're home. It's Robert. I hope I didn't wake you."

"Of course you woke me! It's four o'clock in the morning!"

"Sorry, I'm overseas."

They don't teach time zones at Harvard?

"I'm in some trouble, Jonas, and I need a favor." Langdon's voice sounded tense. "It involves your corporate NetJets card."

"NetJets?" Faukman gave an incredulous laugh. "Robert, we're in book publishing. We don't have access to private jets."

"We both know you're lying, my friend."

Faukman sighed. "Okay, let me rephrase that. We don't have access to private jets for authors of tomes about religious history. If you want to write **Fifty Shades of Iconography**, we can talk."

"Jonas, whatever the flight costs, I'll pay you back. You have my word. Have I ever broken a promise to you?"

Other than missing your last deadline by three years? Nevertheless Faukman sensed the urgency in Langdon's tone. "Tell me what's going on. I'll try to help."

"I don't have time to explain, but I really need you to do this for me. It's a matter of life and death."

Faukman had worked with Langdon long enough to be familiar with his wry sense of humor, but he heard no trace of joking in Langdon's anxious tone at that moment. **The man is dead serious.** Faukman exhaled, and made up his mind. **My finance manager is going to crucify me.** Thirty seconds later, Faukman had written down the details of Langdon's specific flight request.

"Is everything okay?" Langdon asked, apparently sensing his editor's hesitation and surprise over the details of the flight request.

"Yeah, I just thought you were in the States," Faukman said. "I'm surprised to learn you're in Italy."

"You and me both," Langdon said. "Thanks again, Jonas. I'm heading for the airport now."

———

NetJets' U.S. operations center is located in Columbus, Ohio, with a flight support team on call around the clock.

Owner services representative Deb Kier had just received a call from a corporate fractional owner in New York. "One moment, sir," she said, adjusting her headset and typing at her terminal. "Technically that would be a NetJets Europe flight, but I can help you with it." She quickly patched into the NetJets Europe system, centered in Paço de Arcos, Portugal, and checked the current positioning of their jets in and around Italy.

"Okay, sir," she said, "it looks like we have a Citation Excel positioned in Monaco, which we could have routed to Florence in just under an hour. Would that be adequate for Mr. Langdon?"

"Let's hope so," the man from the publishing company replied, sounding exhausted and a bit annoyed. "We do appreciate it."

"Entirely our pleasure," Deb said. "And Mr. Langdon would like to fly to Geneva?"

"Apparently."

Deb kept typing. "All set," she finally said. "Mr. Langdon is confirmed out of Tassignano FBO in Lucca, which is about fifty miles west of Florence. He will be departing at eleven-twenty A.M. local time. Mr. Langdon needs to be at the FBO ten minutes before wheels up. You've requested no ground transportation, no catering, and you've given me his passport information, so we're all set. Will there be anything else?"

"A new job?" he said with a laugh. "Thanks. You've been very helpful."

"Our pleasure. Have a nice night." Deb ended the

call and turned back to her screen to complete the reservation. She entered Robert Langdon's passport information and was about to continue when her screen began flashing a red alert box. Deb read the message, her eyes widening.

This must be a mistake.

She tried entering Langdon's passport again. The blinking warning came up again. This same alert would have shown up on any airline computer in the world had Langdon tried to book a flight.

Deb Kier stared a long moment in disbelief. She knew NetJets took customer privacy very seriously, and yet this alert trumped all of their corporate privacy regulations.

Deb Kier immediately called the authorities.

———

Agent Brüder snapped his mobile phone shut and began herding his men back into the vans.

"Langdon's on the move," he announced. "He's taking a private jet to Geneva. Wheels up in just under an hour out of Lucca FBO, fifty miles west. If we move, we can get there before he takes off."

———

At that same moment a hired Fiat sedan was racing northward along the Via dei Panzani, leaving the Piazza del Duomo behind and making its way toward Florence's Santa Maria Novella train station.

In the backseat, Langdon and Sienna huddled low while Dr. Ferris sat in front with the driver. The reservation with NetJets had been Sienna's idea. With luck, it would provide enough misdirection to allow the three of them to pass safely through the Florence train station, which undoubtedly would otherwise have been packed with police. Fortunately, Venice was only two hours away by train, and domestic train travel required no passport.

Langdon looked to Sienna, who seemed to be studying Dr. Ferris with concern. The man was in obvious pain, his breathing labored, as if it hurt every time he inhaled.

I hope she's right about his ailment, Langdon thought, eyeing the man's rash and picturing all the germs floating around in the cramped little car. Even his fingertips looked like they were puffy and red. Langdon pushed the concern from his mind and looked out the window.

As they approached the train station, they passed the Grand Hotel Baglioni, which often hosted events for an art conference Langdon attended every year. Seeing it, Langdon realized he was about to do something he had never before done in his life.

I'm leaving Florence without visiting the David.

With quiet apologies to Michelangelo, Langdon turned his eyes to the train station ahead . . . and his thoughts to Venice.

CHAPTER 61

Langdon's going to Geneva?

Dr. Elizabeth Sinskey felt increasingly ill as she rocked groggily in the backseat of the van, which was now racing out of Florence, heading west toward a private airfield outside of the city.

Geneva makes no sense, Sinskey told herself.

The only relevant connection to Geneva was that it was the site of the WHO's world headquarters. **Is Langdon looking for me there?** It seemed nonsensical considering that Langdon knew Sinskey was here in Florence.

Another thought now struck her.

My God . . . is Zobrist targeting Geneva?

Zobrist was a man who was attuned to symbolism, and creating a "ground zero" at the World Health Organization's headquarters admittedly had some elegance to it, considering his yearlong battle with Sinskey. Then again, if Zobrist was looking for a receptive flash point for a plague, Geneva was a poor choice. Relative to other metropolises, the city was geographically isolated and was rather cold this time of year. Most plagues took root in overcrowded, warmer environments. Geneva was more than a thousand feet above sea level, and hardly a suitable place to start a pandemic. **No matter how much Zobrist despises me.**

So the question remained—why was Langdon going there? The American professor's bizarre travel destination was yet another entry in the growing list of his inexplicable behaviors that began last night, and despite her best efforts, Sinskey was having a very hard time coming up with any rational explanation for them.

Whose side is he on?

Admittedly, Sinskey had known Langdon only a few days, but she was usually a good judge of character, and she refused to believe that a man like Robert Langdon could be seduced with money. **And yet, he broke contact with us last night.** Now he seemed to be running around like some kind of rogue operative. **Was he somehow persuaded to think that Zobrist's actions make some kind of twisted sense?**

The thought gave her a chill.

No, she assured herself. **I know his reputation too well; he's better than that.**

Sinskey had first met Robert Langdon four nights before in the gutted hull of a retasked C-130 transport plane, which served as the World Health Organization's mobile coordination center.

It had been just past seven when the plane landed at Hanscom Field, less than fifteen miles from Cambridge, Massachusetts. Sinskey was not sure what to expect from the celebrated academic whom she had contacted by phone, but she was pleasantly surprised when he strode confidently up the gangplank into the rear of the plane and greeted her with a carefree smile.

"Dr. Sinskey, I presume?" Langdon firmly shook her hand.

"Professor, it's an honor to meet you."

"The honor's mine. Thanks for all you do."

Langdon was a tall man, with urbane good looks and a deep voice. His clothing at the moment, Sinskey had to assume, was his classroom attire—a tweed jacket, khaki slacks, and loafers—which made sense considering the man had essentially been scooped off his campus with no warning. He also looked younger and far more fit than she'd imagined, which only served to remind Elizabeth of her own age. **I could almost be his mother.**

She gave him a tired smile. "Thank you for coming, Professor."

Langdon motioned to the humorless associate whom Sinskey had sent to collect him. "Your friend here didn't give me much chance to reconsider."

"Good. That's what I pay him for."

"Nice amulet," Langdon said, eyeing her necklace. "Lapis lazuli?"

Sinskey nodded and glanced down at her blue stone amulet, fashioned into the iconic symbol of a snake wrapped around a vertical rod. "The modern symbol for medicine. As I'm sure you know, it's called a caduceus."

Langdon glanced up suddenly, as if there was something he wanted to say.

She waited. **Yes?**

Apparently thinking better of his impulse, he gave a polite smile and changed the subject. "So why am I here?"

Elizabeth motioned to a makeshift conference area around a stainless-steel table. "Please, sit. I have something I need you to look at."

Langdon ambled toward the table, and Elizabeth noted that while the professor seemed intrigued by the prospect of a secret meeting, he did not appear at all unsettled by it. **Here is a man comfortable in his own skin.** She wondered if he would appear as relaxed once he found out why he had been brought here.

Elizabeth got Langdon settled and then, with no preamble, she presented the object she and her team had confiscated from a Florence safe-deposit box less than twelve hours earlier.

Langdon studied the small carved cylinder for a long moment before giving her a quick synopsis of what she already knew. The object was an ancient cylinder seal that could be used for printmaking. It bore a particularly gruesome image of a three-headed Satan along with a single word: **saligia**.

"Saligia," Langdon said, "is a Latin mnemonic for—"

"The Seven Deadly Sins," Elizabeth said. "Yes, we looked it up."

"Okay . . ." Langdon sounded puzzled. "Is there some reason you wanted me to look at this?"

"Actually, yes." Sinskey took the cylinder back and began shaking it violently, the agitator ball rattling back and forth.

Langdon looked puzzled by her action, but before he could ask what she was doing, the end of the cylinder began to glow, and she pointed it at a smooth patch of insulation on the wall of the gutted plane.

Langdon let out a low whistle and moved toward the projected image.

"Botticelli's **Map of Hell**," Langdon announced. "Based on Dante's **Inferno**. Although I'm guessing you probably already know that."

Elizabeth nodded. She and her team had used the Internet to identify the painting, which Sinskey had been surprised to learn was a Botticelli, a painter best known for his bright, idealized masterpieces **Birth of Venus** and **Springtime**. Sinskey loved both of those works despite the fact that they portrayed fertility and the creation of life, which only served to remind her of her own tragic inability to conceive—the lone significant regret in her otherwise very productive life.

"I was hoping," Sinskey said, "that you could tell me about the symbolism hidden in this painting."

Langdon looked irritated for the first time all night. "Is that why you called me in? I thought you said it was an emergency."

"Humor me."

Langdon heaved a patient sigh. "Dr. Sinskey, generally speaking, if you want to know about a specific painting, you should contact the museum that contains the original. In this case, that would be the Vatican's Biblioteca Apostolica. The Vatican has a number of superb iconographers who—"

"The Vatican hates me."

Langdon gave her a startled look. "You, too? I thought I was the only one."

She smiled sadly. "The WHO feels strongly that the widespread availability of contraception is one of the keys to global health—both to combat sexually transmitted diseases like AIDS and also for general population control."

"And the Vatican feels differently."

"Quite. They have spent enormous amounts of energy and money indoctrinating third-world countries into a belief in the evils of contraception."

"Ah, yes," Langdon said with a knowing smile. "Who better than a bunch of celibate male octogenarians to tell the world how to have sex?"

Sinskey was liking the professor more and more every second.

She shook the cylinder to recharge it and then projected the image on the wall again. "Professor, take a closer look."

Langdon walked toward the image, studying it, still moving closer. Suddenly he stopped short. "That's strange. It's been altered."

That didn't take him long. "Yes, it has, and I want you to tell me what the alterations mean."

Langdon fell silent, scanning the entire image, pausing to take in the ten letters that spelled **catrovacer** . . . and then the plague mask . . . and also the strange quote around the border about "the eyes of death."

"Who did this?" Langdon demanded. "Where did it come from?"

"Actually, the less you know right now the better. What I'm hoping is that you'll be able to analyze these alterations and tell us what they mean." She motioned to a desk in the corner.

"Here? Right now?"

She nodded. "I know it's an imposition, but I can't stress enough how important this is to us." She paused. "It could well be a matter of life and death."

Langdon studied her with concern. "Deciphering this may take a while, but I suppose if it's that important to you—"

"Thank you," Sinskey interjected before he could change his mind. "Is there anyone you need to call?"

Langdon shook his head and told her he had been planning on a quiet weekend alone.

Perfect. Sinskey got him settled at his desk with the projector, paper, pencil, and a laptop with a secure satellite connection. Langdon looked deeply puzzled about why the WHO would be interested in a modified painting by Botticelli, but he dutifully set to work.

Dr. Sinskey imagined he might end up studying the image for hours with no breakthrough, and so she settled in to get some work of her own done. From time to time she could hear him shaking the projector and scribbling on his notepad. Barely ten minutes had passed when Langdon set down his pencil and announced, **"Cerca trova."**

Sinskey glanced over. "What?"

"**Cerca trova,**" he repeated. "Seek and ye shall find. That's what this code says."

Sinskey hurried over and sat down close beside him, listening with fascination as Langdon explained how the levels of Dante's inferno had been scrambled, and that, when they were replaced in their proper sequence, they spelled the Italian phrase **cerca trova.**

Seek and find? Sinskey wondered. **That's this lunatic's message to me?** The phrase sounded like a direct challenge. The disturbing memory of the madman's final words to her during their meeting at the Council on Foreign Relations replayed in her mind: **Then it appears our dance has begun.**

"You just went white," Langdon said, studying her thoughtfully. "I take it this is not the message you were hoping for?"

Sinskey gathered herself, straightening the amulet on her neck. "Not exactly. Tell me . . . do you believe this map of hell is suggesting I **seek** something?"

"Yes. **Cerca trova.**"

"And does it suggest **where** I seek?"

Langdon stroked his chin as other WHO staff began gathering around, looking eager for information. "Not overtly . . . no, although I've got a pretty good idea where you'll want to start."

"Tell me," Sinskey demanded, more forcefully than Langdon would have expected.

"Well, how do you feel about Florence, Italy?"

Sinskey set her jaw, doing her best not to react.

Her staff members, however, were less controlled. All of them exchanged startled glances. One grabbed a phone and placed a call. Another hurried through a door toward the front of the plane.

Langdon looked bewildered. "Was it something I said?"

Absolutely, Sinskey thought. "What makes you say Florence?"

"**Cerca trova,**" he replied, quickly recounting a long-standing mystery involving a Vasari fresco at the Palazzo Vecchio.

Florence it is, Sinskey thought, having heard enough. Obviously, it could not be mere coincidence that her nemesis had jumped to his death not more than three blocks from the Palazzo Vecchio in Florence.

"Professor," she said, "when I showed you my amulet earlier and called it a caduceus, you paused, as if you wanted to say something, but then you hesitated and seemed to change your mind. What were you going to say?"

Langdon shook his head. "Nothing. It's foolish. Sometimes the professor in me can be a little overbearing."

Sinskey stared into his eyes. "I ask because I need to know I can trust you. What were you going to say?"

Langdon swallowed and cleared his throat. "Not that it matters, but you said your amulet is the ancient symbol of medicine, which is correct. But when you called it a caduceus, you made a very common mistake. The caduceus has two snakes on the staff and wings at the top. Your amulet has a single snake and no wings. Your symbol is called—"

"The Rod of Asclepius."

Langdon cocked his head in surprise. "Yes. Exactly."

"I know. I was testing your truthfulness."

"I'm sorry?"

"I was curious to know if you would tell me the truth, no matter how uncomfortable it might make me."

"Sounds like I failed."

"Don't do it again. Total honesty is the only way you and I will be able to work together on this."

"Work together? Aren't we done here?"

"No, Professor, we're not done. I need you to come to Florence to help me find something."

Langdon stared in disbelief. "Tonight?"

"I'm afraid so. I have yet to tell you about the truly critical nature of this situation."

Langdon shook his head. "It doesn't matter what you tell me. I don't want to fly to Florence."

"Neither do I," she said grimly. "But unfortunately our time is running out."

CHAPTER 62

T he noon sun glinted off the sleek roof of Italy's high-velocity Frecciargento train as it raced northward, cutting a graceful arc across the Tuscan countryside. Despite traveling away from Florence at 174 miles per hour, the "silver arrow" train made almost no noise, its soft repetitive clicking and gently swaying motion having an almost soothing effect on those who rode it.

For Robert Langdon, the last hour had been a blur.

Now, aboard the high-speed train, Langdon, Sienna, and Dr. Ferris were seated in one of the Frecciargento's private **salottini**—a small, executive-class berth with four leather seats and a foldout table. Ferris had rented the entire cabin using his credit card, along with an assortment of sandwiches and mineral water, which Langdon and Sienna had ravenously consumed after cleaning up in the restroom next to their private berth.

As the three of them settled in for the two-hour train ride to Venice, Dr. Ferris immediately turned his gaze to the Dante death mask, which sat on the table between them in its Ziploc bag. "We need to figure out precisely where in Venice this mask is leading us."

"And quickly," Sienna added, urgency in her voice. "It's probably our only hope of preventing Zobrist's plague."

"Hold on," Langdon said, placing a defensive hand atop the mask. "You promised that once we were safely aboard this train you would give me some answers about the last few days. So far, all I know is that the WHO recruited me in Cambridge to help decipher Zobrist's version of **La Mappa**. Other than that, you've told me nothing."

Dr. Ferris shifted uncomfortably and began scratching again at the rash on his face and neck. "I can see you're frustrated," he said. "I'm sure it's unsettling not to remember what happened, but medically speaking . . ." He glanced over at Sienna for confirmation and then continued. "I strongly recommend you not expend energy trying to recall specifics you can't remember. With amnesia victims, it's best just to let the forgotten past remain forgotten."

"Let it be?!" Langdon felt his anger rising. "The hell with that! I need some answers! Your organization brought me to Italy, where I was shot and lost several days of my life! I want to know how it happened!"

"Robert," Sienna intervened, speaking softly in a clear attempt to calm him down. "Dr. Ferris is right. It definitely would not be healthy for you to be overwhelmed by a deluge of information all at once. Think about the tiny snippets you **do** remember—the silver-haired woman, 'seek and find,' the writhing bodies from **La Mappa**—those images flooded into your mind in a series of jumbled, uncontrollable flashbacks that left you nearly incapacitated. If Dr. Ferris starts recounting the past few days, he will almost certainly dislodge other memories, and your hallucinations could start all over again. Retrograde amnesia is a serious condition. Triggering misplaced memories can be extremely disruptive to the psyche."

The thought had not occurred to Langdon.

"You must feel quite disoriented," Ferris added, "but at the moment we need your psyche intact so we can move forward. It's imperative that we figure out what this mask is trying to tell us."

Sienna nodded.

The doctors, Langdon noted silently, seemed to agree.

Langdon sat quietly, trying to overcome his feelings of uncertainty. It was a strange sensation to meet a total stranger and realize you had actually known him for several days. **Then again**, Langdon thought, **there is something vaguely familiar about his eyes.**

"Professor," Ferris said sympathetically, "I can see that you're not sure you trust me, and this is understandable considering all you've been through. One of the common side effects of amnesia is mild paranoia and distrust."

That makes sense, Langdon thought, **considering I can't even trust my own mind.**

"Speaking of paranoia," Sienna joked, clearly trying to lighten the mood, "Robert saw your rash and thought you'd been stricken with the Black Plague."

Ferris's puffy eyes widened, and he laughed out loud. "This rash? Believe me, Professor, if I had the plague, I would not be treating it with an over-the-counter antihistamine." He pulled a small tube of medicine from his pocket and tossed it to Langdon. Sure enough, it was a half-empty tube of anti-itch cream for allergic reactions.

"Sorry about that," Langdon said, feeling foolish. "Long day."

"No worries," Ferris said.

Langdon turned toward the window, watching the muted hues of the Italian countryside blur together in a peaceful collage. The vineyards and farms were becoming scarcer now as the flatlands gave way to the foothills of the Apennines. Soon the train would navigate the sinuous mountain pass and then descend again, powering eastward toward the Adriatic Sea.

I'm headed for Venice, he thought. **To look for a plague.**

This strange day had left Langdon feeling as if he were moving through a landscape composed of nothing but vague shapes with no particular details. Like a dream. Ironically, nightmares usually woke people up . . . but Langdon felt as if he had awoken **into** one.

"Lira for your thoughts," Sienna whispered beside him.

Langdon glanced up, smiling wearily. "I keep thinking I'll wake up at home and discover this was all a bad dream."

Sienna cocked her head, looking demure. "You wouldn't miss me if you woke up and found out I wasn't real?"

Langdon had to grin. "Yes, actually, I **would** miss you a little."

She patted his knee. "Stop daydreaming, Professor, and get to work."

Langdon reluctantly turned his eyes to the crinkled face of Dante Alighieri, which stared blankly up from the table before him. Gently, Langdon picked up the plaster mask and turned it over in his hands, gazing down into the concave interior at the first line of spiral text:

O you possessed of sturdy intellect . . .

Langdon doubted he qualified at the moment. Nonetheless, he set to work.

———

Two hundred miles ahead of the speeding train, **The Mendacium** remained anchored in the Adriatic. Belowdecks, facilitator Laurence Knowlton heard the soft rap of knuckles on his glass cubicle and touched a button beneath his desk, turning the opaque wall into a transparent one. Outside, a small, tanned form materialized.

The provost.

He looked grim.

Without a word, he entered, locked the cubicle door, and threw the switch that turned the glass room opaque again. He smelled of alcohol.

"The video that Zobrist left us," the provost said.

"Yes, sir?"

"I want to see it. Now."

CHAPTER 63

Robert Langdon had now finished transcribing the spiral text from the death mask onto paper so they could analyze it more closely. Sienna and Dr. Ferris huddled in close to help, and Langdon did his best to ignore Ferris's ongoing scratching and labored breathing.

He's fine, Langdon told himself, forcing his attention to the verse before him.

O you possessed of sturdy intellect,
observe the teaching that is hidden
  here . . .
beneath the veil of verses so obscure.

"As I mentioned earlier," Langdon began, "the opening stanza of Zobrist's poem is taken verbatim from Dante's **Inferno**—an admonition to the reader that the words carry a deeper meaning."

Dante's allegorical work was so replete with veiled commentary on religion, politics, and philosophy that Langdon often suggested to his students that the Italian poet be studied much as one might study the Bible—reading between the lines in an effort to understand the deeper meaning.

"Scholars of medieval allegory," Langdon continued, "generally divide their analyses into two categories—'text' and 'image' . . . text being the literal content of the work, and image being the symbolic message."

"Okay," Ferris said eagerly. "So the fact that the poem begins with this line—"

"Suggests," Sienna interjected, "that our superficial reading may reveal only part of the story. The true meaning may be hidden."

"Something like that, yes." Langdon returned his gaze to the text and continued reading aloud.

Seek the treacherous doge of Venice
who severed the heads from horses . . .
and plucked up the bones of the blind.

"Well," Langdon said, "I'm not sure about headless horses and the bones of the blind, but it sounds like we're supposed to locate a specific doge."

"I assume . . . a doge's grave?" Sienna asked.

"Or a statue or portrait?" Langdon replied. "There haven't been doges for centuries."

The doges of Venice were similar to the dukes of the other Italian city-states, and more than a hundred of them had ruled Venice over the course of a thousand years, beginning in A.D. 697. Their lineage had ended in the late eighteenth century with Napoleon's conquest, but their glory and power still remain subjects of intense fascination for historians.

"As you may know," Langdon said, "Venice's two

most popular tourist attractions—the Doge's Palace and St. Mark's Basilica—were built by the doges, for the doges. Many of them are buried right there."

"And do you know," Sienna asked, eyeing the poem, "if there was a doge who was considered to be particularly dangerous?"

Langdon glanced down at the line in question. **Seek the treacherous doge of Venice.** "None that I know of, but the poem doesn't use the word 'dangerous'; it uses the word 'treacherous.' There's a difference, at least in the world of Dante. Treachery is one of the Seven Deadly Sins—the worst of them, actually—punished in the ninth and final ring of hell."

Treachery, as defined by Dante, was the act of betraying a loved one. History's most notorious example of the sin had been Judas's betrayal of his beloved Jesus, an act Dante considered so vile that he had Judas banished to the inferno's innermost core—a region named Judecca, after its most dishonorable resident.

"Okay," Ferris said, "so we're looking for a doge who committed an act of treachery."

Sienna nodded her agreement. "That will help us limit the list of possibilities." She paused, eyeing the text. "But this next line . . . a doge who 'severed the heads from horses'?" She raised her eyes to Langdon. "Is there a doge who cut off horses' heads?"

The image Sienna evoked in his mind reminded Langdon of the gruesome scene from **The Godfather.** "Doesn't ring a bell. But according to this, he also 'plucked up the bones of the blind.'" He glanced over at Ferris. "Your phone has Internet, right?"

Ferris quickly pulled out his phone and held up his swollen, rashy fingertips. "The buttons might be difficult for me to manage."

"I've got it," Sienna said, taking his phone. "I'll run a search for Venetian doges, cross-referenced with headless horses and the bones of the blind." She began typing rapidly on the tiny keyboard.

Langdon skimmed the poem another time, and then continued reading aloud.

Kneel within the gilded **mouseion** of
   holy wisdom,
and place thine ear to the ground,
listening for the sounds of trickling
   water.

"I've never heard of a **mouseion**," Ferris said.

"It's an ancient word meaning a temple protected by muses," Langdon replied. "In the days of the early Greeks, a **mouseion** was a place where the enlightened gathered to share ideas, and discuss literature, music, and art. The first mouseion was built by Ptolemy at the Library of Alexandria centuries before the birth of Christ, and then hundreds more cropped up around the world."

"Dr. Brooks," Ferris said, glancing hopefully at Sienna. "Can you look and see if there's a mouseion in Venice?"

"Actually there are dozens of them," Langdon said with a playful smile. "Now they're called museums."

"Ahhh . . ." Ferris replied. "I guess we'll have to cast a wider net."

Sienna kept typing into the phone, having no trouble multitasking as she calmly took inventory. "Okay, so we're looking for a museum where we can find a doge who severed the heads from horses and plucked up the bones of the blind. Robert, is there a particular museum that might be a good place to look?"

Langdon was already considering all of Venice's best-known museums—the Gallerie dell'Accademia, the Ca' Rezzonico, the Palazzo Grassi, the Peggy Guggenheim Collection, the Museo Correr—but none of them seemed to fit the description.

He glanced back at the text.

*Kneel within the gilded **mouseion** of holy wisdom . . .*

Langdon smiled wryly. "Venice does have one museum that perfectly qualifies as a 'gilded mouseion of holy wisdom.'"

Both Ferris and Sienna looked at him expectantly.

"St. Mark's Basilica," he declared. "The largest church in Venice."

Ferris looked uncertain. "The church is a museum?"

Langdon nodded. "Much like the Vatican Museum. And what's more, the interior of St. Mark's is famous for being adorned, in its entirety, in solid gold tiles."

"A **gilded mouseion**," Sienna said, sounding genuinely excited.

Langdon nodded, having no doubt that St. Mark's was the gilded temple referenced in the poem. For centuries, the Venetians had called St. Mark's La Chiesa d'Oro—the Church of Gold—and Langdon considered its interior the most dazzling of any church in the world.

"The poem says to 'kneel' there," Ferris added. "And a church is a logical place to kneel."

Sienna was typing furiously again. "I'll add St. Mark's to the search. That must be where we need to look for the doge."

Langdon knew they would find no shortage of doges in St. Mark's—which was, quite literally, the basilica of the doges. He felt encouraged as he returned his eyes to the poem.

Kneel within the gilded *mouseion* of
    holy wisdom,
and place thine ear to the ground,
listening for the sounds of trickling
    water.

Trickling water? Langdon wondered. **Is there water under St. Mark's?** The question, he realized, was foolish. There was water under the entire city. Every building in Venice was slowly sinking and leaking. Langdon pictured the basilica and tried to imagine where inside one might kneel to listen for trickling water. **And once we hear it . . . what do we do?**

Langdon returned to the poem and finished reading aloud.

Follow deep into the sunken palace . . .
for here, in the darkness, the chthonic
*   monster waits,*
submerged in the bloodred waters . . .
of the lagoon that reflects no stars.

"Okay," Langdon said, disturbed by the image, "apparently, we follow the sounds of trickling water . . . to some kind of sunken palace."

Ferris scratched at his face, looking unnerved. "What's a chthonic monster?"

"Subterranean," Sienna offered, her fingers still working the phone. " 'Chthonic' means 'beneath the earth.' "

"Partly, yes," Langdon said. "Although the word has a further historic implication—one commonly associated with myths and monsters. **Chthonics** are an entire category of mythical gods and monsters— Erinyes, Hecate, and Medusa, for example. They're called chthonics because they reside in the under- world and are associated with hell." Langdon paused. "Historically, they emerge from the earth and come aboveground to wreak havoc in the human world."

There was a long silence, and Langdon sensed they were all thinking the same thing. **This chthonic monster . . . could only be Zobrist's plague.**

for here, in the darkness, the chthonic
*   monster waits,*
submerged in the bloodred waters . . .
of the lagoon that reflects no stars.

"Anyway," Langdon said, trying to stay on track, "we're obviously looking for an underground location, which at least explains the last line of the poem referencing 'the lagoon that reflects no stars.'"

"Good point," Sienna said, glancing up now from Ferris's phone. "If a lagoon is subterranean, it couldn't reflect the sky. But does Venice have subterranean lagoons?"

"None that I know of," Langdon replied. "But in a city built on water, there are probably endless possibilities."

"What if the lagoon is indoors?" Sienna asked suddenly, eyeing them both. "The poem refers to 'the darkness' of 'the sunken palace.' You mentioned earlier that the Doge's Palace is connected to the basilica, right? That means those structures have a lot of what the poem mentions—a mouseion of holy wisdom, a palace, relevance to doges—and it's all located right there on Venice's main lagoon, at sea level."

Langdon considered this. "You think the poem's 'sunken palace' is the Doge's Palace?"

"Why not? The poem tells us first to kneel at St. Mark's Basilica, then to follow the sounds of trickling water. Maybe the sounds of water lead next door to the Doge's Palace. It could have a submerged foundation or something."

Langdon had visited the Doge's Palace many times and knew that it was absolutely massive. A sprawling complex of buildings, the palace housed a grand-scale museum, a veritable labyrinth of institutional chambers, apartments, and courtyards, and a prison net-work so vast that it was housed in multiple buildings.

"You may be right," Langdon said, "but a blind search of that palace would take days. I suggest we do exactly as the poem tells us. First, we go to St. Mark's Basilica and find the tomb or statue of this treacherous doge, and then we kneel down."

"And then?" Sienna asked.

"And then," Langdon said with a sigh, "we pray like hell that we hear trickling water . . . and it leads us somewhere."

In the silence that followed, Langdon pictured the anxious face of Elizabeth Sinskey as he had seen it in his hallucinations, calling to him across the water. **Time is short. Seek and find!** He wondered where Sinskey was now . . . and if she was all right. The soldiers in black had no doubt realized by now that Langdon and Sienna had escaped. **How long until they come after us?**

As Langdon returned his eyes to the poem, he fought off a wave of exhaustion. He eyed the final line of verse, and another thought occurred to him. He wondered if it was even worth mentioning. **The lagoon that reflects no stars.** It was probably irrel-evant to their search, but he decided to share it none-theless. "There's another point I should mention."

Sienna glanced up from the cell phone.

"The three sections of Dante's **Divine Comedy,**" Langdon said. "**Inferno, Purgatorio,** and **Paradiso.** They **all** end with the exact same word."

Sienna looked surprised.

"What word is that?" Ferris asked.

Langdon pointed to the bottom of the text he had transcribed. "The same word that ends **this** poem—'stars.'" He picked up Dante's death mask and pointed to the very center of the spiral text.

The lagoon that reflects no stars.

"What's more," Langdon continued, "in the finale of the **Inferno**, we find Dante listening to the sound of trickling water inside a chasm and following it through an opening . . . which leads him out of hell."

Ferris blanched slightly. "Jesus."

Just then, a deafening rush of air filled the cabin as the Frecciargento plunged into a mountain tunnel.

In the darkness, Langdon closed his eyes and tried to allow his mind to relax. **Zobrist may have been a lunatic**, he thought, **but he certainly had a sophisticated grasp of Dante.**

CHAPTER 64

Laurence Knowlton felt a wave of relief wash over him.

The provost changed his mind about watching Zobrist's video.

Knowlton practically dove for the crimson memory stick and inserted it into his computer so he could share it with his boss. The weight of Zobrist's bizarre nine-minute message had been haunting the facilitator, and he was eager to have another set of eyes watch it.

This will no longer be on me.

Knowlton held his breath as he began the playback.

The screen darkened, and the sounds of gently lapping water filled the cubicle. The camera moved through the reddish haze of the underground cavern, and although the provost showed no visible reaction, Knowlton sensed that the man was as alarmed as he was bewildered.

The camera paused its forward motion and tipped downward at the surface of the lagoon, where it plunged beneath the water, diving several feet to reveal the polished titanium plaque bolted to the floor.

IN THIS PLACE, ON THIS DATE,
THE WORLD WAS CHANGED FOREVER.

The provost flinched ever so slightly. "Tomorrow,"
he whispered, eyeing the date. "And do we know
where 'this place' might be?"

Knowlton shook his head.

The camera panned left now, revealing the submerged plastic sack of gelatinous, yellow-brown fluid.

"What in God's name?!" The provost pulled up a
chair and settled in, staring at the undulating bubble,
suspended like a tethered balloon beneath the water.

An uncomfortable silence settled over the room as
the video progressed. Soon the screen went dark, and
then a strange, beak-nosed shadow appeared on the
cavern wall and began talking in its arcane language.

> I am the Shade . . .
> Driven underground, I must speak to the world
> from deep within the earth, exiled to this gloomy
> cavern where the bloodred waters collect in the
> lagoon that reflects no stars.
> But this is my paradise . . . the perfect womb
> for my fragile child.
> Inferno.

The provost glanced up. "Inferno?"

Knowlton shrugged. "As I said, it's disturbing."

The provost returned his eyes to the screen, watching intently.

The beak-nosed shadow continued speaking for several minutes, talking of plagues, of the population's need for purging, of his own glorious role in the future, of his battle against the ignorant souls who had been trying to stop him, and of the faithful few who realized that drastic action was the only way to save the planet.

Whatever this war was about, Knowlton had been wondering all morning if the Consortium might be fighting on the wrong side.

The voice continued.

I have forged a masterpiece of salvation, and yet my efforts have been rewarded not with trumpets and laurels . . . but with threats of death.

I do not fear death . . . for death transforms visionaries into martyrs . . . converts noble ideas into powerful movements.

Jesus. Socrates. Martin Luther King.

One day soon I will join them.

The masterpiece I have created is the work of God Himself . . . a gift from the One who imbued me with the intellect, tools, and courage required to forge such a creation.

Now the day grows near.

Inferno sleeps beneath me, preparing to spring from its watery womb . . . under the watchful eye of the chthonic monster and all her Furies.

Despite the virtue of my deeds, like you, I

am no stranger to Sin. Even I am guilty of the darkest of the seven—that lone temptation from which so few find sanctuary.

Pride.

By recording this very message I have succumbed to Pride's goading pull . . . eager to ensure that the world would know my work.

And why not?

Mankind should know the source of his own salvation . . . the name of he who sealed the yawning gates of hell forever!

With each passing hour, the outcome grows more certain. Mathematics—as relentless as the law of gravity—is nonnegotiable. The same exponential blossoming of life that has nearly killed Mankind shall also be his deliverance. The beauty of a living organism—be it good or evil—is that it will follow the law of God with singular vision.

Be fruitful and multiply.

And so I fight fire . . . with fire.

"That's enough," the provost interrupted so quietly that Knowlton barely heard him.

"Sir?"

"Stop the video."

Knowlton paused the playback. "Sir, the end is actually the most frightening part."

"I've seen enough." The provost looked ill. He paced the cubicle for several moments and then turned suddenly. "We need to make contact with FS-2080."

Knowlton considered the move.

FS-2080 was the code name of one of the provost's trusted contacts—the same contact who had referred Zobrist to the Consortium as a client. The provost was no doubt at this very moment chiding himself for trusting FS-2080's judgment; the recommendation of Bertrand Zobrist as a client had brought chaos into the Consortium's delicately structured world.

FS-2080 is the reason for this crisis.

The growing chain of calamities surrounding Zobrist only seemed to be getting worse, not merely for the Consortium, but quite possibly . . . for the world.

"We need to discover Zobrist's true intentions," the provost declared. "I want to know exactly what he created, and if this threat is real."

Knowlton knew that if anyone had the answers to these questions, it would be FS-2080. Nobody knew Bertrand Zobrist better. It was time for the Consortium to break protocol and assess what kind of insanity the organization might have unwittingly supported over the past year.

Knowlton considered the possible ramifications of confronting FS-2080 directly. The mere act of initiating contact carried certain risks.

"Obviously, sir," Knowlton said, "if you reach out to FS-2080, you'll need to do so very delicately."

The provost's eyes flashed with anger as he pulled out his cell phone. "We're well past delicate."

———

Seated with his two traveling partners in the Frecciargento's private cabin, the man with the paisley necktie and Plume Paris glasses did his best not to scratch at his still-worsening rash. The pain in his chest seemed to have increased as well.

As the train finally emerged from the tunnel, the man gazed over at Langdon, who opened his eyes slowly, apparently returning from far-off thoughts. Beside him, Sienna began eyeing the man's cell phone, which she had set down as the train sped through the tunnel, while there was no signal.

Sienna appeared eager to continue her Internet search, but before she could reach for the phone, it suddenly began vibrating, emitting a series of staccato pings.

Knowing the ring well, the man with the rash immediately grabbed the phone and eyed the illuminated screen, doing his best to hide his surprise.

"Sorry," he said, standing up. "Ailing mother. I've got to take this."

Sienna and Langdon gave him understanding nods as the man excused himself and exited the cabin, moving quickly down the passageway into a nearby restroom.

The man with the rash locked the restroom door as he took the call. "Hello?"

The voice on the line was grave. "It's the provost."

CHAPTER 65

The Frecciargento's restroom was no larger than the restroom on a commercial airliner, with barely enough room to turn around. The man with the skin rash finished his phone call with the provost and pocketed his phone.

The ground has shifted, he realized. The entire landscape was suddenly upside down, and he needed a moment to get his bearings.

My friends are now my enemies.

The man loosened his paisley tie and stared at his pustuled face in the mirror. He looked worse than he thought. His face was of little concern, though, compared to the pain in his chest.

Hesitantly, he unfastened several buttons and pulled open his shirt.

He forced his eyes to the mirror . . . and studied his bare chest.

Jesus.

The black area was growing.

The skin on the center of his chest was a deep hue of bluish black. The area had begun last night as the size of a golf ball, but now it was the size of an orange. He gently touched the tender flesh and winced.

Hurriedly, he rebuttoned his shirt, hoping he would have the strength to carry out what he needed to do.

The next hour will be critical, he thought. **A delicate series of maneuvers.**

He closed his eyes and gathered himself, working through what needed to happen. **My friends have become my enemies**, he thought again.

He took several deep, painful breaths, hoping it might calm his nerves. He knew he needed to stay serene if he was going to keep his intentions hidden. **Inner calm is critical to persuasive acting.**

The man was no stranger to deception, and yet his heart was pounding wildly now. He took another deep, throbbing breath. **You've been deceiving people for years**, he reminded himself. **It's what you do.**

Steeling himself, he prepared to return to Langdon and Sienna.

My final performance, he thought.

As a final precaution before exiting the restroom, he removed the battery from his cell phone, making sure the device was now inoperative.

———

He looks pale, Sienna thought as the man with the rash reentered the cabin and settled into his seat with a pained sigh.

"Is everything okay?" Sienna asked, genuinely concerned.

He nodded. "Thanks, yes. Everything's fine."

Apparently having received all the information

the man intended to share, Sienna changed tacks. "I need your phone again," she said. "If you don't mind, I want to keep searching for more on the doge. Maybe we can get some answers before we visit St. Mark's."

"No problem," he said, taking his phone from his pocket and checking the display. "Oh, damn. My battery was dying during that call. Looks like it's dead now." He glanced at his watch. "We'll be in Venice soon. We'll just have to wait."

———

Five miles off the coast of Italy, aboard **The Mendacium**, facilitator Knowlton watched in silence as the provost stalked around the perimeter of the cubicle like a caged animal. Following the phone call, the provost's wheels were clearly turning, and Knowlton knew better than to utter a sound while the provost was thinking.

Finally, the deeply tanned man spoke, his voice as tight as Knowlton could remember. "We have no choice. We need to share this video with Dr. Elizabeth Sinskey."

Knowlton sat stock-still, not wanting to show his surprise. **The silver-haired devil? The one we've helped Zobrist evade all year?** "Okay, sir. Should I find a way to e-mail the video to her?"

"God, no! And risk leaking the video to the public? It would be mass hysteria. I want Dr. Sinskey aboard this ship as soon as you can get her here."

Knowlton stared in disbelief. **He wants to bring the director of the WHO on board** The Mendacium? "Sir, this breach of our secrecy protocol obviously risks—"

"Just do it, Knowlton! NOW!"

CHAPTER 66

F S-2080 gazed out the window of the speed-ing Frecciargento, watching Robert Langdon's reflection in the glass. The professor was still brainstorming possible solutions to the death-mask riddle that Bertrand Zobrist had composed.

Bertrand, thought FS-2080. **God, I miss him.**

The pangs of loss felt fresh. The night the two had met still felt like a magical dream.

Chicago. The blizzard.

January, six years ago . . . but it still feels like yesterday. I am trudging through snowbanks along the windswept Magnificent Mile, collar upturned against the blinding whiteout. Despite the cold, I tell myself that nothing will keep me from my des-tination. Tonight is my chance to hear the great Bertrand Zobrist speak . . . in person.

I have read everything the man has ever written, and I know I am lucky to have one of the five hun-dred tickets that were printed for the event.

When I arrive at the hall, half numb from the wind, I feel a surge of panic to discover the room nearly empty. Has the speech been canceled?! The city is in near shutdown due to the weather . . . has it kept Zobrist from coming tonight?!

Then he is there.

A towering, elegant form takes the stage.

He is tall . . . so very tall . . . with vibrant green eyes that seem to hold all the mysteries of the world in their depths. He looks out over the empty hall—only a dozen or so stalwart fans—and I feel ashamed that the hall is nearly empty.

This is Bertrand Zobrist!

There is a terrible moment of silence as he stares at us, his face stern.

Then, without warning, he bursts out laughing, his green eyes glimmering. "To hell with this empty auditorium," he declares. "My hotel is next door. Let's go to the bar!"

A cheer goes up, and a small group migrates next door to a hotel bar, where we crowd into a big booth and order drinks. Zobrist regales us with tales of his research, his rise to celebrity, and his thoughts about the future of genetic engineering. As the drinks flow, the topic turns to Zobrist's newfound passion for Transhumanist philosophy.

"I believe Transhumanism is mankind's only hope for long-term survival," Zobrist preaches, pulling aside his shirt and showing them all the "H+" tattoo inscribed on his shoulder. "As you can see, I'm fully committed."

I feel as if I'm having a private audience with a rock star. I never imagined the lauded "genius of genetics" would be so charismatic or beguiling in person. Every time Zobrist glances over at me, his green eyes ignite a wholly unexpected feeling inside me . . . the deep pull of sexual attraction.

As the night wears on, the group slowly thins as the guests excuse themselves to get back to reality. By midnight, I am seated all alone with Bertrand Zobrist.

"Thank you for tonight," I say to him, a little tipsy from one drink too many. "You're an amazing teacher."

"Flattery?" Zobrist smiles and leans closer, our legs touching now. "It will get you everywhere."

The flirtation is clearly inappropriate, but it is a snowy night in a deserted Chicago hotel, and it feels as if the entire world has stopped.

"So what do you think?" Zobrist says. "Nightcap in my room?"

I freeze, knowing I must look like a deer in the headlights.

Zobrist's eyes twinkle warmly. "Let me guess," he whispers. "You've never been with a famous man."

I feel myself flush, fighting to hide a surge of emotions—embarrassment, excitement, fear. "Actually, to be honest," I say to him, "I've never been with any man."

Zobrist smiles and inches closer. "I'm not sure what you've been waiting for, but please let me be your first."

In that moment all the awkward sexual fears and frustrations of my childhood disappear . . . evaporating into the snowy night.

For the first time ever, I feel a yearning unfettered by shame.

I want him.

Ten minutes later, we are in Zobrist's hotel room, naked in each other's arms. Zobrist takes his time, his patient hands coaxing sensations I've never felt before out of my inexperienced body.

This is my choice. He didn't force me.

In the cocoon of Zobrist's embrace, I feel as if everything is right in the world. Lying there, staring out the window at the snowy night, I know I will follow this man anywhere.

The Frecciargento train slowed suddenly, and FS-2080 emerged from the blissful memory and back into the depressing present.

Bertrand . . . you're gone.

Their first night together had been the first step of an incredible journey.

I became more than his lover. I became his disciple.

"Libertà Bridge," Langdon said. "We're almost there."

FS-2080 nodded mournfully, staring out at the waters of the Laguna Veneta, remembering sailing here once with Bertrand . . . a peaceful image that dissolved now into a horrific memory from a week before.

I was there when he jumped off the Badia tower.

Mine were the last eyes he ever saw.

CHAPTER 67

The NetJets Citation Excel bounced through heavy turbulence as it rocketed skyward out of Tassignano Airport and banked toward Venice. On board, Dr. Elizabeth Sinskey barely noticed the bumpy departure as she absently stroked her amulet and gazed out the window into empty space.

They had finally stopped giving her the injections, and Sinskey's mind was already feeling clearer. In the seat beside her, Agent Brüder remained silent, probably pondering the bizarre turn of events that had just transpired.

Everything is upside down, Sinskey thought, still struggling to believe what she had just witnessed.

Thirty minutes ago, they had stormed the tiny airfield to intercept Langdon as he boarded the private jet he had summoned. Instead of finding the professor, however, they discovered an idling Citation Excel and two NetJets pilots pacing the tarmac and checking their watches.

Robert Langdon was a no-show.

Then came the phone call.

When the cell phone rang, Sinskey was where she had been all day—in the backseat of the black van.

Agent Brüder entered the vehicle with a stupefied look on his face as he handed her his phone.

"Urgent call for you, ma'am."

"Who is it?" she asked.

"He asked me to tell you only that he has pressing information to give you about Bertrand Zobrist."

Sinskey grabbed the phone. "This is Dr. Elizabeth Sinskey."

"Dr. Sinskey, you and I have never met, but my organization has been responsible for hiding Bertrand Zobrist from you for the last year."

Sinskey sat bolt upright. "Whoever the hell you are, you've been harboring a criminal!"

"We've done nothing illegal, but that's not—"

"The hell you haven't!"

The man on the line took a long, patient breath, speaking very softly now. "You and I will have plenty of time to debate the ethics of my actions. I know you don't know me, but I do know quite a bit about you. Mr. Zobrist has been paying me handsomely to keep you and others away from him for the past year. I am now breaching my own strict protocol by contacting you. And yet, I believe we have no choice but to pool our resources. Bertrand Zobrist, I fear, may have done something terrible."

Sinskey could not fathom who this man was. "You're just figuring this out now?!"

"Yes, that is correct. Just now." His tone was earnest.

Sinskey tried to shake off the cobwebs. "Who are you?"

"Someone who wants to help you before it's too late. I'm in possession of a video message created by Bertrand Zobrist. He asked me to release it to the world . . . tomorrow. I think you need to see it immediately."

"What does it say?"

"Not on the phone. We need to meet."

"How do I know I can trust you?"

"Because I'm about to tell you where Robert Langdon is . . . and why he's acting so strangely."

Sinskey reeled at the mention of Langdon's name, and she listened in astonishment to the outlandish explanation. This man seemed to have been complicit with her enemy for the last year, and yet, as she listened to the details, Sinskey's gut told her she needed to trust what he was saying.

I have no choice but to comply.

Their combined resources made short work of commandeering the "jilted" NetJets Citation Excel. Sinskey and the soldiers were now in pursuit, racing toward Venice, where, according to this man's information, Langdon and his two traveling companions were at this very moment arriving by train. It was too late to summon the local authorities, but the man on the line claimed to know where Langdon was headed.

St. Mark's Square? Sinskey felt a chill as she imagined the crowds in Venice's most populated area. "How do you know this?"

"Not on the phone," the man said. "But you should be aware that Robert Langdon is unwittingly traveling with a very dangerous individual."

"Who?!" Sinskey demanded.

"One of Zobrist's closest confidants." The man sighed heavily. "Someone I trusted. Foolishly, apparently. Someone I believe may now be a severe threat."

As the private jet headed for Venice's Marco Polo Airport carrying Sinskey and the six soldiers, Sinskey's thoughts returned to Robert Langdon. **He lost his memory? He recalls nothing?** The strange news, while explaining several things, made Sinskey feel even worse than she already did about involving the distinguished academic in this crisis.

I left him no choice.

Almost two days ago, when Sinskey recruited Langdon, she hadn't even let him go back to his house for his passport. Instead, she had arranged for his quiet passage through the Florence Airport as a special liaison to the World Health Organization.

As the C-130 lumbered into the air and pointed east across the Atlantic, Sinskey had glanced at Langdon beside her and noticed he did not look well. He was staring intently at the sidewall of the windowless hull.

"Professor, you **do** realize this plane has no windows? Until recently, it was used as a military transport."

Langdon turned, his face ashen. "Yes, I noticed that the moment I stepped aboard. I'm not so good in enclosed spaces."

"So you're pretending to look out an imaginary window?"

He gave a sheepish smile. "Something like that, yes."

"Well, look at this instead." She pulled out a photo of her lanky, green-eyed nemesis and laid it in front of him. "This is Bertrand Zobrist."

Sinskey had already told Langdon about her confrontation with Zobrist at the Council on Foreign Relations, the man's passion for the Population Apocalypse Equation, his widely circulated comments about the global benefits of the Black Plague, and, most ominously, his total disappearance from sight over the past year.

"How does someone that prominent stay hidden for so long?" Langdon asked.

"He had a lot of help. Professional help. Maybe even a foreign government."

"What government would condone the creation of a plague?"

"The same governments that try to obtain nuclear warheads on the black market. Don't forget that an effective plague is the ultimate biochemical weapon, and it's worth a fortune. Zobrist easily could have lied to his partners and assured them his creation had a limited range. Zobrist would be the only one who had any idea what his creation actually did."

Langdon fell silent.

"In any case," Sinskey continued, "if not for power or money, those helping Zobrist could have helped because they shared his **ideology**. Zobrist has no shortage of disciples who would do anything for him.

He was quite a celebrity. In fact, he gave a speech at your university not long ago."

"At Harvard?"

Sinskey took out a pen and wrote on the border of Zobrist's photo—the letter **H** followed by a plus sign. "You're good with symbols," she said. "Do you recognize this one?"

H+

"H-plus," Langdon whispered, nodding vaguely. "Sure, a few summers ago it was posted all over campus. I assumed it was some kind of chemistry conference."

Sinskey chuckled. "No, those were signs for the 2010 'Humanity-plus' Summit—one of the largest Transhumanism gatherings ever. H-plus is the symbol of the Transhumanist movement."

Langdon cocked his head, as if trying to place the term.

"Transhumanism," Sinskey said, "is an intellectual movement, a philosophy of sorts, and it's quickly taking root in the scientific community. It essentially states that humans should use technology to transcend the weaknesses inherent in our human bodies. In other words, the next step in human evolution should be that we begin biologically engineering **ourselves.**"

"Sounds ominous," Langdon said.

"Like all change, it's just a matter of degree. Technically, we've been engineering ourselves for years now—developing vaccines that make children immune to certain diseases . . . polio, smallpox, typhoid. The difference is that now, with Zobrist's breakthroughs in germ-line genetic engineering, we're learning how to create **inheritable** immunizations, those that would affect the recipient at the core germ-line level—making all subsequent generations immune to that disease."

Langdon looked startled. "So the human species would essentially undergo an **evolution** that makes it immune to typhoid, for example?"

"It's more of an **assisted** evolution," Sinskey corrected. "Normally, the evolutionary process—whether it be a lungfish developing feet or an ape developing opposable thumbs—takes millennia to occur. Now we can make radical genetic adaptations in a single generation. Proponents of the technology consider it the ultimate expression of Darwinian 'survival of the fittest'—humans becoming a species that learns to improve its own evolutionary process."

"Sounds more like playing God," Langdon replied.

"I agree wholeheartedly," Sinskey said. "Zobrist, however, like many other Transhumanists, argued strongly that it is mankind's evolutionary **obligation** to use all the powers at our disposal—germ-line genetic mutation, for one—to improve as a species. The problem is that our genetic makeup is like a house of cards—each piece connected to and supported by countless others—often in ways we don't understand. If we try to remove a single human trait, we can cause hundreds of others to shift simultaneously, possibly with catastrophic effects."

Langdon nodded. "There's a reason evolution is a gradual process."

"Precisely!" Sinskey said, feeling her admiration for the professor growing with each passing moment. "We're tinkering with a process that took aeons to build. These are dangerous times. We now literally have the capacity to activate certain gene sequences that will result in our descendants having increased dexterity, stamina, strength, even intelligence— essentially a super-race. These hypothetical 'enhanced' individuals are what Transhumanists refer to as **post- humans**, which some believe will be the future of our species."

"Sounds eerily like eugenics," Langdon replied.

The reference made Sinskey's skin crawl.

In the 1940s, Nazi scientists had dabbled in a technology they'd dubbed eugenics—an attempt to use rudimentary genetic engineering to increase the birth rate of those with certain "desirable" genetic traits, while decreasing the birth rate of those with "less desirable" ethnic traits.

Ethnic cleansing at the genetic level.

"There are similarities," Sinskey admitted, "and while it's hard to fathom how one would engineer a new human race, there are a lot of smart people who believe it is critical to our survival that we begin that very process. One of the contributors to the Trans- humanist magazine **H+** described germ-line genetic engineering as 'the clear next step,' and claimed it 'epitomized the true potential of our species.'" Sinskey paused. "Then again, in the magazine's defense, they also ran a **Discover** magazine piece called 'The Most Dangerous Idea in the World.'"

"I think I'd side with the latter," Langdon said. "At least from the sociocultural standpoint."

"How so?"

"Well, I assume that genetic enhancements—much like cosmetic surgery—cost a lot of money, right?"

"Of course. Not everyone could afford to improve themselves or their children."

"Which means that legalized genetic enhancements would immediately create a world of haves and have-nots. We already have a growing chasm between the rich and the poor, but genetic engineering would create a race of superhumans and . . . perceived subhumans. You think people are concerned about the ultrarich one percent running the world? Just imagine if that one percent were also, quite literally, a superior **species**—smarter, stronger, healthier. It's the kind of situation that would be ripe for slavery or ethnic cleansing."

Sinskey smiled at the handsome academic beside her. "Professor, you have very quickly grasped what I believe to be the most serious pitfall of genetic engineering."

"Well, I may have grasped that, but I'm still confused about Zobrist. All of this Transhumanist thinking seems to be about bettering humankind, making us more healthy, curing fatal diseases, extending our longevity. And yet Zobrist's views on overpopulation seem to endorse killing off people. His ideas on Transhumanism and overpopulation seem to be in conflict, don't they?"

Sinskey gave a solemn sigh. It was a good question, and unfortunately it had a clear and troubling answer. "Zobrist believed wholeheartedly in Transhumanism—in bettering the species through technology; however, he also believed our species would go extinct before we got a chance to do that. In effect, if nobody takes action, our sheer numbers will kill off the species before we get a chance to realize the promise of genetic engineering."

Langdon's eyes went wide. "So Zobrist wanted to thin the herd . . . in order to buy more time?"

Sinskey nodded. "He once described himself as being trapped on a ship where the passengers double in number every hour, while he is desperately trying to build a lifeboat before the ship sinks under its own weight." She paused. "He advocated throwing half the people overboard."

Langdon winced. "Frightening thought."

"Quite. Make no mistake about it," she said. "Zobrist firmly believed that a drastic curbing of the human population will be remembered one day as the ultimate act of heroism . . . the moment the human race chose to survive."

"As I said, frightening."

"More so because Zobrist was not alone in his thinking. When Zobrist died, he became a martyr for a lot of people. I have no idea who we're going to run into when we arrive in Florence, but we'll need to be very careful. We won't be the only ones trying to find this plague, and for your own safety, we can't let a soul know you're in Italy looking for it."

Langdon told her about his friend Ignazio Busoni, a Dante specialist, who Langdon believed could get him into Palazzo Vecchio for a quiet after-hours look at the painting that contained the words **cerca trova**, from Zobrist's little projector. Busoni might also be able to help Langdon understand the strange quote about the eyes of death.

Sinskey pulled back her long silver hair and looked intently at Langdon. "Seek and find, Professor. Time is running out."

Sinskey went to an onboard storeroom and retrieved the WHO's most secure hazmat tube—a model with biometric sealing capability.

"Give me your thumb," she said, setting the canister in front of Langdon.

Langdon looked puzzled but obliged.

Sinskey programmed the tube so that Langdon would be the only person who could open it. Then she took the little projector and placed it safely inside.

"Think of it as a portable lockbox," she said with a smile.

"With a biohazard symbol?" Langdon looked uneasy.

"It's all we have. On the bright side, nobody will mess with it."

Langdon excused himself to stretch his legs and use the restroom. While he was gone, Sinskey tried to slip the sealed canister into his jacket pocket. Unfortunately it didn't fit.

He can't be carrying this projector around in plain sight. She thought a moment and then headed back to the storeroom for a scalpel and a stitch kit. With expert precision, she cut a slit in the lining of Langdon's jacket and carefully sewed a hidden pocket that was the exact size required to conceal the biotube.

When Langdon returned, she was just finishing the final stitches.

The professor stopped and stared as if she had defaced the **Mona Lisa**. "You sliced into the lining of my Harris Tweed?"

"Relax, Professor," she said. "I'm a trained surgeon. The stitches are quite professional."

CHAPTER 68

Venice's Santa Lucia Train Station is an elegant, low-slung structure made of gray stone and concrete. It was designed in a modern, minimalist style, with a facade that is gracefully devoid of all signage except for one symbol—the winged letters **FS**—the icon of the state railway system, the Ferrovie dello Stato.

Because the station is located at the westernmost end of the Grand Canal, passengers arriving in Venice need take only a single step out of the station to find themselves fully immersed in the distinctive sights, smells, and sounds of Venice.

For Langdon, it was always the salty air that struck him first—a clean ocean breeze spiced by the aroma of the white pizza sold by the street vendors outside the station. Today, the wind was from the east, and the air also carried the tang of diesel fuel from the long line of water taxis idling nearby on the turgid waters of the Grand Canal. Dozens of boat captains waved their arms and shouted to tourists, hoping to lure a new fare onto their taxis, gondolas, vaporetti, and private speedboats.

Chaos on the water, Langdon mused, eyeing the

floating traffic jam. Somehow, the congestion that would be maddening in Boston felt quaint in Venice.

A stone's throw across the canal, the iconic verdigris cupola of San Simeone Piccolo rose into the afternoon sky. The church was one of the most architecturally eclectic in all of Europe. Its unusually steep dome and circular sanctuary were Byzantine in style, while its columned marble pronaos was clearly modeled on the classical Greek entryway to Rome's Pantheon. The main entrance was topped by a spectacular pediment of intricate marble relief portraying a host of martyred saints.

Venice is an outdoor museum, Langdon thought, his gaze dropping to the canal water that lapped at the church's stairs. **A slowly sinking museum**. Even so, the potential of flooding seemed inconsequential compared to the threat that Langdon feared was now lurking beneath the city.

And nobody has any idea . . .

The poem on the back of Dante's death mask still played in Langdon's mind, and he wondered where the verses would lead them. He had the transcription of the poem in his pocket, but the plaster mask itself—at Sienna's suggestion—Langdon had wrapped in newspaper and discreetly sealed inside a self-serve locker in the train station. Although an egregiously inadequate resting place for such a precious artifact, the locker was certainly far safer than carrying the priceless plaster mask around a water-filled city.

"Robert?" Sienna was up ahead with Ferris, motioning toward the water taxis. "We don't have much time."

Langdon hurried toward them, although as an architecture enthusiast, he found it almost unthinkable to rush a trip along the Grand Canal. Few Venetian experiences were more pleasurable than boarding vaporetto no. 1—the city's primary open-air water bus—preferably at night, and sitting up front in the open air as the floodlit cathedrals and palaces drifted past.

No vaporetto today, Langdon thought. The vaporetti water buses were notoriously slow, and water taxi would be a faster option. Unfortunately, the taxi queue outside the train station looked interminable at the moment.

Ferris, in no apparent mood to wait, quickly took matters into his own hands. With a generous stack of bills, he quickly summoned over a water limousine—a highly polished Veneziano Convertible made of South African mahogany. While the elegant craft was certainly overkill, the journey would be both private and swift—a mere fifteen minutes along the Grand Canal to St. Mark's Square.

Their driver was a strikingly handsome man in a tailored Armani suit. He looked more like a movie star than a skipper, but this was, after all, Venice, the land of Italian elegance.

"Maurizio Pimponi," the man said, winking at Sienna as he welcomed them all aboard. "Prosecco? Limoncello? Champagne?"

"**No, grazie,**" Sienna replied, instructing him in

rapid-fire Italian to get them to St. Mark's Square as fast as he possibly could.

"**Ma certo!**" Maurizio winked again. "My boat, she is the fastest in all of Venezia . . ."

As Langdon and the others settled into plush seats in the open-air stern, Maurizio reversed the boat's Volvo Penta motor, expertly backing away from the bank. Then he spun the wheel to the right and gunned the engines forward, maneuvering his large craft through a throng of gondolas, leaving a number of stripe-shirted **gondolieri** shaking their fists as their sleek black crafts bobbed up and down in his wake.

"**Scusate!**" Maurizio called apologetically. "VIPs!"

Within seconds, Maurizio had pulled away from the congestion at Santa Lucia Station and was skimming eastward along the Grand Canal. As they accelerated beneath the graceful expanse of the Ponte degli Scalzi, Langdon smelled the distinctively sweet aroma of the local delicacy **seppie al nero**—squid in its own ink—which was wafting out of the canopied restaurants along the bank nearby. As they rounded a bend in the canal, the massive, domed Church of San Geremia came into view.

"Saint Lucia," Langdon whispered, reading the saint's name from the inscription on the side of the church. "The bones of the blind."

"I'm sorry?" Sienna glanced over, looking hopeful that Langdon might have figured out something more about the mysterious poem.

"Nothing," Langdon said. "Strange thought. Probably nothing." He pointed to the church. "See the inscription? Saint Lucia is buried there. I sometimes lecture on hagiographic art—art depicting Christian saints—and it just occurred to me that Saint Lucia is the patron saint of the blind."

"Sì, santa Lucia!" Maurizio chimed in, eager to be of service. "Saint for the blind! You know the story, no?" Their driver looked back at them and shouted over the sound of the engines. "Lucia was so beautiful that all men have lust for her. So, Lucia, for to be pure to God and keep virginity, she cut out her own eyes."

Sienna groaned. "There's commitment."

"As reward for her sacrifice," Maurizio added, "God gave Lucia an even more beautiful set of eyes!"

Sienna looked at Langdon. "He **does** know that makes no sense, right?"

"The Lord works in mysterious ways," Langdon observed, picturing the twenty or so famous Old Master paintings depicting Saint Lucia carrying her own eyeballs on a platter.

While there were numerous versions of the Saint Lucia tale, they all involved Lucia cutting out her lust-inducing eyes and placing them on a platter for her ardent suitor and defiantly declaring: "Here hast thou, what thou so much desired . . . and, for the rest, I beseech thee, leave me now in peace!" Eerily, it had been Holy Scripture that had inspired Lucia's self-mutilation, forever linking her to Christ's famous admonition "If thine eye offend thee, pluck it out and cast it from thee."

Pluck, Langdon thought, realizing the same word

was used in the poem. **Seek the treacherous doge of Venice who . . . plucked up the bones of the blind.**

Puzzled by the coincidence, he wondered if perhaps this was a cryptic indication that Saint Lucia was the blind person being referenced in the poem.

"Maurizio," Langdon shouted, pointing to the Church of San Geremia. "The bones of Saint Lucia are in that church, no?"

"A few, yes," Maurizio said, driving skillfully with one hand and looking back at his passengers, ignoring the boat traffic ahead. "But mostly no. Saint Lucia is so beloved, her body has spread in churches all over the world. Venetians love Saint Lucia the most, of course, and so we celebrate—"

"Maurizio!" Ferris shouted. "Saint Lucia is blind, not you. Eyes front!"

Maurizio laughed good-naturedly and turned forward just in time to handily avoid colliding with an oncoming boat.

Sienna was studying Langdon. "What are you getting at? The treacherous doge who plucked up the bones of the blind?"

Langdon pursed his lips. "I'm not sure."

He quickly told Sienna and Ferris the history of Saint Lucia's relics—her bones—which was among the strangest in all of hagiography. Allegedly, when the beautiful Lucia refused the advances of an influential suitor, the man denounced her and had her burned at the stake, where, according to legend, her body refused to burn. Because her flesh had been resistant to fire, her relics were believed to have special powers, and whoever possessed them would enjoy an unusually long life.

"Magic bones?" Sienna said.

"Believed to be, yes, which is the reason her relics have been spread all over the world. For two millennia, powerful leaders have tried to thwart aging and death by possessing the bones of Saint Lucia. Her skeleton has been stolen, restolen, relocated, and divided up more times than that of any other saint in history. Her bones have passed through the hands of at least a dozen of history's most powerful people."

"Including," Sienna inquired, "a treacherous doge?"

Seek the treacherous doge of Venice who severed the heads from horses . . . and plucked up the bones of the blind.

"Quite possibly," Langdon said, now realizing that Dante's **Inferno** mentioned Saint Lucia very prominently. Lucia was one of the three blessed women—**le "tre donne benedette"**—who helped summon Virgil to help Dante escape the underworld. As the other two women were the Virgin Mary and Dante's beloved Beatrice, Dante had placed Saint Lucia in the highest of all company.

"If you're right about this," Sienna said, excitement in her voice, "then the same treacherous doge who severed the heads from horses . . ."

". . . also stole the bones of Saint Lucia," Langdon concluded.

Sienna nodded. "Which should narrow our list

considerably." She glanced over at Ferris. "Are you sure your phone's not working? We might be able to search online for—"

"Stone dead," Ferris said. "I just checked. Sorry."

"We'll be there soon," Langdon said. "I have no doubt we'll be able to find some answers at St. Mark's Basilica."

St. Mark's was the only piece of the puzzle that felt rock solid to Langdon. **The mouseion of holy wisdom.** Langdon was counting on the basilica to reveal the identity of their mysterious doge . . . and from there, with luck, the specific palace that Zobrist had chosen to release his plague. **For here, in the darkness, the chthonic monster waits.**

Langdon tried to push from his mind any images of the plague, but it was no use. He had often wondered what this incredible city had been like in its heyday . . . before the plague weakened it enough for it to be conquered by the Ottomans, and then by Napoleon . . . back when Venice reigned gloriously as the commercial center of Europe. By all accounts, there was no more beautiful city in the world, the wealth and culture of its population unparalleled.

Ironically, it was the population's taste for foreign luxuries that brought about its demise—the deadly plague traveling from China to Venice on the backs of rats stowed away on trading vessels. The same plague that destroyed an unfathomable **two-thirds** of China's population arrived in Europe and very quickly killed one in three—young and old, rich and poor alike.

Langdon had read descriptions of life in Venice during the plague outbreaks. With little or no dry land in which to bury the dead, bloated bodies floated in the canals, with some areas so densely packed with corpses that workers had to labor like log rollers and prod the bodies out to sea. It seemed no amount of praying could diminish the plague's wrath. By the time city officials realized it was the rats that were causing the disease, it was too late, but Venice still enforced a decree by which all incoming vessels had to anchor offshore for a full forty days before they would be permitted to unload. To this day, the number forty—**quaranta** in Italian—served as a grim reminder of the origins of the word **quarantine**.

As their boat sped onward around another bend in the canal, a festive red awning luffed in the breeze, pulling Langdon's attention away from his grim thoughts of death toward an elegant, three-tiered structure on his left.

CASINÒ DI VENEZIA: AN INFINITE EMOTION.

While Langdon had never quite understood the words on the casino's banner, the spectacular Renaissance-style palace had been part of the Venetian landscape since the sixteenth century. Once a private mansion, it was now a black-tie gaming hall that was famous for being the site at which, in 1883, composer Richard Wagner had collapsed dead of a heart attack shortly after composing his opera **Parsifal**.

Beyond the casino on the right, a Baroque, rusticated facade bore an even larger banner, this one deep blue, announcing the CA' PESARO: GALLERIA INTER-NAZIONALE D'ARTE MODERNA. Years ago, Langdon had been inside and seen Gustav Klimt's masterpiece **The Kiss** while it was on loan from Vienna. Klimt's dazzling gold-leaf rendering of intertwined lovers had sparked in him a passion for the artist's work, and to this day, Langdon credited Venice's Ca' Pesaro with arousing his lifelong gusto for modern art.

Maurizio drove on, powering faster now in the wide canal.

Ahead, the famous Rialto Bridge loomed—the halfway point to St. Mark's Square. As they neared the bridge, preparing to pass beneath it, Langdon looked up and saw a lone figure standing motionless at the railing, peering down at them with a somber visage.

The face was both familiar . . . and terrifying.

Langdon recoiled on instinct.

Grayish and elongated, the face had cold dead eyes and a long beaked nose.

The boat slipped beneath the ominous figure just as Langdon realized it was nothing more than a tourist showing off a recent purchase—one of the hundreds of plague masks sold every day in the nearby Rialto Market.

Today, however, the costume seemed anything but charming.

CHAPTER 69

St. Mark's Square lies at the southernmost tip of Venice's Grand Canal, where the sheltered waterway merges with the open sea. Overlooking this perilous intersection is the austere triangular fortress of Dogana da Mar—the Maritime Customs Office—whose watchtower once guarded Venice against foreign invasion. Nowadays, the tower has been replaced by a massive golden globe and a weather vane depicting the goddess of fortune, whose shifting directions on the breeze serve as a reminder to ocean-bound sailors of the unpredictability of fate.

As Maurizio steered the sleek boat toward the end of the canal, the choppy sea opened ominously before them. Robert Langdon had traveled this route many times before, although always in a much larger vaporetto, and he felt uneasy as their limo lurched on the growing swells.

To reach the docks at St. Mark's Square, their boat would need to cross an expanse of open lagoon whose waters were congested with hundreds of craft—everything from luxury yachts, to tankers, to private sailboats, to massive cruise liners. It felt as if they were leaving a country road and merging onto an eight-lane superhighway.

Sienna seemed equally uncertain as she eyed the towering ten-story cruise liner that was now passing in front of them, only three hundred yards off. The ship's decks were crawling with passengers, all packed against the railings, taking photos of St. Mark's Square from the water. In the churning wake of this ship, three others were lined up, awaiting their chance to drive past Venice's best-known landmark. Langdon had heard that in recent years, the number of ships had multiplied so quickly that an endless line of cruises passed all day and all night.

At the helm, Maurizio studied the line of oncoming cruise liners and then glanced to his left at a canopied dock not far away. "I park at Harry's Bar?" He motioned to the restaurant famous for having invented the Bellini. "St. Mark's Square is very short walking."

"No, take us all the way," Ferris commanded, pointing across the lagoon toward the docks at St. Mark's Square.

Maurizio shrugged good-naturedly. "Your choice. Hold on!"

The engines revved and the limo began cutting through the heavy chop, falling into one of the travel lanes marked by buoys. The passing cruise liners looked like floating apartment buildings, their wakes tossing the other boats like corks.

To Langdon's surprise, dozens of gondolas were making this same crossing. Their slender hulls—at nearly forty feet in length and almost fourteen hundred pounds—appeared remarkably stable in the rough waters. Each vessel was piloted by a sure-footed gondolier who stood on a platform on the left side of the stern in his traditional black-and-white-striped shirt and rowed a single oar attached to the right-hand gunwale. Even in the rough water, it was evident that every gondola listed mysteriously to the left, an oddity that Langdon had learned was caused by the boat's asymmetrical construction; every gondola's hull was curved to the right, away from the gondolier, to resist the boat's tendency to turn left from the right-sided rowing.

Maurizio pointed proudly to one of the gondolas as they powered past it. "You see the metal design on the front?" he called over his shoulder, motioning to the elegant ornament protruding from the bow. "It's the only metal on a gondola—called **ferro di prua**—the iron of the prow. It is a picture of Venice!"

Maurizio explained that the scythelike decoration that protruded from the bow of every gondola in Venice had a symbolic meaning. The **ferro**'s curved shape represented the Grand Canal, its six teeth reflected the six **sestieri** or districts of Venice, and its oblong blade was the stylized headpiece of the Venetian doge.

The doge, Langdon thought, his thoughts returning to the task ahead. **Seek the treacherous doge of Venice who severed the heads from horses . . . and plucked up the bones of the blind.**

Langdon raised his gaze to the shoreline ahead, where a small wooded park met the water's edge. Above the trees, silhouetted against a cloudless sky, rose the redbrick spire of St. Mark's bell tower, atop which a golden Archangel Gabriel peered down from a dizzying three hundred feet.

In a city where high-rises were nonexistent as a result of their tendency to sink, the towering Campanile di San Marco served as a navigational beacon to all who ventured into Venice's maze of canals and passageways; a lost traveler, with a single glance skyward, would see the way back to St. Mark's Square. Langdon still found it hard to believe that this massive tower had collapsed in 1902, leaving an enormous pile of rubble on St. Mark's Square. Remarkably, the lone casualty in the disaster had been a cat.

Visitors to Venice could experience the city's inimitable atmosphere in any number of breathtaking locales, and yet Langdon's favorite had always been the Riva degli Schiavoni. The wide stone promenade that sat along the water's edge had been built in the ninth century from dredged silt and ran from the old Arsenal all the way to St. Mark's Square.

Lined with fine cafés, elegant hotels, and even the home church of Antonio Vivaldi, the Riva began its course at the Arsenal—Venice's ancient shipbuilding yards—where the piney scent of boiling tree sap had once filled the air as boatbuilders smeared hot pitch on their unsound vessels to plug the holes. Allegedly it had been a visit to these very shipyards that had inspired Dante Alighieri to include rivers of boiling pitch as a torture device in his **Inferno**.

Langdon's gaze moved to the right, tracing the Riva along the waterfront, and coming to rest on the promenade's dramatic ending. Here, at the southern-most edge of St. Mark's Square, the vast expanse of pavement met the open sea. During Venice's golden age, this stark precipice had been proudly dubbed "the edge of all civilization."

Today, the three-hundred-yard-long stretch where St. Mark's Square met the sea was lined, as it always was, with no fewer than a hundred black gondolas, which bobbed against their moorings, their scythe-like bow ornaments rising and falling against the white marble buildings of the piazza.

Langdon still found it hard to fathom that this tiny city—just twice the size of Central Park in New York—had somehow risen out of the sea to become the largest and richest empire in the west.

As Maurizio powered the boat closer, Lang-don could see that the main square was absolutely mobbed with people. Napoleon had once referred to St. Mark's Square as "the drawing room of Europe," and from the looks of things, this "room" was host-ing a party for far too many guests. The entire piazza looked almost as if it would sink beneath the weight of its admirers.

"My God," Sienna whispered, gazing out at the throngs of people.

Langdon wasn't sure whether she was saying this out of fear that Zobrist might have chosen such a heavily populated location to release his plague . . . or because she sensed that Zobrist might actually have had a point in warning about the dangers of over-population.

Venice hosted a staggering number of tourists every year—an estimated one-third of 1 percent of the world's population—some twenty million visitors in the year 2000. With the additional billion added to the earth's population since that year, the city was now groaning under the weight of three million more tourists per year. Venice, like the planet itself, had only a finite amount of space, and at some point would no longer be able to import enough food, dispose of enough waste, or find enough beds for all those who wanted to visit it.

Ferris stood nearby, his eyes turned not toward the mainland, but out to sea, watching all the incoming ships.

"You okay?" Sienna asked, eyeing him curiously.

Ferris turned abruptly. "Yeah, fine . . . just thinking." He faced front and called up to Maurizio: "Park as close to St. Mark's as you can."

"No problem!" Their driver gave a wave. "Two minutes!"

The limo had now come even with St. Mark's Square, and the Doge's Palace rose majestically to their right, dominating the shoreline.

A perfect example of Venetian Gothic architecture, the palace was an exercise in understated elegance. With none of the turrets or spires normally associated with the palaces of France or England, it was conceived as a massive rectangular prism, which provided for the largest possible amount of interior square footage in which to house the doge's substantial government and support staff.

Viewed from the ocean, the palace's massive expanse of white limestone would have been overbearing had the effect not been carefully muted by the addition of porticos, columns, a loggia, and quatrefoil perforations. Geometric patterns of pink limestone ran throughout the exterior, reminding Langdon of the Alhambra in Spain.

As the boat pulled closer to the moorings, Ferris seemed concerned by a gathering of people in front of the palace. A dense crowd had gathered on a bridge, and all of its members were pointing down a narrow canal that sliced between two large sections of the Doge's Palace.

"What are they looking at?" Ferris demanded, sounding nervous.

"Il Ponte dei Sospiri," Sienna replied. "A famous Venetian bridge."

Langdon peered down the cramped waterway and saw the beautifully carved, enclosed tunnel that arched between the two buildings. **The Bridge of Sighs**, he thought, recalling one of his favorite boyhood movies, **A Little Romance**, which was based on the legend that if two young lovers kissed beneath this bridge at sunset while the bells of St. Mark's were ringing, they would love each other forever. The deeply romantic notion had stayed with Langdon his entire life. Of course, it hadn't hurt that the film also starred an adorable fourteen-year-old newcomer named Diane Lane, on whom Langdon had immediately developed a boyhood crush . . . a crush that, admittedly, he had never quite shaken.

Years later, Langdon had been horrified to learn that the Bridge of Sighs drew its name not from sighs of passion . . . but instead from sighs of misery. As it turned out, the enclosed walkway served as the connector between the Doge's Palace and the doge's prison, where the incarcerated languished and died, their groans of anguish echoing out of the grated windows along the narrow canal.

Langdon had visited the prison once, and was surprised to learn that the most terrifying cells were not those at water level, which often flooded, but those next door on the top floor of the palace proper—called **piombi** after their lead-tiled roofs—which made them torturously hot in the summer and freezing cold in the winter. The great lover Casanova had once been a prisoner in the **piombi**; charged by the Inquisition with adultery and spying, he had survived fifteen months of incarceration only to escape by beguiling his keeper.

"Sta' attento!" Maurizio shouted to the pilot of a gondola as their limo slid into the berth the gondola was just vacating. He had found a spot in front of the Hotel Danieli, only a hundred yards from St. Mark's Square and the Doge's Palace.

Maurizio threw a line around a mooring post and leaped ashore as if he were auditioning for a swashbuckling movie. Once he had secured the boat, he turned and extended a hand down into the boat, offering to help his passengers out.

"Thanks," Langdon said as the muscular Italian pulled him ashore.

Ferris followed, looking vaguely distracted and again glancing out to sea.

Sienna was the last to disembark. As the devilishly handsome Maurizio hoisted her ashore, he fixed her with a deep stare that seemed to imply that she'd have a better time if she ditched her two companions and stayed aboard with him. Sienna seemed not to notice.

"**Grazie,** Maurizio," she said absently, her gaze focused on the nearby Doge's Palace.

Then, without missing a stride, she led Langdon and Ferris into the crowd.

CHAPTER 70

A ptly named after one of history's most famed travelers, the Marco Polo International Airport is located four miles north of St. Mark's Square on the waters of the Laguna Veneta.

Because of the luxuries of private air travel, Elizabeth Sinskey had deplaned only ten minutes earlier and was already skimming across the lagoon in a futuristic black tender—a Dubois SR52 Blackbird—which had been sent by the stranger who had phoned earlier.

The provost.

For Sinskey, after being immobilized in the back of the van all day, the open air of the ocean felt invigorating. She turned her face to the salty wind and let her silver hair stream out behind her. Nearly two hours had passed since her last injection, and she was finally feeling alert. For the first time since last night, Elizabeth Sinskey was herself.

Agent Brüder was seated beside her along with his team of men. None of them said a word. If they had concerns about this unusual rendezvous, they knew their thoughts were irrelevant; the decision was not theirs to make.

As the tender raced on, a large island loomed up to them on the right, its shoreline dotted with squat brick buildings and smokestacks. **Murano**, Elizabeth realized, recognizing the illustrious glassblowing factories.

I can't believe I'm back, she thought, enduring a sharp pang of sadness. **Full circle.**

Years ago, while in med school, she had come to Venice with her fiancé and stopped to visit the Murano Glass Museum. There, her fiancé had spied a beautiful handblown mobile and innocently commented that he wanted to hang one just like it someday in their baby's nursery. Overcome with guilt for having kept a painful secret far too long, Elizabeth finally leveled with him about her childhood asthma and the tragic glucocorticoid treatments that had destroyed her reproductive system.

Whether it had been her dishonesty or her infertility that turned the young man's heart to stone, Elizabeth would never know. But one week later, she left Venice without her engagement ring.

Her only memento of the heartbreaking trip had been a lapis lazuli amulet. The Rod of Asclepius was a fitting symbol of medicine—bitter medicine in this case—but she had worn it every day since.

My precious amulet, she thought. **A parting gift from the man who wanted me to bear his children.**

Nowadays, the Venetian islands carried no romance for her at all, their isolated villages sparking thoughts not of love but of the quarantine colonies that had once been established on them in an effort to curb the Black Death.

As the Blackbird tender raced on past Isola San Pietro, Elizabeth realized they were homing in on a massive gray yacht, which seemed to be anchored in a deep channel, awaiting their arrival.

The gunmetal-gray ship looked like something out of the U.S. military's stealth program. The name emblazoned across the back offered no clue as to what kind of ship it might be.

The Mendacium?

The ship loomed larger and larger, and soon Sinskey could see a lone figure on the rear deck—a small, solitary man, deeply tanned, watching them through binoculars. As the tender arrived at **The Mendacium**'s expansive rear docking platform, the man descended the stairs to greet them.

"Dr. Sinskey, welcome aboard." The sun-drenched man politely shook her hand, his palms soft and smooth, hardly the hands of a boatman. "I appreciate your coming. Follow me, please."

As the group ascended several decks, Sinskey caught fleeting glimpses of what looked like busy cubicle farms. This strange ship was actually packed with people, but none were relaxing—they were all working.

Working on what?

As they continued climbing, Sinksey could hear the ship's massive engines power up, churning a deep wake as the yacht began moving again.

Where are we going? she wondered, alarmed.

"I'd like to speak to Dr. Sinskey alone," the man said to the soldiers, pausing to glance at Sinskey. "If that's okay with you?"

Elizabeth nodded.

"Sir," Brüder said forcefully, "I'd like to recommend Dr. Sinskey be examined by your onboard physician. She's had some medical—"

"I'm fine," Sinskey interjected. "Truly. Thank you, though."

The provost eyed Brüder a long moment and then motioned to a table of food and drink being set up on the deck. "Catch your breath. You're going to need it. You'll be going back ashore very shortly."

Without further ado, the provost turned his back on the agent and ushered Sinskey into an elegant stateroom and study, closing the door behind him.

"Drink?" he asked, motioning to a bar.

She shook her head, still trying to take in her bizarre surroundings. **Who is this man? What does he do here?**

Her host was studying her now, his fingers steepled beneath his chin. "Are you aware that my client Bertrand Zobrist referred to you as 'the silver-haired devil'?"

"I have a few choice names for him as well."

The man showed no emotion as he walked over to his desk and pointed down at a large book. "I'd like you to look at this."

Sinskey walked over and eyed the tome. **Dante's**

Inferno? She recalled the horrifying images of death that Zobrist had shown her during their encounter at the Council on Foreign Relations.

"Zobrist gave this to me two weeks ago. There's an inscription."

Sinskey studied the handwritten text on the title page. It was signed by Zobrist.

My dear friend, thank you for helping me find the
  path.
The world thanks you, too.

Sinskey felt a chill. "What path did you help him find?"

"I have no idea. Or rather, until a few hours ago I had no idea."

"And now?"

"Now I've made a rare exception to my protocol . . . and I've reached out to you."

Sinskey had traveled a long way and was in no mood for a cryptic conversation. "Sir, I don't know who you are, or what the hell you do on this ship, but you owe me an explanation. Tell me why you harbored a man who was being actively pursued by the World Health Organization."

Despite Sinskey's heated tone, the man replied in a measured whisper: "I realize you and I have been working at cross-purposes, but I would suggest that we forget the past. The past is the past. The future, I sense, is what demands our immediate attention."

With that, the man produced a tiny red flash drive

and inserted it into his computer, motioning for her to sit down. "Bertrand Zobrist made this video. He was hoping I would release it for him tomorrow."

Before Sinskey could respond, the computer monitor dimmed, and she heard the soft sounds of lapping water. Emerging from the blackness, a scene began to take shape . . . the interior of a water-filled cavern . . . like a subterranean pond. Strangely, the water appeared to be illuminated from within . . . glowing with an odd crimson luminescence.

As the lapping continued, the camera tilted downward and descended into the water, focusing in on the cavern's silt-covered floor. Bolted to the floor was a shiny rectangular plaque bearing an inscription, a date, and a name.

IN THIS PLACE, ON THIS DATE,
THE WORLD WAS CHANGED FOREVER.

The date was tomorrow. The name was Bertrand Zobrist.

Elizabeth Sinskey felt herself shudder. "What is this place?!" she demanded. "**Where** is this place?!"

In response, the provost showed his first bit of emotion—a deep sigh of disappointment and concern. "Dr. Sinskey," he replied, "I was hoping you might know the answer to that same question."

———

One mile away, on the waterfront walkway of Riva degli Schiavoni, the view out to sea had changed ever so slightly. To anyone looking carefully, an enormous gray yacht had just eased around a spit of land to the east. It was now bearing down on St. Mark's Square.

The **Mendacium**, FS-2080 realized with a surge of fear.

Its gray hull was unmistakable.

The provost is coming . . . and time is running out.

CHAPTER 71

Snaking through heavy crowds on the Riva degli Schiavoni, Langdon, Sienna, and Ferris hugged the water's edge, making their way into St. Mark's Square and arriving at its southernmost border, the edge where the piazza met the sea.

Here the throng of tourists was almost impenetrable, creating a claustrophobic crush around Langdon as the multitudes gravitated over to photograph the two massive columns that stood here, framing the square.

The official gateway to the city, Langdon thought ironically, knowing the spot had also been used for public executions until as late as the eighteenth century.

Atop one of the gateway's columns he could see a bizarre statue of St. Theodore, posing proudly with his slain dragon of legendary repute, which always looked to Langdon much more like a crocodile.

Atop the second column stood the ubiquitous symbol of Venice—the winged lion. Throughout the city, the winged lion could be seen with his paw resting proudly on an open book bearing the Latin inscription **Pax tibi Marce, evangelista meus (May Peace Be with You, Mark, My Evangelist)**. According to legend, these words were spoken by an angel upon St. Mark's arrival in Venice, along with the prediction that his body would one day rest here. This apocryphal legend was later used by Venetians to justify plundering St. Mark's bones from Alexandria for reburial in St. Mark's Basilica. To this day, the winged lion endures as the city's symbol and is visible at nearly every turn.

Langdon motioned to his right, past the columns, across St. Mark's Square. "If we get separated, meet at the front door of the basilica."

The others agreed and quickly began skirting the edges of the crowd and following the western wall of the Doge's Palace into the square. Despite the laws forbidding feeding them, the celebrated pigeons of Venice appeared to be alive and well, some pecking about at the feet of the crowds and others swooping into the outdoor cafés to pillage unprotected bread baskets and torment the tuxedoed waiters.

This grand piazza, unlike most in Europe, was shaped not in the form of a square but rather in that of the letter L. The shorter leg—known as the **piazzetta**—connected the ocean to St. Mark's Basilica. Up ahead, the square took a ninety-degree left turn into its larger leg, which ran from the basilica toward the Museo Correr. Strangely, rather than being rectilinear, the square was an irregular trapezoid, narrowing substantially at one end. This funhouse-type illusion made the piazza look far longer than it was, an effect that was accentuated by the grid of tiles whose patterns outlined the original stalls of fifteenth-century street merchants.

As Langdon continued on toward the elbow of the square, he could see, directly ahead in the distance, the shimmering blue glass dial of the St. Mark's Clock Tower—the same astronomical clock through which James Bond had thrown a villain in the film **Moonraker.**

It was not until this moment, as he entered the sheltered square, that Langdon could fully appreciate this city's most unique offering.

Sound.

With virtually no cars or motorized vehicles of any kind, Venice enjoyed a blissful absence of the usual civic traffic, subways, and sirens, leaving sonic space for the distinctly unmechanical tapestry of human voices, cooing pigeons, and lilting violins serenading patrons at the outdoor cafés. Venice sounded like no other metropolitan center in the world.

As the late-afternoon sun streamed into St. Mark's from the west, casting long shadows across the tiled square, Langdon glanced up at the towering spire of the campanile, which rose high over the square and dominated the ancient Venetian skyline. The upper loggia of the tower was packed with hundreds of people. Even the mere thought of being up there made him shiver, and he put his head back down and continued through the sea of humanity.

———

Sienna could easily have kept up with Langdon, but Ferris was lagging behind, and Sienna had decided to split the difference in order to keep both men in sight. Now, however, as the distance between them grew more pronounced, she looked back impatiently. Ferris pointed to his chest, indicating he was winded, and motioned for her to go on ahead.

Sienna complied, moving quickly after Langdon and losing sight of Ferris. Yet as she wove her way through the crowd, a nagging feeling held her back— the strange suspicion that Ferris was lagging behind intentionally . . . as if he were trying to put distance between them.

Having learned long ago to trust her instincts, Sienna ducked into an alcove and looked out from the shadows, scanning the crowd behind her and looking for Ferris.

Where did he go?!

It was as if he were no longer even trying to follow them. Sienna studied the faces in the crowd, and finally she saw him. To her surprise, Ferris had stopped and was crouched low, typing into his phone.

The same phone he told me had a dead battery.

A visceral fear gripped her, and again she knew she should trust it.

He lied to me on the train.

As Sienna watched him, she tried to imagine what he was doing. Secretly texting someone? Researching behind her back? Trying to solve the mystery of Zobrist's poem before Langdon and Sienna could do so?

Whatever his rationale, he had blatantly lied to her.
I can't trust him.

Sienna wondered if she should storm over and confront him, but she quickly decided to slip back into the crowd before he spotted her. She headed again toward the basilica, searching for Langdon. **I've got to warn him not to reveal anything else to Ferris.**

She was only fifty yards from the basilica when she felt a strong hand tugging on her sweater from behind.

She spun around and found herself face-to-face with Ferris.

The man with the rash was panting heavily, clearly having dashed through the mob to catch up with her. There was a frantic quality about him that Sienna hadn't seen before.

"Sorry," he said, barely able to breathe. "I got lost in the crowd."

The instant Sienna looked in his eyes, she knew.

He's hiding something.

———

When Langdon arrived in front of St. Mark's Basilica, he was surprised to discover that his two companions were no longer behind him. Also of surprise to Langdon was the absence of a line of tourists waiting to enter the church. Then again, Langdon realized, this was late afternoon in Venice, the hour when most tourists—their energy flagging from heavy lunches of pasta and wine—decided to stroll the piazzas or sip coffee rather than trying to absorb any more history.

Assuming that Sienna and Ferris would be arriving at any moment, Langdon turned his eyes to the entrance of the basilica before him. Sometimes accused of offering "an embarrassing surfeit of ingress," the building's lower facade was almost entirely taken up by a phalanx of five recessed entrances whose clustered columns, vaulted archways, and gaping bronze doors arguably made the building, if nothing else, eminently welcoming.

One of Europe's finest specimens of Byzantine architecture, St. Mark's had a decidedly soft and whimsical appearance. In contrast to the austere gray towers of Notre-Dame or Chartres, St. Mark's seemed imposing and yet, somehow, far more down-to-earth. Wider than it was tall, the church was topped by five bulging whitewashed domes that exuded an airy, almost festive appearance, causing more than a few of the guidebooks to compare St. Mark's to a meringue-topped wedding cake.

High atop the central peak of the church, a slender statue of St. Mark gazed down into the square that bore his name. His feet rested atop a crested arch that was painted midnight blue and dotted with golden stars. Against this colorful backdrop, the golden winged lion of Venice stood as the shimmering mascot of the city.

It was beneath the golden lion, however, that St. Mark's displayed one of its most famous treasures—four mammoth copper stallions—which at the moment were glinting in the afternoon sun.

The Horses of St. Mark's.

Poised as if prepared to leap down at any moment into the square, these four priceless stallions—like so many treasures here in Venice—had been pillaged from Constantinople during the Crusades. Another similarly looted work of art was on display beneath the horses at the southwest corner of the church—a purple porphyry carving known as **The Tetrarchs**. The statue was well known for its missing foot, broken off while it was being plundered from Constantinople in the thirteenth century. Miraculously, in the 1960s, the foot was unearthed in Istanbul. Venice petitioned for the missing piece of statue, but the Turkish authorities replied with a simple message: **You stole the statue—we're keeping our foot.**

"Mister, you buy?" a woman's voice said, drawing Langdon's gaze downward.

A heavyset Gypsy woman was holding up a tall pole on which hung a collection of Venetian masks. Most were in the popular **volto intero** style—the stylized full-faced, white masks often worn by women during Carnevale. Her collection also contained some playful half-faced Colombina masks, a few triangle-chinned bautas, and a strapless Moretta. Despite her colorful offerings, though, it was a single, grayish-black mask at the top of the pole that seized Langdon's attention, its menacing dead eyes seeming to stare directly down at him over a long, beaked nose.

The plague doctor. Langdon averted his eyes, needing no reminder of what he was doing here in Venice.

"You buy?" the Gypsy repeated.

Langdon smiled weakly and shook his head. "**Sono molto belle, ma no, grazie.**"

As the woman departed, Langdon's gaze followed the ominous plague mask as it bobbed above the crowd. He sighed heavily and raised his eyes back to the four copper stallions on the second-floor balcony.

In a flash, it hit him.

Langdon felt a sudden rush of elements crashing together—Horses of St. Mark's, Venetian masks, and pillaged treasures from Constantinople.

"My God," he whispered. "That's it!"

CHAPTER 72

Robert Langdon was transfixed.

The Horses of St. Mark's!

These four magnificent horses—with their regal necks and bold collars—had sparked in Langdon a sudden and unexpected memory, one he now realized held the explanation of a critical element of the mysterious poem printed on Dante's death mask.

Langdon had once attended a celebrity wedding reception at New Hampshire's historic Runnymede Farm—home to Kentucky Derby winner Dancer's Image. As part of the lavish entertainment, the guests were treated to a performance by the prominent equine theatrical troupe Behind the Mask—a stunning spectacle in which riders performed in dazzling Venetian costumes with their faces hidden behind **volto intero** masks. The troupe's jet-black Friesian mounts were the largest horses Langdon had ever seen. Colossal in stature, these stunning animals thundered across the field in a blur of rippling muscles, feathered hooves, and three-foot manes flowing wildly behind their long, graceful necks.

The beauty of these creatures left such an impression on Langdon that upon returning home, he researched them online, discovering the breed had once been a favorite of medieval kings for use as war-horses and had been brought back from the brink of extinction in recent years. Originally known as **Equus robustus**, the breed's modern name, Friesian, was a tribute to their homeland of Friesland, the Dutch province that was the birthplace of the brilliant graphic artist M. C. Escher.

As it turned out, the powerful bodies of the early Friesian horses had inspired the robust aesthetic of the Horses of St. Mark's in Venice. According to the Web site, the Horses of St. Mark's were so beautiful that they had become "history's most frequently stolen pieces of art."

Langdon had always believed that this dubious honor belonged to the **Ghent Altarpiece** and paid a quick visit to the ARCA Web site to confirm his theory. The Association for Research into Crimes Against Art offered no definitive ranking, but they did offer a concise history of the sculptures' troubled life as a target of pillage and plunder.

The four copper horses had been cast in the fourth century by an unknown Greek sculptor on the island of Chios, where they remained until Theodosius II whisked them off to Constantinople for display at the Hippodrome. Then, during the Fourth Crusade, when Venetian forces sacked Constantinople, the ruling doge demanded the four precious statues be transported via ship all the way back to Venice, a nearly impossible feat because of their size and weight. The horses arrived in Venice in 1254, and were installed in front of the facade of St. Mark's Cathedral.

More than half a millennium later, in 1797, Napoleon conquered Venice and took the horses for himself. They were transported to Paris and prominently displayed atop the Arc de Triomphe. Finally, in 1815, following Napoleon's defeat at Waterloo and his exile, the horses were winched down from the Arc de Triomphe and shipped on a barge back to Venice, where they were reinstalled on the front balcony of St. Mark's Basilica.

Although Langdon had been fairly familiar with the history of the horses, the ARCA site contained a passage that startled him.

The decorative collars were added to the horses' necks in 1204 by the Venetians to conceal where the heads had been severed to facilitate their transportation by ship from Constantinople to Venice.

The doge ordered the heads cut off the Horses of St. Mark's? It seemed unthinkable to Langdon.

"Robert?!" Sienna's voice was calling.

Langdon emerged from his thoughts, turning to see Sienna pushing her way through the crowd with Ferris close at her side.

"The horses in the poem!" Langdon shouted excitedly. "I figured it out!"

"What?" Sienna looked confused.

"We're looking for a treacherous doge who severed the heads from horses!"

"Yes?"

"The poem isn't referring to **live** horses." Langdon pointed high on the facade of St. Mark's, where a shaft of bright sun was illuminating the four copper statues. "It's referring to **those** horses!"

CHAPTER 73

On board **The Mendacium**, Dr. Elizabeth Sinskey's hands were trembling. She watched the video in the provost's study, and although she had seen some terrifying things in her life, this inexplicable movie that Bertrand Zobrist had made before his suicide left her feeling as cold as death.

On the screen before her, the shadow of a beaked face wavered, projected on the dripping wall of an underground cavern. The silhouette continued speaking, proudly describing his masterpiece—the creation called Inferno—which would save the world by culling the population.

God save us, Sinskey thought. "We must . . ." she said, her voice quavering. "We **must** find that underground location. It may not be too late."

"Keep watching," the provost replied. "It gets stranger."

Suddenly the shadow of the mask grew larger on the wet wall, looming hugely before her, until a figure stepped suddenly into the frame.

Holy shit.

Sinskey was staring at a fully outfitted plague doctor—complete with the black cloak and chilling beaked mask. The plague doctor was walking directly toward the camera, his mask filling the entire screen to terrifying effect.

"'The darkest places in hell,'" he whispered, "'are reserved for those who maintain their neutrality in times of moral crisis.'"

Sinskey felt goose bumps on her neck. It was the same quotation that Zobrist had left for her at the airline counter when she had eluded him in New York a year ago.

"I know," the plague doctor continued, "that there are those who call me monster." He paused, and Sinskey sensed his words were directed at her. "I know there are those who think me a heartless beast who hides behind a mask." He paused again, stepping closer still to the camera. "But I am not faceless. Nor am I heartless."

With that, Zobrist pulled off his mask and lowered the hood of his cloak—his face laid bare. Sinskey stiffened, staring into the familiar green eyes she had last seen in the darkness of the CFR. His eyes in the video had the same passion and fire, but there was something else in them now—the wild zeal of a madman.

"My name is Bertrand Zobrist," he said, staring into the camera. "And this is my face, unveiled and naked for the world to see. As for my soul . . . if I could hold aloft my flaming heart, as did Dante's Lord for his beloved Beatrice, you would see I am overflowing with love. The deepest kind of love. For all of you. And, above all, for **one** of you."

Zobrist stepped closer still, gazing deep into the camera and speaking softly, as if to a lover.

"My love," he whispered, "my precious love. You are my beatitude, my destroyer of all vices, my endorser of all virtue, my salvation. You are the one who lay naked at my side and unwittingly helped me across the abyss, giving me the strength to do what I now have done."

Sinskey listened with repulsion.

"My love," Zobrist continued in a doleful whisper that echoed in the ghostly subterranean cavern in which he spoke. "You are my inspiration and my guide, my Virgil and my Beatrice all in one, and this masterpiece is as much yours as it is mine. If you and I, as star-crossed lovers, never touch again, I shall find my peace in knowing that I have left the future in your gentle hands. My work below is done. And now the hour has come for me to climb again to the world above . . . and rebehold the stars."

Zobrist stopped talking, and the word **stars** echoed a moment in the cavern. Then, very calmly, Zobrist reached out and touched the camera, ending his transmission.

The screen went black.

"The underground location," the provost said, turning off the monitor. "We don't recognize it. Do you?"

Sinskey shook her head. **I've never seen anything like it.** She thought of Robert Langdon, wondering if he had made any more headway in deciphering Zobrist's clues.

"If it's of any help," the provost said, "I believe I know who Zobrist's lover is." He paused. "An individual code-named FS-2080."

Sinskey jumped up. "FS-2080?!" She stared at the provost in shock.

The provost looked equally startled. "That means something to you?"

Sinskey gave an incredulous nod. "It most certainly does."

Sinskey's heart was pounding. **FS-2080**. While she didn't know the identity of the individual, she certainly knew what the code name stood for. The WHO had been monitoring similar code names for years.

"The Transhumanist movement," she said. "Are you familiar with it?"

The provost shook his head.

"In the simplest terms," Sinskey explained, "Transhumanism is a philosophy stating that humans should use all available technologies to engineer our own species to make it stronger. Survival of the fittest."

The provost shrugged as if unmoved.

"Generally speaking," she continued, "the Transhumanist movement is made up of responsible individuals—ethically accountable scientists, futurists, visionaries—but, as in many movements, there exists a small but militant faction that believes the movement is not moving fast enough. They are apocalyptic thinkers who believe the end is coming and that someone needs to take drastic action to save the future of the species."

"And I'm guessing," the provost said, "that Bertrand Zobrist was one of these people?"

"Absolutely," Sinskey said. "A leader of the movement. In addition to being highly intelligent, he was enormously charismatic and penned doomsday articles that spawned an entire cult of zealots for Transhumanism. Today, many of his fanatical disciples use these code names, all of which take a similar form—two letters and a four-digit number—for example, DG-2064, BA-2105, or the one you just mentioned."

"FS-2080."

Sinskey nodded. "That could **only** be a Transhumanist code name."

"Do the numbers and letters have meaning?"

Sinskey motioned to his computer. "Pull up your browser. I'll show you."

The provost looked uncertain but went to his computer and launched a search engine.

"Search for 'FM-2030,'" Sinskey said, settling in behind him.

The provost typed **FM-2030**, and thousands of Web pages appeared.

"Click any of them," Sinskey said.

The provost clicked the top hit, which returned a Wikipedia page showing a picture of a handsome Iranian man—**Fereidoun M. Esfandiary**—whom it described as an author, philosopher, futurist, and forefather of the Transhumanist movement. Born in

1930, he was credited with introducing Transhumanist philosophy to the multitudes, as well as presciently predicting in vitro fertilization, genetic engineering, and the globalization of civilization.

According to Wikipedia, Esfandiary's boldest claim was that new technologies would enable him to live to be a hundred years old, a rarity for his generation. As a display of his confidence in future technology, Fereidoun M. Esfandiary changed his name to FM-2030, a code name created by combining his first and middle initials along with the year in which he would turn one hundred. Sadly, he succumbed to pancreatic cancer at age seventy and never reached his goal, but in honor of his memory, zealous Transhumanist followers still paid tribute to FM-2030 by adopting his naming technique.

When the provost finished reading, he stood up and walked to the window, staring blankly out at the ocean for a long moment.

"So," he finally whispered, as if thinking aloud. "Bertrand Zobrist's lover—this FS-2080—is obviously one of these . . . **Transhumanists**."

"Without a doubt," Sinskey replied. "I'm sorry I don't know exactly who this FS-2080 is, but—"

"That was my point," the provost interrupted, still staring out to sea. "I **do** know. I know exactly who it is."

CHAPTER 74

The air itself seems fashioned of gold.

Robert Langdon had visited many magnificent cathedrals in his life, but the ambience of St. Mark's Chiesa d'Oro always struck him as truly singular. For centuries it had been claimed that simply breathing the air of St. Mark's would make you a richer person. The statement was intended to be understood not only metaphorically, but also literally.

With an interior veneer consisting of several **million** ancient gold tiles, many of the dust particles hovering in the air were said to be actual flecks of gold. This suspended gold dust, combined with the bright sunlight that streamed through the large western window, made for a vibrant atmosphere that helped the faithful attain both spiritual wealth and, provided they inhaled deeply, a more worldly enrichment in the form of gilding their lungs.

At this hour, the low sun piercing the west window spread out over Langdon's head like a broad, gleaming fan, or an awning of radiant silk. Langdon could not help but draw an awestruck breath, and he sensed Sienna and Ferris do the same beside him.

"Which way?" Sienna whispered.

Langdon motioned toward a set of ascending stairs.

The museum section of the church was on the upper level and contained an extensive exhibit devoted to the Horses of St. Mark's, which Langdon believed would quickly reveal the identity of the mysterious doge who had severed the animals' heads.

As they climbed the stairs, he could see that Ferris was struggling again with his breathing, and Sienna caught Langdon's eye, which she had been trying to do for several minutes now. Her expression was cautionary as she nodded discreetly toward Ferris and mouthed something Langdon couldn't understand. Before he could ask her for clarification, though, Ferris glanced back, a split second too late, for Sienna had already averted her eyes and was staring directly at Ferris.

"You okay, Doctor?" she asked innocently.

Ferris nodded and climbed faster.

The talented actress, Langdon thought, **but what was she trying to tell me?**

When they reached the second tier, they could see the entire basilica spread out beneath them. The sanctuary had been constructed in the form of a Greek Cross, far more square in appearance than the elongated rectangles of St. Peter's or Notre-Dame. With a shorter distance from narthex to altar, St. Mark's exuded a robust, sturdy quality, as well as a feeling of greater accessibility.

Not to appear **too** accessible, however, the church's altar resided behind a columned screen topped by an imposing crucifix. It was sheltered by an elegant ciborium and boasted one of the most valuable altarpieces in the world—the famed **Pala d'Oro.** An expansive backdrop of gilded silver, this "golden cloth" was a fabric only in the sense that it was a fused tapestry of previous works—primarily Byzantine enamel—all interwoven into a single Gothic frame. Adorned with some thirteen hundred pearls, four hundred garnets, three hundred sapphires, as well as emeralds, amethysts, and rubies, the **Pala d'Oro** was considered, along with the Horses of St. Mark's, to be one of the finest treasures in Venice.

Architecturally speaking, the word **basilica** defined any eastern, Byzantine-style church erected in Europe or the West. Being a replica of Justinian's Basilica of the Holy Apostles in Constantinople, St. Mark's was so eastern in style that guidebooks often suggested it as a viable alternative to visiting Turkish mosques, many of which were Byzantine cathedrals that had been turned into Muslim houses of worship.

While Langdon would never consider St. Mark's a stand-in for the spectacular mosques of Turkey, he did have to admit that one's passion for Byzantine art could be satisfied with a visit to the secret suite of rooms just off the right transept in this church, in which was hidden the so-called Treasure of St. Mark—a glittering collection of 283 precious icons, jewels, and chalices acquired during the looting of Constantinople.

Langdon was pleased to find the basilica relatively quiet this afternoon. There were still throngs of people, but at least there was room to maneuver. Weaving in and out of various groups, Langdon guided Ferris and Sienna toward the west window, where visitors could step outside and see the horses on the balcony. Despite Langdon's confidence in their ability to identify the doge in question, he remained concerned about the step they'd have to take **after** that—locating the doge himself. **His tomb? His statue?** This would probably require some form of assistance, considering the hundreds of statues housed in the church proper, the lower crypt, and the domed tombs along the church's north arm.

Langdon spotted a young female docent giving a tour, and he politely interrupted her talk. "Excuse me," he said. "Is Ettore Vio here this afternoon?"

"Ettore Vio?" The woman gave Langdon an odd look. "**Sì, certo, ma—**" She stopped short, her eyes brightening. "**Lei è Robert Langdon, vero?!**" *You're Robert Langdon, aren't you?*

Langdon smiled patiently. "**Sì, sono io.** Is it possible to speak with Ettore?"

"**Sì, sì!**" The woman motioned for her tour group to wait a moment and hurried off.

Langdon and the museum's curator, Ettore Vio, had once appeared together in a short documentary about the basilica, and they had kept in touch ever since. "Ettore wrote the book on this basilica," Langdon explained to Sienna. "Several of them, actually."

Sienna still looked strangely unnerved by Ferris, who stayed close while Langdon led the group across the upper register toward the west window, from which the horses could be seen. As they reached the window, the stallions' muscular hindquarters became visible in silhouette against the afternoon sun. Out on the balcony, wandering tourists enjoyed close contact with the horses as well as a spectacular panorama of St. Mark's Square.

"There they are!" Sienna exclaimed, moving toward the door that led to the balcony.

"Not exactly," Langdon said. "The horses we see on the balcony are actually just replicas. The **real** Horses of St. Mark's are kept inside for safety and preservation."

Langdon guided Sienna and Ferris along a corridor toward a well-lit alcove where an identical grouping of four stallions appeared to be trotting toward them out of a backdrop of brick archways.

Langdon motioned admiringly to the statues. "Here are the originals."

Every time Langdon saw these horses up close, he couldn't help but marvel at the texture and detail of their musculature. Only intensifying the dramatic appearance of their rippling skin was the sumptuous, golden-green verdigris that entirely covered their surface. For Langdon, seeing these four stallions perfectly maintained despite their tumultuous past was always a reminder of the importance of preserving great art.

"Their collars," Sienna said, motioning to the decorative breast collars around their necks. "You said those were added? To cover the seam?"

Langdon had told Sienna and Ferris about the strange "severed head" detail he had read about on the ARCA Web site.

"Apparently, yes," Langdon said, moving toward an informational placard posted nearby.

"Roberto!" a friendly voice bellowed behind them. "You insult me!"

Langdon turned to see Ettore Vio, a jovial-looking, white-haired man in a blue suit, with eyeglasses on a chain around his neck, pushing his way through the crowd. "You dare to come to my Venice and not call me?"

Langdon smiled and shook the man's hand. "I like to surprise you, Ettore. You look good. These are my friends Dr. Brooks and Dr. Ferris."

Ettore greeted them and then stood back, appraising Langdon. "Traveling with doctors? Are you sick? And your clothing? Are you turning Italian?"

"Neither," Langdon said, chuckling. "I've come for some information on the horses."

Ettore looked intrigued. "There is something the famous professor does not already know?"

Langdon laughed. "I need to learn about the severing of these horses' heads for transport during the Crusades."

Ettore Vio looked as if Langdon had just inquired about the Queen's hemorrhoids. "Heavens, Robert," he whispered, "we don't speak of that. If you want to see severed heads, I can show you the famed decapitated **Carmagnola** or—"

"Ettore, I need to know **which** Venetian doge cut off these heads."

"It never happened," Ettore countered defensively. "I've heard the tales, of course, but historically there is little to suggest that any doge committed—"

"Ettore, please, humor me," Langdon said. "According to the tale, which doge was it?"

Ettore put on his glasses and eyed Langdon. "Well, according to the **tale**, our beloved horses were transported by Venice's most clever and deceitful doge."

"Deceitful?"

"Yes, the doge who tricked everyone into the Crusades." He eyed Langdon expectantly. "The doge who took state money to sail to Egypt . . . but redirected his troops and sacked Constantinople instead."

Sounds like treachery, Langdon mused. "And what was his name?"

Ettore frowned. "Robert, I thought you were a student of world history."

"Yes, but the world is large, and history is long. I could use some help."

"Very well then, a final clue."

Langdon was going to protest, but he sensed that he'd be wasting his breath.

"Your doge lived for nearly a century," Ettore said. "A miracle in his day. Superstition attributed his longevity to his brave act of rescuing the bones of Saint Lucia from Constantinople and bringing them back to Venice. Saint Lucia lost her eyes to—"

"He plucked up the bones of the blind!" Sienna blurted, glancing at Langdon, who had just had the same thought.

Ettore gave Sienna an odd look. "In a manner of speaking, I suppose."

Ferris looked suddenly wan, as if he had not yet

caught his breath from the long walk across the plaza and the climb up the stairs.

"I should add," Ettore said, "that the doge loved Saint Lucia so much because the doge himself was blind. At the age of ninety, he stood out in this very square, unable to see a thing, and preached the Crusade."

"I know who it is," Langdon said.

"Well, I should hope so!" Ettore replied with a smile.

Because his eidetic memory was better suited to images rather than uncontextualized ideas, Langdon's revelation had arrived in the form of a piece of artwork—a famous illustration by Gustave Doré depicting a wizened, blind doge, arms raised high overhead as he incited a gathered crowd to join the Crusade. The name of Doré's illustration was clear in his mind: **Dandolo Preaching the Crusade.**

"Enrico Dandolo," Langdon declared. "The doge who lived forever."

"**Finalmente!**" Ettore said. "I fear your mind has aged, my friend."

"Along with the rest of me. Is he buried here?"

"Dandolo?" Ettore shook his head. "No, not here."

"Where?" Sienna demanded. "At the Doge's Palace?"

Ettore took off his glasses, thinking a moment. "Give me a moment. There are so many doges, I can't recall—"

Before Ettore could finish, a frightened-looking docent came running over and ushered him aside, whispering in his ear. Ettore stiffened, looking alarmed, and immediately hurried over to a railing, where he peered down into the sanctuary below. After a moment he turned back toward Langdon.

"I'll be right back," Ettore shouted, and then hurried off without another word.

Puzzled, Langdon went over to the railing and peered over. **What's going on down there?**

At first he saw nothing at all, just tourists milling around. After a moment, though, he realized that many of the visitors were staring in the same direction, toward the main entrance, through which an imposing group of black-clad soldiers had just entered the church and was fanning out across the narthex, blocking all the exits.

The soldiers in black. Langdon felt his hands tighten on the railing.

"Robert!" Sienna called out behind him.

Langdon remained fixated on the soldiers. **How did they find us?!**

"Robert," she called more urgently. "Something's wrong! Help me!"

Langdon turned from the railing, puzzled by her cries for help.

Where did she go?

An instant later, his eyes found both Sienna and Ferris. On the floor in front of the Horses of St. Mark's, Sienna was kneeling over Dr. Ferris . . . who had collapsed in convulsions, clutching his chest.

CHAPTER 75

I think he's having a heart attack!" Sienna shouted.
Langdon hurried over to where Dr. Ferris lay
sprawled on the floor. The man was gasping,
unable to catch his breath.

What happened to him?! For Langdon, everything had come to a head in a single moment. With
the soldiers' arrival downstairs and Ferris thrashing
on the floor, Langdon felt momentarily paralyzed,
unsure which way to turn.

Sienna crouched down over Ferris and loosened his
necktie, tearing open the top few buttons of his shirt
to help him breathe. But as the man's shirt parted,
Sienna recoiled and let out a sharp cry of alarm, covering her mouth as she staggered backward, staring
down at the bare flesh of his chest.

Langdon saw it, too.

The skin of Ferris's chest was deeply discolored. An
ominous-looking bluish-black blemish the circum-
ference of a grapefruit spread out across his sternum.
Ferris looked like he'd been hit in the chest with a
cannonball.

"That's internal bleeding," Sienna said, glancing up
at Langdon with a look of shock. "No wonder he's
been having trouble breathing all day."

Ferris twisted his head, clearly trying to speak, but he could only make faint wheezing sounds. Tourists had started gathering around, and Langdon sensed that the situation was about to get chaotic.

"The soldiers are downstairs," Langdon warned Sienna. "I don't know how they found us."

The look of surprise and fear on Sienna's face turned quickly to anger, and she glared back down at Ferris. "You've been lying to us, haven't you?"

Ferris attempted to speak again, but he could barely make a sound. Sienna roughly searched Ferris's pockets and pulled out his wallet and phone, which she slipped into her own pocket, standing over him now with an accusatory glower.

At that moment an elderly Italian woman pushed through the crowd, shouting angrily at Sienna. "**L'hai colpito al petto!**" She made a forceful motion with her fist against her own chest.

"**No!**" Sienna snapped. "CPR will kill him! Look at his chest!" She turned to Langdon. "Robert, we need to get out of here. Now."

Langdon looked down at Ferris, who desperately locked eyes with him, pleading, as if he wanted to communicate something.

"We can't just leave him!" Langdon said frantically.

"Trust me," Sienna said. "That's not a heart attack. And we're leaving. **Now.**"

As the crowd closed in, tourists began shouting for help. Sienna gripped Langdon's arm with startling force and dragged him away from the chaos, out into the fresh air of the balcony.

For a moment Langdon was blinded. The sun was directly in front of his eyes, sinking low over the western end of St. Mark's Square, bathing the entire balcony in a golden light. Sienna led Langdon to their left along the second-story terrace, snaking through the tourists who had stepped outside to admire the piazza and the replicas of the Horses of St. Mark's.

As they rushed along the front of the basilica, the lagoon was straight ahead. Out on the water, a strange silhouette caught Langdon's eye—an ultramodern yacht that looked like some kind of futuristic warship.

Before he could give it a second thought, he and Sienna had cut left again, following the balcony around the southwest corner of the basilica toward the "Paper Door"—the annex connecting the basilica to the Doge's Palace—so named because the doges posted decrees there for the public to read.

Not a heart attack? The image of Ferris's black-and-blue chest was imprinted in Langdon's mind, and he suddenly felt fearful at the prospect of hearing Sienna's diagnosis of the man's actual illness. Moreover, it seemed something had shifted, and Sienna no longer trusted Ferris. **Was that why she was trying to catch my eye earlier?**

Sienna suddenly skidded to a stop and leaned out over the elegant balustrade, peering down into a cloistered corner of St. Mark's Square far below.

"Damn it," she said. "We're higher up than I thought."

Langdon stared at her. **You were thinking of jumping?!**

Sienna looked frightened. "We can't let them catch us, Robert."

Langdon turned back toward the basilica, eyeing the heavy door of wrought iron and glass directly behind them. Tourists were entering and exiting, and if Langdon's estimate was correct, passing through the door would deposit them back inside the museum near the back of the church.

"They'll have all the exits covered," Sienna said.

Langdon considered their escape options and arrived at only one. "I think I saw something inside that could solve that problem."

Barely able to fathom what he was even now considering, Langdon guided Sienna back inside the basilica. They skirted the perimeter of the museum, trying to stay out of sight among the crowd, many of whom were now looking diagonally across the vast open space of the central nave toward the commotion going on around Ferris. Langdon spied the angry old Italian woman directing a pair of black-clad soldiers out onto the balcony, revealing Langdon and Sienna's escape route.

We'll have to hurry, Langdon thought, scanning the walls and finally spotting what he was looking for near a large display of tapestries.

The device on the wall was bright yellow with a red warning sticker: ALLARME ANTINCENDIO.

"A fire alarm?" Sienna said. "That's your plan?"

"We can slip out with the crowd." Langdon reached up and grabbed the alarm lever. **Here goes nothing**. Acting quickly before he could think better of it, he pulled down hard, seeing the mechanism cleanly shatter the small glass cylinder inside.

The sirens and pandemonium that Langdon expected never came.

Only silence.

He pulled again.

Nothing.

Sienna stared at him like he was crazy. "Robert, we're in a stone cathedral packed with tourists! You think these public fire alarms are **active** when a single prankster could—"

"Of course! Fire laws in the U.S.—"

"You're in Europe. We have fewer lawyers." She pointed over Langdon's shoulder. "And we're also out of time."

Langdon turned toward the glass door through which they'd just entered and saw two soldiers hurrying in from the balcony, their hard eyes scanning the area. Langdon recognized one as the same muscular agent who had fired at them on the Trike as they were fleeing Sienna's apartment.

With precious few options, Langdon and Sienna slipped out of sight in an enclosed spiral stairwell, descending back to the ground floor. When they reached the landing, they paused in the shadows of the stairwell. Across the sanctuary, several soldiers stood guarding the exits, their eyes intently sweeping the entire room.

"If we step out of this stairwell, they'll see us," Langdon said.

"The stairs go farther down," Sienna whispered, motioning to an ACCESSO VIETATO swag that cordoned off the stairs beneath them. Beyond the swag, the stairs descended in an even tighter spiral toward pitch blackness.

Bad idea, Langdon thought. **Subterranean crypt with no exit.**

Sienna had already stepped over the swag and was groping her way down the spiral tunnel, disappearing into the void.

"It's open," Sienna whispered from below.

Langdon was not surprised. The crypt of St. Mark's was different from many other such places in that it was also a working chapel, where regular services were held in the presence of the bones of St. Mark.

"I think I see natural light!" Sienna whispered.

How is that possible? Langdon tried to recall his previous visits to this sacred underground space and guessed that Sienna was probably seeing the **lux eterna**—an electric light that remained lit on St. Mark's tomb in the center of the crypt. With footsteps approaching from above him, though, Langdon didn't have time to think. He quickly stepped over the swag, making sure he didn't move it, and then he placed his palm on the rough-hewn stone wall, feeling his way down around the curve and out of sight.

Sienna was waiting for him at the bottom of the stairs. Behind her, the crypt was barely visible in the darkness. It was a squat subterranean chamber with an alarmingly low stone ceiling supported by ancient pillars and brick-vaulted archways. **The weight of the entire basilica rests on these pillars**, Langdon thought, already feeling claustrophobic.

"Told you," Sienna whispered, her pretty face faintly illuminated by the hint of muted natural light. She pointed to several small, arched transoms, high on the wall.

Light wells, Langdon realized, having forgotten they were here. The wells—designed to bring light and fresh air into this cramped crypt—opened into deep shafts that dropped down from St. Mark's Square above. The window glass was reinforced with a tight ironwork pattern of fifteen interlocking circles, and although Langdon suspected that they could be opened from inside, they were shoulder height and would be a tight fit. Even if they somehow managed to get through the window into the shaft, climbing out of the shafts would be impossible, since they were ten feet deep and covered by heavy security grates at the top.

In the dim light that filtered through the wells, St. Mark's crypt resembled a moonlit forest—a dense grove of trunklike pillars that cast long and heavy-looking shadows across the ground. Langdon turned his gaze to the center of the crypt, where a lone light burned at St. Mark's tomb. The basilica's namesake rested in a stone sarcophagus behind an altar, before which there were lines of pews for those lucky few invited to worship here at the heart of Venetian Christendom.

A tiny light suddenly flickered to life beside him and Langdon turned to see Sienna holding the illuminated screen of Ferris's phone.

Langdon did a double take. "I thought Ferris said his battery was dead!"

"He lied," Sienna said, still typing. "About a lot of things." She frowned at the phone and shook her head. "No signal. I thought maybe I could find the location of Enrico Dandolo's tomb." She hurried over to the light well and held the phone high overhead near the glass, trying to get a signal.

Enrico Dandolo, Langdon thought, having barely had a chance to consider the doge before having to flee the area. Despite their current predicament, their visit to St. Mark's had indeed served its purpose—revealing the identity of the treacherous doge who severed the heads from horses . . . and plucked up the bones of the blind.

Unfortunately, Langdon had no idea where Enrico Dandolo's tomb was located, and apparently neither did Ettore Vio. **He knows every inch of this basilica . . . probably of the Doge's Palace, too.** The fact that Ettore hadn't immediately located Dandolo's tomb suggested to Langdon that the tomb was probably nowhere near St. Mark's or the Doge's Palace.

So where is it?

Langdon glanced over at Sienna, who was now standing on a pew that she had moved under one of the light wells. She unlatched the window, swung it open, and held Ferris's phone out into the open air of the shaft itself.

The outdoor sounds of St. Mark's Square filtered down from above, and Langdon suddenly wondered if maybe there **was** some way out of here after all. There was a line of folding chairs behind the pews, and Langdon sensed that he might be able to hoist one up into the light well. **Maybe the upper grates unlatch from inside as well?**

Langdon hurried through the darkness toward Sienna. He had taken only a few steps when a powerful blow to his forehead knocked him backward. Crumpling to his knees, he thought for an instant that he had been attacked. He had not, he quickly realized, cursing himself for not anticipating that his six-foot frame far exceeded the height of vaults built for the average human height of more than a thousand years ago.

As he knelt there on the hard stone and let the stars clear, he found himself gazing at an inscription on the floor.

Sanctus Marcus.

He stared at it a long moment. It was not St. Mark's name in the inscription that struck him but rather the language in which it was written.

Latin.

After his daylong immersion in modern Italian, Langdon found himself vaguely disoriented to see St. Mark's name written in Latin, a quick reminder that the dead language was the lingua franca of the Roman Empire at the time of St. Mark's death.

Then a second thought hit Langdon.

During the early thirteenth century—the time of Enrico Dandolo and the Fourth Crusade—the language of power was still very much Latin. A Venetian doge who had brought great glory to the Roman Empire by recapturing Constantinople would never have been buried under the name of Enrico Dandolo . . . instead his Latin name would have been used.

Henricus Dandolo.

And with that, a long-forgotten image struck him like a jolt of electricity. Although the revelation had come while he was kneeling in a chapel, he knew it was not divinely inspired. More likely, it was nothing more than a visual cue that sparked his mind to make a sudden connection. The image that leaped suddenly from the depths of Langdon's memory was that of Dandolo's Latin name . . . engraved in a worn marble slab, embedded in an ornate tile floor.

Henricus Dandolo.

Langdon could barely breathe as he pictured the doge's simple tomb marker. **I've been there.** Precisely as the poem had promised, Enrico Dandolo was indeed buried in a gilded museum—a mouseion of holy wisdom—but it was not St. Mark's Basilica.

As the truth settled in, Langdon clambered slowly to his feet.

"I can't get a signal," Sienna said, climbing down from the light well and coming toward him.

"You don't need one," Langdon managed. "The gilded mouseion of holy wisdom . . ." He took a deep breath. "I . . . made a mistake."

Sienna went pale. "Don't tell me we're in the wrong museum."

"Sienna," Langdon whispered, feeling ill. "We're in the wrong country."

CHAPTER 76

Out in St. Mark's Square, the Gypsy woman selling Venetian masks was taking a break, leaning against the outer wall of the basilica to rest. As always, she had claimed her favorite spot—a small niche between two metal grates in the pavement—an ideal spot to set down her heavy wares and watch the setting sun.

She had witnessed many things in St. Mark's Square over the years, and yet the bizarre event that now drew her attention was not transpiring **in** the square . . . it was happening instead beneath it. Startled by a loud sound at her feet, the woman peered down through a grate into a narrow well, maybe ten feet deep. The window at the bottom was open and a folding chair had been shoved out into the bottom of the well, scraping against the pavement.

To the Gypsy's surprise, the chair was followed by a pretty woman with a blond ponytail who was apparently being hoisted from within and was now clambering through the window into the tiny opening.

The blond woman scrambled to her feet and immediately looked up, clearly startled to see the Gypsy staring down at her through the grate. The blond woman raised a finger to her lips and gave a tight

smile. Then she unfolded the chair and climbed onto
it, reaching up toward the grate.

You're far too short, the Gypsy thought. **And just
what are you doing?**

The blond woman climbed back down off the chair
and spoke to someone inside the building. Although
she barely had room to stand in the narrow well
beside the chair, she now stepped aside as a second
person—a tall, dark-haired man in a fancy suit—
heaved himself up out of the basilica basement and
into the crowded shaft.

He, too, looked up, making eye contact with the
Gypsy through the iron grate. Then, in an awkward
twist of limbs, he exchanged positions with the blond
woman and climbed up on top of the rickety chair.
He was taller, and when he reached up, he was able
to unlatch the security bar beneath the grate. Standing on tiptoe, he placed his hands on the grate and
heaved upward. The grate rose an inch or so before
he had to set it down.

"**Può darci una mano?**" the blond woman called
up to the Gypsy.

Give you a hand? the Gypsy wondered, having no
intention of getting involved. **What are you doing?**

The blond woman pulled out a man's wallet and
extracted a hundred-euro bill, waving it as an offering. It was more money than the vendor made with
her masks in three days. No stranger to negotiation,
she shook her head and held up two fingers. The
blond woman produced a second bill.

Disbelieving of her good fortune, the Gypsy

shrugged a reluctant yes, trying to look indifferent as she crouched down and grabbed the bars, looking into the man's eyes so they could synchronize their efforts.

As the man heaved again, the Gypsy pulled upward with arms made strong from years of carrying her wares, and the grate swung upward . . . halfway. Just as she thought they had it, there was a loud crash beneath her, and the man disappeared, plummeting back down into the well as the folding chair collapsed beneath him.

The iron grate grew instantly heavier in her hands, and she thought she would have to drop it, but the promise of two hundred euros gave her strength, and she managed to heave the grate up against the side of the basilica, where it came to rest with a loud clang.

Breathless, the Gypsy peered down into the well at the twist of bodies and broken furniture. As the man got back up and brushed himself off, she reached down into the well, holding out her hand for her money.

The ponytailed woman nodded appreciatively and raised the two bills over her head. The Gypsy reached down, but it was too far.

Give the money to the man.

Suddenly there was a commotion in the shaft— angry voices shouting from inside the basilica. The man and woman both spun in fear, recoiling from the window.

Then everything turned to chaos.

The dark-haired man took charge, crouching down and firmly ordering the woman to place her foot into a cradle formed by his fingers. She stepped in, and he heaved upward. She skimmed up the side of the shaft, stuffing the bills in her teeth to free her hands as she strained to reach the lip. The man heaved, higher . . . higher . . . lifting her until her hands curled over the edge.

With enormous effort, she heaved herself up into the square like a woman climbing out of a swimming pool. She shoved the money into the Gypsy's hands and immediately spun around and knelt at the edge of the well, reaching back down for the man.

It was too late.

Powerful arms in long black sleeves were reaching into the well like the thrashing tentacles of some hungry monster, grasping at the man's legs, pulling him back toward the window.

"Run, Sienna!" shouted the struggling man. "Now!"

The Gypsy saw their eyes lock in an exchange of pained regret . . . and then it was over.

The man was dragged roughly down through the window and back into the basilica.

The blond woman stared down in shock, her eyes welling with tears. "I'm so sorry, Robert," she whispered. Then, after a pause, she added, "For everything."

A moment later, the woman sprinted off into the crowd, her ponytail swinging as she raced down the narrow alleyway of the Merceria dell'Orologio . . . disappearing into the heart of Venice.

CHAPTER 77

The soft sounds of lapping water eased Robert Langdon gently back to consciousness. He smelled the sterile tang of antiseptics mixed with salty sea air and felt the world swaying beneath him.

Where am I?

Only moments before, it seemed, he had been locked in a death struggle against powerful hands that were dragging him out of the light well and back into the crypt. Now, strangely, he no longer felt the cold stone floor of St. Mark's beneath him . . . instead he felt a soft mattress.

Langdon opened his eyes and took in his surroundings—a small, hygienic-looking room with a single portal window. The rocking motion continued.

I'm on a boat?

Langdon's last recollection was of being pinned to the crypt floor by one of the black-clad soldiers, who hissed angrily at him, "Stop trying to escape!"

Langdon had shouted wildly, calling for help as the soldiers tried to muffle his voice.

"We need to get him out of here," one soldier had said to another.

His partner gave a reluctant nod. "Do it."

Langdon felt powerful fingertips expertly probing the arteries and veins on his neck. Then, having
located a precise spot on the carotid, the fingers began
applying a firm, focused pressure. Within seconds,
Langdon's vision began to blur, and he felt himself
slipping away, his brain being starved of oxygen.

They're killing me, Langdon thought. **Right here
beside the tomb of St. Mark.**

The blackness came, but it seemed incomplete . . .
more of a wash of grays punctuated by muted shapes
and sounds.

Langdon had little sense of how much time had
passed, but the world was now starting to come back
into focus for him. From all he could tell, he was in
an onboard infirmary of some sort. His sterile surroundings and the scent of isopropyl alcohol created
a strange sense of déjà vu—as if Langdon had come
full circle, awakening as he had the previous night,
in a strange hospital bed with only muted memories.

His thoughts turned instantly to Sienna and her
safety. He could still see her soft brown eyes gazing
down at him, filled with remorse and fear. Langdon
prayed that she had escaped and would find her way
safely out of Venice.

We're in the wrong country, Langdon had told
her, having realized to his shock the actual location
of Enrico Dandolo's tomb. The poem's mysterious
mouseion of holy wisdom was not in Venice after
all . . . but a world away. Precisely as Dante's text had
warned, the cryptic poem's meaning had been hidden "beneath the veil of verses so obscure."

Langdon had intended to explain everything to Sienna as soon as they'd escaped the crypt, but he'd never had the chance.

She ran off knowing only that I failed.

Langdon felt a knot tighten in his stomach.

The plague is still out there . . . a world away.

From outside the infirmary, he heard loud boot steps in the hall, and Langdon turned to see a man in black entering his berth. It was the same muscular soldier who had pinned him to the crypt floor. His eyes were ice cold. Langdon's instinct was to recoil as the man approached, but there was nowhere to run. **Whatever these people want to do to me, they can do.**

"Where am I?" Langdon demanded, putting as much defiance into his voice as he could muster.

"On a yacht anchored off Venice."

Langdon eyed the green medallion on the man's uniform—a globe of the world, encircled by the letters **ECDC**. Langdon had never seen the symbol or the acronym.

"We need information from you," the soldier said, "and we don't have much time."

"Why would I tell you anything?" Langdon asked. "You almost killed me."

"Not even close. We used a judo demobilization technique called **shime waza**. We had no intention of harming you."

"You **shot** at me this morning!" Langdon declared, clearly recalling the clang of the bullet on the fender of Sienna's speeding Trike. "Your bullet barely missed the base of my spine!"

The man's eyes narrowed. "If I had **wanted** to hit the base of your spine, I would have hit it. I took a single shot trying to puncture your moped's rear tire so I could stop you from running away. I was under orders to establish contact with you and figure out why the hell you were acting so erratically."

Before Langdon could fully process his words, two more soldiers came through the door, moving toward his bed.

Walking between them was a woman.

An apparition.

Ethereal and otherworldly.

Langdon immediately recognized her as the vision from his hallucinations. The woman before him was beautiful, with long silver hair and a blue lapis lazuli amulet. Because she had previously appeared against a horrifying landscape of dying bodies, Langdon needed a moment to believe she was truly standing before him in the flesh.

"Professor Langdon," the woman said, smiling wearily as she arrived at his bedside. "I'm relieved that you're okay." She sat down and took his pulse. "I've been advised that you have amnesia. Do you remember me?"

Langdon studied the woman for a moment. "I've had . . . visions of you, although I don't remember meeting."

The woman leaned toward him, her expression empathetic. "My name is Elizabeth Sinskey. I'm director of the World Health Organization, and I recruited you to help me find—"

"A plague," Langdon managed. "Created by Bertrand Zobrist."

Sinskey nodded, looking encouraged. "You remember?"

"No, I woke up in a hospital with a strange little projector and visions of **you** telling me to seek and find. That's what I was trying to do when these men tried to kill me." Langdon motioned to the soldiers.

The muscular one bristled, clearly ready to respond, but Elizabeth Sinskey silenced him with a wave.

"Professor," she said softly, "I have no doubt you are very confused. As the person who pulled you into all this, I'm horrified by what has transpired, and I'm thankful you're safe."

"Safe?" Langdon replied. "I'm captive on a ship!"

And so are you!

The silver-haired woman gave an understanding nod. "I'm afraid that due to your amnesia, many aspects of what I am about to tell you will be disorienting. Nonetheless, our time is short, and a lot of people need your help."

Sinskey hesitated, as if uncertain how to continue. "First off," she began, "I need you to understand that Agent Brüder and his team never tried to harm you. They were under direct orders to reestablish contact with you by whatever means were necessary."

"Reestablish? I don't—"

"Please, Professor, just listen. Everything will be made clear. I promise."

Langdon settled back into the infirmary bed, his thoughts spinning as Dr. Sinskey continued.

"Agent Brüder and his men are an SRS team—Surveillance and Response Support. They work under the auspices of the European Centre for Disease Prevention and Control."

Langdon glanced over at the ECDC medallions on their uniforms. **Disease Prevention and Control?**

"His group," she continued, "specializes in detecting and containing communicable-disease threats. Essentially, they are a SWAT team for the mitigation of acute, large-scale health risks. You were my main hope of locating the contagion Zobrist has created, and so when you vanished, I tasked the SRS team with locating you . . . I summoned them to Florence to support me."

Langdon was stunned. "Those soldiers work for **you?**"

She nodded. "On loan from the ECDC. Last night, when you disappeared and stopped calling in, we thought something had happened to you. It was not until early this morning, when our tech support team saw that you had checked your Harvard e-mail account, that we knew you were alive. At that point our only explanation for your strange behavior was that you had switched sides . . . possibly having been offered large sums of money to locate the contagion for someone else."

Langdon shook his head. "That's preposterous!"

"Yes, it seemed an unlikely scenario, but it was the only logical explanation—and with the stakes being so high, we couldn't take any chances. Of course, we never imagined you were suffering from amnesia. When our tech support saw your Harvard e-mail account suddenly activate, we tracked the computer IP address to the apartment in Florence and moved in. But you fled on a moped, with the woman, which increased our suspicions that you were now working for someone else."

"We drove right past you!" Langdon choked. "I saw you in the back of a black van, surrounded by soldiers. I thought you were a **captive**. You seemed delirious, like they had drugged you."

"You saw us?" Dr. Sinskey looked surprised. "Strangely, you're right . . . they **had** medicated me." She paused. "But only because I ordered them to."

Langdon was now wholly confused. **She told them to drug her?**

"You may not remember this," Sinskey said, "but as our C-130 landed in Florence, the pressure changed, and I suffered an episode of what is known as paroxysmal positional vertigo—a severely debilitating inner-ear condition that I've experienced in the past. It's temporary and not serious, but it causes victims to become so dizzy and nauseated they can barely hold their heads up. Normally I'd go to bed and endure intense nausea, but we were facing the Zobrist crisis, and so I prescribed myself hourly injections of metoclopramide to keep me from vomiting. The drug has the serious side effect of causing intense drowsiness, but it enabled me at least to run operations by phone from the back of the van. The SRS team wanted to take me to a hospital, but I ordered them not to do so until we had completed our mission of reacquiring you. Fortunately, the vertigo finally passed during the flight up to Venice."

Langdon slumped into the bed, unnerved. **I've been running all day from the World Health Organization—the very people who recruited me in the first place.**

"Now we have to focus, Professor," Sinskey declared, her tone urgent. "Zobrist's plague . . . do you have any idea where it is?" She gazed down at him with an expression of intense expectation. "We have very little time."

It's far away, Langdon wanted to say, but something stopped him. He glanced up at Brüder, a man who had fired a gun at him this morning and nearly strangled him a little while earlier. For Langdon, the ground had been shifting so quickly beneath him that he had no idea whom to believe anymore.

Sinskey leaned in, her expression still more intense. "We are under the impression that the contagion is here in Venice. Is that correct? Tell us where, and I'll send a team ashore."

Langdon hesitated.

"Sir!" Brüder barked impatiently. "You obviously know **something** . . . tell us where it is! Don't you understand what's about to happen?"

"Agent Brüder!" Sinskey spun angrily on the man. "That's enough," she commanded, then turned back to Langdon and spoke quietly. "Considering what you've been through, it's entirely understandable that you're disoriented, and uncertain whom to trust."

She paused, staring deep into his eyes. "But our time is short, and I'm asking you to trust **me**."

"Can Langdon stand?" a new voice asked.

A small, well-tended man with a deep tan appeared in the doorway. He studied Langdon with a practiced calm, but Langdon saw danger in his eyes.

Sinskey motioned for Langdon to stand up. "Professor, this is a man with whom I'd prefer not to collaborate, but the situation is serious enough that we have no choice."

Uncertain, Langdon swung his legs over the side of the bed and stood erect, taking a moment to get his balance back.

"Follow me," the man said, moving toward the door. "There's something you need to see."

Langdon held his ground. "Who are you?"

The man paused and steepled his fingers. "Names are not important. You can call me the provost. I run an organization . . . which, I'm sorry to say, made the mistake of helping Bertrand Zobrist achieve his goals. Now I am trying to fix that mistake before it's too late."

"What is it you want to show me?" Langdon asked.

The man fixed Langdon with an unyielding stare. "Something that will leave no doubt in your mind that we're all on the same side."

CHAPTER 78

Langdon followed the tanned man through a maze of claustrophobic corridors belowdecks with Dr. Sinskey and the ECDC soldiers trailing behind in a single file. As the group neared a staircase, Langdon hoped they were about to ascend toward daylight, but instead they descended deeper into the ship.

Deep in the bowels of the vessel now, their guide led them through a cubicle farm of sealed glass chambers—some with transparent walls and some with opaque ones. Inside each soundproofed room, various employees were hard at work typing on computers or speaking on telephones. Those who glanced up and noticed the group passing through looked seriously alarmed to see strangers in this part of the ship. The tanned man gave them a nod of reassurance and pressed on.

What is this place? Langdon wondered as they continued through another series of tightly configured work areas.

Finally, their host arrived at a large conference room, and they all filed in. As the group sat down, the man pressed a button, and the glass walls suddenly hissed and turned opaque, sealing them inside. Langdon startled, having never seen anything like it.

"Where are we?" Langdon finally demanded.

"This is my ship—**The Mendacium**."

"**Mendacium?**" Langdon asked. "As in . . . the Latin word for Pseudologos—the Greek god of deception?"

The man looked impressed. "Not many people know that."

Hardly a noble appellation, Langdon thought. Mendacium was the shadowy deity who reigned over all the **pseudologoi**—the daimones specializing in falsehoods, lies, and fabrications.

The man produced a tiny red flash drive and inserted it into a rack of electronic gear at the back of the room. A huge flat-panel LCD flickered to life, and the overhead lights dimmed.

In the expectant silence, Langdon heard soft lapping sounds of water. At first, he thought they were coming from outside the ship, but then he realized the sound was coming through the speakers on the LCD screen. Slowly, a picture materialized—a dripping cavern wall, illuminated by wavering reddish light.

"Bertrand Zobrist created this video," their host said. "And he asked me to release it to the world tomorrow."

In mute disbelief, Langdon watched the bizarre home movie . . . a cavernous space with a rippling lagoon . . . into which the camera plunged . . . diving beneath the surface to a silt-covered tile floor on which was bolted a plaque that read IN THIS PLACE, ON THIS DATE, THE WORLD WAS CHANGED FOREVER.

The plaque was signed: BERTRAND ZOBRIST.

The date was **tomorrow.**

My God! Langdon turned to Sinskey in the darkness, but she was just staring blankly at the floor, apparently having seen the film already, and clearly unable to watch it again.

The camera panned left now, and Langdon was baffled to see, hovering beneath the water, an undulating bubble of transparent plastic containing a gelatinous, yellow-brown liquid. The delicate sphere appeared to be tethered to the floor so it could not rise to the surface.

What the hell? Langdon studied the distended bag. The viscous contents seemed to be slowly swirling . . . smoldering almost.

When it hit him, Langdon stopped breathing. **Zobrist's plague.**

"Stop the playback," Sinskey said in the darkness.

The image froze—a tethered plastic sac hovering beneath the water—a sealed cloud of liquid suspended in space.

"I think you can guess what that is," Sinskey said. "The question is, how long will it remain contained?" She walked up to the LCD and pointed to a tiny marking on the transparent bag. "Unfortunately, this tells us what the bag is made of. Can you read that?"

Pulse racing, Langdon squinted at the text, which appeared to be a manufacturer's trademark notice: Solublon®.

"World's largest manufacturer of water-soluble plastics," Sinskey said.

Langdon felt his stomach knot. "You're saying this bag is . . . **dissolving?!**"

Sinskey gave him a grim nod. "We've been in touch with the manufacturer, from whom we learned, unfortunately, that they make dozens of different grades of this plastic, dissolving in anywhere from ten minutes to ten weeks, depending on the application. Decay rates vary slightly based on water type and temperature, but we have no doubt that Zobrist took those factors into careful account." She paused. "This bag, we believe, will dissolve by—"

"Tomorrow," the provost interrupted. "Tomorrow is the date Zobrist circled in my calendar. And also the date on the plaque."

Langdon sat speechless in the dark.

"Show him the rest," Sinskey said.

On the LCD screen, the video image refreshed, the camera now panning along the glowing waters and cavernous darkness. Langdon had no doubt that this was the location referenced in the poem. **The lagoon that reflects no stars.**

The scene conjured images of Dante's visions of hell . . . the river Cocytus flowing through the caverns of the underworld.

Wherever this lagoon was located, its waters were contained by steep, mossy walls, which, Langdon sensed, had to be man-made. He also sensed that the camera was revealing only a small corner of the massive interior space, and this notion was supported by the presence of very faint vertical shadows on the wall. The shadows were broad, columnar, and evenly spaced.

Pillars, Langdon realized.

The ceiling of this cavern is supported by pillars.

This lagoon was not in a cavern, it was in a massive room.

Follow deep into the sunken palace . . .

Before he could say a word, his attention shifted to the arrival of a new shadow on the wall . . . a humanoid shape with a long, beaked nose.

Oh, dear God . . .

The shadow began speaking now, its words muffled, whispering across the water with an eerily poetic rhythm.

"I am your salvation. I am the Shade."

For the next several minutes, Langdon watched the most terrifying film he had ever witnessed. Clearly the ravings of a lunatic genius, the soliloquy of Bertrand Zobrist—delivered in the guise of the plague doctor—was laden with references to Dante's **Inferno** and carried a very clear message: human population growth was out of control, and the very survival of mankind was hanging in the balance.

Onscreen, the voice intoned:

"To do nothing is to welcome Dante's hell . . .
cramped and starving, weltering in Sin. And
so boldly I have taken action. Some will recoil

in horror, but all salvation comes at a price.
One day the world will grasp the beauty of my
sacrifice."

Langdon recoiled as Zobrist himself abruptly
appeared, dressed as the plague doctor, and then tore
off his mask. Langdon stared at the gaunt face and
wild green eyes, realizing that he was finally seeing
the face of the man who was at the center of this crisis. Zobrist began professing his love to someone he
called his inspiration.

"I have left the future in your gentle hands. My
work below is done. And now the hour has come
for me to climb again to the world above ... and
rebehold the stars."

As the video ended, Langdon recognized Zobrist's
final words as a near duplicate of Dante's final words
in the **Inferno**.

In the darkness of the conference room, Langdon
realized that all the moments of fear he had experienced today had just crystallized into a single, terrifying reality.

Bertrand Zobrist now had a face ... and a voice.

The conference room lights came up, and Langdon
saw all eyes trained expectantly on him.

Elizabeth Sinskey's expression seemed frozen as she
stood up and nervously stroked her amulet. "Professor, obviously our time is very short. The only good
news so far is that we've had no cases of pathogen

detection, or reported illness, so we're assuming the suspended Solublon bag is still intact. But we don't know where to **look**. Our goal is to neutralize this threat by containing the bag before it ruptures. The only way we can do that, of course, is to find its location immediately."

Agent Brüder stood up now, staring intently at Langdon. "We're assuming you came to Venice because you learned that this is where Zobrist hid his plague."

Langdon gazed out at the assembly before him, faces taut with fear, everyone hoping for a miracle, and he wished he had better news to offer them.

"We're in the wrong country," Langdon announced. "What you're looking for is nearly a thousand miles from here."

———

Langdon's insides reverberated with the deep thrum of **The Mendacium**'s engines as the ship powered through its wide turn, banking back toward the Venice Airport. On board, all hell had broken loose. The provost had dashed off, shouting orders to his crew. Elizabeth Sinskey had grabbed her phone and called the pilots of the WHO's C-130 transport plane, demanding they be prepped as soon as possible to fly out of the Venice Airport. And Agent Brüder had jumped on a laptop to see if he could coordinate some kind of international advance team at their final destination.

A world away.

The provost now returned to the conference room and urgently addressed Brüder. "Any further word from the Venetian authorities?"

Brüder shook his head. "No trace. They're looking, but Sienna Brooks has vanished."

Langdon did a double take. **They're looking for Sienna?**

Sinskey finished her phone call and also joined the conversation. "No luck finding her?"

The provost shook his head. "If you're agreeable, I think the WHO should authorize the use of force if necessary to bring her in."

Langdon jumped to his feet. "Why?! Sienna Brooks is not involved in any of this!"

The provost's dark eyes cut to Langdon. "Professor, there are some things I have to tell you about Ms. Brooks."

CHAPTER 79

Pushing past the crush of tourists on the Rialto Bridge, Sienna Brooks began running again, sprinting west along the canal-front walkway of the Fondamenta Vin Castello.

They've got Robert.

She could still see his desperate eyes gazing up at her as the soldiers dragged him back down the light well into the crypt. She had little doubt that his captors would quickly persuade him, one way or another, to reveal everything he had figured out.

We're in the wrong country.

Far more tragic, though, was her knowledge that his captors would waste no time revealing to Langdon the true nature of the situation.

I'm so sorry, Robert.

For everything.

Please know I had no choice.

Strangely, Sienna missed him already. Here, amid the masses of Venice, she felt a familiar loneliness settling in.

The feeling was nothing new.

Since childhood, Sienna Brooks had felt alone.

Growing up with an exceptional intellect, Sienna had spent her youth feeling like a stranger in a strange land . . . an alien trapped on a lonely world. She tried to make friends, but her peers immersed themselves in frivolities that held no interest to her. She tried to respect her elders, but most adults seemed like nothing more than aging children, lacking even the most basic understanding of the world around them, and, most troubling, lacking any curiosity or concern about it.

I felt I was a part of nothing.

And so Sienna Brooks learned how to be a ghost. Invisible. She learned how to be a chameleon, a performer, playing just another face in the crowd. Her childhood passion for stage acting, she had no doubt, stemmed from what would become her life-long dream of becoming someone else.

Someone normal.

Her performance in Shakespeare's **A Midsummer Night's Dream** helped her feel a part of something, and the adult actors were supportive without being condescending. Her joy, however, was short-lived, evaporating the moment she left the stage on opening night and faced throngs of wide-eyed media people while her costars quietly skulked out the back door unnoticed.

Now they hate me, too.

By the age of seven, Sienna had read enough to diagnose herself with deep depression. When she told her parents, they seemed dumbfounded, as they usually were by the strangeness of their own daughter. Nonetheless, they sent her to a psychiatrist. The doctor asked her a lot of questions, which Sienna had already asked herself, and then he prescribed a combination of amitriptyline and chlordiazepoxide.

Furious, Sienna jumped off his couch. "Amitriptyline?!" she challenged. "I want to be happier—not a zombie!"

The psychiatrist, to his great credit, remained very calm in the face of her outburst and offered a second suggestion. "Sienna, if you prefer not to take pharmaceuticals, we can try a more holistic approach." He paused. "It sounds as if you are trapped in a cycle of thinking about yourself and how you don't belong in the world."

"That's true," Sienna replied. "I try to stop, but I can't!"

He smiled calmly. "Of course you can't stop. It is physically impossible for the human mind to think of nothing. The soul craves emotion, and it will continue to seek fuel for that emotion—good or bad. Your problem is that you're giving it the wrong fuel."

Sienna had never heard anyone talk about the mind in such mechanical terms, and she was instantly intrigued. "How do I give it a different fuel?"

"You need to shift your intellectual focus," he said. "Currently, you think mainly about yourself. You wonder why **you** don't fit . . . and what is wrong with **you**."

"That's true," Sienna said again, "but I'm trying to solve the problem. I'm trying to fit in. I can't solve the problem if I don't think about it."

He chuckled. "I believe that thinking about the problem . . . **is** your problem." The doctor suggested that she try to shift her focus away from herself and her own problems . . . turning her attention instead to the world around her . . . and its problems.

That's when everything changed.

She began pouring all of her energy not into feeling sorry for herself . . . but into feeling sorry for other people. She began a philanthropic initiative, ladled soup at homeless shelters, and read books to the blind. Incredibly, none of the people Sienna helped even seemed to notice that she was different. They were just grateful that somebody cared.

Sienna worked harder every week, barely able to sleep because of the realization that so many people needed her help.

"Sienna, slow down!" people would urge her. "You can't save the world!"

What a terrible thing to say.

Through her acts of public service, Sienna came in contact with several members of a local humanitarian group. When they invited her to join them on a monthlong trip to the Philippines, she jumped at the chance.

Sienna imagined they were going to feed poor fishermen or farmers in the countryside, which she had read was a wonderland of geological beauty, with vibrant seabeds and dazzling plains. And so when the group settled in among the throngs in the city of Manila—the most densely populated city on earth— Sienna could only gape in horror. She had never seen poverty on this scale.

How can one person possibly make a difference?

For every one person Sienna fed, there were hundreds more who gazed at her with desolate eyes. Manila had six-hour traffic jams, suffocating pollution, and a horrifying sex trade, whose workers consisted primarily of young children, many of whom had been sold to pimps by parents who took solace in knowing that at least their children would be fed.

Amid this chaos of child prostitution, panhandlers, pickpockets, and worse, Sienna found herself suddenly paralyzed. All around her, she could see humanity overrun by its primal instinct for survival. **When they face desperation . . . human beings become animals.**

For Sienna, all the dark depression came flooding back. She had suddenly understood mankind for what it was—a species on the brink.

I was wrong, she thought. **I can't save the world.**

Overwhelmed by a rush of frantic mania, Sienna broke into a sprint through the city streets, thrusting her way through the masses of people, knocking them over, pressing on, searching for open space.

I'm being suffocated by human flesh!

As she ran, she could feel the eyes upon her again. She no longer blended in. She was tall and fair-skinned with a blond ponytail waving behind her. Men stared at her as if she were naked.

When her legs finally gave out, she had no idea how far she had run or where she had gone. She cleared the tears and grime from her eyes and saw that she was standing in a kind of shantytown—a city made of pieces of corrugated metal and cardboard propped up and held together. All around her the wails of crying babies and the stench of human excrement hung in the air.

I've run through the gates of hell.

"Turista," a deep voice sneered behind her. "**Magkano?**" How much?

Sienna spun to see three young men approaching, salivating like wolves. She instantly knew she was in danger and she tried to back away, but they corralled her, like predators hunting in a pack.

Sienna shouted for help, but nobody paid attention to her cries. Only fifteen feet away, she saw an old woman sitting on a tire, carving the rot off an old onion with a rusty knife. The woman did not even glance up when Sienna shouted.

When the men seized her and dragged her inside a little shack, Sienna had no illusions about what was going to happen, and the terror was all-consuming. She fought with everything she had, but they were strong, quickly pinning her down on an old, soiled mattress.

They tore open her shirt, clawing at her soft skin. When she screamed, they stuffed her torn shirt so deep into her mouth that she thought she would choke. Then they flipped her onto her stomach, forcing her face into the putrid bed.

Sienna Brooks had always felt pity for the ignorant souls who could believe in God amid a world of such suffering, and yet now she herself was praying . . . praying with all her heart.

Please, God, deliver me from evil.

Even as she prayed, she could hear the men laughing, taunting her as their filthy hands hauled her jeans down over her flailing legs. One of them climbed onto her back, sweaty and heavy, his perspiration dripping onto her skin.

I'm a virgin, Sienna thought. **This is how it is going to happen for me.**

Suddenly the man on her back leaped off her, and the taunting jeers turned to shouts of anger and fear. The warm sweat rolling onto Sienna's back from above suddenly began gushing . . . spilling onto the mattress in splatters of red.

When Sienna rolled over to see what was happening, she saw the old woman with the half-peeled onion and the rusty knife standing over her attacker, who was now bleeding profusely from his back.

The old woman glared threateningly at the others, whipping her bloody knife through the air until the three men scampered off.

Without a word, the old woman helped Sienna gather her clothes and get dressed.

"**Salamat,**" Sienna whispered tearfully. "Thank you."

The old woman tapped her ear, indicating she was deaf.

Sienna placed her palms together, closed her eyes, and bowed her head in a gesture of respect. When she opened her eyes, the woman was gone.

Sienna left the Philippines at once, without even saying good-bye to the other members of the group. She never once spoke of what had happened to her.

She hoped that ignoring the incident would make it fade away, but it seemed only to make it worse. Months later, she was still haunted by night terrors, and she no longer felt safe anywhere. She took up martial arts, and despite quickly mastering the deadly skill of **dim mak**, she still felt at risk everywhere she went.

Her depression returned, surging tenfold, and eventually she stopped sleeping altogether. Every time she combed her hair, she noticed that huge clumps were falling out, more hair every day. To her horror, within weeks, she was half bald, having developed symptoms that she self-diagnosed as telegenic effluvium—a stress-related alopecia with no cure other than curing one's stress. Every time she looked in the mirror, though, she saw her balding head and felt her heart race.

I look like an old woman!

Finally, she had no choice but to shave her head. At least she no longer looked old. She simply looked ill. Not wanting to look like a cancer victim, she purchased a wig, which she wore in a blond ponytail, and at least looked like herself again.

Inside, however, Sienna Brooks was changed.

I am damaged goods.

In a desperate attempt to leave her life behind, she traveled to America and attended medical school. She had always had an affinity for medicine, and she hoped that being a doctor would make her feel like she was being of service . . . as if she were doing **something** at least to ease the pain of this troubled world.

Despite the long hours, school had been easy for her, and while her classmates were studying, Sienna took a part-time acting job to earn some extra money. The gig definitely wasn't Shakespeare, but her skills with language and memorization meant that instead of feeling like work, acting felt like a sanctuary where Sienna could forget who she was . . . and be **someone else**.

Anybody else.

Sienna had been trying to escape her identity since she could first speak. As a child, she had shunned her given name, Felicity, in favor of her middle name, Sienna. **Felicity** meant "fortunate," and she knew she was anything but.

Remove the focus on your own problems, she reminded herself. **Focus on the problems of the world.**

Her panic attack in the crowded streets of Manila had sparked in Sienna a deep concern about overcrowding and world population. It was then that she discovered the writings of Bertrand Zobrist, a genetic engineer who had proposed some very progressive theories about world population.

He's a genius, she realized, reading his work. Sienna had never felt that way about another human being, and the more of Zobrist she read, the more she felt like she was looking into the heart of a soul mate. His article "You Can't Save the World" reminded Sienna of what everyone used to tell her as a child . . . and yet Zobrist believed the exact opposite.

You CAN save the world, Zobrist wrote. **If not you, then who? If not now, when?**

Sienna studied Zobrist's mathematical equations carefully, educating herself on his predictions of a Malthusian catastrophe and the impending collapse of the species. Her intellect loved the high-level speculations, but she felt her stress level climbing as she saw the entire future before her . . . mathematically guaranteed . . . so obvious . . . inevitable.

Why doesn't anyone else see this coming?

Though she was frightened by his ideas, Sienna became obsessed with Zobrist, watching videos of his presentations, reading everything he had ever written. When Sienna heard that he had a speaking engagement in the United States, she knew she had to go see him. And that was the night her entire world had changed.

A smile lit up her face, a rare moment of happiness, as she again pictured that magical evening . . . an evening she had vividly recalled only hours earlier while sitting on the train with Langdon and Ferris.

Chicago. The blizzard.

January, six years ago . . . but it still feels like yesterday. I am trudging through snowbanks along the windswept Magnificent Mile, collar upturned against the blinding whiteout. Despite the cold, I tell myself that nothing will keep me from my destination. Tonight is my chance to hear the great Bertrand Zobrist speak . . . in person.

The hall is nearly deserted when Bertrand takes

the stage, and he is tall . . . so very tall . . . with vibrant green eyes that seem to hold all the mysteries of the world.

"To hell with this empty auditorium," he declares. "Let's go to the bar!"

And then we are there, a handful of us, in a quiet booth, as he speaks of genetics, of population, and of his newest passion . . . Transhumanism.

As the drinks flow, I feel as if I'm having a private audience with a rock star. Every time Zobrist glances over at me, his green eyes ignite a wholly unexpected feeling inside me . . . the deep pull of sexual attraction.

It is a wholly new sensation for me.

And then we are alone.

"Thank you for tonight," I say to him, feeling a little tipsy. "You're an amazing teacher."

"Flattery?" Zobrist smiles and leans closer, our legs touching now. "It will get you everywhere."

The flirtation is clearly inappropriate, but it is a snowy night in a deserted Chicago hotel, and it feels as if the entire world has stopped.

"So what do you think?" Zobrist says. "Nightcap in my room?"

I freeze, knowing I must look like a deer in the headlights. I don't know how to do this!

Zobrist's eyes twinkle warmly. "Let me guess," he whispers. "You've never been with a famous man."

I feel myself flush, fighting to hide a surge of emotions—embarrassment, excitement, fear. "Actually, to be honest," I say to him, "I've never been with any man."

Zobrist smiles and inches closer. "I'm not sure what you've been waiting for, but please let me be your first."

In that moment all the awkward sexual fears and frustrations of my childhood disappear . . . evaporating into the snowy night.

Then, I am naked in his arms.

"Relax, Sienna," he whispers, and then, with patient hands, he coaxes from my inexperienced body a torrent of sensations that I have never imagined existed.

Basking in the cocoon of Zobrist's embrace, I feel as if everything is finally right in the world, and I know my life has purpose.

I have found Love.

And I will follow it anywhere.

CHAPTER 80

Abovedecks on **The Mendacium**, Langdon gripped the polished teak railing, steadied his wavering legs, and tried to catch his breath. The sea air had grown colder, and the roar of low-flying commercial jets told him they were nearing the Venice Airport.

There are some things I have to tell you about Ms. Brooks.

Beside him at the railing, the provost and Dr. Sinskey remained silent but attentive, giving him a moment to get his bearings. What they had told Langdon downstairs had left him so disoriented and upset that Sinskey had brought him outside for some air.

The sea air was bracing, and yet Langdon felt no clearer in his head. All he could do was stare vacantly down at the churning wake of the ship, trying to find a shred of logic to what he had just heard.

According to the provost, Sienna Brooks and Bertrand Zobrist had been longtime lovers. They were active together in some kind of underground Transhumanist movement. Her full name was Felicity Sienna Brooks, but she also went by the code name FS-2080 . . . which had something to do with her initials, and the year of her one-hundredth birthday.

None of it makes any sense!

"I knew Sienna Brooks through a different source," the provost had told Langdon, "and I trusted her. So, when she came to me last year and asked me to meet a wealthy potential client, I agreed. That prospect turned out to be Bertrand Zobrist. He hired me to provide him a safe haven where he could work undetected on his 'masterpiece.' I assumed he was developing a new technology that he didn't want pirated . . . or maybe he was performing some cutting-edge genetic research that was in conflict with the WHO's ethics regulations . . . I didn't ask questions, but believe me, I never imagined he was creating . . . a plague."

Langdon had only been able to nod vacantly . . . bewildered.

"Zobrist was a Dante fanatic," the provost continued, "and he therefore chose Florence as the city in which he wanted to hide. So my organization set him up with everything he needed—a discreet lab facility with living quarters, various aliases and secure communication avenues, and a personal attaché who oversaw everything from his security to buying food and supplies. Zobrist never used his own credit cards or appeared in public, so he was impossible to track. We even provided him disguises, aliases, and alternate documentation for traveling unnoticed." He paused. "Which he apparently did when he placed the Solublon bag."

Sinskey exhaled, making little effort to hide her frustration. "The WHO has been trying to keep tabs on him since last year, but he seemed to have vanished off the face of the earth."

"Even hiding from Sienna," the provost said.

"I'm sorry?" Langdon glanced up, clearing the knot in his throat. "I thought you said they were lovers?"

"They were, but he cut her off suddenly when he went into hiding. Even though Sienna was the one who sent him to us, my agreement was with Zobrist himself, and part of our deal was that when he disappeared, he would disappear from the whole world, including Sienna. Apparently after he went into hiding, he sent her a farewell letter revealing that he was very ill, would be dead in a year or so, and didn't want her to see him deteriorate."

Zobrist abandoned Sienna?

"Sienna tried to contact me for information," the provost said, "but I refused to take her calls. I had to respect my client's wishes."

"Two weeks ago," Sinskey continued, "Zobrist walked into a bank in Florence and anonymously rented a safe-deposit box. After he left, our watch list got word that the bank's new facial-recognition software had identified the disguised man as Bertrand Zobrist. My team flew to Florence and it took a week to locate his safe house, which was empty, but inside we found evidence that he had created some kind of highly contagious pathogen and hidden it somewhere else."

Sinskey paused. "We were desperate to find him. The following morning, before sunrise, we spotted him walking along the Arno, and we immediately gave chase. That's when he fled up the Badia tower and jumped to his death."

"He may have been planning to do that anyway," the provost added. "He was convinced he did not have long to live."

"As it turned out," Sinskey said, "Sienna had been searching for him as well. Somehow, she found out that we had mobilized to Florence, and she tailed our movements, thinking we might have located him. Unfortunately, she was there in time to see Zobrist jump." Sinskey sighed. "I suspect it was very traumatic for her to watch her lover and mentor fall to his death."

Langdon felt ill, barely able to comprehend what they were telling him. The only person in this entire scenario whom he trusted was Sienna, and these people were telling him that she was not who she claimed to be? No matter what they said, he could not believe Sienna would condone Zobrist's desire to create a plague.

Or would she?

Would you kill half the population today, Sienna had asked him, **in order to save our species from extinction?**

Langdon felt a chill.

"Once Zobrist was dead," Sinskey explained, "I used my influence to force the bank to open Zobrist's safe-deposit box, which ironically turned out to contain a letter to me . . . along with a strange little device."

"The projector," Langdon ventured.

"Exactly. His letter said he wanted me to be the first to visit ground zero, which nobody would ever find without following his **Map of Hell.**"

Langdon pictured the modified Botticelli painting that shone out of the tiny projector.

The provost added, "Zobrist had contracted me to deliver to Dr. Sinskey the contents of the safe-deposit box, but not until **after** tomorrow morning. When Dr. Sinskey came into possession of it early, we panicked and took action, trying to recover it in accordance with our client's wishes."

Sinskey looked at Langdon. "I didn't have much hope of understanding the map in time, so I recruited you to help me. Are you remembering any of this, now?"

Langdon shook his head.

"We flew you quietly to Florence, where you had made an appointment with someone you thought could help."

Ignazio Busoni.

"You met with him last night," Sinskey said, "and then you disappeared. We thought something had happened to you."

"And in fact," the provost said, "something **did** happen to you. In an effort to recover the projector, we had an agent of mine named Vayentha tail you from the airport. She lost you somewhere around the Piazza della Signoria." He scowled. "Losing you was a critical error. And Vayentha had the nerve to blame it on a bird."

"I'm sorry?"

"A cooing dove. By Vayentha's account, she was in perfect position, watching you from a darkened alcove, when a group of tourists passed. She said a dove suddenly cooed loudly from a window box over her head, causing the tourists to stop and block Vayentha in. By the time she could slip back into the alley, you were gone." He shook his head in disgust. "Anyway, she lost you for several hours. Finally, she picked up your trail again—and by this time you had been joined by another man."

Ignazio, Langdon thought. **He and I must have been exiting the Palazzo Vecchio with the mask.**

"She successfully tailed you both in the direction of the Piazza della Signoria, but the two of you apparently saw her and decided to flee, going in separate directions."

That makes sense, Langdon thought. **Ignazio fled with the mask and hid it in the baptistry before he had a heart attack.**

"Then Vayentha made a terrible mistake," the provost said.

"She shot me in the head?"

"No, she revealed herself too early. She pulled you in for interrogation before you actually knew anything. We needed to know if you had deciphered the map or told Dr. Sinskey what she needed to know. You refused to say a word. You said you would die first."

I was looking for a deadly plague! I probably thought you were mercenaries looking to obtain a biological weapon!

The ship's massive engines suddenly shifted into reverse, slowing the vessel as it neared the loading dock for the airport. In the distance, Langdon could see the nondescript hull of a C-130 transport plane fueling. The fuselage bore the inscription WORLD HEALTH ORGANIZATION.

At that moment Brüder arrived, his expression grim. "I've just learned that the only qualified response team within five hours of the site is **us**, which means we're on our own."

Sinskey slumped. "Coordination with local authorities?"

Brüder looked wary. "Not yet. That's my recommendation. We don't have an exact location at the moment, so there's nothing they could do. Moreover, a containment operation is well beyond the scope of their expertise, and we run the real risk of their doing more damage than good."

"**Primum non nocere**," Sinskey whispered with a nod, repeating the fundamental precept of medical ethics: **First, do no harm.**

"Lastly," Brüder said, "we still have no word on Sienna Brooks." He eyed the provost. "Do you know if Sienna has contacts in Venice who might assist her?"

"It wouldn't surprise me," he replied. "Zobrist had disciples everywhere, and if I know Sienna, she'll be using all available resources to carry out her directive."

"You can't let her get out of Venice," Sinskey said. "We have no idea what condition that Solublon bag is currently in. If anyone discovers it, all that would be needed at this point is a slight touch to burst the plastic and release the contagion into the water."

There was a moment of silence as the gravity of the situation settled in.

"I'm afraid I've got more bad news," Langdon said. "The gilded mouseion of holy wisdom." He paused. "Sienna knows where it is. She **knows** where we're going."

"What?!" Sinskey's voice rose in alarm. "I thought you said you didn't have a chance to tell Sienna what you'd figured out! You said all you told her is that you were in the wrong country!"

"That's true," Langdon said, "but she knew we were looking for the tomb of Enrico Dandolo. A quick Web search can tell her where that is. And once she finds Dandolo's tomb . . . the dissolving canister can't be far away. The poem said to follow the sounds of trickling water to the sunken palace."

"Damn it!" Brüder erupted, and stormed off.

"She'll never beat us there," the provost said. "We have a head start."

Sinskey sighed heavily. "I wouldn't be so sure. Our transport is slow, and it appears Sienna Brooks is extremely resourceful."

As **The Mendacium** docked, Langdon found himself staring uneasily at the cumbersome C-130 on the runway. It barely looked airworthy and had no windows. **I've been on this thing already?** Langdon didn't remember a thing.

Whether it was because of the movement of the

docking boat, or growing reservations about the claustrophobic aircraft, Langdon didn't know, but he was suddenly hit by an upsurge of nausea.

He turned to Sinskey. "I'm not sure I feel well enough to fly."

"You're fine," she said. "You've been through the wringer today, and of course, you've got the toxins in your body."

"**Toxins?**" Langdon took a wavering step backward. "What are you talking about?"

Sinskey glanced away, clearly having said more than she intended.

"Professor, I'm sorry. Unfortunately, I've just learned that your medical condition is a bit more complicated than a simple head wound."

Langdon felt a spike of fear as he pictured the black flesh on Ferris's chest when the man collapsed in the basilica.

"What's wrong with me?" Langdon demanded.

Sinskey hesitated, as if uncertain how to proceed. "Let's get you onto the plane first."

CHAPTER **81**

ocated just east of the spectacular Frari church, the Atelier Pietro Longhi has always been one of Venice's premier providers of historical costumes, wigs, and accessories. Its client list includes film companies and theatrical troupes, as well as influential members of the public who rely on the staff's expertise to dress them for Carnevale's most extravagant balls.

The clerk was just about to lock up for the evening when the door jingled loudly. He glanced up to see an attractive woman with a blond ponytail come bursting in. She was breathless, as if she'd been running for miles. She hurried to the counter, her brown eyes wild and desperate.

"I want to speak to Giorgio Venci," she had said, panting.

Don't we all, the clerk thought. **But nobody gets to see the wizard.**

Giorgio Venci—the atelier's chief designer—worked his magic from behind the curtain, speaking to clients very rarely and never without an appointment. As a man of great wealth and influence, Giorgio was allowed certain eccentricities, including his passion for solitude. He dined privately, flew pri-

vately, and constantly complained about the rising
number of tourists in Venice. He was not one who
liked company.

"I'm sorry," the clerk said with a practiced smile.
"I'm afraid Signor Venci is not here. Perhaps I can
help you?"

"Giorgio's here," she declared. "His flat is upstairs.
I saw his light on. I'm a friend. It's an emergency."

There was a burning intensity about the woman. **A
friend? she claims.** "Might I tell Giorgio your name?"

The woman took a scrap of paper off the counter
and jotted down a series of letters and numbers.

"Just give him this," she said, handing the clerk the
paper. "And please hurry. I don't have much time."

The clerk hesitantly carried the paper upstairs and
laid it on the long altering table, where Giorgio was
hunched intently at his sewing machine.

"Signore," he whispered. "Someone is here to see
you. She says it's an emergency."

Without breaking off from his work or looking up,
the man reached out with one hand and took the
paper, reading the text.

His sewing machine rattled to a stop.

"Send her up immediately," Giorgio commanded
as he tore the paper into tiny shreds.

CHAPTER 82

The massive C-130 transport plane was still ascending as it banked southeast, thundering out across the Adriatic. On board, Robert Langdon was feeling simultaneously cramped and adrift—oppressed by the absence of windows in the aircraft and bewildered by all of the unanswered questions swirling around in his brain.

Your medical condition, Sinskey had told him, **is a bit more complicated than a simple head wound.**

Langdon's pulse quickened at the thought of what she might tell him, and yet at the moment she was busy discussing containment strategies with the SRS team. Brüder was on the phone nearby, speaking with government agencies about Sienna Brooks, following up on everyone's attempts to locate her.

Sienna . . .

Langdon was still trying to make sense of the claim that she was intricately involved in all of this. As the plane leveled out from its ascent, the small man who called himself the provost walked across the cabin and sat down opposite Langdon. He steepled his fingers beneath his chin and pursed his lips. "Dr. Sinskey asked me to fill you in . . . make an attempt to bring clarity to your situation."

Langdon wondered what this man could possibly say to make any of this confusion even remotely clear.

"As I began to say earlier," the provost said, "much of this started after my agent Vayentha pulled you in prematurely. We had no idea how much progress you had made on Dr. Sinskey's behalf, or how much you had shared with her. But we were afraid if she learned the location of the project our client had hired us to protect, she was going to confiscate or destroy it. We had to find it before she did, and so we needed you to work on **our** behalf . . . rather than on Sinskey's." The provost paused, tapping his fingertips together. "Unfortunately, we had already shown our cards . . . and you most certainly did not trust us."

"So you shot me in the head?" Langdon replied angrily.

"We came up with a plan to make you **trust** us."

Langdon felt lost. "How do you **make** someone trust you . . . after you've kidnapped and interrogated him?"

The man shifted uncomfortably now. "Professor, are you familiar with the family of chemicals known as benzodiazepines?"

Langdon shook his head.

"They are a breed of pharmaceutical that are used for, among other things, the treatment of post-traumatic stress. As you may know, when someone endures a horrific event like a car accident or a sexual assault, the long-term memories can be permanently debilitating. Through the use of benzodiazepines, neuroscientists are now able to treat post-traumatic stress, as it were, before it happens."

Langdon listened in silence, unable to imagine where this conversation might be going.

"When new memories are formed," the provost continued, "those events are stored in your short-term memory for about forty-eight hours before they migrate to your long-term memory. Using new blends of benzodiazepines, one can easily **refresh** the short-term memory . . . essentially deleting its content before those recent memories migrate, so to speak, into long-term memories. A victim of assault, for example, if administered a benzodiazepine within a few hours after the attack, can have those memories expunged forever, and the trauma never becomes part of her psyche. The only downside is that she loses all recollection of several days of her life."

Langdon stared at the tiny man in disbelief. "You **gave** me amnesia!"

The provost let out an apologetic sigh. "I'm afraid so. Chemically induced. Very safe. But yes, a deletion of your short-term memory." He paused. "While you were out, you mumbled something about a plague, which we assumed was on account of your viewing the projector images. We never imagined that Zobrist had created a real plague." He paused. "You also kept mumbling a phrase that sounded to us like 'Very sorry. Very sorry.'"

Vasari. It must have been all he had figured out about the projector at that point. **Cerca trova.**

"But . . . I thought my amnesia was caused by my head wound. Somebody shot me."

The provost shook his head. "Nobody shot you, Professor. There was no head wound."

"What?!" Langdon's fingers groped instinctively for the stitches and the swollen injury on the back of his head. "Then what the hell is this!" He raised his hair to reveal the shaved area.

"Part of the illusion. We made a small incision in your scalp and then immediately closed it up with stitches. You had to believe you had been attacked."

This isn't a bullet wound?!

"When you woke up," the provost said, "we wanted you to believe that people were trying to kill you . . . that you were in peril."

"People **were** trying to kill me!" Langdon shouted, his outburst drawing gazes from elsewhere in the plane. "I saw the hospital's doctor—Dr. Marconi—gunned down in cold blood!"

"That's what you **saw**," the provost said evenly, "but that's not what happened. Vayentha worked for me. She had a superb skill set for this kind of work."

"Killing people?" Langdon demanded.

"No," the provost said calmly. "**Pretending** to kill people."

Langdon stared at the man for a long moment, picturing the gray-bearded doctor with the bushy eyebrows who had collapsed on the floor, blood gushing from his chest.

"Vayentha's gun was loaded with blanks," the provost said. "It triggered a radio-controlled squib that detonated a blood pack on Dr. Marconi's chest. He is fine, by the way."

Langdon closed his eyes, dumbstruck by what he was hearing. "And the . . . hospital room?"

"A quickly improvised set," the provost said. "Professor, I know this is all very difficult to absorb. We were working quickly, and you were groggy, so it didn't need to be perfect. When you woke up, you saw what we wanted you to see—hospital props, a few actors, and a choreographed attack scene."

Langdon was reeling.

"This is what my company does," the provost said. "We're very good at creating illusions."

"What about Sienna?" Langdon asked, rubbing his eyes.

"I needed to make a judgment call, and I chose to work with her. My priority was to protect my client's project from Dr. Sinskey, and Sienna and I shared that desire. To gain your trust, Sienna saved you from the assassin and helped you escape into a rear alleyway. The waiting taxi was also ours, with another radio-controlled squib on the rear windshield to create the final effect as you fled. The taxi took you to an apartment that we had hastily put together."

Sienna's meager apartment, Langdon thought, now understanding why it looked like it had been furnished from a yard sale. And it also explained the convenient coincidence of Sienna's "neighbor" having clothing that fit him perfectly.

The entire thing had been staged.

Even the desperate phone call from Sienna's friend

at the hospital had been phony. **Sienna, eez Dani-kova!**

"When you phoned the U.S. Consulate," the provost said, "you phoned a number that Sienna looked up for you. It was a number that rang on **The Mendacium.**"

"I never reached the consulate . . ."

"No, you didn't."

Stay where you are, the fake consulate employee had urged him. **I'll send someone for you right away.** Then, when Vayentha showed up, Sienna had conveniently spotted her across the street and connected the dots. **Robert, your own government is trying to kill you! You can't involve any authorities! Your only hope is to figure out what that projector means.**

The provost and his mysterious organization—whatever the hell it was—had effectively retasked Langdon to stop working for Sinskey and start working for them. Their illusion was complete.

Sienna played me perfectly, he thought, feeling more sad than angry. He had grown fond of her in the short time they'd been together. Most troubling to Langdon was the distressing question of how a soul as bright and warm as Sienna's could give itself over entirely to Zobrist's maniacal solution for overpopulation.

I can tell you without a doubt, Sienna had said to him earlier, **that without some kind of drastic change, the end of our species is coming . . . The mathematics is indisputable.**

"And the articles about Sienna?" Langdon asked, recalling the Shakespeare playbill and the pieces about her staggeringly high IQ.

"Authentic," the provost replied. "The best illusions involve as much of the real world as possible. We didn't have much time to set up, and so Sienna's computer and real-world personal files were almost all we had to work with. You were never really intended to see any of that unless you began doubting her authenticity."

"Nor use her computer," Langdon said.

"Yes, that was where we lost control. Sienna never expected Sinskey's SRS team to find the apartment, so when the soldiers moved in, Sienna panicked and had to improvise. She fled on the moped with you, trying to keep the illusion alive. As the entire mission unraveled, I had no choice but to disavow Vayentha, although she broke protocol and pursued you."

"She almost killed me," Langdon said, recounting for the provost the showdown in the attic of the Palazzo Vecchio, when Vayentha raised her handgun and aimed point-blank at Langdon's chest. **This will only hurt for an instant . . . but it's my only choice.** Sienna had then darted out and pushed her over the railing, where Vayentha plunged to her death.

The provost sighed audibly, considering what Langdon had just said. "I doubt Vayentha was trying to kill you . . . her gun fires only blanks. Her only hope of redemption at that point was to take control of you. She probably thought if she shot you with a blank, she could make you understand she was not an assassin after all and that you were caught up in an illusion."

The provost paused, thinking a bit, and then continued. "Whether Sienna actually meant to kill Vayentha or was only trying to interfere with the shot, I won't venture to guess. I'm beginning to realize that I don't know Sienna Brooks as well as I thought."

Me neither, Langdon agreed, although as he recalled the look of shock and remorse on the young woman's face, he sensed that what she had done to the spike-haired operative was very likely a mistake.

Langdon felt unmoored . . . and utterly alone. He turned toward the window, longing to gaze out at the world below, but all he could see was the wall of the fuselage.

I've got to get out of here.

"Are you okay?" the provost asked, eyeing Langdon with concern.

"No," Langdon replied. "Not even close."

————

He'll survive, the provost thought. **He's merely trying to process his new reality.**

The American professor looked as if he had just been snatched up off the ground by a tornado, spun around, and dumped in a foreign land, leaving him shell-shocked and disoriented.

Individuals targeted by the Consortium seldom realized the truth behind the staged events they had witnessed, and if they did, the provost certainly was never present to view the aftermath. Today, in addition to the guilt he felt at seeing firsthand Langdon's bewilderment, the man was burdened by an overwhelming sense of responsibility for the current crisis.

I accepted the wrong client. Bertrand Zobrist.

I trusted the wrong person. Sienna Brooks.

Now the provost was flying toward the eye of the storm—the epicenter of what might well be a deadly plague that had the potential to wreak havoc across the entire world. If he emerged alive from all this, he suspected that his Consortium would never survive the fallout. There would be endless inquiries and accusations.

Is this how it all ends for me?

CHAPTER 83

I need air, Robert Langdon thought. **A vista . . . anything.**

The windowless fuselage felt as if it were closing in around him. Of course, the strange tale of what had actually happened to him today was not helping at all. His brain throbbed with unanswered questions . . . most of them about Sienna.

Strangely, he missed her.

She was acting, he reminded himself. **Using me.**

Without a word, Langdon left the provost and walked toward the front of the plane. The cockpit door was open, and the natural light streaming through it pulled him like a beacon. Standing in the doorway, undetected by the pilots, Langdon let the sunlight warm his face. The wide-open space before him felt like manna from heaven. The clear blue sky looked so peaceful . . . so permanent.

Nothing is permanent, he reminded himself, still struggling to accept the potential catastrophe they were facing.

"Professor?" a quiet voice said behind him, and he turned.

Langdon took a startled step backward. Standing before him was Dr. Ferris. The last time Langdon had seen the man, he was writhing on the floor of St. Mark's Basilica, unable to breathe. Now here he was in the aircraft leaning against the bulkhead, wearing a baseball cap, his face, covered in calamine lotion, a pasty pink. His chest and torso were heavily bandaged, and his breathing was shallow. If Ferris had the plague, nobody seemed too concerned that he was going to spread it.

"You're . . . **alive**?" Langdon said, staring at the man.

Ferris gave a tired nod. "More or less." The man's demeanor had changed dramatically, seeming far more relaxed.

"But I thought—" Langdon stopped. "Actually . . . I'm not sure what to think anymore."

Ferris gave him an empathetic smile. "You've heard a lot of lies today. I thought I'd take a moment to apologize. As you may have guessed, I don't work for the WHO, and I didn't go to recruit you in Cambridge."

Langdon nodded, too tired to be surprised by anything at this point. "You work for the provost."

"I do. He sent me in to offer emergency field support to you and Sienna . . . and help you escape the SRS team."

"Then I guess you did your job perfectly," Langdon said, recalling how Ferris had shown up at the baptistry, convinced Langdon he was a WHO employee, and then facilitated his and Sienna's transportation out of Florence and away from Sinskey's team. "Obviously you're not a doctor."

The man shook his head. "No, but I played that part today. My job was to help Sienna keep the illusion going so you could figure out where the projector was pointing. The provost was intent on finding Zobrist's creation so he could protect it from Sinskey."

"You had no idea it was a plague?" Langdon said, still curious about Ferris's strange rash and internal bleeding.

"Of course not! When you mentioned the plague, I figured it was just a story Sienna had told you to keep you motivated. So I played along. I got us all onto the train to Venice . . . and then, everything changed."

"How so?"

"The provost saw Zobrist's bizarre video."

That could do it. "He realized Zobrist was a madman."

"Exactly. The provost suddenly comprehended what the Consortium had been involved in, and he was horrified. He immediately demanded to speak to the person who knew Zobrist best—FS-2080—to see if she knew what Zobrist had done."

"FS-2080?"

"Sorry, Sienna Brooks. That was the code name she chose for this operation. It's apparently a Transhumanist thing. And the provost had no way to reach Sienna except through me."

"The phone call on the train," Langdon said. "Your 'ailing mother.'"

"Well, I obviously couldn't take the provost's call

in front of you, so I stepped out. He told me about the video, and I was terrified. He was hoping Sienna had been duped as well, but when I told him you and Sienna had been talking about plagues and seemed to have no intention of breaking off the mission, he knew Sienna and Zobrist were in this together. Sienna instantly became an adversary. He told me to keep him abreast of our position in Venice . . . and that he was sending in a team to detain her. Agent Brüder's team almost had her at St. Mark's Basilica . . . but she managed to escape."

Langdon stared blankly at the floor, still able to see Sienna's pretty brown eyes gazing down at him before she fled.

I'm so sorry, Robert. For everything.

"She's tough," the man said. "You probably didn't see her attack me at the basilica."

"Attack you?"

"Yes, when the soldiers entered, I was about to shout out and reveal Sienna's location, but she must have sensed it coming. She drove the heel of her hand straight into the center of my chest."

"What?!"

"I didn't know what hit me. Some kind of martial-arts move, I guess. Because I was already badly bruised there, the pain was excruciating. It took me five minutes to get my wind back. Sienna dragged you out onto the balcony before any witnesses could reveal what had happened."

Stunned, Langdon thought back to the elderly

Italian woman who had shouted at Sienna—"**L'hai colpito al petto!**"—and made a forceful motion of her fist on her own chest.

I can't! Sienna had replied. **CPR will kill him! Look at his chest!**

As Langdon replayed the scene in his mind, he realized just how quickly Sienna Brooks thought on her feet. Sienna had cleverly mistranslated the old woman's Italian. **L'hai colpito al petto** was not a suggestion that Sienna apply chest compressions . . . it was an angry accusation: **You punched him in the chest!**

With all the chaos of the moment, Langdon had not even noticed.

Ferris gave him a pained smile. "As you may have heard, Sienna Brooks is pretty sharp."

Langdon nodded. **I've heard.**

"Sinskey's men brought me back to **The Mendacium** and bandaged me up. The provost asked me to come along for intel support because I'm the only person other than you who spent time with Sienna today."

Langdon nodded, distracted by the man's rash. "Your face?" Langdon asked. "And the bruise on your chest? It's not . . ."

"The plague?" Ferris laughed and shook his head. "I'm not sure if you've been told yet, but I actually played the part of **two** doctors today."

"I'm sorry?"

"When I showed up at the baptistry, you said I looked vaguely familiar."

"You did. Vaguely. Your eyes, I think. You told me that's because you were the one who recruited me in Cambridge . . ." Langdon paused. "Which I know now is untrue, so . . ."

"I looked familiar because we had already met. But not in Cambridge." The man's eyes probed Langdon's for any hint of recognition. "I was actually the first person you saw when you woke up this morning in the hospital."

Langdon pictured the grim little hospital room. He had been groggy and his eyesight was compromised, so he was pretty certain that the first person he saw when he awoke was a pale, older doctor with bushy eyebrows and a shaggy graying beard who spoke only Italian.

"No," Langdon said. "Dr. Marconi was the first person I saw when—"

"**Scusi, professore**," the man interrupted with a flawless Italian accent. "**Ma non si ricorda di me?**" He hunched over like an older man, smoothing back imaginary bushy eyebrows and stroking a nonexistent graying beard. "**Sono il dottor Marconi.**"

Langdon's mouth fell open. "Dr. Marconi was . . . **you?**"

"That's why my eyes looked familiar. I had never worn a fake beard and eyebrows, and unfortunately had no idea until it was too late that I was severely allergic to the bonding cement—a latex spirit gum— which left my skin raw and burning. I'm sure you were horrified when you saw me . . . considering you were on alert for a possible plague."

Langdon could only stare, recalling now how Dr. Marconi had scratched at his beard before Vayentha's attack left him lying on the hospital floor, bleeding from the chest.

"To make matters worse," the man said, motioning to the bandages around his chest, "my squib shifted while the operation was already under way. I couldn't get it back into position in time, and when it detonated, it was at an angle. Broke a rib and left me badly bruised. I've been having trouble breathing all day."

And here I thought you had the plague.

The man inhaled deeply and winced. "In fact, I think it's time for me to sit down again." As he departed, he motioned behind Langdon. "It looks like you have company anyway."

Langdon turned to see Dr. Sinskey striding up the cabin, her long silver hair streaming behind her. "Professor, there you are!"

The director of the WHO looked exhausted, and yet strangely, Langdon detected a fresh glint of hope in her eyes. **She's found something.**

"I'm sorry to have left you," Sinskey said, arriving beside Langdon. "We've been coordinating and doing some research." She motioned to the open cockpit door. "I see you're getting some sunlight?"

Langdon shrugged. "Your plane needs windows."

She gave him a compassionate smile. "On the topic of light, I hope the provost was able to shed some for you on recent events?"

"Yes, although nothing I'm pleased about."

"Nor I," she concurred, glancing around to make sure they were alone. "Trust me," she whispered, "there **will** be serious ramifications for him and for his organization. I will see to it. At the moment, however, we all need to remain focused on locating that container before it dissolves and the contagion is released."

Or before Sienna gets there and helps it dissolve.

"I need to talk to you about the building that houses Dandolo's tomb."

Langdon had been picturing the spectacular structure ever since he realized it was their destination. The mouseion of holy wisdom.

"I just learned something exciting," Sinskey said. "We've been on the phone with a local historian," she said. "He has no idea why we're inquiring about Dandolo's tomb, of course, but I asked him if he had any idea what was beneath the tomb, and guess what he said." She smiled. "Water."

Langdon was surprised. "Really?"

"Yes, it sounds like the building's lower levels are flooded. Over the centuries the water table beneath the building has risen, submerging at least two lower levels. He said there are definitely all kinds of air pockets and partially submerged spaces down there."

My God. Langdon pictured Zobrist's video and the strangely lit underground cavern on whose mossy walls he had seen the faint vertical shadows of pillars. "It's a submerged room."

"Exactly."

"But then . . . how did Zobrist get down there?"

Sinskey's eyes twinkled. "That's the amazing part. You won't believe what we just discovered."

———

At that moment, less than a mile off the coast of Venice, on the slender island known as the Lido, a sleek Cessna Citation Mustang lifted off the tarmac of Nicelli Airport and streaked into the darkening twilight sky.

The jet's owner, prominent costume designer Giorgio Venci, was not on board, but he had ordered his pilots to take their attractive young passenger wherever she needed to go.

CHAPTER 84

Night had fallen on the ancient Byzantine capital.

All along the banks of the Sea of Marmara, floodlights flickered to life, illuminating a skyline of glistening mosques and slender minarets. This was the hour of the **akşam**, and loudspeakers across the city reverberated with the haunting intonations of the **adhān**, the call to prayer.

La-ilaha-illa-Allah.

There is no god but the God.

While the faithful scurried to mosques, the rest of the city carried on without a glance; raucous university students drank beer, businessmen closed deals, merchants hawked spices and rugs, and tourists watched it all in wonder.

This was a world divided, a city of opposing forces—religious, secular; ancient, modern; Eastern, Western. Straddling the geographic boundary between Europe and Asia, this timeless city was quite literally the bridge from the Old World . . . to a world that was even older.

Istanbul.

While no longer the capital of Turkey, it had served over the centuries as the epicenter of three distinct

empires—the Byzantine, the Roman, and the Ottoman. For this reason, Istanbul was arguably one of
the most historically diverse locations on earth. From
Topkapi Palace to the Blue Mosque to the Castle of
the Seven Towers, the city is teeming with folkloric
tales of battle, glory, and defeat.

Tonight, high in the night sky above its bustling
masses, a C-130 transport plane was descending
through a gathering storm front, on final approach
to Atatürk Airport. Inside the cockpit, buckled into
the jump seat behind the pilots, Robert Langdon
peered out through the windshield, relieved that he
had been offered a seat with a view.

He was feeling somewhat refreshed after having
had something to eat and then dozing at the rear of
the plane for nearly an hour of much-needed rest.

Now, off to his right, Langdon could see the lights
of Istanbul, a glistening, horn-shaped peninsula jutting into the blackness of the Sea of Marmara. This
was the European side, separated from its Asian sister by a sinuous ribbon of darkness.

The Bosporus waterway.

At a glance, the Bosporus appeared as a wide gash
that severed Istanbul in two. In fact, Langdon knew
the channel was the lifeblood of Istanbul's commerce.
In addition to providing the city with two coastlines
rather than one, the Bosporus enabled ship passage
from the Mediterranean to the Black Sea, allowing
Istanbul to serve as a way station between two worlds.

As the plane descended through a layer of mist,
Langdon's eyes intently scanned the distant city, try-

ing to catch a glimpse of the massive building they had come to search.

The site of Enrico Dandolo's tomb.

As it turned out, Enrico Dandolo—the treacherous doge of Venice—had not been buried in Venice; rather, his remains had been interred in the heart of the stronghold he had conquered in 1202 . . . the sprawling city beneath them. Fittingly, Dandolo had been laid to rest in the most spectacular shrine his captured city had to offer—a building that to this day remained the crown jewel of the region.

Hagia Sophia.

Originally built in A.D. 360, Hagia Sophia had served as an Eastern Orthodox cathedral until 1204, when Enrico Dandolo and the Fourth Crusade conquered the city and turned it into a Catholic church. Later, in the fifteenth century, following the conquest of Constantinople by Fatih Sultan Mehmed, it had become a mosque, remaining an Islamic house of worship until 1935, when the building was secularized and became a museum.

A gilded mouseion of holy wisdom, Langdon thought.

Not only was Hagia Sophia adorned with more gold tile than St. Mark's, its name—Hagia Sophia—literally meant "Holy Wisdom."

Langdon pictured the colossal building and tried to fathom the fact that somewhere beneath it, a darkened lagoon contained a tethered, undulating sac, hovering underwater, slowly dissolving and preparing to release its contents.

Langdon prayed they were not too late.

"The building's lower levels are flooded," Sinskey had announced earlier in the flight, excitedly motioning for Langdon to follow her back to her work area. "You won't believe what we just discovered. Have you ever heard of a documentary film director named Göksel Gülensoy?"

Langdon shook his head.

"While I was researching Hagia Sophia," Sinskey explained, "I discovered that a film had been made about it. A documentary made by Gülensoy a few years back."

"Dozens of films have been made about Hagia Sophia."

"Yes," she said, arriving at her work area, "but none like this." She spun her laptop so he could see it. "Read this."

Langdon sat down and eyed the article—a composite of various news sources including the **Hürriyet Daily News**—discussing Gülensoy's newest film: **In the Depths of Hagia Sophia.**

As Langdon began to read, he immediately realized why Sinskey was excited. The first two words alone made Langdon glance up at her in surprise. **Scuba diving?**

"I know," she said. "Just read."

Langdon turned his eyes back to the article.

SCUBA DIVING BENEATH HAGIA SOPHIA: Documentary filmmaker Göksel Gülensoy and his exploratory scuba team have located remote flooded basins lying hundreds of feet beneath Istanbul's heavily touristed religious structure.

In the process, they discovered numerous architectural wonders, including the 800-year-old submerged graves of martyred children, as well as submerged tunnels connecting Hagia Sophia to Topkapi Palace, Tekfur Palace, and the rumored subterranean extensions of the Anemas Dungeons.

"I believe what is beneath Hagia Sophia is much more exciting than what is above the surface," Gülensoy explained, describing how he had been inspired to make the film after seeing an old photograph of researchers examining the foundations of Hagia Sophia by boat, paddling through a large, partially submerged hall.

"You've obviously found the right building!" Sinskey exclaimed. "And it sounds like there are huge pockets of navigable space beneath that building, many of them accessible without scuba gear . . . which may explain what we're seeing in Zobrist's video."

Agent Brüder stood behind them, studying the laptop screen. "It also sounds like the waterways beneath the building spider outward to all kinds of other areas. If that Solublon bag dissolves before we arrive, there will be no way to stop the contents from spreading."

"The contents . . ." Langdon ventured. "Do you have any idea what it is? I mean **exactly**? I know we're dealing with a pathogen, but—"

"We've been analyzing the footage," Brüder said,

"which suggests that it's indeed biological rather than chemical . . . that is to say, something **living**. Considering the small amount in the bag, we assume it's highly contagious and has the ability to replicate. Whether it's a waterborne contagion like a bacterium, or whether it has the potential to go airborne like a virus once it's released, we're not sure, but either is possible."

Sinskey said, "We're now gathering data on water-table temperatures in the area, trying to assess what kinds of contagious substances might thrive in those subterranean areas, but Zobrist was exceptionally talented and easily could have engineered something with unique capabilities. And I have to suspect that there was a reason Zobrist chose this location."

Brüder gave a resigned nod and quickly relayed his assessment of the unusual dispersal mechanism—the submerged Solublon bag—the simple brilliance of which was just starting to dawn on them all. By suspending the bag underground and underwater, Zobrist had created an exceptionally stable incubation environment: one with consistent water temperature, no solar radiation, a kinetic buffer, and total privacy. By choosing a bag of the correct durability, Zobrist could leave the contagion unattended to mature for a specific duration before it self-released on schedule.

Even if Zobrist never returned to the site.

The sudden jolt of the plane touching down jarred Langdon back to his jump seat in the cockpit. The pilots braked hard and then taxied to a remote hangar, where they brought the massive plane to a stop.

Langdon half expected to be greeted by an army of WHO employees in hazmat suits. Strangely, the only party awaiting their arrival was the driver of a large white van that bore the emblem of a bright red, equal-armed cross.

The Red Cross is here? Langdon looked again, realizing it was the other entity that used the red cross. **The Swiss embassy.**

He unbuckled and located Sinskey as everyone prepared to deplane. "Where is everyone?" Langdon demanded. "The WHO team? The Turkish authorities? Is everyone already over at Hagia Sophia?"

Sinskey gave him an uneasy glance. "Actually," she explained, "we have decided against alerting local authorities. We already have the ECDC's finest SRS team with us, and it seems preferable to keep this a quiet operation for the moment, rather than creating a possible widespread panic."

Nearby, Langdon could see Brüder and his team zipping up large black duffel bags that contained all kinds of hazmat gear—biosuits, respirators, and electronic detection equipment.

Brüder heaved his bag over his shoulder and came over. "We're a go. We'll enter the building, find Dandolo's tomb, listen for water as the poem suggests, and then my team and I will reassess and decide whether to call in other authorities for support."

Langdon already saw problems with the plan.

"Hagia Sophia closes at sunset, so without local authorities, we can't even get in."

"We're fine," Sinskey said. "I have a contact in the Swiss embassy who contacted the Hagia Sophia Museum curator and asked for a private VIP tour as soon as we arrive. The curator agreed."

Langdon almost laughed out loud. "A VIP tour for the director of the World Health Organization? And an army of soldiers carrying hazmat duffels? You don't think that might raise a few eyebrows?"

"The SRS team and gear will stay in the car while Brüder, you, and I assess the situation," Sinskey said. "Also, for the record, I'm not the VIP. **You** are."

"I beg your pardon?!"

"We told the museum that a famous American professor had flown in with a research team to write an article on the symbols of Hagia Sofia, but their plane was delayed five hours and he missed his window to see the building. Since he and his team were leaving tomorrow morning, we were hoping—"

"Okay," Langdon said. "I get the gist."

"The museum is sending an employee to meet us there personally. As it turns out, he's a big fan of your writings on Islamic art." Sinskey gave him a tired smile, clearly trying to look optimistic. "We've been assured that you'll have access to every corner of the building."

"And more important," Brüder declared, "we'll have the entire place to ourselves."

CHAPTER 85

Robert Langdon gazed blankly out the window of the van as it sped along the waterfront highway connecting Atatürk Airport to the center of Istanbul. The Swiss officials had somehow facilitated a modified customs process, and Langdon, Sinskey, and the others in the group had been en route in a matter of minutes.

Sinskey had ordered the provost and Ferris to remain aboard the C-130 with several WHO staff members and to continue trying to track the whereabouts of Sienna Brooks.

While nobody truly believed Sienna could reach Istanbul in time, there were fears she might phone one of Zobrist's disciples in Turkey and ask for assistance in realizing Zobrist's delusional plan before Sinskey's team could interfere.

Would Sienna really commit mass murder? Langdon was still struggling to accept all that had happened today. It pained him to do so, but he was forced to accept the truth. **You never knew her, Robert. She played you.**

A light rain had begun to fall over the city, and Langdon felt suddenly weary as he listened to the repetitive swish of the windshield wipers. To his right, out on the Sea of Marmara, he could see the running lights of luxury yachts and massive tankers powering to and from the city port up ahead. All along the waterfront, illuminated minarets rose slender and elegant above their domed mosques, silent reminders that while Istanbul was a modern, secular city, its core was grounded in religion.

Langdon had always found this ten-mile strip of highway one of the prettiest drives in Europe. A perfect example of Istanbul's clash of old and new, the road followed part of Constantine's wall, which had been built more than sixteen centuries before the birth of the man for whom this avenue was now named—John F. Kennedy. The U.S. president had been a great admirer of Kemal Atatürk's vision for a Turkish republic springing from the ashes of a fallen empire.

Providing unparalleled views of the sea, Kennedy Avenue wound through spectacular groves and historic parks, past the harbor in Yenikapi, and eventually threaded its way between the city limits and the Strait of Bosporus, where it continued northward all the way around the Golden Horn. There, high above the city, rose the Ottoman stronghold of Topkapi Palace. With its strategic view of the Bosporus waterway, the palace was a favorite among tourists, who visited to admire both the vistas and the staggering collection of Ottoman treasure that included the cloak and sword said to have belonged to the Prophet Muhammad himself.

We won't be going that far, Langdon knew, picturing their destination, Hagia Sophia, which rose out of the city center not far ahead.

As they pulled off Kennedy Avenue and began snaking into the densely populated city, Langdon stared out at the crowds of people on the streets and sidewalks and felt haunted by the day's conversations.

Overpopulation.

The plague.

Zobrist's twisted aspirations.

Even though Langdon had understood all along exactly where this SRS mission was headed, he had not fully processed it until this moment. **We are going to ground zero.** He pictured the slowly dissolving bag of yellow-brown fluid and wondered how he had let himself get into this position.

The strange poem that Langdon and Sienna had unveiled on the back of Dante's death mask had eventually guided him here, to Istanbul. Langdon had directed the SRS team to Hagia Sophia, and knew there would be more to do once they arrived.

Kneel within the gilded mouseion of holy wisdom,
and place thine ear to the ground,
listening for the sounds of trickling water.
Follow deep into the sunken palace . . .
for here, in the darkness, the chthonic monster waits,
submerged in the bloodred waters . . .
of the lagoon that reflects no stars.

Langdon again felt troubled to know that the final canto of Dante's **Inferno** ended in a nearly identical scene: After a long descent through the underworld, Dante and Virgil reach the lowest point of hell. Here, with no way out, they hear the sounds of trickling water running through stones beneath them, and they follow the rivulet through cracks and crevices . . . ultimately finding safety.

Dante wrote: **"A place is there below . . . which not by sight is known, but by the sound of a rivulet, which descends along the hollow of a rock . . . and by that hidden way, my guide and I did enter, to return to the fair world."**

Dante's scene had clearly been the inspiration for Zobrist's poem, although in this case, it seemed Zobrist had flipped everything upside down. Langdon and the others would indeed be following the sounds of trickling water, but unlike Dante, they would not be heading away from the inferno . . . but directly **into** it.

As the van maneuvered through tighter streets and more densely populated neighborhoods, Langdon began to grasp the perverse logic that had led Zobrist to choose downtown Istanbul as the epicenter of a pandemic.

East meets West.

The crossroads of the world.

Istanbul had, at numerous times in history, succumbed to deadly plagues that killed off enormous portions of its population. In fact, during the final phase of the Black Death, this very city had been called the "plague hub" of the empire, and the disease was said to have killed more than ten thousand residents a day. Several famous Ottoman paintings depicted townspeople desperately digging plague pits to bury mounds of corpses in the nearby fields of Taksim.

Langdon hoped Karl Marx was wrong when he said, "History repeats itself."

All along the rainy streets, unsuspecting souls were bustling about their evening's business. A pretty Turkish woman called her children in to dinner; two old men shared a drink at an outdoor café; a well-dressed couple walked hand in hand beneath an umbrella; and a tuxedoed man leaped off a bus and ran down the street, sheltering his violin case beneath his jacket, apparently late for a concert.

Langdon found himself studying the faces around him, trying to imagine the intricacies of each person's life.

The masses are made up of individuals.

He closed his eyes, turning from the window and trying to abandon the morbid turn his thoughts had taken. But the damage was done. In the darkness of his mind, an unwanted image materialized—the desolate landscape of Bruegel's **Triumph of Death**—a hideous panorama of pestilence, misery, and torture laying ruin to a seaside city.

The van turned to the right onto Torun Avenue, and for a moment Langdon thought they had arrived at their destination. On his left, rising out of the mist, a great mosque appeared.

But it was not Hagia Sophia.

The Blue Mosque, he quickly realized, spotting the building's six fluted, pencil-shaped minarets, which had multiple şerefe balconies and climbed skyward to end in piercing spires. Langdon had once read that the exotic, fairy-tale quality of the Blue Mosque's balconied minarets had inspired the design for Cinderella's iconic castle at Disney World. The Blue Mosque drew its name from the dazzling sea of blue tiles that adorned its interior walls.

We're close, Langdon thought as the van sped onward, turning onto Kabasakal Avenue and running along the expansive plaza of Sultanahmet Park, which was situated halfway between the Blue Mosque and Hagia Sophia and famous for its views of both.

Langdon squinted through the rain-swept windshield, searching the horizon for the outline of Hagia Sofia, but the rain and headlights made visibility difficult. Worse still, traffic along the avenue seemed to have stopped.

Up ahead, Langdon saw nothing but a line of glowing brake lights.

"An event of some sort," the driver announced. "A concert, I think. It may be faster on foot."

"How far?" Sinskey demanded.

"Just through the park here. Three minutes. Very safe."

Sinskey nodded to Brüder and then turned to the SRS team. "Stay in the van. Get as close as you can to the building. Agent Brüder will be in touch very soon."

With that, Sinskey, Brüder, and Langdon jumped out of the van into the street and headed across the park.

The broad-leaved trees in Sultanahmet Park offered a bit of cover from the worsening weather as the group hurried along its canopied paths. The walkways were dotted with signage directing visitors to the park's many attractions—an Egyptian obelisk from Luxor, the Serpent Column from the Temple of Apollo at Delphi, and the Milion Column that once served as the "point zero" from which all distances were measured in the Byzantine Empire.

Finally, they emerged from the trees at the foot of a circular reflecting pool that marked the center of the park. Langdon stepped into the opening and raised his eyes to the east.

Hagia Sophia.

Not so much a building . . . as a mountain.

Glistening in the rain, the colossal silhouette of Hagia Sophia appeared to be a city unto itself. Its central dome—impossibly broad and ribbed in silver gray—seemed to rest upon a conglomeration of other domed buildings that had been piled up around it. Four towering minarets—each with a single balcony and a silver-gray spire—rose from the corners of the building, so far from the central dome that one could barely determine that they were part of a single structure.

Sinskey and Brüder, who until this point had been

maintaining a steady focused jog, both pulled up suddenly, their eyes craning upward . . . upward . . . as their minds struggled to absorb the full height and breadth of the structure looming before them.

"Dear God." Brüder let out a soft groan of disbelief. "We're going to be searching . . . **that?**"

CHAPTER 86

I'm being held captive, the provost sensed as he paced the interior of the parked C-130 transport plane. He had agreed to go to Istanbul to help Sinskey avert this crisis before it went completely out of control.

Not lost on the provost was the fact that cooperating with Sinskey might help mitigate any punitive backlash he might suffer for his inadvertent involvement in this crisis. **But now Sinskey has me in custody.**

As soon as the plane had parked inside the government hangar at Atatürk Airport, Sinskey and her team had deplaned, and the head of the WHO ordered the provost and his few Consortium staff members to stay aboard.

The provost had attempted to step outside for a breath of air but had been blocked by the stone-faced pilots, who reminded him that Dr. Sinskey had requested that everyone remain aboard.

Not good, the provost thought, taking a seat as the uncertainty of his future truly began to settle in.

The provost had long been accustomed to being the puppet master, the ultimate force that pulled the strings, and yet suddenly all of his power had been snatched from him.

Zobrist, Sienna, Sinskey.

They had all defied him . . . manipulated him even.

Now, trapped in the strange windowless holding cell of the WHO's transport jet, he began to wonder if his luck had run out . . . if his current situation might be a kind of karmic retribution for a lifetime of dishonesty.

I lie for a living.

I am a purveyor of disinformation.

While the provost was not the only one selling lies in this world, he had established himself as the biggest fish in the pond. The smaller fish were a different breed altogether, and the provost disliked even to be associated with them.

Available online, businesses with names like the Alibi Company and Alibi Network made fortunes all over the world by providing unfaithful spouses with a way to cheat and not get caught. Promising to briefly "stop time" so their clients could slip away from husband, wife, or kids, these organizations were masters at creating illusions—fake business conventions, fake doctor's appointments, even fake weddings—all of which included phony invitations, brochures, plane tickets, hotel confirmation forms, and even special contact numbers that rang at Alibi Company switchboards, where trained professionals pretended to be whatever receptionist or contact the illusion required.

The provost, however, had never wasted his time

with such petty artifice. He dealt solely with large-scale deception, plying his trade for those who could afford to pay millions of dollars in order to receive the best service.

Governments.

Major corporations.

The occasional ultrawealthy VIP.

To achieve their goals, these clients would have at their disposal all of the Consortium's assets, personnel, experience, and creativity. Above all, though, they were given deniability—the assurance that whatever illusion was fabricated in support of their deception could never be traced to them.

Whether trying to prop up a stock market, justify a war, win an election, or lure a terrorist out of hiding, the world's power brokers relied on massive disinformation schemes to help shape public perception.

It had always been this way.

In the sixties, the Russians built an entire fake spy network that dead-dropped bad intel that the British intercepted for years. In 1947, the U.S. Air Force manufactured an elaborate UFO hoax to divert attention from a classified plane crash in Roswell, New Mexico. And more recently, the world had been led to believe that weapons of mass destruction existed in Iraq.

For nearly three decades, the provost had helped powerful people protect, retain, and increase their power. Although he was exceptionally careful about the jobs he accepted, the provost had always feared that one day he would take the wrong job.

And now that day has arrived.

Every epic collapse, the provost believed, could be traced back to a single moment—a chance meeting, a bad decision, an indiscreet glance.

In this case, he realized, that instant had come almost a dozen years before, when he agreed to hire a young med school student who was looking for some extra money. The woman's keen intellect, dazzling language skills, and knack for improvisation made her an instantaneous standout at the Consortium.

Sienna Brooks was a natural.

Sienna had immediately understood his operation, and the provost sensed that the young woman was no stranger to keeping secrets herself. Sienna worked for him for almost two years, earned a generous paycheck that helped her pay her med school tuition, and then, without warning, she announced that she was done. She wanted to save the world, and as she had told him, she couldn't do it there.

The provost never imagined Sienna Brooks would resurface nearly a decade later, bringing with her a gift of sorts—an ultrawealthy prospective client.

Bertrand Zobrist.

The provost bristled at the memory.

This is Sienna's fault.

She was party to Zobrist's plan all along.

Nearby, at the C-130's makeshift conference table, the conversation was becoming heated, with WHO officials talking on phones and arguing.

"Sienna Brooks?!" one demanded, shouting into

the phone. "Are you sure?" The official listened a moment, frowning. "Okay, get me the details. I'll hold."

He covered the receiver and turned to his colleagues. "It sounds like Sienna Brooks departed Italy shortly after we did."

Everyone at the table stiffened.

"How?" one female employee demanded. "We covered the airport, bridges, train station . . ."

"Nicelli airfield," he replied. "On the Lido."

"Not possible," the woman countered, shaking her head. "Nicelli is tiny. There are no flights out. It handles only local helicopter tours and—"

"Somehow Sienna Brooks had access to a private jet that was hangared at Nicelli. They're still looking into it." He raised the receiver to his mouth again. "Yes, I'm here. What do you have?" As he listened to the update, his shoulders slumped lower and lower until finally he took a seat. "I understand. Thank you." He ended the call.

His colleagues all stared at him expectantly.

"Sienna's jet was headed for Turkey," the man said, rubbing his eyes.

"Then call European Air Transport Command!" someone declared. "Have them turn the jet around!"

"I can't," the man said. "It landed twelve minutes ago at Hezarfen private airfield, only fifteen miles from here. Sienna Brooks is gone."

CHAPTER 87

Rain was now pelting the ancient dome of Hagia
Sophia.

For nearly a thousand years, it had been the
largest church in the world, and even now it was hard
to imagine anything larger. Seeing it again, Langdon
was reminded that the Emperor Justinian, upon the
completion of Hagia Sophia, had stepped back and
proudly proclaimed, "Solomon, I have outdone thee!"

Sinskey and Brüder were marching with intensifying purpose toward the monumental building, which
only seemed to swell in size as they approached.

The walkways here were lined with the ancient
cannonballs used by the forces of Mehmet the Con-
queror—a decorative reminder that the history of
this building had been filled with violence as it was
conquered and then retasked to serve the spiritual
needs of assorted victorious powers.

As they neared the southern facade, Langdon
glanced to his right at the three domed, silolike
appendages jutting off the building. These were
the Mausoleums of the Sultans, one of whom—
Murad III—was said to have fathered over a hundred children.

The ring of a cell phone cut the night air, and

Brüder fished his out, checking the caller ID, and answered tersely: "Anything?"

As he listened to the report, he shook his head in disbelief. "How is that possible?" He listened further and sighed. "Okay, keep me posted. We're about to go inside." He hung up.

"What is it?" Sinskey demanded.

"Keep your eyes open," Brüder said, glancing around the area. "We may have company." He returned his gaze to Sinskey. "It sounds like Sienna Brooks is in Istanbul."

Langdon stared at the man, incredulous to hear both that Sienna had found a way to get to Turkey, and also that, having successfully escaped from Venice, she would risk capture and possible death to ensure that Bertrand Zobrist's plan succeeded.

Sinskey looked equally alarmed and drew a breath as if preparing to interrogate Brüder further, but she apparently thought better of it, turning instead to Langdon. "Which way?"

Langdon pointed to their left around the southwest corner of the building. "The Fountain of Ablutions is over here," he said.

Their rendezvous point with the museum contact was an ornately latticed wellhead that had once been used for ritual washing before Muslim prayer.

"Professor Langdon!" a man's voice shouted as they drew near.

A smiling Turkish man stepped out from under the octagonal cupola that covered the fountain. He was waving his arms excitedly. "Professor, over here!"

Langdon and the others hurried over.

"Hello, my name is Mirsat," he said, his accented English voice brimming with enthusiasm. He was a slight man with thinning hair, scholarly-looking glasses, and a gray suit. "This is a great honor for me."

"The honor is ours," Langdon replied, shaking Mirsat's hand. "Thank you for your hospitality on such short notice."

"Yes, yes!"

"I'm Elizabeth Sinskey," Dr. Sinskey said, shaking Mirsat's hand and then motioning to Brüder. "And this is Cristoph Brüder. We're here to assist Professor Langdon. I'm so sorry our plane was delayed. You're very kind to accommodate us."

"Please! Think nothing of it!" Mirsat gushed. "For Professor Langdon I would give a private tour at any hour. His little book **Christian Symbols in the Muslim World** is a favorite in our museum gift shop."

Really? Langdon thought. **Now I know the one place on earth that carries that book.**

"Shall we?" Mirsat said, motioning for them to follow.

The group hurried across a small open space, passing the regular tourist entrance and continuing on to what had originally been the building's main entrance—three deeply recessed archways with massive bronze doors.

Two armed security guards were waiting to greet them. Upon seeing Mirsat, the guards unlocked one of the doors and swung it open.

"**Sağ olun**," Mirsat said, uttering one of a handful of Turkish phrases Langdon was familiar with—an especially polite form of "thank you."

The group stepped through, and the guards closed the heavy doors behind them, the thud resonating through the stone interior.

Langdon and the others were now standing in Hagia Sophia's narthex—a narrow antechamber that was common in Christian churches and served as an architectural buffer between the divine and the profane.

Spiritual moats, Langdon often called them.

The group crossed toward another set of doors, and Mirsat pulled one open. Beyond it, instead of the sanctuary he had anticipated seeing, Langdon beheld a secondary narthex, slightly larger than the first.

An esonarthex, Langdon realized, having forgotten that Hagia Sophia's sanctuary enjoyed two levels of protection from the outside world.

As if to prepare the visitor for what lay ahead, the esonarthex was significantly more ornate than the narthex, its walls made of burnished stone that glowed in the light of elegant chandeliers. On the far side of the serene space stood four doors, above which were spectacular mosaics, which Langdon found himself intently admiring.

Mirsat walked to the largest door—a colossal, bronze-plated portal. "The Imperial Doorway," Mirsat whispered, his voice almost giddy with enthusiasm. "In Byzantine times, this door was reserved for sole use of the emperor. Tourists don't usually go through it, but this is a special night."

Mirsat reached for the door, but paused. "Before we enter," he whispered, "let me ask, is there something in particular you would like to see inside?"

Langdon, Sinskey, and Brüder all glanced at one another.

"Yes," Langdon said. "There's so much to see, of course, but if we could, we'd like to begin with the tomb of Enrico Dandolo."

Mirsat cocked his head as if he had misunderstood. "I'm sorry? You want to see . . . Dandolo's tomb?"

"We do."

Mirsat looked downcast. "But, sir . . . Dandolo's tomb is very plain. No symbols at all. Not our finest offering."

"I realize that," Langdon said politely. "All the same, we'd be most grateful if you could take us to it."

Mirsat studied Langdon a long moment, and then his eyes drifted upward to the mosaic directly over the door, which Langdon had just been admiring. The mosaic was a ninth-century image of the Pantocrator Christ—the iconic image of Christ holding the New Testament in his left hand while making a blessing with his right.

Then, as if a light had suddenly dawned for their guide, the corners of Mirsat's lips curled into a knowing smile, and he began wagging his finger. "Clever man! Very clever!"

Langdon stared. "I'm sorry?"

"Don't worry, Professor," Mirsat said in a conspiratorial whisper. "I won't tell anyone why you're **really** here."

Sinskey and Brüder shot Langdon a puzzled look.

All Langdon could do was shrug as Mirsat heaved open the door and ushered them inside.

CHAPTER 88

The Eighth Wonder of the World, some had called this space, and standing in it now, Langdon was not about to argue with that assessment.

As the group stepped across the threshold into the colossal sanctuary, Langdon was reminded that Hagia Sophia required only an instant to impress upon its visitors the sheer magnitude of its proportions.

So vast was this room that it seemed to dwarf even the great cathedrals of Europe. The staggering force of its enormity was, Langdon knew, partly an illusion, a dramatic side effect of its Byzantine floor plan, with a centralized **naos** that concentrated all of its interior space in a single square room rather than extending it along the four arms of a cruciform, as was the style adopted in later cathedrals.

This building is seven hundred years older than Notre-Dame, Langdon thought.

After taking a moment to absorb the breadth of the room's dimensions, Langdon let his eyes climb skyward, more than a hundred and fifty feet overhead, to the sprawling, golden dome that crowned the room. From its central point, forty ribs radiated outward like rays of the sun, extending to a circular arcade of forty arched windows. During daylight hours, the light that streamed through these windows reflected—and re-reflected—off glass shards embedded in the golden tile work, creating the "mystical light" for which Hagia Sophia was most famous.

Langdon had seen the gilded ambience of this room captured accurately in painting only once. **John Singer Sargent**. Not surprisingly, in creating his famous painting of Hagia Sophia, the American artist had limited his palette only to multiple shades of a single color.

Gold.

The glistening golden cupola was often called "the dome of heaven itself" and was supported by four tremendous arches, which in turn were sustained by a series of semidomes and tympana. These supports were then carried by yet another descending tier of smaller semidomes and arcades, creating the effect of a cascade of architectural forms working their way from heaven toward earth.

Moving from heaven to earth, albeit by a more direct route, long cables descended straight down from the dome and supported a sea of gleaming chandeliers, which seemed to hang so low to the floor that tall visitors risked colliding with them. In reality, this was another illusion created by the sheer magnitude of the space, for the fixtures hung more than twelve feet off the floor.

As with all great shrines, Hagia Sophia's prodigious size served two purposes. First, it was proof to God of the great lengths to which Man would go to pay tribute to Him. And second, it served as a kind of shock treatment for worshippers—a physical space so imposing that those who entered felt dwarfed, their egos erased, their physical being and cosmic importance shrinking to the size of a mere speck in the face of God . . . an atom in the hands of the Creator.

Until a man is nothing, God can make nothing out of him. Martin Luther had spoken those words in the sixteenth century, but the concept had been part of the mind-set of builders since the earliest examples of religious architecture.

Langdon glanced over at Brüder and Sinskey, who had been staring upward and who now lowered their eyes to earth.

"Jesus," Brüder said.

"Yes!" Mirsat said excitedly. "And Allah and Muhammad, too!"

Langdon chuckled as their guide directed Brüder's gaze to the main altar, where a towering mosaic of Jesus was flanked by two massive disks bearing the Arabic names of Muhammad and Allah in ornate calligraphy.

"This museum," Mirsat explained, "in an effort to remind visitors of the diverse uses of this sacred space, displays in tandem both the Christian iconography, from the days when Hagia Sophia was a basilica, and the Islamic iconography, from its days as a mosque." He gave a proud smile. "Despite the friction between the religions in the real world, we think their symbols work quite nicely together. I know you agree, Professor."

Langdon gave a heartfelt nod, recalling that all of the Christian iconography had been covered in whitewash when the building became a mosque. The restoration of the Christian symbols next to the Muslim symbols had created a mesmerizing effect, particularly because the styles and sensibilities of the two iconographies are polar opposites.

While Christian tradition favored literal images of its gods and saints, Islam focused on calligraphy and geometric patterns to represent the beauty of God's universe. Islamic tradition held that only God could create life, and therefore man has no place creating images of life—not gods, not people, not even animals.

Langdon recalled once trying to explain this concept to his students: "A Muslim Michelangelo, for example, would never have painted God's face on the ceiling of the Sistine Chapel; he would have inscribed the **name** of God. Depicting God's face would be considered blasphemy."

Langdon had gone on to explain the reason for this.

"Both Christianity and Islam are logocentric," he told his students, "meaning they are focused on **the Word.** In Christian tradition, the Word became flesh in the book of John: 'And the Word was made flesh, and He dwelt among us.' Therefore, it was acceptable to depict the Word as having a human form. In

Islamic tradition, however, the Word did **not** become
flesh, and therefore the Word needs to remain in the
form of a **word** . . . in most cases, calligraphic render-
ings of the names of the holy figures of Islam."

One of Langdon's students had summed up the
complex history with an amusingly accurate marginal
note: "Christians like faces; Muslims like words."

"Here before us," Mirsat went on, motioning across
the spectacular room, "you see a unique blending of
Christianity with Islam."

He quickly pointed out the fusion of symbols
in the massive apse, most notably the Virgin and
Child gazing down upon a **mihrab**—the semicir-
cular niche in a mosque that indicates the direction
of Mecca. Nearby, a staircase rose up to an orator's
pulpit, which resembled the kind from which Christian sermons are delivered, but in fact was a **minbar**,
the holy platform from which an imam leads Fri-
day services. Similarly, the daislike structure nearby
resembled a Christian choir stall but in reality was a
müezzin mahfili, a raised platform where a muezzin
kneels and chants in response to the imam's prayers.

"Mosques and cathedrals are startlingly similar,"
Mirsat proclaimed. "The traditions of East and West
are not as divergent as you might think!"

"Mirsat?" Brüder pressed, sounding impatient.
"We'd really like to see Dandolo's tomb, if we may?"

Mirsat looked mildly annoyed, as if the man's haste
were somehow a display of disrespect to the building.

"Yes," Langdon said. "I'm sorry to rush, but we're
on a very tight schedule."

"Very well, then," Mirsat said, pointing to a high balcony to their right. "Let's head upstairs and see the tomb."

"Up?" Langdon replied, startled. "Isn't Enrico Dandolo buried down in the crypt?" Langdon recalled the tomb itself, but not the precise place in the building where it was located. He had been picturing the dark underground areas of the building.

Mirsat seemed confounded by the query. "No, Professor, the tomb of Enrico Dandolo is most certainly upstairs."

———

What the devil is going on here? Mirsat wondered.

When Langdon had asked to see Dandolo's tomb, Mirsat had sensed that the request was a kind of decoy. **Nobody wants to see Dandolo's tomb.** Mirsat had assumed what Langdon really wanted to see was the enigmatic treasure directly beside Dandolo's tomb—the **Deesis Mosaic**—an ancient Pantocrator Christ that was arguably one of the most mysterious pieces of art in the building.

Langdon is researching the mosaic, and trying to be discreet about it, Mirsat had guessed, imagining that the professor was probably writing a secret piece on the **Deesis.**

Now, however, Mirsat was confused. Certainly Langdon knew the **Deesis Mosaic** was on the second floor, so why was he acting so surprised?

Unless he is indeed looking for Dandolo's tomb?

Puzzled, Mirsat guided them toward the staircase,

passing one of Hagia Sophia's two famous urns—a 330-gallon behemoth carved out of a single piece of marble during the Hellenistic period.

Climbing in silence now with his entourage, Mirsat found himself feeling unsettled. Langdon's colleagues did not seem like academics at all. One of them looked like a soldier of some sort, muscular and rigid, dressed all in black. And the woman with the silver hair, Mirsat sensed . . . he had seen her before. **Maybe on television?**

He was starting to suspect that the purpose of this visit was not what it appeared to be. **Why are they really here?**

"One more flight," Mirsat announced cheerily as they reached the landing. "Upstairs we shall find the tomb of Enrico Dandolo, and of course"—he paused, eyeing Langdon—"the famed **Deesis Mosaic.**"

Not even a flinch.

Langdon, it appeared, was not, in fact, here for the **Deesis Mosaic** at all. He and his guests seemed inexplicably fixated on Dandolo's tomb.

CHAPTER 89

As Mirsat led the way up the stairs, Langdon could tell that Brüder and Sinskey were worried. Admittedly, ascending to the second floor seemed to make no sense. Langdon kept picturing Zobrist's subterranean video . . . and the documentary film about the submerged areas beneath Hagia Sophia.

We need to go down!

Even so, if this was the location of Dandolo's tomb, they had no choice but to follow Zobrist's directions. **Kneel within the gilded mouseion of holy wisdom, and place thine ear to the ground, listening for the sounds of trickling water.**

When they finally reached the second level, Mirsat led them to the right along the balcony's edge, which offered breathtaking views of the sanctuary below. Langdon faced front, remaining focused.

Mirsat was talking fervently about the **Deesis Mosaic** again, but Langdon tuned him out.

He could now see his target.

Dandolo's tomb.

The tomb appeared exactly as Langdon remembered it—a rectangular piece of white marble, inlaid in the polished stone floor and cordoned off by stanchions and chains.

Langdon rushed over and examined the carved inscription.

HENRICUS DANDOLO

As the others arrived behind him, Langdon sprang into action, stepping over the protective chain and placing his feet directly in front of the tombstone.

Mirsat protested loudly, but Langdon continued, dropping quickly to his knees as if preparing to pray at the feet of the treacherous doge.

Next, in a move that elicited shouts of horror from Mirsat, Langdon placed his palms flat on the tomb and prostrated himself. As he lowered his face to the ground, Langdon realized that he looked like he was bowing to Mecca. The maneuver apparently stunned Mirsat, who fell mute, and a sudden hush seemed to pervade the entire building.

Taking a deep breath, Langdon turned his head to the right and gently pressed his left ear to the tomb. The stone felt cold on his flesh.

The sound he heard echoing up through the stone was as clear as day.

My God.

The finale of Dante's **Inferno** seemed to be echoing up from below.

Slowly, Langdon turned his head, gazing up at Brüder and Sinskey.

"I hear it," he whispered. "The sounds of trickling water."

Brüder vaulted the chain and crouched down beside Langdon to listen. After a moment he was nodding intently.

Now that they could hear the water flowing downward, one question remained. **Where is it flowing?**

Langdon's mind was suddenly flooded with images of a half-submerged cavern, bathed in an eerie red light . . . somewhere beneath them.

Follow deep into the sunken palace . . .
for here, in the darkness, the chthonic
  monster waits,
submerged in the bloodred waters . . .
of the lagoon that reflects no stars.

When Langdon stood and stepped back over the stanchions, Mirsat was glaring up at him with a look of alarm and betrayal on his face. Langdon stood almost a foot taller than the Turkish guide.

"Mirsat," Langdon began. "I'm sorry. As you can see, this is a very unusual situation. I don't have time to explain, but I have a very important question to ask you about this building."

Mirsat managed a weak nod. "Okay."

"Here at Dandolo's tomb, we can hear a rivulet of water flowing somewhere under the stone. We need to know **where** this water flows."

Mirsat shook his head. "I don't understand. Water

can be heard beneath the floors everywhere in Hagia Sophia."

Everyone stiffened.

"Yes," Mirsat told them, "especially when it rains. Hagia Sophia has approximately one hundred thousand square feet of rooftops that need to drain, and it often takes days. And usually it rains again before the drainage is complete. The sounds of trickling water are quite common here. Perhaps you are aware that Hagia Sofia sits on vast caverns of water. There was a documentary even, which—"

"Yes, yes," Langdon said, "but do you know if the water that is audible here at Dandolo's tomb flows somewhere **specific**?"

"Of course," Mirsat said. "It flows to the same place that **all** the water shedding from Hagia Sophia flows. To the city cistern."

"No," Brüder declared, stepping back over the stanchion. "We're not looking for a cistern. We're looking for a large, underground space, perhaps with columns?"

"Yes," Mirsat said. "The city's ancient cistern is precisely that—a large underground space with columns. Quite impressive actually. It was built in the sixth century to house the city's water supply. Nowadays it contains only about four feet of water, but—"

"Where is it!" Brüder demanded, his voice echoing across the empty hall.

"The . . . cistern?" Mirsat asked, looking frightened. "It's a block away, just east of this building." He pointed outside. "It's called Yerebatan Sarayi."

Sarayi? Langdon wondered. As in Topkapi Sarayi? Signage for the Topkapi Palace had been ubiquitous as they were driving in. "But . . . doesn't sarayi mean 'palace'?"

Mirsat nodded. "Yes. The name of our ancient cistern is Yerebatan Sarayi. It means—the sunken palace."

CHAPTER 90

The rain was falling in sheets as Dr. Elizabeth Sinskey burst out of Hagia Sophia with Langdon, Brüder, and their bewildered guide, Mirsat.

Follow deep into the sunken palace, Sinskey thought.

The site of the city's cistern—Yerebatan Sarayi— was apparently back toward the Blue Mosque and a bit to the north.

Mirsat led the way.

Sinskey had seen no other option but to tell Mirsat who they were and that they were racing to thwart a possible health crisis within the sunken palace.

"This way!" Mirsat called, leading them across the darkened park. The mountain of Hagia Sophia was behind them now, and the fairy-tale spires of the Blue Mosque glistened ahead.

Hurrying beside Sinskey, Agent Brüder was shouting into his phone, updating the SRS team and ordering them to rendezvous at the cistern's entrance. "It sounds like Zobrist is targeting the city's water supply," Brüder said, breathless. "I'm going to need schematics of all conduits in and out of the cistern. We'll run full isolation and containment protocols.

We'll need physical and chemical barriers along with vacuum—"

"Wait," Mirsat called over to him. "You misunderstood me. The cistern is not the city water supply. Not anymore!"

Brüder lowered his phone, glaring at their guide. "What?"

"In ancient times, the cistern held the water supply," Mirsat clarified. "But no longer. We modernized."

Brüder came to a stop under a sheltering tree, and everyone halted with him.

"Mirsat," Sinskey said, "you're sure that nobody drinks the water out of the cistern?"

"Heavens no," Mirsat said. "The water pretty much just sits there . . . eventually filtering down into the earth."

Sinskey, Langdon, and Brüder all exchanged uncertain looks. Sinskey didn't know whether to feel relieved or alarmed. **If nobody comes in regular contact with the water, why would Zobrist choose to contaminate it?**

"When we modernized our water supply decades ago," Mirsat explained, "the cistern fell out of use and became just a big pond in an underground room." He shrugged. "These days it's nothing more than a tourist attraction."

Sinskey spun toward Mirsat. **A tourist attraction?** "Hold on . . . people can go **down** there? Into the cistern?"

"Of course," he said. "Many thousands visit every

day. The cavern is quite striking. There are board-walks over the water . . . and even a small café. There's limited ventilation, so the air is quite stuffy and humid, but it's still very popular."

Sinskey's eyes locked on Brüder, and she could tell that she and the trained SRS agent were picturing the same thing—a dark, humid cavern filled with stagnant water in which a pathogen was incubating. Completing the nightmare was the presence of boardwalks over which tourists moved all day long, just above the water's surface.

"He created a bioaerosol," Brüder declared.

Sinskey nodded, slumping.

"Meaning?" Langdon demanded.

"Meaning," Brüder replied, "that it can go **airborne.**"

Langdon fell silent, and Sinskey could see that he was now grasping the potential magnitude of this crisis.

An airborne pathogen had been on Sinskey's mind as a possible scenario for some time, and yet when she believed that the cistern was the city's water supply, she had hoped maybe this meant that Zobrist had chosen a water-bound bioform. Water-dwelling bacteria were robust and weather-resistant, but they were also slow to propagate.

Airborne pathogens spread fast.

Very fast.

"If it's airborne," Brüder said, "it's probably viral."

A virus, Sinskey agreed. **The fastest-spreading pathogen Zobrist could choose.**

Releasing an airborne virus underwater was admittedly unusual, and yet there were many life-forms that incubated in liquid and then hatched into the air—mosquitoes, mold spores, the bacterium that caused Legionnaires' disease, mycotoxins, red tide, even human beings. Sinskey grimly pictured the virus permeating the cistern's lagoon . . . and then the infected microdroplets rising into the damp air.

Mirsat was now staring across a traffic-jammed street with a look of apprehension on his face. Sinskey followed his gaze to a squat, red-and-white brick building whose single door was open, revealing what looked to be a stairwell. A scattering of well-dressed people seemed to be waiting outside under umbrellas while a doorman controlled the flow of guests who were descending the stairs.

Some kind of underground dance club?

Sinskey saw the gold lettering on the building and felt a sudden tightness in her chest. Unless this club was called the Cistern and had been built in A.D. 523, she realized why Mirsat was looking so concerned.

"The sunken palace," Mirsat stammered. "It seems . . . there is a concert tonight."

Sinskey was incredulous. "A concert in a cistern?!"

"It's a large indoor space," he replied. "It is often used as a cultural center."

Brüder had apparently heard enough. He dashed toward the building, sidestepping his way through snarled traffic on Alemdar Avenue. Sinskey and the others broke into a run as well, close on the agent's heels.

When they arrived at the cistern entrance, the doorway was blocked by a handful of concertgoers who were waiting to be let in—a trio of women in burkas, a pair of tourists holding hands, a man in a tuxedo. They were all clustered together in the doorway, trying to keep out of the rain.

Sinskey could hear the melodic strains of a classical music composition lilting up from below. **Berlioz,** she guessed from the idiosyncratic orchestration, but whatever it was, it felt out of place here in the streets of Istanbul.

As they drew closer to the doorway, she felt a warm wind rushing up the stairs, billowing from deep inside the earth and escaping from the enclosed cavern. The wind brought to the surface not only the sound of violins, but the unmistakable scents of humidity and masses of people.

It also brought to Sinskey a deep sense of foreboding.

As a group of tourists emerged from the stairs, chatting happily as they exited the building, the doorman allowed the next group to descend.

Brüder immediately moved to enter, but the doorman stopped him with a pleasant wave. "One moment, sir. The cistern is at capacity. It should be less than a minute until another visitor exits. Thank you."

Brüder looked ready to force his way in, but Sinskey placed a hand on his shoulder and pulled him off to one side.

"Wait," she commanded. "Your team is on the way and you can't search this place alone." She motioned to the plaque on the wall beside the door. "The cistern is enormous."

The informational plaque described a cathedral-size subterranean room—nearly two football fields in length—with a ceiling spanning more than a hundred thousand square feet and supported by a forest of 336 marble columns.

"Look at this," Langdon said, standing a few yards away. "You're not going to believe it."

Sinskey turned. Langdon motioned to a concert poster on the wall.

Oh, dear God.

The WHO director had been correct in identifying the style of the music as Romantic, but the piece that was being performed had not been composed by Berlioz. It was by a different Romantic composer—Franz Liszt.

Tonight, deep within the earth, the Istanbul State Symphony Orchestra was performing one of Franz Liszt's most famous works—the Dante Symphony—an entire composition inspired by Dante's descent into and return from hell.

"It's being performed here for a week," Langdon said, scrutinizing the poster's fine print. "A free concert. Underwritten by an anonymous donor."

Sinskey suspected that she could guess the identity of the anonymous donor. Bertrand Zobrist's flair for the dramatic, it seemed, was also a ruthless practical strategy. This week of free concerts would lure thousands more tourists than usual down into the cistern and place them in a congested area . . . where they would breathe the contaminated air, then travel back to their homes both here and abroad.

"Sir?" the doorman called to Brüder. "We have room for a couple more."

Brüder turned to Sinskey. "Call the local authorities. Whatever we find down there, we'll need support. When my team arrives, have them radio me for an update. I'll go down and see if I can get a sense of where Zobrist might have tethered this thing."

"Without a respirator?" Sinskey asked. "You don't know for a fact the Solublon bag is intact."

Brüder frowned, holding his hand up in the warm wind that was blowing out of the doorway. "I hate to say this, but if this contagion is out, I'm guessing everyone in this city is probably infected."

Sinskey had been thinking the same thing but hadn't wanted to say it in front of Langdon and Mirsat.

"Besides," Brüder added, "I've seen what happens to crowds when my team marches in wearing hazmat suits. We'd have full-scale panic and a stampede."

Sinskey decided to defer to Brüder; he was, after all, the specialist and had been in situations like this before.

"Our only realistic option," Brüder told her, "is to assume it's still safe down there, and make a play to contain this."

"Okay," Sinskey said. "Do it."

"There's another problem," Langdon interjected. "What about Sienna?"

"What about her?" Brüder demanded.

"Whatever her intentions may be here in Istanbul, she's very good with languages and possibly speaks some Turkish."

"So?"

"Sienna knows the poem references the 'sunken palace,'" Langdon said. "And in Turkish, 'sunken palace' literally points . . ." He motioned to the "Yerebatan Sarayi" sign over the doorway. ". . . here."

"That's true," Sinskey agreed wearily. "She may have figured this out and bypassed Hagia Sophia altogether."

Brüder glanced at the lone doorway and cursed under his breath. "Okay, if she's down there and plans to break the Solublon bag before we can contain it, at least she hasn't been there long. It's a huge area, and she probably has no idea where to look. And with all those people around, she probably can't just dive into the water unnoticed."

"Sir?" the doorman called again to Brüder. "Would you like to enter now?"

Brüder could see another group of concertgoers approaching from across the street, and nodded to the doorman that he was indeed coming.

"I'm coming with you," Langdon said, following.

Brüder turned and faced him. "No chance."

Langdon's tone was unyielding. "Agent Brüder, one of the reasons we're in this situation is that Sienna Brooks has been playing me all day. And as you said, we may all be infected already. I'm helping you whether you like it or not."

Brüder stared at him a moment and then relented.

As Langdon passed through the doorway and began descending the steep staircase behind Brüder, he could feel the warm wind rushing past them from the bowels of the cistern. The humid breeze carried on it the strains of Liszt's Dante Symphony as well as a familiar, yet ineffable scent . . . that of a massive crush of people congregated together in an enclosed space.

Langdon suddenly felt a ghostly pall envelop him, as if the long fingers of an unseen hand were reaching out of the earth and raking his flesh.

The music.

The symphony chorus—a hundred voices strong—was now singing a well-known passage, articulating every syllable of Dante's gloomy text.

"Lasciate ogne speranza," they were now chanting, **"voi ch'entrate."**

These six words—the most famous line in all of Dante's **Inferno**—welled up from the bottom of the stairs like the ominous stench of death.

Accompanied by a swell of trumpets and horns, the choir intoned the warning again. **"Lasciate ogne speranza voi ch'entrate!"**

Abandon all hope, ye who enter here!

CHAPTER 91

Bathed in red light, the subterranean cavern resonated with the sounds of hell-inspired music—the wail of voices, the dissonant pinch of strings, and the deep roll of timpani, which thundered through the grotto like a seismic tremor.

As far as Langdon could see, the floor of this underground world was a glassy sheet of water—dark, still, smooth—like black ice on a frozen New England pond.

The lagoon that reflects no stars.

Rising out of the water, meticulously arranged in seemingly endless rows, were hundreds upon hundreds of thick Doric columns, each climbing thirty feet to support the cavern's vaulted ceiling. The columns were lit from below by a series of individual red spotlights, creating a surreal forest of illuminated trunks that telescoped off into the darkness like some kind of mirrored illusion.

Langdon and Brüder paused at the bottom of the stairs, momentarily stalled on the threshold of the spectral hollow before them. The cavern itself seemed to glow with a reddish hue, and as Langdon took it all in, he could feel himself breathing as shallowly as possible.

The air down here was heavier than he'd imagined.

Langdon could see the crowd in the distance to their left. The concert was taking place deep in the underground space, halfway back against the far wall, its audience seated on an expanse of platforms. Several hundred spectators sat in concentric rings that had been arranged around the orchestra while a hundred more stood around the perimeter. Still others had taken up positions out on the near boardwalks, leaning on the sturdy railings and gazing down into the water as they listened to the music.

Langdon found himself scanning the sea of amorphous silhouettes, his eyes searching for Sienna. She was nowhere in sight. Instead he saw figures in tuxedos, gowns, **bishts**, burkas, and even tourists in shorts and sweatshirts. The cross section of humanity, gathered in the crimson light, looked to Langdon like celebrants in some kind of occult mass.

If Sienna's down here, he realized, **it will be nearly impossible to spot her.**

At that moment a heavyset man moved past them, exiting up the stairs, coughing as he went. Brüder spun and watched him go, scrutinizing him carefully. Langdon felt a faint tickle in his own throat but told himself it was his imagination.

Brüder now took a tentative step forward on the boardwalk, eyeing their numerous options. The path before them looked like the entrance to the Minotaur's labyrinth. The single boardwalk quickly forked into three, each of those branching off again, creating a suspended maze, hovering over the water, weaving in and out of the columns and snaking into the darkness.

I found myself within a forest dark, Langdon thought, recalling the ominous first canto of Dante's masterwork, **for the straightforward pathway had been lost.**

Langdon peered over the walkway's railing into the water. It was about four feet deep and surprisingly clear. The stone tile floor was visible, blanketed by a fine layer of silt.

Brüder took a quick look down, gave a noncommittal grunt, and then raised his eyes back to the room. "Do you see anything that looks like the area in Zobrist's video?"

Everything, Langdon thought, surveying the steep, damp walls around them. He motioned to the most remote corner of the cavern, far off to the right, away from the congestion of the orchestral platform. "I'm guessing back there somewhere."

Brüder nodded. "My instinct as well."

The two of them hurried down the boardwalk, choosing the right-hand fork, which carried them away from the crowd, in the direction of the farthest reaches of the sunken palace.

As they walked, Langdon realized how easy it would be to hide overnight in this space, undetected. Zobrist could have done just that to make his video. Of course, if he had generously underwritten this weeklong concert series, he also could have simply requested some private time in the cistern.

Not that it matters anymore.

Brüder was striding faster now, as if subconsciously keeping pace with the symphony's tempo, which had increased into a cascading series of descending semitone suspensions.

Dante and Virgil's descent into hell.

Langdon intently scanned the steep, mossy walls in the distance to their right, trying to match them up with what they had seen in the video. At each new fork in the boardwalk, they turned right, moving farther from the crowd, heading for the cavern's most remote corner. Langdon looked back and was astounded by the distance they had covered.

They advanced at almost a jog now, passing a handful of meandering visitors, but by the time they entered the deepest parts of the cistern, the number of people had thinned to nothing.

Brüder and Langdon were alone.

"It all looks the same," Brüder despaired. "Where do we start?"

Langdon shared his frustration. He remembered the video vividly, but nothing down here leaped out as a recognizable feature.

Langdon studied the softly lit informational signs that dotted the boardwalk as they moved ahead. One described the twenty-one-million-gallon capacity of the room. Another pointed out a nonmatching pillar that had been looted from a nearby structure during construction. And still another offered a diagram of an ancient carving now faded from view—the Crying Hen's Eye symbol, which wept for all the slaves who died while building the cistern.

Strangely, it was a sign that bore a single word that now stopped Langdon dead in his tracks.

Brüder halted, too, turning. "What's wrong?"

Langdon pointed.

On the sign, accompanied by a directional arrow, was the name of a fearsome Gorgon—an infamous female monster.

MEDUSA⇒

Brüder read the sign and shrugged. "So what?"

Langdon's heart was pounding. He knew Medusa was not only the fearsome snake-haired spirit whose gaze could turn anyone who looked at her to stone, but was also a prominent member of the Greek pantheon of subterranean spirits . . . a specific category known as the chthonic monsters.

Follow deep into the sunken palace . . . for here, in the darkness, the chthonic monster waits . . .

She's pointing the way, Langdon realized, breaking into a run along the boardwalk. Brüder could barely keep up with him as Langdon zigzagged into the darkness, following the signs for Medusa. Finally, he reached a dead end at a small viewing platform near the base of the cistern's rightmost wall.

There before him was an incredible sight.

Rising out of the water was a colossal carved marble block—the head of Medusa—her hair writhing with snakes. Making her presence here even more bizarre was the fact that her head had been placed on her neck upside down.

Inverted as the damned, Langdon realized, picturing Botticelli's **Map of Hell** and the inverted sinners he had placed in the Malebolge.

Brüder arrived breathless beside Langdon at the railing, staring out at the upside-down Medusa with a look of bewilderment.

Langdon suspected that this carved head, which now served as a plinth supporting one of the columns, had probably been pillaged from elsewhere and used here as an inexpensive building supply. The reason for Medusa's inverted position was no doubt the superstitious belief that the inversion would rob her of her evil powers. Even so, Langdon could not shake off the barrage of haunting thoughts that assailed him.

Dante's Inferno. The finale. The center of the earth. Where gravity inverts itself. Where up becomes down.

His skin now prickling with foreboding, Langdon squinted through the reddish haze that surrounded the sculpted head. Most of Medusa's serpent-infested hair was submerged underwater, but her eyes were above the surface, facing to the left, staring out across the lagoon.

Fearfully, Langdon leaned over the railing and

turned his head, letting his gaze follow the statue's out into the familiar empty corner of the sunken palace.

In an instant, he knew.

This was the spot.

Zobrist's ground zero.

CHAPTER 92

Agent Brüder lowered himself stealthily, sliding beneath the railing and dropping down into the chest-deep water. As the rush of cool liquid permeated his clothing, his muscles tensed against the chill. The floor of the cistern was slippery beneath his boots, but it felt solid. He stood a moment, taking stock, watching the concentric circles of water rippling away from his body like shock waves across the lagoon.

For a moment Brüder didn't breathe. **Move slowly,** he told himself. **Create no turbulence.**

Above him on the boardwalk, Langdon stood at the railing, scanning the surrounding boardwalks.

"All set," Langdon whispered. "Nobody sees you."

Brüder turned and faced the huge upside-down head of Medusa, which was brightly lit by a red spotlight. The inverted monster looked even larger now that Brüder was down at her level.

"Follow Medusa's gaze across the lagoon," Langdon whispered. "Zobrist had a flair for symbolism and dramatics . . . I wouldn't be surprised if he placed his creation directly in the lethal sight line of Medusa."

Great minds think alike. Brüder felt grateful that the American professor had insisted on making the descent with him; Langdon's expertise had guided them almost immediately to this distant corner of the cistern.

As the strains of the Dante Symphony continued to reverberate in the distance, Brüder took out his waterproof Tovatec penlight and submerged it beneath the water, flipping the switch. A bright halogen beam pierced the water, illuminating the cistern floor before him.

Easy, Brüder reminded himself. **Don't disturb a thing.**

Without another word, he began his careful journey out into the lagoon, wading in slow motion through the water, moving his flashlight methodically back and forth like an underwater minesweeper.

———

At the railing, Langdon had begun to feel an unsettling tightness in his throat. The air in the cistern, despite the humidity, tasted stale and oxygen-depleted to him. As Brüder waded carefully out into the lagoon, the professor reassured himself that everything would be fine.

We arrived in time.

It's all intact.

Brüder's team can contain this.

Even so, Langdon felt jumpy. As a lifelong claustrophobe, he knew he would be anxious down here under any circumstances. **Something about thousands of tons of earth hovering overhead . . . supported by nothing but decaying pillars.**

He pushed the thought from his mind and took another glance behind him for anyone taking undue interest.

Nothing.

The only people nearby were standing on various other boardwalks, and they were all looking in the opposite direction, toward the orchestra. No one seemed to have noticed Brüder slowly wading across the water in this deep corner of the cistern.

Langdon returned his gaze to the SRS team leader, whose submerged halogen beam still oscillated eerily in front of him, lighting the way.

As Langdon looked on, his peripheral vision suddenly picked up movement to his left—an ominous black form rising out of the water in front of Brüder. Langdon wheeled and stared into the looming darkness, half expecting to see some kind of leviathan rearing up from beneath the surface.

Brüder had stopped short, apparently having seen it, too.

In the far corner, a wavering black shape rose some thirty feet up the wall. The ghostly silhouette looked nearly identical to that of the plague doctor who'd appeared in Zobrist's video.

It's a shadow, Langdon realized, exhaling. **Brüder's shadow.**

The shadow had been cast as Brüder moved past a submerged spotlight in the lagoon, exactly, it seemed, as Zobrist's shadow had done in the video.

"This is the spot," Langdon called out to Brüder. "You're close."

Brüder nodded and continued inching his way out into the lagoon. Langdon moved along the railing, staying even with him. As the agent moved farther and farther away, Langdon stole another quick glance toward the orchestra to make sure Brüder had not been noticed.

Nothing.

As Langdon again returned his gaze to the lagoon, a glint of reflected light caught his eye on the boardwalk at his feet.

He looked down and saw a tiny puddle of red liquid.

Blood.

Strangely, Langdon was standing in it.

Am I bleeding?

Langdon felt no pain, and yet he frantically began searching himself for some injury or possible reaction to an unseen toxin in the air. He checked his nose for a possible bleed, his fingernails, his ears.

Baffled as to where the blood had come from, Langdon glanced around, confirming that he was indeed alone on the deserted walkway.

Langdon looked down at the puddle again, and this time he noticed a tiny rivulet flowing along the boardwalk and collecting in the low spot at his feet. The red liquid, it seemed, was coming from somewhere up ahead and trickling down an incline in the boardwalk.

Someone is injured up there, Langdon sensed. He glanced quickly out at Brüder, who was nearing the center of the lagoon.

Langdon strode quickly up the boardwalk, following the rivulet. As he advanced toward the dead end, the rivulet became wider, flowing freely. **What in the world?** At this point it turned into a small stream. He broke into a jog, following the flowing liquid all the way to the wall, where the boardwalk suddenly ended.

Dead end.

In the murky darkness, he found a large pool, which was glistening red, as if someone had just been slaughtered here.

In that instant, as Langdon watched the red liquid dripping off the boardwalk into the cistern, he realized that his original assessment was mistaken.

It's not blood.

The red lights of the vast space, combined with the red hue of the boardwalk, had created an illusion, giving these clear droplets a reddish-black tint.

It's just water.

Instead of bringing a sense of relief, the revelation infused him with blunt fear. He stared down at the puddle of water, now seeing splashes on the banister . . . and footprints.

Someone climbed out of the water here.

Langdon spun to call out to Brüder, but he was too far away and the music had progressed into a fortissimo of brass and timpani. It was deafening. Langdon suddenly felt a presence beside him.

I'm not alone out here.

In slow motion, Langdon turned toward the wall where the boardwalk dead-ended. Ten feet away, shrouded in dark shadows, he was able to discern a rounded form, like a large stone cloaked in black cloth, dripping in a pool of water. The form was motionless.

And then it moved.

The form elongated, its featureless head rotating upward from its bowed position.

A person huddled in a black burka, Langdon realized.

The traditional Islamic body covering left no skin showing, but as the veiled head turned toward Langdon, two dark eyes materialized, staring out through the narrow slit of the burka's face covering, locking intently on Langdon.

In an instant, he knew.

Sienna Brooks exploded from her hiding place. She accelerated to a sprint in a single stride, plowing into Langdon and driving him to the ground as she raced off down the boardwalk.

CHAPTER 93

Out in the lagoon, Agent Brüder had stopped in his tracks. The halogen beam of his Tovatec penlight had just picked up the sharp glint of metal up ahead on the submerged cistern floor.

Barely breathing, Brüder took a delicate step closer, cautious not to create any turbulence in the water. Through the glassy surface, he could now make out a sleek rectangle of titanium, bolted to the floor.

Zobrist's plaque.

The water was so clear he could almost read tomorrow's date and accompanying text:

IN THIS PLACE, ON THIS DATE,
THE WORLD WAS CHANGED FOREVER.

Think again, Brüder mused, his confidence rising. **We have several hours to stop this before tomorrow.**

Picturing Zobrist's video, Brüder gently inched the flashlight beam to the left of the plaque, searching for the tethered Solublon bag. As the beam illuminated the darkened water, Brüder strained his gaze in confusion.

No bag.

He moved the beam farther to the left, to the precise spot where the bag had appeared on the video.

Still nothing.

But . . . it was right here!

Brüder's jaw clenched as he took another tentative step closer, sweeping the beam slowly around the entire area.

There was no bag. Only the plaque.

For a brief, hopeful instant, Brüder wondered if perhaps this threat, like so many things today, had been nothing but an illusion.

Was it all a hoax?!

Did Zobrist just want to scare us?!

And then he saw it.

To the left of the plaque, barely visible on the lagoon floor, lay a limp tether. The flaccid string looked like a lifeless worm in the water. At the far end of the string was a tiny plastic clasp, from which hung a few tatters of Solublon plastic.

Brüder stared down at the frayed relic of the transparent bag. It clung to the end of the tether like the tattered knot of a popped party balloon.

The truth settled slowly in his gut.

We're too late.

He pictured the submerged bag dissolving and breaking apart . . . its deadly contents spreading out into the water . . . and bubbling up to the surface of the lagoon.

With a tremulous finger, he flicked off his flashlight and stood a moment in the darkness, trying to gather his thoughts.

Those thoughts turned quickly to prayer.

God help us all.

———

"Agent Brüder, repeat!" Sinskey shouted into her radio, descending halfway down the stairwell into the cistern, trying to get better reception. "I didn't copy that!"

The warm wind rushed past her, up the stairs toward the open doorway above. Outside, the SRS team had arrived and its members were prepping behind the building in an effort to keep their hazmat gear out of sight while they waited to receive Brüder's assessment.

". . . ruptured bag . . ." Brüder's voice crackled in Sinskey's comm. ". . . and . . . released."

What?! Sinskey prayed she was misunderstanding as she rushed farther down the stairs. "Repeat!" she commanded, nearing the base of the stairwell, where the orchestral music grew louder.

Brüder's voice was much clearer this time. ". . . and I repeat . . . the contagion has been dispersed!"

Sinskey lurched forward, nearly falling into the cistern's entryway at the base of the stairwell. **How can that be?!**

"The bag has dissolved," Brüder's voice snapped loudly. "The contagion is in the water!"

A cold sweat gripped Dr. Sinskey as she raised her eyes and tried to process the sprawling underground world now spread out before her. Through the reddish haze, she saw a vast expanse of water from which sprang hundreds of columns. Most of all, however, she saw people.

Hundreds of people.

Sinskey stared out at the unsuspecting crowd, all of them confined in Zobrist's underground death trap. She reacted on instinct. "Agent Brüder, come up at once. We'll begin evacuating people immediately."

Brüder's reply was instantaneous. "Absolutely not! Seal the doors! Nobody gets out of here!"

As director of the World Health Organization, Elizabeth Sinskey was accustomed to having her orders followed without question. For an instant, she thought she had misunderstood the lead SRS agent's words. **Seal the doors?!**

"Dr. Sinskey!" Brüder shouted over the music. "Do you read me?! Close the goddamn doors!"

Brüder repeated the command, but it was unnecessary. Sinskey knew he was correct. In the face of a possible pandemic, containment was the only viable option.

Sinskey reflexively reached up and gripped her lapis lazuli amulet. **Sacrifice the few to save the many.** With a hardening resolve, she raised the radio to her lips. "Confirmed, Agent Brüder. I'll give the order to seal the doors."

Sinskey was about to turn away from the horror of the cistern and give the command to seal the area when she sensed a sudden commotion in the crowd.

Not far away, a woman in a black burka was dashing toward her along a crowded boardwalk, knocking people out of the way as she ran. The veiled woman seemed to be headed directly for Sinskey and the exit.

She's being chased, Sinskey realized, spotting a man running behind her.

Then Sinskey froze. **That's Langdon!**

Sinskey's eyes whipped back to the woman in the burka, who was approaching fast and now shouting something in Turkish to all the people on the boardwalk. Sinskey didn't speak Turkish, but judging from the panicked reaction of the people, the woman's words were the equivalent of shouting "Fire!" in a crowded theater.

A ripple of panic swept through the crowd, and suddenly it was not only the veiled woman and Langdon who were dashing for the stairs. Everyone was.

Sinskey turned her back to the oncoming stampede and began shouting desperately up the stairs to her team.

"Lock the doors!" Sinskey screamed. "Seal the cistern! NOW!"

———

By the time Langdon skidded around the corner into the stairwell, Sinskey was halfway up the stairs, clambering toward the surface, shouting wildly to close the doors. Sienna Brooks was close on her heels, struggling with her heavy, wet burka as she lumbered up the stairs.

Bounding after them, Langdon could feel a tidal wave of terrified concertgoers surging up behind him.

"Seal the exit!" Sinskey shouted again.

Langdon's long legs carried him three steps at a time, gaining fast on Sienna. Above, he could see the cistern's heavy double doors begin to swing inward.

Too slow.

Sienna overtook Sinskey, grabbing her shoulder and using it as leverage to launch past her, clambering wildly over her toward the exit. Sinskey stumbled forward onto her knees, her beloved amulet hitting the cement stairs and breaking in half.

Langdon fought the instinct to stop and help the fallen woman, but instead, he hurtled past her, sprinting toward the top landing.

Sienna was only a few feet away now, almost within reach, but she had attained the landing, and the doors were not closing fast enough. Without breaking stride, Sienna deftly angled her slender body and leaped sideways through the narrow opening.

She was halfway through the doors when her burka snagged on a latch, halting her in her tracks, wedged in the middle of the doorway, mere inches from freedom. As she writhed to escape, Langdon's hand shot out and seized a clump of her burka. He held fast, pulling back, trying to reel her in, but she wriggled frantically and suddenly Langdon was holding only a wet clump of fabric.

The doors slammed onto the fabric, barely missing Langdon's hands. The wadded cloth was now pinched in the doorway, making it impossible for the men outside to push the doors all the way closed.

Through the narrow slit, Langdon could see Sienna

Brooks sprinting across a busy street, her bald head shining in the streetlights. She was wearing the same sweater and blue jeans she had been wearing all day, and Langdon suddenly felt a fiery, upwelling sense of betrayal.

The feeling lasted only an instant. A sudden, crushing weight rammed Langdon hard against the door.

The stampede had arrived behind him.

The stairwell echoed with shouts of terror and confusion as the sounds of the symphony orchestra deteriorated into a confused cacophony below. Langdon could feel the pressure on his back increasing as the bottleneck thickened. His rib cage began to compress painfully against the door.

Then the doors exploded outward, and Langdon was launched into the night like a cork from a bottle of champagne. He stumbled across the sidewalk, nearly falling into the street. Behind him, a stream of humanity was flowing up out of the earth like ants escaping from a poisoned anthill.

The SRS agents, hearing the sounds of chaos, now emerged from behind the building. Their appearance in full hazmat gear and respirators immediately amplified the panic.

Langdon turned away and peered across the street after Sienna. All he could see was traffic and lights and confusion.

Then, for a fleeting instant, down the street to his left, the pale flash of a bald head shone in the night, darting along a crowded sidewalk and disappearing around a corner.

Langdon shot a desperate glance behind him, searching for Sinskey, or the police, or an SRS agent who was not wearing a bulky hazmat suit.

Nothing.

Langdon knew he was on his own.

Without hesitation, he sprinted after Sienna.

———

Far below, in the deepest recesses of the cistern, Agent Brüder stood all alone in the waist-deep water. The sounds of pandemonium echoed through the darkness as frenzied tourists and musicians shoved their way toward the exit and disappeared up the stairs.

The doors were never sealed, Brüder realized to his horror. **Containment has failed.**

CHAPTER 94

Robert Langdon was not a runner, but years of swimming made for powerful legs, and his stride was long. He reached the corner in a matter of seconds and rounded it, finding himself on a wider avenue. His eyes urgently scanned the sidewalks.

She's got to be here!

The rain had stopped, and from this corner, Langdon could clearly see the entire well-lit street. There was nowhere to hide.

And yet Sienna seemed to have vanished.

Langdon came to a stop, hands on his hips, panting as he surveyed the rain-soaked street before him. The only movement he saw was fifty yards ahead, where one of Istanbul's modern **otobüse**s was pulling away from the curb and powering up the avenue.

Did Sienna jump on a city bus?

It seemed far too risky. Would she really trap herself on a bus when she knew everyone would be looking for her? Then again, if she believed nobody had seen her round the corner, and if the bus had been just pulling away by chance, offering a perfectly timed opportunity . . .

Maybe.

Affixed to the top of the bus was a destination sign—a programmable matrix of lights displaying a single word: GALATA.

Langdon rushed up the street toward an elderly man who was standing outside a restaurant under an awning. He was nicely dressed in an embroidered tunic and a white turban.

"Excuse me," Langdon said breathless, arriving before him. "Do you speak English?"

"Of course," the man said, looking unnerved by the urgency of Langdon's tone.

"**Galata?!** That's a place?"

"Galata?" the man replied. "Galata Bridge? Galata Tower? Galataport?"

Langdon pointed to the departing **otobüs.** "Galata! Where is the bus going!"

The man in the turban looked after the departing bus and considered it a moment. "Galata Bridge," he replied. "It departs the old city and crosses the waterway."

Langdon groaned, his eyes making another frantic pass of the street but seeing no hint of Sienna. Sirens blared everywhere now, as emergency response vehicles tore past them in the direction of the cistern.

"What's happening?" the man demanded, looking alarmed. "Is everything okay?"

Langdon took another look at the departing bus and knew it was a gamble, but he had no other choice.

"No, sir," Langdon replied. "There's an emergency, and I need your help." He motioned to the curb, where a valet had just delivered a slick, silver Bentley. "Is that your car?"

"It is, but—"

"I need a ride," Langdon said. "I know we've never met, but something catastrophic is happening. It's a matter of life and death."

The turbaned man stared into the professor's eyes a long moment, as if searching his soul. Finally he nodded. "Then you'd better get in."

As the Bentley roared away from the curb, Langdon found himself gripping his seat. The man was clearly an experienced driver and seemed to enjoy the challenge of weaving in and out of traffic, playing catch-up with the bus.

It took him less than three blocks to position his Bentley directly behind the **otobüs**. Langdon leaned forward in his seat, squinting at the rear window. The interior lights were dim, and the only things Langdon could make out were the vague silhouettes of the passengers.

"Stay with the bus, please," Langdon said. "And do you have a phone?"

The man produced a cell phone from his pocket and handed it to his passenger, who thanked him profusely before realizing that he had no idea whom to call. He had no contact numbers for Sinskey or Brüder, and calling the WHO's offices in Switzerland could take forever.

"How do I reach the local police?" Langdon asked.

"One-five-five," the man replied. "Anywhere in Istanbul."

Langdon dialed the three numbers and waited. The line seemed to ring forever. Finally a recorded voice answered, conveying both in Turkish and English that due to high call volume, he would need to hold. Langdon wondered if the reason for the call volume was the crisis at the cistern.

The sunken palace was now probably in a state of total pandemonium. He pictured Brüder wading out in the lagoon and wondered what he had discovered out there. Langdon had a sinking feeling he already knew.

Sienna had gotten into the water before him.

Up ahead, the bus's brake lights flashed, and the transport pulled over to a curbside bus stop. The Bentley's driver pulled over as well, idling about fifty feet behind the bus, providing Langdon a perfect view of the passengers getting on and off. Only three people disembarked—all of them men—and yet Langdon studied each carefully, fully aware of Sienna's skills for disguise.

His eyes shifted again to the rear window. It was tinted, but the lights inside were now fully illuminated, and Langdon could see the people on board more clearly. He leaned forward, craning his neck, holding his face close to the Bentley's windshield as he searched for Sienna.

Please don't tell me I gambled wrong!

Then he saw her.

In the rearmost part of the vehicle, facing away from him, a pair of slender shoulders sloped up to the back of a shaved head.

It could only be Sienna.

As the bus accelerated, the interior lights faded once more. In the fleeting second before it disappeared into darkness, the head turned backward, glancing out the rear window.

Langdon lowered himself down in the seat, into the shadows of the Bentley. **Did she see me?** His turbaned driver was already pulling out again, tailing the bus.

The road was descending toward the water now, and up ahead Langdon could see the lights of a low-slung bridge that stretched out over the water. The bridge looked completely deadlocked with traffic. In fact, the entire area near its entrance looked congested.

"Spice Bazaar," the man said. "Very popular on rainy nights."

The man pointed down to the water's edge, where an incredibly long building sat in the shadow of one of Istanbul's more spectacular mosques—the New Mosque, if Langdon were not mistaken, judging from the height of its famed twin minarets. The Spice Bazaar looked larger than most American malls, and Langdon could see people streaming in and out of its enormous arched doorway.

"Alo?!" a tiny voice declared somewhere in the car. "Acil Durum! Alo?!"

Langdon glanced down at the phone in his hand. **The police.**

"Yes, hello!" Langdon blurted, raising the receiver. "My name is Robert Langdon. I'm working with the

World Health Organization. You have a major crisis at the city cistern, and I'm tailing the person responsible. She's on a bus near the Spice Bazaar, heading for—"

"One moment, please," the operator said. "Let me connect you with dispatch."

"No, wait!" But Langdon was on hold again.

The Bentley's driver turned to him with a look of fear. "A crisis at the cistern?!"

Langdon was about to explain when the driver's face suddenly glowed red, like a demon.

Brake lights!

The driver's head whipped around and the Bentley skidded to a stop directly behind the bus. The interior lights flickered on again and Langdon could see Sienna as plain as day. She was standing at the back door, yanking repeatedly on the emergency stop cord and banging to get off the bus.

She saw me, Langdon realized. No doubt Sienna had also seen the traffic on Galata Bridge and knew she could not afford to get caught in it.

Langdon opened his door in a flash, but Sienna had already bolted from the bus and was sprinting into the night. Langdon tossed the cell phone back to its owner. "Tell the police what happened! Tell them to surround this area!"

The turbaned man gave a frightened nod.

"And thank you!" Langdon shouted. "**Teşekkürler!**"

With that, Langdon dashed down the hill after Sienna, who was running directly toward the crowds milling around the Spice Bazaar.

CHAPTER 95

Istanbul's three-hundred-year-old Spice Bazaar is one of the largest covered marketplaces in the world. Built in the shape of an L, the sprawling complex has eighty-eight vaulted rooms divided into hundreds of stalls, where local merchants zealously hawk a mind-boggling array of edible pleasures from around the world—spices, fruits, herbs, and Istanbul's ubiquitous candylike confection, Turkish delight.

The bazaar's entryway—a massive stone portal with a Gothic arch—is located on the corner of Çiçek Pazari and Tahmis Street, and is said to witness the passage of more than three hundred thousand visitors a day.

Tonight, as Langdon approached the swarming entrance, he felt as if all three hundred thousand were here at that very moment. He was still running hard, his eyes never leaving Sienna. She was now only twenty yards ahead of him, racing directly toward the bazaar's gateway and showing no signs of stopping.

Sienna reached the arched portal and came up hard against the crowd. She snaked through the people, clawing her way inside. The moment she crossed the threshold, she stole a glance backward. Langdon saw in her eyes a frightened little girl, running scared . . . desperate and out of control.

"Sienna!" he shouted.

But she plunged into the sea of humanity and was gone.

Langdon dove in after her, bumping, pushing, craning his neck until he spotted her weaving down the bazaar's western hallway to his left.

Burgeoning casks of exotic spices lined the way—Indian curry, Iranian saffron, Chinese flower tea—their dazzling colors creating a tunnel of yellows, browns, and golds. With every step, Langdon smelled a new aroma—pungent mushrooms, bitter roots, musky oils—all wafting through the air with a deafening chorus of languages from around the world. The result was an overwhelming rush of sensory stimuli . . . set against the unceasing thrum of people.

Thousands of people.

A wrenching feeling of claustrophobia gripped Langdon, and he almost pulled up before gathering himself again and forcing his way deeper into the bazaar. He could see Sienna just ahead, pushing through the masses with adamant force. She clearly was taking this ride to the end . . . wherever that might be for her.

For a moment Langdon wondered why he was chasing her.

For justice? Considering what Sienna had done, Langdon could not begin to fathom what kind of punishment awaited her if she were caught.

To prevent a pandemic? Whatever had been done was done.

As Langdon pushed through the ocean of strangers, he suddenly realized why he wanted so badly to stop Sienna Brooks.

I want answers.

Only ten yards ahead, Sienna was headed for an exit door at the end of the western arm of the bazaar. She stole another quick glance behind her, looking alarmed to see Langdon so close. As she turned again, facing front, she tripped and fell.

Sienna's head snapped forward, colliding with the shoulder of the person in front of her. As he went down, her right hand shot out, searching for anything to break her fall. She found only the rim of a barrel of dried chestnuts, which she seized in desperation, pulling it over on top of her and sending a landslide of nuts across the floor.

It took Langdon three strides to reach the spot where she had fallen. He looked down at the floor but saw only the toppled barrel and the chestnuts. No Sienna.

The shopkeeper was screaming wildly.

Where did she go?!

Langdon spun in a circle, but Sienna had somehow vanished. By the time his gaze landed on the western exit only fifteen yards ahead, he knew that her dramatic fall had been anything but accidental.

Langdon raced to the exit and burst out into an enormous plaza, also crowded with people. He stared into the plaza, searching in vain.

Directly ahead, on the far side of a multilane highway, Galata Bridge stretched out across the wide
waters of the Golden Horn. The dual minarets of
the New Mosque rose to Langdon's right, shining
brightly over the plaza. And to his left was nothing
but open plaza . . . packed with people.

The sound of blaring car horns drew Langdon's
gaze ahead again, toward the highway that separated
the plaza from the water. He saw Sienna, already a
hundred yards away, darting through speeding traffic and narrowly avoiding being crushed between
two trucks. She was headed for the sea.

To Langdon's left, on the banks of the Golden
Horn, a transportation hub bustled with activity—
ferry docks, **otobüs**es, taxis, tour boats.

Langdon sprinted hard across the plaza toward the
highway. When he reached the guardrail, he timed
his leap with the oncoming headlights and safely
bounded across the first of several two-lane highways.
For fifteen seconds, assaulted by blinding headlights
and angry car horns, Langdon managed to advance
from median to median—stopping, starting, weaving, until he finally vaulted over the final guardrail
onto the grassy banks of the sea.

Although he could still see her, Sienna was a long
way ahead, eschewing the taxi stand and idling buses
and heading directly for the docks, where Langdon
saw all manner of boats moving in and out—tourist
barges, water taxis, private fishing boats, speedboats.
Out across the water, city lights twinkled on the
western side of the Golden Horn, and Langdon had

no doubt that if Sienna reached the other side, there would be no hope of finding her, probably ever.

When Langdon finally reached the waterfront, he turned left and dashed along the boardwalk, drawing startled looks from tourists who were queued up waiting to board a flotilla of gaudily decorated dinner barges, complete with mosquelike domes, faux-gold flourishes, and blinking neon trim.

Las Vegas on the Bosporus, Langdon moaned, powering past.

He saw Sienna far ahead, and she was no longer running. She was stopped on the dock in an area cluttered by private powerboats, pleading with one of the owners.

Don't let her aboard!

As he closed the gap, he could see that Sienna's appeal was directed at a young man who stood at the helm of a sleek powerboat that was just preparing to pull away from the dock. The man was smiling but politely shaking his head no. Sienna continued gesticulating, but the boater appeared to decline with finality, and he turned back to his controls.

As Langdon dashed closer, Sienna glanced at him, her face a mask of desperation. Below her, the boat's twin outboards revved, churning the water and moving the craft away from the dock.

Sienna was suddenly airborne, leaping off the dock over the open water. She landed with a crash on the boat's fiberglass stern. Feeling the impact, the driver turned with an expression of disbelief on his face. He yanked back the throttle, idling the boat, which was now twenty yards from the dock. Yelling angrily, he marched back toward his unwanted passenger.

As the driver advanced on her, Sienna effortlessly stepped aside, seizing the man's wrist and using his own momentum to launch him up and over the stern gunwale. The man plunged headlong into the water. Moments later, he rose to the surface, sputtering and thrashing wildly, and shouting a string of what were no doubt Turkish obscenities.

Sienna seemed detached as she tossed a flotation cushion into the water, moved to the helm of the boat, and pushed the dual throttles forward.

The engines roared and the boat sped off.

Langdon stood on the dock, catching his breath as he watched the sleek white hull skimming away across the water, becoming a ghostly shadow in the night. Langdon raised his eyes toward the horizon and knew that Sienna now had access not only to the distant shores, but also to an almost endless web of waterways that stretched from the Black Sea to the Mediterranean.

She's gone.

Nearby, the boat's owner climbed out of the water, got to his feet, and hurried off to call the police.

Langdon felt starkly alone as he watched the lights of the stolen boat growing faint. The whine of the powerful engines was growing distant as well.

And then the engines faded abruptly to silence.

Langdon peered into the distance. **Did she kill the motor?**

The boat's lights seemed to have stopped receding

and were now bobbing gently in the small waves of the Golden Horn. For some unknown reason, Sienna Brooks had stopped.

Did she run out of gas?

He cupped his hands and listened, now able to hear the faint thrum of her engines idling.

If she's not out of gas, what is she doing?

Langdon waited.

Ten seconds. Fifteen seconds. Thirty seconds.

Then, without warning, the engines revved up again, reluctantly at first, and then more decidedly. To Langdon's bewilderment, the boat's lights began banking into a wide turn, and the bow swung around toward him.

She's coming back.

As the boat approached, Langdon could see Sienna at the wheel, staring blankly ahead. Thirty yards away, she throttled down and eased the boat safely back to the dock it had just left. Then she killed the engines.

Silence.

Above her, Langdon stared down in disbelief.

Sienna never looked up.

Instead, she buried her face in her hands. She began trembling, her shoulders hunched and shuddering. When she finally looked at Langdon, her eyes were overflowing with tears.

"Robert," she sobbed. "I can't run away anymore. I have nowhere left to go."

CHAPTER 96

It's out.

Elizabeth Sinskey stood at the bottom of the cistern stairwell and gazed at the void of the evacuated cavern. Her breathing felt strained through the respirator she was wearing. Although she had probably already been exposed to whatever pathogen might be down here, Sinskey felt relieved to be wearing a hazmat suit as she and the SRS team entered the desolate space. They were dressed in bulbous white jumpsuits that locked into airtight helmets, and the group looked like a team of astronauts breaching an alien spacecraft.

Sinskey knew that upstairs on the street, hundreds of frightened concertgoers and musicians were huddling in confusion, many being treated for injuries suffered in the stampede. Others had fled the area entirely. She felt lucky to have escaped with only a bruised knee and a broken amulet.

Only one form of contagion travels faster than a virus, Sinskey thought. **And that's fear.**

The doors upstairs were now locked, hermetically sealed, and guarded by local authorities. Sinskey had anticipated a jurisdictional showdown with the arriving local police, but any potential conflicts had evaporated instantly when they saw the SRS team's biohazard gear and heard Sinskey's warnings of a possible plague.

We're on our own, the director of the WHO thought, staring out at the forest of columns reflected in the lagoon. **Nobody wants to come down here.**

Behind her, two agents were stretching a huge polyurethane sheet across the bottom of the stairwell and sealing it to the wall with a heat gun. Two others had found an open area of boardwalk planks and had begun setting up an array of electronic gear as if preparing to analyze a crime scene.

That's exactly what this is, Sinskey thought. **A crime scene.**

She again pictured the woman in the wet burka who had fled the cistern. By all appearances, Sienna Brooks had risked her own life in order to sabotage the WHO's containment efforts and fulfill Zobrist's twisted mission. **She came down here and broke the Solublon bag . . .**

Langdon had chased Sienna off into the night, and Sinskey had still not received word regarding what had happened to either of them.

I hope Professor Langdon is safe, she thought.

———

Agent Brüder stood dripping on the boardwalk, staring blankly out at the inverted head of Medusa and wondering how to proceed.

As an SRS agent, Brüder had been trained to think on the macrocosmic level, setting aside any immediate ethical or personal concerns and focusing on saving as many lives as possible over the long term. Threats to his own health had barely registered on him until this moment. **I waded into this stuff,** he thought, chastising himself for the risky action he had taken and yet knowing he'd had little choice. **We needed an immediate assessment.**

Brüder forced his thoughts to the task at hand—implement Plan B. Unfortunately, in a containment crisis, Plan B was always the same: **widen the radius.** Fighting communicable disease was often like fighting a forest fire: sometimes you had to drop back and surrender a battle in hopes of winning the war.

At this point, Brüder had still not given up the idea that a full containment was possible. Most likely Sienna Brooks had ruptured the bag only minutes before the mass hysteria and evacuation. If that were true, even though hundreds of people had fled the scene, everyone might have been located far enough away from the source to avoid contamination.

Everyone except Langdon and Sienna, Brüder realized. **Both of whom were here at ground zero, and are now someplace out in the city.**

Brüder had another concern as well—a gap in logic that continued to nag at him. While in the water, he had never found the actual breached Solublon bag. It seemed to Brüder that if Sienna had broken the bag—by kicking it or ripping it or whatever she had done—he would have found the damaged, deflated remnants floating somewhere in the area.

But Brüder had found nothing. Any remains of

the bag seemed to have vanished. Brüder strongly doubted that Sienna would have carried off the Solublon bag with her, since by this point it would have been no more than a slimy, dissolving mess.

So where did it go?

Brüder had an uneasy sense that he was missing something. Even so, he focused on a new containment strategy, which required him to answer one critical question.

What is the contagion's current dispersal radius?

Brüder knew the question would be answered in a matter of minutes. His team had set up a series of portable virus-detection devices along the boardwalks at increasing distances from the lagoon. These devices—known as PCR units—used what was called a polymerase chain reaction to detect the presence of viral contamination.

The SRS agent remained hopeful. With no movement of the water in the lagoon, and the passage of very little time, he was confident that the PCR devices would detect a relatively small region of contamination, which they could then attack with chemicals and the use of suction.

"Ready?" a technician called out through a megaphone.

Agents stationed around the cistern gave the thumbs-up.

"Run your samples," the megaphone crackled.

Throughout the cavern, analysts crouched down and started their individual PCR machines. Each device began analyzing a sample from the point at which its operator was located on the boardwalk, spaced in ever-widening arcs around Zobrist's plaque.

A hush fell across the cistern as everyone waited, praying to see only green lights.

And then it happened.

On the machine closest to Brüder, a virus-detection light began flashing red. His muscles tensed, and his eyes shifted to the next machine.

It, too, began blinking red.

No.

Stunned murmurs reverberated throughout the cavern. Brüder watched in horror as, one by one, every PCR device began blinking red, all the way across the cistern to the entrance.

Oh, God . . . he thought. The sea of blinking red detection lights painted an unmistakable picture.

The radius of contamination was enormous.

The entire cistern was teeming with virus.

CHAPTER 97

Robert Langdon stared down at Sienna Brooks, huddled at the wheel of the stolen powerboat, and struggled to make sense of what he had just witnessed.

"I'm sure you despise me," she sobbed, looking up at him through tearful eyes.

"Despise you?!" Langdon exclaimed. "I don't have the slightest idea **who** you are! All you've done is lie to me!"

"I know," she said softly. "I'm sorry. I've been trying to do the right thing."

"By releasing a plague?"

"No, Robert, you don't understand."

"I **do** understand!" Langdon replied. "I understand you waded out into the water to break that Solublon bag! You wanted to release Zobrist's virus before anyone could contain it!"

"Solublon bag?" Sienna's eyes flashed confusion. "I don't know what you're talking about. Robert, I went to the cistern to **stop** Bertrand's virus . . . to **steal** it and make it disappear forever . . . so nobody could ever study it, including Dr. Sinskey and the WHO."

"Steal it? Why keep it from the WHO?"

Sienna took a long breath. "There's so much you

don't know, but it's all moot now. We arrived much too late, Robert. We never had a chance."

"Of course we had a chance! The virus was not going to be released until **tomorrow**! That's the date Zobrist chose, and if you hadn't gone into the water—"

"Robert, I **didn't** release the virus!" Sienna yelled. "When I went into the water, I was trying to find it, but it was too late. There was nothing there."

"I don't believe you," Langdon said.

"I know you don't. And I don't blame you." She reached into her pocket and pulled out a soggy pamphlet. "But maybe this will help." She tossed the paper to Langdon. "I found this just before I waded into the lagoon."

He caught it and opened it up. It was a concert program for the cistern's seven performances of the Dante Symphony.

"Look at the dates," she said.

Langdon read the dates and then reread them, puzzled by what he saw. For some reason, he had been under the impression that this evening's performance was opening night—the first of seven performances to be given during the week, designed to lure people into a plague-infested cistern. This program, however, told a different story.

"Tonight was **closing** night?" Langdon asked, glancing up from the paper. "The orchestra has been playing all week?"

Sienna nodded. "I was as surprised as you are." She paused, her eyes somber. "The virus is already out, Robert. It **has** been for a week."

"That can't be true," Langdon argued. "**Tomorrow** is the date. Zobrist even made a plaque with tomorrow's date on it."

"Yes, I saw the plaque in the water."

"Then you know he was fixated on **tomorrow**."

Sienna sighed. "Robert, I knew Bertrand well, better than I ever admitted to you. He was a scientist, a results-oriented person. I now realize that the date on the plaque is not the virus's **release** date. It's something else, something more important to his goal."

"And that would be . . . ?"

Sienna gazed up solemnly from the boat. "It's a global-saturation date—a mathematical projection of the date after which his virus will have propagated across the world . . . and infected every individual."

The prospect sent a visceral tremor through Langdon, and yet he couldn't help but suspect that she was lying. Her story contained a fatal flaw, and Sienna Brooks had already proven she'd lie about anything.

"One problem, Sienna," he said, staring down at her. "If this plague has already spread all over the world, then why aren't people getting sick?"

Sienna glanced away, suddenly unable to meet his gaze.

"If this plague has been out a week," Langdon repeated, "why aren't people dying?"

She turned slowly back to him. "Because . . . " she began, the words catching in her throat. "Bertrand didn't create a plague." Her eyes welled up again with tears. "He created something far more dangerous."

CHAPTER **98**

Despite the flow of oxygen that passed through her respirator, Elizabeth Sinskey felt light-headed. Five minutes had passed since Brüder's PCR devices had revealed the horrifying truth.

Our window for containment closed long ago.

The Solublon bag had apparently dissolved sometime last week, most likely on the opening night of the concert, which Sinskey now knew had been playing for seven nights straight. The few remaining shreds of Solublon attached to the tether had not disappered, only because they had been coated with an adhesive to help secure them to the tether's clasp.

The contagion has been out for a week.

Now, with no possibility of isolating the pathogen, the SRS agents huddled over samples in the cistern's makeshift lab and assumed their usual fallback position—analysis, classification, and threat assessment. So far, the PCR units had revealed only one solid piece of data, and the discovery surprised no one.

The virus was now airborne.

The contents of the Solublon bag had apparently bubbled up to the surface and aerosolized viral particles into the air. **It wouldn't take many,** Sinskey knew. **Especially in such an enclosed area.**

A virus—unlike a bacteria or chemical pathogen—could spread through a population with astounding speed and penetration. Parasitic in their behavior, viruses entered an organism and attached to a host cell in a process called adsorption. They then injected their own DNA or RNA into that cell, recruiting the invaded cell, and forcing it to replicate multiple versions of the virus. Once a sufficient number of copies existed, the new virus particles would kill the cell and burst through the cell wall, speeding off to find new host cells to attack, and the process would be repeated.

An infected individual would then exhale or sneeze, sending respiratory droplets out of his body; these droplets would remain suspended in the air until they were inhaled by other hosts, and the process began all over again.

Exponential growth, Sinskey mused, recalling Zobrist's graphs illustrating the human population explosion. **Zobrist is using the exponential growth of viruses to combat the exponential growth of people.**

The burning question now, however, was: How would this virus behave?

Coldly stated: **How will it attack its host?**

The Ebola virus impaired the blood's ability to coagulate, resulting in unstoppable hemorrhaging. The hantavirus triggered the lungs to fail. A whole host of viruses known as **oncoviruses** caused cancer.

And the HIV virus attacked the immune system, causing the disease AIDS. It was no secret in the medical community that, had the HIV virus gone airborne, it could have been an extinction event.

So what the hell does Zobrist's virus do?

Whatever it did, the effects clearly took time to reveal themselves . . . and nearby hospitals had reported no cases of patients showing symptoms that were out of the ordinary.

Impatient for answers, Sinskey moved toward the lab. She saw Brüder standing near the stairwell, having found a faint signal for his cell phone. He was speaking to someone in hushed tones.

She hurried over, arriving just as he was finishing his call.

"Okay, understood," Brüder said, the look on his face expressing an emotion between disbelief and terror. "And once again, I cannot stress strongly enough the confidentiality of this information. **Your** eyes only at this point. Call me when you know more. Thanks." He hung up.

"What's going on?" Sinskey demanded.

Brüder blew out a slow breath. "I just spoke to an old friend of mine who is a top virologist at the CDC in Atlanta."

Sinskey bristled. "You alerted the CDC without my authorization?"

"I made a judgment call," he replied. "My contact will be discreet, and we're going to need far better data than we can get from this makeshift lab."

Sinskey glanced over at the handful of SRS agents

who were taking water samples and huddling over portable electronics. **He's right.**

"My CDC contact," Brüder continued, "is standing in a fully equipped microbiology lab and has already confirmed the existence of an extremely contagious and never-before-seen viral pathogen."

"Hold on!" Sinskey interjected. "How did you get him a sample so fast?"

"I didn't," Brüder said tautly. "He tested his own blood."

Sinskey needed only a moment for the meaning to register.

It's already gone global.

CHAPTER 99

Langdon walked slowly, feeling strangely disembodied, as if he were moving through a particularly vivid nightmare. **What could be more dangerous than a plague?**

Sienna had said nothing more since she had climbed out of the boat and motioned for Langdon to follow her away from the docks, along a quiet gravel path, farther away from the water and the crowds.

Although Sienna's tears had stopped, Langdon sensed a torrent of emotion building up within her. He could hear sirens wailing in the distance, but Sienna appeared not to notice. She was staring blankly at the ground, seemingly hypnotized by the rhythmic crunch of the gravel beneath their feet.

They entered a small park, and Sienna guided him into a dense grove of trees, where they were hidden away from the world. Here they sat on a bench that overlooked the water. On the far shore, the ancient Galata Tower glistened above the quiet residences that dotted the hillside. The world looked strangely peaceful from here, a far cry, Langdon imagined, from what was probably transpiring at the cistern. By now, he suspected, Sinskey and the SRS team had realized that they had arrived too late to stop the plague.

Beside him, Sienna stared out across the sea. "I don't have much time, Robert," she said. "The authorities will eventually figure out where I went. But before they do, I need you to hear the truth . . . all of it."

Langdon gave her a silent nod.

Sienna wiped her eyes and shifted on the bench to face him fully. "Bertrand Zobrist . . ." she began. "He was my first love. He became my mentor."

"I've already been told, Sienna," Langdon said.

She gave him a startled look but continued speaking, as if afraid to lose her momentum. "I met him at an impressionable age, and his ideas and intellect bewitched me. Bertrand believed, as I do, that our species is on the brink of collapse . . . that we're facing a horrifying end, which is racing toward us so much faster than anyone dares accept."

Langdon made no reply.

"My entire childhood," Sienna said, "I wanted to save the world. And all I was ever told was: 'You can't save the world, so don't sacrifice your happiness trying.' " She paused, her face taut, holding back tears. "Then I met Bertrand—a beautiful, brilliant man who told me not only that saving the world was **possible** . . . but that doing so was a moral imperative. He introduced me to an entire circle of like-minded individuals—people of staggering abilities and intellect . . . people who really **could** change the future. For the first time in my life, I no longer felt all alone, Robert."

Langdon offered a soft smile, sensing the pain in her words.

"I've endured some terrible things in my life," Sienna continued, her voice increasingly unsteady. "Things I've had trouble moving past . . ." She broke his gaze and ran an anxious palm across her bald scalp before collecting herself and turning back to him. "And maybe that's why the only thing that keeps me going is my belief that we are capable of being better than we are . . . capable of taking action to avoid a catastrophic future."

"And Bertrand believed that, too?" Langdon asked.

"Absolutely. Bertrand had boundless hope for humankind. He was a Transhumanist who believed we are living on the threshold of a glittering 'posthuman' age—an era of true transformation. He had the mind of a futurist, eyes that could see down the road in ways few others could even imagine. He understood the astonishing powers of technology and believed that in the span of several generations, our species would become a different animal entirely—genetically enhanced to be healthier, smarter, stronger, even more compassionate." She paused. "Except for one problem. He didn't think we'd live long enough as a species to realize that possibility."

"Due to overpopulation . . ." Langdon said.

She nodded. "The Malthusian catastrophe. Bertrand used to tell me he felt like St. George trying to slay the chthonic monster."

Langdon didn't follow her meaning. "Medusa?"

"Metaphorically, yes. Medusa and the entire class

of chthonic deities live underground because they're associated directly with Mother Earth. In allegory, chthonics are always symbols of—"

"Fertility," Langdon said, startled that the parallel had not occurred to him earlier. **Fruitfulness. Population.**

"Yes, fertility," Sienna replied. "Bertrand used the term 'chthonic monster' to represent the ominous threat of our own fecundity. He described our over-production of offspring as a monster looming on the horizon . . . a monster we needed to contain imme-diately, before it consumed us all."

Our own virility stalks us, Langdon realized. **The chthonic monster.** "And Bertrand battled this mon-ster . . . how?"

"Please understand," she said defensively, "these are not easy problems to solve. Triage is always a messy process. A man who severs the leg of a three-year-old child is a horrific criminal . . . until that man is a doctor who saves the child from gangrene. Some-times the only choice is the lesser of two evils." She began tearing up again. "I believe Bertrand had a noble goal . . . but his methods . . ." She looked away, on the verge of breaking down.

"Sienna," Langdon whispered gently. "I need to understand all of this. I need you to explain to me what Bertrand did. **What** did he release into the world?"

Sienna faced him again, her soft brown eyes radi-ating a darker fear. "He released a virus," she whis-pered. "A very specific kind of virus."

Langdon held his breath. "Tell me."

"Bertrand created something known as a viral **vector**. It's a virus intentionally designed to install genetic information into the cell it's attacking." Sienna paused to let him process the idea. "A vector virus . . . rather than **killing** its host cell . . . inserts a piece of predetermined DNA into that cell, essentially **modifying** the cell's genome."

Langdon struggled to grasp her meaning. **This virus changes our DNA?**

"The insidious nature of this virus," Sienna continued, "is that none of us know it has infected us. No one gets sick. It causes no overt symptoms to suggest that it's changing us genetically."

For a moment Langdon could feel the blood pulsing in his veins. "And what **changes** does it make?"

Sienna closed her eyes for a moment. "Robert," she whispered, "as soon as this virus was released into the cistern's lagoon, a chain reaction began. Every person who descended into that cavern and breathed the air became infected. They became viral hosts . . . unwitting accomplices who transferred the virus to others, sparking an exponential proliferation of disease that will now have torn across the planet like a forest fire. By now, the virus will have penetrated the global population. You, me . . . **everyone**."

Langdon rose from the bench and began pacing frantically before her. "And what does it **do** to us?" he repeated.

Sienna was silent for a long moment. "The virus has the ability to render the human body . . . infertile." She shifted uncomfortably. "Bertrand created a sterility plague."

Her words struck Langdon hard. **A virus that makes us infertile?** Langdon knew there existed viruses that could cause sterility, but a highly contagious airborne pathogen that could do so by altering us **genetically** seemed to belong in another world . . . some kind of Orwellian dystopia of the future.

"Bertrand often theorized about a virus like this," Sienna said quietly, "but I never imagined he would attempt to create it . . . much less succeed. When I got his letter and learned what he had done, I was in shock. I tried desperately to find him, to beg him to destroy his creation. But I arrived too late."

"Hold on," Langdon interjected, finally finding his voice. "If the virus makes **everyone** on earth infertile, there will be no new generations, and the human race will start dying out . . . immediately."

"Correct," she responded, her voice sounding small. "Except extinction was not Bertrand's goal—quite the opposite, in fact—which is why he created a **randomly** activating virus. Even though Inferno is now endemic in all human DNA and will be passed along by all of us from this generation forward, it will 'activate' only in a certain percentage of people. In other words, the virus is now carried by everyone on earth, and yet it will cause sterility in only a randomly selected **part** of the population."

"What . . . **part?**" Langdon heard himself say, incredulous even to be asking such a question.

"Well, as you know, Bertrand was fixated on the

Black Death—the plague that indiscriminately killed one third of the European population. Nature, he believed, knew how to cull itself. When Bertrand did the math on infertility, he was exhilarated to discover that the plague's death rate of **one in three** seemed to be the precise ratio required to start winnowing the human population at a manageable rate."

That's monstrous, Langdon thought.

"The Black Plague thinned the herd and paved the way for the Renaissance," she said, "and Bertrand created Inferno as a kind of modern-day catalyst for global renewal—a Transhumanist Black Death—the difference being that those manifesting the disease, rather than perishing, would simply become infertile. Assuming Bertrand's virus has taken hold, one third of the world's population is now sterile . . . and one third of the population will continue to be sterile for all time. The effect would be similar to that of a recessive gene . . . which gets passed along to all offspring, and yet exerts its influence in only a small percentage of them."

Sienna's hands were shaking as she continued. "In Bertrand's letter to me, he sounded quite proud, saying he considered Inferno to be a very elegant and humane resolution of the problem." Fresh tears formed in her eyes, and she wiped them away. "Compared to the virulence of the Black Death, I admit there is some compassion in this approach. There will be no hospitals overflowing with the sick and dying, no bodies rotting in the streets, and no anguished survivors enduring the death of loved ones. Humans will simply stop having so many babies. Our planet will experience a steady reduction in our birth rate until the population curve actually inverts, and our total numbers begin to decrease." She paused. "The result will be far more potent than the plague, which only briefly curbed our numbers, creating a temporary dip in the graph of human expansion. With Inferno, Bertrand created a long-term solution, a permanent solution . . . a **Transhumanist** solution. He was a germ-line genetic engineer. He solved problems at the root level."

"It's genetic terrorism . . ." Langdon whispered. "It's changing who we are, who we've always been, at the most fundamental level."

"Bertrand didn't see it that way. He dreamed of fixing the fatal flaw in human evolution . . . the fact that our species is simply too prolific. We are an organism that, despite our unmatched intellect, cannot seem to control our own numbers. No amount of free contraception, education, or government enticement works. We keep having babies . . . whether we want to or not. Did you know the CDC just announced that nearly **half** of all pregnancies in the U.S. are unplanned? And, in underdeveloped nations, that number is over seventy percent!"

Langdon had seen these statistics before and yet only now was he starting to understand their implications. As a species, humans were like the rabbits that were introduced on certain Pacific islands and allowed to reproduce unchecked to the point that they decimated their ecosystem and finally went extinct.

Bertrand Zobrist has redesigned our species . . . in an attempt to save us . . . transforming us into a less fruitful population.

Langdon took a deep breath and stared out at the Bosporus, feeling as ungrounded as the boats sailing in the distance. The sirens were growing still louder, coming from the direction of the docks, and Langdon sensed that time was running out.

"The most frightening thing of all," Sienna said, "is **not** that Inferno causes sterility, but rather that it has the **ability** to do so. An airborne viral vector is a quantum leap—years ahead of its time. Bertrand has suddenly lifted us out of the dark ages of genetic engineering and launched us headlong into the future. He has unlocked the evolutionary process and given humankind the ability to redefine our species in broad, sweeping strokes. Pandora is out of the box, and there's no putting her back in. Bertrand has created the keys to modify the human race . . . and if those keys fall into the wrong hands, then God help us. This technology should **never** have been created. As soon as I read Bertrand's letter explaining how he had achieved his goals, I burned it. Then I vowed to find his virus and destroy all traces of it."

"I don't understand," Langdon declared, his voice laced with anger. "If you wanted to destroy the virus, why didn't you cooperate with Dr. Sinskey and the WHO? You should have called the CDC or **someone**."

"You can't be serious! Government agencies are the **last** entities on earth that should have access to this technology! Think about it, Robert. Throughout all of human history, every groundbreaking technology ever discovered by science has been **weaponized**—from simple fire to nuclear power—and almost **always** at the hands of powerful governments. Where do you think our biological weapons come from? They originate from research done at places like the WHO and CDC. Bertrand's technology—a pandemic virus used as a genetic vector—is the most powerful weapon ever created. It paves the way for horrors we can't yet even imagine, including **targeted** biological weapons. Imagine a pathogen that attacks only those people whose genetic code contains certain ethnic markers. It could enable widespread ethnic cleansing on the genetic level!"

"I see your concerns, Sienna, I do, but this technology could also be used for **good**, couldn't it? Isn't this discovery a godsend for genetic medicine? A new way to deliver global inoculations, for example?"

"Perhaps, but unfortunately, I've learned to expect the worst from people who hold power."

In the distance Langdon could hear the whine of a helicopter shatter the air. He peered through the trees back in the direction of the Spice Bazaar and saw the running lights of an aircraft skimming up over the hill and streaking toward the docks.

Sienna tensed. "I need to go," she said, standing up and glancing to the west toward Atatürk Bridge. "I think I can get across the bridge on foot, and from there reach—"

"You're not leaving, Sienna," he said firmly.

"Robert, I came back because I felt I owed you an explanation. Now you have it."

"No, Sienna," Langdon said. "You came back because you've been running your whole life, and you finally realized you can't run anymore."

Sienna seemed to shrink before him. "What choice do I have?" she asked, watching the helicopter scan the water. "They'll put me in prison as soon as they find me."

"You've done nothing wrong, Sienna. You didn't create this virus . . . nor did you release it."

"True, but I went to great lengths to prevent the World Health Organization from finding it. If I don't end up in a Turkish prison, I'll face some kind of international tribunal on charges of biological terrorism."

As the thrum of the helicopter grew louder, Langdon looked toward the docks in the distance. The craft was hovering in place, rotors churning the water as its searchlight strafed the boats.

Sienna looked ready to bolt at any instant.

"Please listen," Langdon said, softening his tone. "I know you've been through a lot, and I know you're scared, but you need to think of the big picture. Bertrand created this virus. **You** tried to stop it."

"But I failed."

"Yes, and now that the virus is out, the scientific and medical communities will need to understand it fully. You're the **only** person who knows anything at all about it. Maybe there's a way to neutralize it . . . or do something to prepare." Langdon's penetrating gaze bore into her. "Sienna, the world **needs** to know what you know. You can't just disappear."

Sienna's slim frame was shaking now, as if the floodgates of sorrow and uncertainty were about to burst wide. "Robert, I . . . I don't know what to do. I don't even know who I am anymore. Look at me." She put a hand on her bald scalp. "I've turned into a monster. How can I possibly face—"

Langdon stepped forward and wrapped his arms around her. He could feel her body trembling, feel her frailty against his chest. He whispered softly in her ear.

"Sienna, I know you want to run, but I'm not going to let you. Sooner or later you need to start trusting **someone**."

"I can't . . . " She was sobbing. "I'm not sure I know how."

Langdon held her tighter. "You start small. You take that first tiny step. You trust **me**."

CHAPTER **100**

The sharp clang of metal on metal rang through the fuselage of the windowless C-130 transport, causing the provost to jump. Outside, someone was banging the butt of a pistol against the aircraft's hatch and demanding entry.

"Everyone stay seated," the C-130 pilot commanded, moving toward the door. "It's the Turkish police. They just drove out to the plane."

The provost and Ferris exchanged a quick glance.

From the flurry of panicked calls among the WHO staff on board, the provost sensed that their containment mission had failed. **Zobrist carried out his plan**, he thought. **And my company made it possible.**

Outside the hatch, authoritative-sounding voices began shouting in Turkish.

The provost jumped to his feet. "Don't open the door!" he ordered the pilot.

The pilot stopped short, glaring at the provost. "Why the hell not?"

"The WHO is an international relief organization," the provost replied, "and this plane is sovereign territory!"

The pilot shook his head. "Sir, this plane is parked

at a Turkish airport, and until it leaves Turkish airspace, it is subject to the laws of the land." The pilot moved to the exit and threw open the hatch.

Two uniformed men stared in. Their humorless eyes showed not the slightest hint of leniency. "Who is the captain of this aircraft?" one of them demanded in a heavy accent.

"I am," the pilot said.

An officer handed the pilot two sheets of paper. "Arrest documents. These two passengers must come with us."

The pilot skimmed the pages and glanced over at the provost and Ferris.

"Call Dr. Sinskey," the provost ordered the WHO pilot. "We're on an international emergency mission."

One of the officers eyed the provost with an amused sneer. "Dr. **Elizabeth** Sinskey? Director of the World Health Organization? **She** is the one who ordered your arrest."

"That can't be," the provost replied. "Mr. Ferris and I are here in Turkey trying to **help** Dr. Sinskey."

"Then you are not doing a very good job," the second officer replied. "Dr. Sinskey contacted us and named you both as conspirators in a bioterrorism plot on Turkish soil." He pulled out handcuffs. "You both are coming to headquarters for questioning."

"I demand an attorney!" the provost shouted.

Thirty seconds later, he and Ferris were shackled, muscled down the gangway, and shoved roughly into the backseat of a black sedan. The sedan raced away, skimming across the tarmac to a remote corner of the airport, where it stopped at a chicken-wire fence that had been cut and pulled apart to allow their car to pass. Once through the perimeter fence, the car bounced across a dusty wasteland of broken airport machinery and came to a halt near an old service building.

The two uniformed men got out of the sedan and scanned the area. Apparently satisfied that they had not been followed, they stripped off their police uniforms and tossed them aside. Then they helped Ferris and the provost out of the car and removed their handcuffs.

The provost rubbed his wrists, realizing that he would not do well in captivity.

"The car keys are under the mat," one of the agents said, motioning to a white van parked nearby. "There's a duffel in the backseat with everything you requested—travel documents, cash, prepaid phones, clothing, as well as a few other items we thought you might appreciate."

"Thank you," the provost said. "You guys are good."

"Just well trained, sir."

With that, the two Turkish men got back into the black sedan and drove off.

Sinskey was never going to let me walk away, the provost reminded himself. Having sensed as much while flying to Istanbul, the provost had e-mailed an alert to the Consortium's local branch, indicating that he and Ferris might need an extraction.

"You think she'll come after us?" Ferris asked.

"Sinskey?" The provost nodded. "Absolutely. Although I suspect she has other concerns at the moment."

The two men climbed into the white van, and the provost rummaged through the contents of the duffel, getting their documentation in order. He pulled out a baseball cap and slipped it on. Wrapped inside the cap, he found a small bottle of Highland Park single malt.

These guys are good.

The provost eyed the amber liquid, telling himself he should wait until tomorrow. Then again, he pictured Zobrist's Solublon bag and wondered what tomorrow would even look like.

I broke my cardinal rule, he thought. **I gave up my client.**

The provost felt strangely adrift, knowing that in the coming days the world would be blanketed with news of a catastrophe in which he had played a very significant role. **This would not have happened without me.**

For the first time in his life, ignorance no longer felt like the moral high ground. His fingers broke the seal on the bottle of Scotch.

Enjoy it, he told himself. **One way or another, your days are numbered.**

The provost took a deep pull on the bottle, relishing the warmth in his throat.

Suddenly the darkness lit up with spotlights and the blue flashing strobes of police cars, which surrounded them on all sides.

The provost looked frantically in every direction . . . and then sat as still as stone.

No escape.

As armed Turkish police officers approached the van, rifles extended, the provost took a final sip of Highland Park and quietly raised his hands over his head.

This time, he knew, the officers were not his own.

CHAPTER 101

The Swiss Consulate in Istanbul is located at One Levent Plaza in a sleek, ultramodern skyscraper. The building's concave, blue-glass facade resembles a futuristic monolith along the skyline of the ancient metropolis.

Nearly an hour had passed since Sinskey had left the cistern to set up a temporary command post in the consulate offices. The local news stations hummed with reports of the panicked stampede at the cistern's final performance of Liszt's Dante Symphony. No specifics had been reported yet, but the presence of an international medical team wearing hazmat suits had sparked wild speculation.

Sinskey stared out the window at the lights of the city and felt utterly alone. Reflexively, she reached to her neck for her amulet necklace, but there was nothing to grasp. The broken talisman now lay on her desk in two fractured halves.

The WHO director had just finished coordinating an array of emergency meetings to be held in Geneva in several hours. Specialists from various agencies were already en route, and Sinskey herself planned to fly there shortly to brief them. Mercifully, someone on the night staff had delivered a piping-hot mug of authentic Turkish coffee, which Sinskey had quickly drained.

A young man on the consulate staff peered in her open door. "Ma'am? Robert Langdon is here to see you."

"Thank you," she replied. "You can send him in."

Twenty minutes earlier, Langdon had contacted Sinskey by phone and explained that Sienna Brooks had eluded him, having stolen a boat and fled out to sea. Sinskey had already heard this news from the authorities, who were still searching the area, but so far had come up empty-handed.

Now, as Langdon's tall frame materialized in the doorway, she barely recognized him. His suit was dirty, his dark hair tousled, and his eyes looked weary and sunken.

"Professor, are you okay?" Sinskey stood up.

Langdon gave her a tired smile. "I've had easier nights."

"Please," she said, motioning to a chair. "Have a seat."

"Zobrist's contagion," Langdon began without preamble as he sat down. "I think it may have been released a week ago."

Sinskey gave a patient nod. "Yes, we've come to the same conclusion. No symptoms have been reported yet, but we've isolated samples and are already gearing up for intensive testing. Unfortunately, it could take days or weeks to get a real grip on what this virus is . . . and what it might do."

"It's a vector virus," Langdon said.

Sinskey cocked her head in surprise, startled to hear that he even knew the term. "I beg your pardon?"

"Zobrist created an airborne vector virus capable of modifying human DNA."

Sinskey rose abruptly, knocking her chair over in the process. **That's not even possible!** "What would ever make you claim such a thing?"

"Sienna," Langdon replied quietly. "She told me. Half an hour ago."

Sinskey leaned her hands on her desk and stared across at Langdon with sudden distrust. "She didn't escape?"

"She certainly **did**," he replied. "She was free, in a boat speeding out to sea, and she easily could have disappeared forever. But she thought better of it. She came back of her own volition. Sienna wants to help with this crisis."

A harsh laugh escaped Sinskey's lips. "Forgive me if I'm not inclined to trust Ms. Brooks, especially when she's making such a far-fetched claim."

"I believe her," Langdon said, his tone unwavering. "And if she claims that this is a vector virus, I think you'd better take her seriously."

Sinskey felt suddenly exhausted, her mind struggling to analyze Langdon's words. She moved to the window and stared out. **A DNA-altering viral vector?** As improbable and horrifying as the prospect sounded, she had to admit there was an eerie logic to it. After all, Zobrist was a genetic engineer and knew firsthand that the smallest mutation in a single gene could have catastrophic effects on the body—cancers, organ failure, and blood disorders. Even a disease as abhorrent as cystic fibrosis—which drowns its victim in mucus—was caused by nothing more than a minuscule hiccup in a regulator gene on chromosome seven.

Specialists had now started treating these genetic conditions with rudimentary vector viruses that were injected directly into the patient. These noncontagious viruses were programmed to travel through the patient's body and install replacement DNA that fixed the damaged sections. This new science, however, like all sciences, had a dark side. The effects of a vector virus could be either favorable or destructive . . . depending on the engineer's intentions. If a virus were maliciously programmed to insert **damaged** DNA into healthy cells, the results would be devastating. Moreover, if that destructive virus were somehow engineered to be highly contagious and airborne . . .

The prospect made Sinskey shudder. **What genetic horror has Zobrist dreamed up? How does he plan to thin the human herd?**

Sinskey knew that finding the answer could take weeks. The human genetic code contained a seemingly infinite labyrinth of chemical permutations. The prospect of searching its entirety in hopes of finding Zobrist's one specific alteration would be like looking for a needle in a haystack . . . without even knowing on what planet that particular haystack was located.

"Elizabeth?" Langdon's deep voice pulled her back.

Sinskey turned from the window and looked at him.

"Did you hear me?" he asked, still seated calmly. "Sienna wanted to destroy this virus as much as you did."

"I sincerely doubt that."

Langdon exhaled, standing now. "I think you should listen to me. Shortly before his death, Zobrist wrote a letter to Sienna, telling her what he had done. He outlined exactly what this virus would do . . . how it would attack us . . . how it would achieve his goals."

Sinskey froze. **There's a letter?!**

"When Sienna read Zobrist's description of what he had created, she was horrified. She wanted to stop him. She considered his virus so dangerous that she didn't want **anybody** to gain access to it, including the World Health Organization. Don't you see? Sienna has been trying to **destroy** the virus . . . not release it."

"There's a letter?" Sinskey demanded, her focus now singular. "With **specifics**?"

"That's what Sienna told me, yes."

"We **need** that letter! Having specifics could save us months in understanding what this thing is and knowing how to handle it."

Langdon shook his head. "You don't understand. When Sienna read Zobrist's letter, she was **terrified**. She burned it immediately. She wanted to be sure nobody—"

Sinskey smacked her hand down on the desk. "She

destroyed the one thing that could help us prepare for this crisis? And you want me to trust her?"

"I know it's asking a lot, in light of her actions, but rather than castigating her, it might be helpful to remember that Sienna has a unique intellect, including a rather startling capacity for recall." Langdon paused. "What if she can re-create enough of Zobrist's letter to be helpful to you?"

Sinskey narrowed her gaze, nodding slightly. "Well, Professor, in that case, what do you suggest I do?"

Langdon motioned to her empty coffee cup. "I suggest you order more coffee . . . and listen to the one condition that Sienna has requested."

Sinskey's pulse quickened, and she glanced at the phone. "You know how to reach her?"

"I do."

"Tell me what she requested."

Langdon told her, and Sinskey fell silent, considering the proposal.

"I think it's the right thing to do," Langdon added. "And what do you have to lose?"

"If everything you're saying is true, then you have my word." Sinskey pushed the phone toward him. "Please make the call."

To Sinskey's surprise, Langdon ignored the phone. Instead, he stood up and headed out the door, stating that he would be back in a minute. Puzzled, Sinskey walked into the hall and observed him striding through the consulate's waiting area, pushing open the glass doors, and exiting into the elevator foyer beyond. For a moment, she thought he was leaving, but then, rather than summoning the elevator, he slipped quietly into the women's restroom.

A few moments later, he emerged with a woman who looked to be in her early thirties. Sinskey needed a long moment to accept the fact that this was truly Sienna Brooks. The pretty ponytailed woman she had seen earlier in the day had been utterly transformed. She was totally bald, as if her scalp had been shaved clean.

When the two entered her office, they silently took seats facing the desk.

"Forgive me," Sienna said quickly. "I know we have a lot to discuss, but first, I was hoping you would permit me to say something that I really need to say."

Sinskey noted the sadness in Sienna's voice. "Of course."

"Ma'am," she began, her voice frail, "you are the director of the World Health Organization. You know better than anyone that we are a species on the edge of collapse . . . a population out of control. For years, Bertrand Zobrist attempted to engage with influential people like yourself to discuss the impending crisis. He visited countless organizations that he believed could effect change—Worldwatch Institute, the Club of Rome, Population Matters, the Council on Foreign Relations—but he never found anyone who dared engage in a meaningful conversation about a **real** solution. You all responded with plans for better contraceptive education, tax incentives for smaller families, and even talk of colonizing the moon! It's no wonder Bertrand lost his mind."

Sinskey stared at her, offering no reaction.

Sienna took a deep breath. "Dr. Sinskey, Bertrand came to you personally. He begged you to acknowledge that we are on the brink . . . begged you to engage in some kind of dialogue. But rather than listening to his ideas, you called him a madman, put him on a watch list, and drove him underground." Sienna's voice grew heavy with emotion. "Bertrand died all alone because people like yourself refused to open your minds enough even to admit that our catastrophic circumstances might actually require an uncomfortable solution. All Bertrand ever did was speak the truth . . . and for that, he was ostracized." Sienna wiped her eyes and gazed across the desk at Sinskey. "Believe me, I know what it's like to feel all alone . . . the worst kind of loneliness in the world is the isolation that comes from being misunderstood. It can make people lose their grasp on reality."

Sienna stopped talking, and a strained silence followed.

"That's all I wanted to say," she whispered.

Sinskey studied her for a long while and then sat down. "Ms. Brooks," she said, as calmly as possible, "you're right. I may not have listened before . . ." She folded her hands on the desk and looked directly at Sienna. "But I'm listening now."

CHAPTER 102

The clock in the Swiss Consulate's lobby had long since chimed 1 A.M.

The notepad on Sinskey's desk was now a patchwork of handwritten text, questions, and diagrams. The director of the World Health Organization had neither moved nor spoken in more than five minutes. She stood at the window, staring out into the night.

Behind her, Langdon and Sienna waited, seated in silence, cradling the last of their Turkish coffee, the heavy aroma of its pulverized grounds and pistachio grains filling the room.

The only sound was the buzz of the fluorescent lights overhead.

Sienna could feel her own heart pounding, and she wondered what Sinskey was thinking, having now heard the truth in brutal detail. **Bertrand's virus is a sterility plague. One third of the human population will be infertile.**

Throughout the explanation, Sienna had watched Sinskey's range of emotions, which, while restrained, had been palpable. First, there was a stunned acceptance of the fact that Zobrist had actually created an airborne vector virus. Next she had displayed fleeting hope when she learned that the virus was not designed to **kill** people. Then . . . slowly, there had been the spiraling horror as the truth set in, and she realized that vast portions of the earth's population would be rendered sterile. It was clear that the revelation that the virus attacked human **fertility** affected Sinskey on a deeply personal level.

In Sienna's case, the overwhelming emotion was relief. She had shared the complete contents of Bertrand's letter with the WHO director. **I have no more secrets.**

"Elizabeth?" Langdon ventured.

Sinskey emerged slowly from her thoughts. When she returned her gaze to them, her face was drawn. "Sienna," she began, speaking in a flat tone, "the information you have provided will be very helpful in preparing a strategy to deal with this crisis. I appreciate your candor. As you know, pandemic vector viruses have been discussed **theoretically** as a possible way to immunize large populations, but everyone believed that the technology was still many years away."

Sinskey returned to her desk, where she sat down.

"Forgive me," she said, shaking her head. "This all feels like science fiction to me at the moment."

Not surprising, Sienna thought. Every quantum leap in medicine had always felt this way—penicillin, anesthesia, X-rays, the first time humans looked through a microscope and saw a cell divide.

Dr. Sinskey gazed down at her notepad. "In a few hours, I will arrive in Geneva to a firestorm of questions. I have no doubt that the first question will be whether there is any way to counteract this virus."

Sienna suspected she was right.

"And," Sinskey continued, "I imagine the first proposed solution will be to analyze Bertrand's virus, understand it as best as we can, and then attempt to engineer a second strain of it—a strain that we **reprogram** in order to change our DNA back to its original form." Sinskey did not look optimistic as she turned her gaze to Sienna. "Whether a countervirus is even possible remains to be seen, but hypothetically speaking, I'd like to hear your thoughts on that approach."

My thoughts? Sienna felt herself glance reflexively at Langdon. The professor gave her a nod, sending a very clear message: **You've come this far. Speak your mind. Tell the truth as you see it.**

Sienna cleared her throat, turned to Sinskey, and spoke in a clear, strong voice. "Ma'am, the world of genetic engineering is one I've inhabited with Bertrand for many years. As you know, the human genome is an extremely delicate structure . . . a house of cards. The more adjustments we make, the greater the chances we mistakenly alter the wrong card and bring the entire thing crashing down. My personal belief is that there is enormous danger in attempting to undo what has already been done. Bertrand was a genetic engineer of exceptional skill and vision. He was years ahead of his peers. At this point in time, I'm not sure I would trust anyone else to go poking around in the human genome, hoping to get it right.

Even if you designed something you thought might work, trying it would involve **reinfecting** the entire population with something new."

"Very true," Sinskey said, seeming unsurprised by what she had just heard. "But of course, there is the bigger issue. We might not even **want** to counteract it."

Her words caught Sienna off guard. "I'm sorry?"

"Ms. Brooks, I may disagree with Bertrand's methods, but his assessment of the state of the world is accurate. This planet is facing a serious overpopulation issue. If we manage to neutralize Bertrand's virus without a viable alternate plan . . . we are simply back at square one."

Sienna's shock must have been apparent, because Sinskey gave her a tired chuckle and added, "Not a viewpoint you expected to hear from me?"

Sienna shook her head. "I guess I'm not sure what to expect anymore."

"Then perhaps I can surprise you again," Sinskey went on. "As I mentioned earlier, leaders from top health agencies around the world will be gathering in Geneva in a matter of hours to discuss this crisis and prepare an action plan. I can't recall a gathering of greater significance in all my years at the WHO." She leveled her gaze at the young doctor. "Sienna, I would like **you** to have a seat at that table."

"Me?" Sienna recoiled. "I'm not a genetic engineer. I've told you everything I know." She pointed to Sinskey's notepad. "Everything I have to offer is right there in your notes."

"Not by a long shot," Langdon interjected. "Sienna, any meaningful debate about this virus will require **context**. Dr. Sinskey and her team will need to develop a moral framework to assess their response to this crisis. She obviously believes you are in a unique position to add to that dialogue."

"My moral framework, I suspect, will not please the WHO."

"Probably not," Langdon replied, "which is all the more reason for you to be there. You are a member of a new breed of thinkers. You provide counterpoint. You can help them understand the mind-set of visionaries like Bertrand—brilliant individuals whose convictions are so strong that they take matters into their own hands."

"Bertrand was hardly the first."

"No," Sinskey interjected, "and he won't be the last. Every month, the WHO uncovers labs where scientists are dabbling in the gray areas of science— everything from manipulating human stem cells to breeding chimeras . . . blended species that don't exist in nature. It's disturbing. Science is progressing so fast that nobody knows where the lines are drawn anymore."

Sienna had to agree. Just recently, two very respected virologists—Fouchier and Kawaoka—had created a highly pathogenic mutant H5N1 virus. Despite the researchers' purely academic intent, their new creation possessed certain capabilities that had alarmed biosecurity specialists and had created a firestorm of controversy online.

"I'm afraid it's only going to get murkier," Sinskey said. "We're on the verge of new technologies that we can't yet even imagine."

"And new philosophies as well," Sienna added. "The Transhumanist movement is about to explode from the shadows into the mainstream. One of its fundamental tenets is that we as humans have a moral obligation to **participate** in our evolutionary process . . . to use our technologies to advance the species, to create better humans—healthier, stronger, with higher-functioning brains. Everything will soon be possible."

"And you don't think that such beliefs are in conflict with the evolutionary process?"

"No," Sienna responded without hesitation. "Humans have evolved incrementally over millennia, inventing new technologies along the way—rubbing sticks together for warmth, developing agriculture to feed ourselves, inventing vaccines to fight disease, and now, creating genetic tools to help engineer our own bodies so we can survive in a changing world." She paused. "I believe genetic engineering is just another step in a long line of human advances."

Sinskey was silent, deep in thought. "So you believe we should embrace these tools with open arms."

"If we **don't** embrace them," Sienna replied, "then we are as undeserving of life as the caveman who freezes to death because he's afraid to start a fire."

Her words seemed to hang in the room for a long time before anyone spoke.

It was Langdon who broke the silence. "Not to

sound old-fashioned," he began, "but I was raised on the theories of Darwin, and I can't help but question the wisdom of attempting to **accelerate** the natural process of evolution."

"Robert," Sienna said emphatically, "genetic engineering is not an acceleration of the evolutionary process. It is the natural course of events! What you forget is that it was **evolution** that created Bertrand Zobrist. His superior intellect was the product of the very process Darwin described . . . an evolution over time. Bertrand's rare insight into genetics did not come as a flash of divine inspiration . . . it was the product of years of human intellectual progress."

Langdon fell silent, apparently considering the notion.

"And as a Darwinist," she continued, "you know that nature has always found a way to keep the human population in check—plagues, famines, floods. But let me ask you this—isn't it possible that nature found a different way this time? Instead of sending us horrific disasters and misery . . . maybe nature, through the process of evolution, created a scientist who invented a different method of decreasing our numbers over time. No plagues. No death. Just a species more in tune with its environment—"

"Sienna," Sinskey interrupted. "It's late. We need to go. But before we do, I need to clarify one more thing. You have told me repeatedly tonight that Bertrand was not an evil man . . . that he loved humankind, and that he simply longed so deeply to save our species that he was able to rationalize taking such drastic measures."

Sienna nodded. "The ends justify the means," she said, quoting the notorious Florentine political theorist Machiavelli.

"So tell me," Sinskey said, "do you believe that the ends justify the means? Do you believe that Bertrand's goal to save the world was so noble that it warranted his releasing this virus?"

A tense silence settled in the room.

Sienna leaned in, close to the desk, her expression forceful. "Dr. Sinskey, as I told you, I believe Bertrand's actions were **reckless** and extremely dangerous. If I could have stopped him, I would have done so in a heartbeat. I **need** you to believe me."

Elizabeth Sinskey reached across the desk and gently grasped both of Sienna's hands in her own. "I do believe you, Sienna. I believe every word you've told me."

CHAPTER 103

The predawn air at Atatürk Airport was cold and laced with mist. A light fog had settled, hugging the tarmac around the private terminal.

Langdon, Sienna, and Sinskey arrived by town car and were met outside by a WHO staffer who helped them out of the vehicle.

"We're ready whenever you are, ma'am," the man said, ushering the trio into a modest terminal building.

"And Mr. Langdon's arrangements?" Sinskey asked.

"Private plane to Florence. His temporary travel documents are already on board."

Sinskey nodded her appreciation. "And the other matter we discussed?"

"Already in motion. The package will be shipped as soon as possible."

Sinskey thanked the man, who now headed out across the tarmac toward the plane. She turned to Langdon. "Are you sure you don't want to join us?" She gave him a tired smile and pulled back her long silver hair, tucking it behind her ears.

"Considering the situation," Langdon said playfully, "I'm not sure an art professor has much to offer."

"You've offered plenty," Sinskey said. "More than you know. Not the least of which being . . ." She motioned beside her to Sienna, but the young woman was no longer with them. Sienna was twenty yards back, having paused at a large window where she was staring out at the waiting C-130, apparently deep in thought.

"Thanks for trusting her," Langdon said quietly. "I sense she hasn't had a lot of that in her life."

"I suspect Sienna Brooks and I will find plenty of things to learn from each other." Sinskey extended her palm. "Godspeed, Professor."

"And to **you**," Langdon said as they shook hands. "Best of luck in Geneva."

"We'll need it," she said, and then nodded toward Sienna. "I'll give you two a moment. Just send her out when you're ready."

As Sinskey headed across the terminal, she reached absently into her pocket and pulled out the two halves of her broken amulet, clutching them tightly in one palm.

"Don't give up on that rod of Asclepius," Langdon called out behind her. "It's fixable."

"Thanks," Sinskey replied with a wave. "I'm hoping everything is."

———

Sienna Brooks stood alone at the window, gazing out at the lights of the runway, which looked ghostly in the low-lying fog and gathering clouds. Atop a control tower in the distance, the Turkish flag fluttered proudly—a field of red emblazoned with the ancient symbols of the crescent and star—vestiges of the Ottoman Empire, still flying proudly in the modern world.

"A Turkish lira for your thoughts?" a deep voice said behind her.

Sienna did not turn. "A storm is coming."

"I know," Langdon responded quietly.

After a long moment, Sienna turned to him. "And I wish you were coming to Geneva."

"Nice of you to say so," he replied. "But you'll be busy talking about the future. The last thing you need is some old-fashioned college professor slowing you down."

She gave him a puzzled look. "You think you're too old for me, don't you?"

Langdon laughed out loud. "Sienna, I am **definitely** too old for you!"

She shifted uncomfortably, feeling embarrassed. "Okay . . . but at least you'll know where to find me." She managed a girlish shrug. "I mean . . . if you ever want to see me again."

He smiled at her. "I'd enjoy that."

She felt her spirits lift a bit, and yet a long silence grew between them, neither of them quite certain how to say good-bye.

As Sienna stared up at the American professor, she felt a surge of emotion she wasn't accustomed to feeling. Without warning, she stood on her tiptoes and kissed him full on the lips. When she pulled away, her eyes were moist with tears. "I'll miss you," she whispered.

Langdon smiled affectionately and wrapped his arms around her. "I'll miss you, too."

They stood for a long while, locked in an embrace that neither seemed willing to end. Finally, Langdon spoke. "There's an ancient saying . . . often attributed to Dante himself . . ." He paused. "'Remember tonight . . . for it's the beginning of forever.'"

"Thank you, Robert," she said, as the tears began to flow. "I finally feel like I have a purpose."

Langdon pulled her closer. "You always said you wanted to save the world, Sienna. This might just be your chance."

Sienna smiled softly and turned away. As she walked alone toward the waiting C-130, Sienna considered everything that had happened . . . everything that might still happen . . . and all the possible futures.

Remember tonight, she repeated to herself, **for it's the beginning of forever.**

As Sienna climbed into the plane, she prayed that Dante was right.

CHAPTER 104

The pale afternoon sun dipped low over the Piazza del Duomo, glinting off the white tiles of Giotto's bell tower and casting long shadows across Florence's magnificent Cathedral of Santa Maria del Fiore.

The funeral for Ignazio Busoni was just getting under way as Robert Langdon slipped into the cathedral and found a seat, pleased that Ignazio's life was to be memorialized here, in the timeless basilica that he had looked after for so many years.

Despite its vibrant facade, the interior of Florence's cathedral was stark, empty, and austere. Nonetheless, the ascetic sanctuary seemed to radiate an air of celebration today. From all over Italy, government officials, friends, and art-world colleagues had flooded into the church to remember the jovial mountain of a man they had lovingly called **il Duomino**.

The media had reported that Busoni passed away while doing what he loved most—taking a late-night stroll around the Duomo.

The tone of the funeral was surprisingly upbeat, with humorous commentary from friends and family, one colleague noting that Busoni's love of Renaissance art, by his own admission, had been matched only by his love of spaghetti Bolognese and caramel **budino**.

After the service, as the mourners mingled and fondly recounted incidents from Ignazio's life, Langdon wandered around the interior of the Duomo, admiring the artwork that Ignazio had so deeply loved . . . Vasari's **Last Judgment** beneath the dome, Donatello and Ghiberti's stained-glass windows, Uccello's clock, and the often-overlooked mosaic pavements that adorned the floor.

At some point Langdon found himself standing before a familiar face—that of Dante Alighieri. Depicted in the legendary fresco by Michelino, the great poet stood before Mount Purgatory and held forth in his hands, as if in humble offering, his masterpiece **The Divine Comedy**.

Langdon couldn't help but wonder what Dante would have thought if he had known the effect his epic poem would have on the world, centuries later, in a future even the Florentine poet himself could never have envisioned.

He found eternal life, Langdon thought, recalling the early Greek philosophers' views on fame. **So long as they speak your name, you shall never die**.

It was early evening when Langdon made his way across Piazza Sant'Elisabetta and returned to Florence's elegant Hotel Brunelleschi. Upstairs in his room, he was relieved to find an oversize package waiting for him.

At last, the delivery had arrived.

The package I requested from Sinskey.

Hurriedly, Langdon cut the tape sealing the box and lifted out the precious contents, reassured to see that it had been meticulously packed and was cushioned in bubble wrapping.

To Langdon's surprise, however, the box contained some additional items. Elizabeth Sinskey, it seemed, had used her substantial influence to recover a bit more than he had requested. The box contained Langdon's own clothing—button-down shirt, khaki pants, and his frayed Harris Tweed jacket—all carefully cleaned and pressed. Even his cordovan loafers were here, newly polished. Inside the box, he was also pleased to find his wallet.

It was the discovery of one final item, however, that made Langdon chuckle. His reaction was part relief that the item had been returned . . . and part sheepishness that he cared so deeply about it.

My Mickey Mouse watch.

Langdon immediately fastened the collector's edition timepiece on his wrist. The feel of the worn leather band against his skin made him feel strangely secure. By the time he had gotten dressed in his own clothes and slipped his feet back into his own loafers, Robert Langdon was feeling almost like himself again.

Langdon exited the hotel, carrying the delicate package with him in a Hotel Brunelleschi tote bag, which he had borrowed from the concierge. The

evening was unusually warm, adding to the dream-
like quality of his walk along the Via dei Calzaiuoli
toward the lone spire of the Palazzo Vecchio.

When he arrived, Langdon checked in at the security office, where his name was on a list to see Marta
Alvarez. He was directed to the Hall of the Five Hundred, which was still bustling with tourists. Langdon
had arrived right on time, expecting Marta to meet
him here in the entryway, but she was nowhere to
be seen.

He flagged down a passing docent.

"Scusi?" Langdon called. "**Dove passo trovare
Marta Alvarez?**"

The docent broke into a broad grin. "**Signora Alvarez?! She no here! She have baby! Catalina! Molto
bella!**"

Langdon was pleased to hear Marta's good news.
"**Ahh . . . che bello,**" he replied. "**Stupendo!**"

As the docent hurried off, Langdon wondered what
he was supposed to do with the package he was carrying.

Quickly making up his mind, he crossed the
crowded Hall of the Five Hundred, passing beneath
Vasari's mural and heading up into the palazzo
museum, staying out of sight of any security guards.

Finally, he arrived outside the museum's narrow
andito. The passage was dark, sealed off with stanchions, a swag, and a sign: CHIUSO/CLOSED.

Langdon took a careful glance around and then
slipped under the swag and into the darkened

space. He reached into his tote bag and carefully extracted the delicate package, peeling away the bubble wrapping.

When the plastic fell away, Dante's death mask stared up at him once again. The fragile plaster was still in its original Ziploc bag, having been retrieved as Langdon had requested from the lockers at the Venice train station. The mask appeared to be in flawless condition with one small exception—the addition of a poem, inscribed in an elegant spiral shape, on its reverse side.

Langdon glanced at the antique display case. **The Dante death mask is displayed face front . . . nobody will notice.**

He carefully removed the mask from the Ziploc bag. Then, very gently, he lifted it back onto the peg inside the display case. The mask sank into place, nestling against its familiar red velvet setting.

Langdon closed the case and stood a moment, gazing at Dante's pale visage, a ghostly presence in the darkened room. **Home at last.**

Before exiting the room, Langdon discreetly removed the stanchions, swag, and sign from the doorway. As he crossed the gallery, he paused to speak to a young female docent.

"**Signorina?**" Langdon said. "The lights above the Dante death mask need to be turned on. It's very hard to see in the dark."

"I'm sorry," the young woman said, "but that exhibit is closed. The Dante death mask is no longer here."

"That's odd." Langdon feigned a look of surprise. "I was just admiring it."

The woman's face registered confusion.

As she rushed off toward the **andito**, Langdon quietly slipped out of the museum.

EPILOGUE

Thirty-four thousand feet above the dark expanse of the Bay of Biscay, Alitalia's red-eye to Boston cruised westward through a moonlit night.

On board, Robert Langdon sat engrossed in a paperback copy of **The Divine Comedy**. The rhythm of the poem's lilting **terza rima** rhyme scheme, along with the hum of the jet engines, had lulled him into a near-hypnotic state. Dante's words seemed to flow off the page, resonating in his heart as if they had been written specifically for him in this very moment.

Dante's poem, Langdon was now reminded, was not so much about the misery of hell as it was about the power of the human spirit to endure any challenge, no matter how daunting.

Outside the window, a full moon had risen, dazzling and bright, blotting out all other heavenly bodies. Langdon gazed out at the expanse, lost in his thoughts of all that had transpired in the last few days.

The darkest places in hell are reserved for those who maintain their neutrality in times of moral crisis. For Langdon, the meaning of these words had never felt so clear: **In dangerous times, there is no sin greater than inaction.**

Langdon knew that he himself, like millions, was guilty of this. When it came to the circumstances of the world, denial had become a global pandemic. Langdon promised himself that he would never forget this.

As the plane streaked west, Langdon thought of the two courageous women who were now in Geneva, meeting the future head-on and navigating the complexities of a changed world.

Outside the window, a bank of clouds appeared on the horizon, inching slowly across the sky, finally slipping across the moon and blocking out its radiant light.

Robert Langdon eased back in his seat, sensing that it was time to sleep.

As he clicked off his overhead light, he turned his eyes one last time to the heavens. Outside, in the newly fallen darkness, the world had been transformed. The sky had become a glistening tapestry of stars.

>⋅⟨⟩⋅○⋅⟨⟩⋅⋅◅

ABOUT THE AUTHOR

Dan Brown is the author of
The Da Vinci Code, one of
the most widely read novels of
all time, as well as the international bestsellers **The Lost
Symbol, Angels & Demons,
Deception Point**, and **Digital Fortress**. He lives in New
England with his wife.

LIKE WHAT YOU'VE READ?

If you enjoyed this large print edition of
INFERNO,
here are a few of Dan Brown's latest
bestsellers also available in large print.

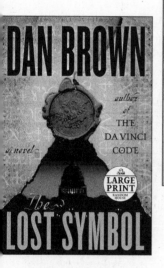

Angels & Demons
(paperback)
978-0-7393-2675-6
($17.95/$21.00C)

The Lost Symbol
(paperback)
978-0-375-43452-5
($31.00/$38.00C)

The Da Vinci Code
(paperback)
978-0-7393-2674-9
($17.95/$25.95C)

Large print books are available wherever books
are sold and at many local libraries.

All prices are subject to change. Check with your
local retailer for current pricing and availability.
For more information on these and other large print titles,
visit www.randomhouse.com/largeprint.

well we work together. She has so many years of experience in publishing and she and her husband, Boris Vallejo, also a renowned artist, were there, encouraging and helping me in every way possible.

I must send my love and thanks to my sister Rochelle Lazarus Saxena, who has loved me and encouraged me always and my two nieces and her daughters, Kiara and Alika Saxena, who are jumping with joy for me right about now. And I want to let Maria Parreiral know how much she means to me. She has helped me run my home smoothly through thick and thin and has always wanted to see this book published and read by children everywhere. Thank you!

One hundred hugs and kisses to my daughter, Kara Lysandra Ross Colón, for being the inspiration for Sara when she herself was 12-years-old. She has continued to be an inspiration as I've watched her grow into the strong, creative, beautiful and accomplished woman she is. She also had the idea for Lucinda to plant the chocolate chips! And another 100 to my wonderful, creative, and handsome son-in-law, Sean Colón, for his continuous support and all he does for our family. He is our son, too.

And saving for last, my husband, my love, my partner in everything and best friend ever, Fred Ross. He has supported me always as I hope I do him. He was there at the beginning, when it was just a concept and he has given me many creative ideas to use and think about along the way, acting as a sounding board and reading several editions of the manuscript. He also contributed to the visual fun of this book with his playful and lively illustration of *Opening the Car Door*. I thank you from the bottom of my heart.

THE AUTHOR

Sherry Ross is the editor-in-chief of the Art Renewal Center (www.artrenewal.org), which is a non-profit art educational website and foundation that offers art scholarships and sponsors a well-known international art contest with art exhibits in Barcelona, Spain and NYC. She also has a cookbook and a book of poetry to her credit, *Seeds of the Pomegranate*, but this is her first novel. Ms. Ross studied art at the Arts Student League in NYC and one of her drawings also appears in this book. She has also had a one-person show of her fantasy sculptures. She lives with her husband, Fred Ross, in the middle of the woods not too far from her daughter Kara, her son-in-law Sean, and her two granddaughters Anna and Kayleigh ... who also live in the middle of the woods. Sherry likes to walk in the woods and be on the lookout for natural "phenomena" in nature. She believes life is indeed miraculous and many surprising twists and turns have probability. The author, like many of her characters, loves the old and the new.

THE ILLUSTRATOR

Julie Bell was born in Beaumont, Texas. As a former nationally ranked competitive body builder, she applies the same discipline and intensity to her art. Her knowledge of anatomy has allowed her to imbue her figures of humans and animals with grace and strength. At the heart of her work is a deep curiosity, honor, and respect for the human body and the world of emotions.

Julie's work is well known throughout the world in the fantasy and science fiction fields and has appeared on hundreds of book covers, comic books, trading cards, and various collectibles. Her work can be seen worldwide in major advertising campaigns, album covers, posters, and collectibles of all kinds.

After having her heart captured by a pack of wolves at Lakota Wolf Preserve in 2001, Julie has also turned her attention to painting wildlife. She has now established her place among the top wildlife and western painters in the world, winning awards and showing her work in exhibits throughout the USA and Europe.

Every year, she and her husband, Boris Vallejo, produce paintings for the highly anticipated Boris Vallejo and Julie Bell Fantasy Calendar published by Workman, now in its 37th year.

Julie shares her life and her studio with Boris and their two dogs, Izze and Stella, in Pennsylvania, USA.